GIRL'S CHOICE

'I have only two shots left, so stand quite still, please . . .'

GIRL'S CHOICE

A collection of stories

Illustrated by
JEANNETTE GIBLIN

Gillian
Douglas

HAMLYN
LONDON · NEW YORK · SYDNEY · TORONTO

ACKNOWLEDGEMENTS

The publishers wish to express their thanks to authors and publishers for permission to include the following stories.

AU PAIR by Elisabeth Kyle from STIRRING STORIES FOR GIRLS (Odhams)

THE BREADTH OF A WHISKER by Janet McNeill from SPECIAL OCCASIONS (Faber & Faber Ltd)

JANE RINGS A BELL © copyright by E. W. Hildick 1965

THE PARK © copyright by Penelope Farmer 1965

SURE MAGIC by Monica Edwards from PONY CLUB ANNUAL 1954 (Max Parrish)

A WOOD BY MOONLIGHT by Geoffrey Trease from COLLINS YOUNG ELIZABETHAN © copyright 1954 Geoffrey Trease

First published 1965
Sixth impression 1973
Published by The Hamlyn Publishing Group Limited
LONDON · NEW YORK · SYDNEY · TORONTO
Hamlyn House, Feltham, Middlesex, England
© Copyright The Hamlyn Publishing Group Limited 1965
ISBN 0 601 08636 8
Printed in Czechoslovakia by Tisk Brno
51096/6

CONTENTS

page

THE WINDOWBOX WALTZ   9
by Joan Aiken

SURE MAGIC   29
by Monica Edwards

ASHVALE GRANGE   45
by Elisabeth Sheppard-Jones

THE LEOPARD   63
by Rosemary Weir

BEING WITCHES   75
by Lorna Wood

LUCINDA'S LONG AFTERNOON   83
by Margaret Biggs

A WOOD BY MOONLIGHT   101
by Geoffrey Trease

THE BEACH HUT   117
by Elizabeth Stucley

THE STOLEN PONIES   135
by John Davies

NO COUNTRY HOLIDAY?   153
by Lois Lamplugh

THE LAND OF TREES AND HEROES   169
by Joan Aiken

PIP AND THE FAMOUS AUTHOR   187
by Margaret Biggs

THE BIGGEST CATCH 203
    by Lois Lamplugh

THE PARK 211
    by Penelope Farmer

A FAIR DEAL 227
    by Alan C. Jenkins

THE BREADTH OF A WHISKER 241
    by Janet McNeill

LAKE ISLAND 249
    by Kathleen Mackenzie

GRANDPA'S GOLD WATCH 267
    by Kathleen O'Farrell

THE LIME TREE DEN 285
    by Anne Barrett

AU PAIR 305
    by Elisabeth Kyle

THE CAT AND THE QUINCE TREE 315
    by Joan Aiken

JANE RINGS A BELL 329
    by E. W. Hildick

LIST OF ILLUSTRATIONS

Page

Wrapping his coat round the tiny creature, he lifted it into his arms   39

They handed out supper to the children as they came downstairs   57

'Get out of here,' Judy shouted at the leopard   73

'The whole village may come to us for a beauty potion!'   79

'Please get me down!' Lucinda wailed   92

It looked as though the magic words had produced the Devil   104

Alice wished for a beach hut more then anything else in the world   123

The men in the field drove the ponies towards the gate   138

The cottage was exactly right   167

The postman and the butcher's boy were asleep in the tree   175

Pip typed as James Travers dictated to her   197

'Marion, look! It's a mine!'   207

I sat on the lawn, as if the park belonged to me   219

Old Joe Floggit was the most colourful character in the village   229

The mouse dipped one whisker in the crucible   246

It seemed as if they were the first people to set foot on the island   253

Susan hated Grandpa's watch   269

Frozen with terror, she heard a rustling   301

The Japanese warrior turned its grinning mask towards them   312

'Do you think it's Miss Eaves in disguise?'   324

Three wild figures were swinging on the bells   355

The Windowbox Waltz

by JOAN AIKEN

Rosemary lay stretched and baking on the sunny beach watching a boat unloading. It was a foreigner — unusual in the small Cornish harbour — with an unpronounceable name, full of s's and y's, and manned by blond Nordic sailors with peeling sunburnt noses. There was a woman with them too, also tall and blonde, with the figure of a goddess in her boiler-suit, and a face like the bottom of a frying-pan, squashed and sour under the golden plaits. She seemed to have authority among the men, who treated her with respect.

A whistle blew, and the creaking and thudding of machinery stopped; peace fell over the harbour and Rosemary almost drifted off to sleep under the noon sun. Then, irritating as a mosquito, came a sound from above. Footsteps walking to and fro, to and fro, on the harbour wall above her and, not talk which she could have ignored, but a thin persistent whistling which repeated again and again a tinselly little theme — pom *pom* pom, pom *pom* pom, pom tiddle om pom, om pom pom — it was vaguely familiar and after a few repetitions she identified it as a tune from early piano lessons called the Windowbox Waltz.

In exasperation she screwed her head round and looked up. It was the pan-faced vikingess, strolling on the harbour wall with a man in bottle-green corduroys; presumably having run out of conversational topics he was whistling to her to fill in the gaps and he seemed all set to go on till two o'clock.

Rosemary had discovered an excellent method of shifting people if she wanted them out of the way: it was to start taking photographs aimed in their direction; nice-minded people always hurried self-consciously away for fear of getting in the picture or spoiling it. Accordingly she scrambled up the sandy steps and levelled her camera at the strolling couple.

She was not prepared for what happened.

The woman gave a sharp exclamation; the man broke away from her, strode over to Rosemary, grabbed the camera, and threw it into the deep water of the harbour.

He and Rosemary stared at one another.

'What the dickens do you think you're doing?' she exclaimed furiously.

'I do not care to have my picture taken by strangers,' he replied harshly.

'Do you realise that camera cost fifty pounds?' Rosemary said. 'It's my father's. You'll have to replace it!'

'I don't care if it cost a hundred pounds. You have no right to take my picture.'

'I haven't the slightest wish to take your picture! You don't improve the view of the cliffs at all. Will you please give me your name and address, unless you happen to have fifty pounds on you?'

The harbour policeman strolled towards them. Rosemary turned to him in relief, but the man spoke first.

'This young woman is annoying us,' he said. 'She seems to think she can get money out of me with some cock-and-bull story of a camera, but she is mistaken. Will you please caution her, or whatever you do?'

'Oh!' exclaimed Rosemary, bursting with rage, but the policeman turned calm, ox-like eyes from one to the other.

'He threw my camera into the harbour!' Rosemary exploded. 'It was worth fifty pounds.'

'Fifty pounds? That's a likely story,' the policeman said. 'What were you doing with a camera worth that?'

'It's my father's. And I'm a photographic student.'

'I did see something chucked in,' the policeman said.

'I threw in a stone,' the man cut in. 'Isn't that so?' he appealed to the woman.

'Ja,' she replied stolidly. 'He throw in a stone.'

'It's two against one, miss,' the policeman pointed out heavily. 'After all, what would the gentleman want to do a thing like you said for?'

Rosemary turned and called to a man who was sprawled on a baulk of timber above them a little way up the cliff path.

'Can you come down a minute please?'

Grinning, the man joined them. He was dark, dressed disreputably, and had a sardonic expression.

'You saw him throw my camera into the harbour, didn't you?' Rosemary asked him. 'You must have, you've been here all along.'

'Nope. Didn't see a thing,' said the man with complete calm.

'You — you absolute so-and-so!' Rosemary exclaimed. Her temper got the better of her and she smacked his face. It was not logical, but it made her feel better.

'Now, now, dear,' the man protested, grinning still more. He put an arm around her and said to the policeman, 'I must apologise for my young sister. She's a bit temperamental — thyroid gland trouble. Nothing to worry about, she'll soon be all right.'

With a little bow to the group he led Rosemary, quite bereft of speech, along the dusty harbour to a small green sports car. He deftly insinuated her into it, slid into the driver's seat, and drove rapidly up the steep winding road until they were on the height of the cliffs and out of sight of Polbissick Harbour.

There he pulled up.

'Now, have a good cry, why don't you?' he suggested mildly. 'It'll help.'

'Have a good cry —' she faced him with stormy eyes.

11

'Do you know you've lost me a—'

'Yes, I know, I know,' he said soothingly. 'I've lost you fifty pounds. But you can set against that the fact that I've probably saved your life, while *you've* just cost me six weeks' work — probably irreplaceable.'

'Saved my life? What on earth do you mean?'

'Quite simple. If you'd stayed round there, pestering that bloke for your fifty pounds, the odds are about a hundred to one that in the next few hours you would have been overtaken by some nasty accident — a hopper full of cement would have landed on you, or you'd have tripped and fallen under the boat, or, simpler still, he'd have taken you off in his car to settle the matter at the nearest lawyer's and you'd never have been seen again.'

'You can't be serious?' Rosemary said. 'Who is he?'

'His name's Peterson.'

'Carl Peterson, I suppose?' she said witheringly. 'Why not Dr No?' She still thought he was joking. 'I suppose you're James Bond?'

'No, seriously, he's a very dangerous man. Do you live round here?'

'I'm on holiday, staying with my Aunt Lou. She has a bungalow above Linhoe.'

'I'll run you back. You're better at home while he's around.'

'But who is he? What does he do?'

'I'd have found out a bit more, but for your interruption with the camera. I was just getting close enough to lip-read when you had to butt in.'

'You wouldn't have heard anything. They weren't talking,' Rosemary said. 'He was only whistling a tune.'

'*Was* he?' said the man with extreme interest. 'You wouldn't remember it?'

'Yes I do, as a matter of fact. I used to play it. It's called the Windowbox Waltz.' She whistled it.

'You wonderful girl! That's well worth a new camera. Do you suppose if I rang up my boss in London you could whistle it to him? I'm tone-deaf,' he confessed. 'Old Waterfalls would never have put me on the job if he'd known music was going to come into it.'

'I expect I could. Are you really not pulling my leg? Are you from Scotland Yard? What's your name?'

'Alan Hawthorne. I've been seconded to the Yard from the Ministry of Defence —' and then suddenly he leaned nearer and hissed, 'Don't look round, but he's followed us up here and he's sitting in his car watching us.'

Rosemary fished out the mirror she kept in her skirt pocket. Holding it at a cautious angle she surveyed the car behind. There was a gleam as something metallic inside it caught the sun, and Alan let out a soft curse.

'There's an old Home Guard slit trench over to your left in the heather,' he said. 'Make for it, wriggle along it on your tummy — it runs all the way to Linhoe — and when you get there, if I'm not about, ring up my boss, Westminster nine thousand, and whistle that tune to him. Say Peterson's here. Okay? Ready?'

He was holding her hand tight. She stared at him in fright, wondering what he meant to do. He stood up, there was a slight whirr, as if a hollow golf ball had buzzed past them, and Alan toppled neatly forward over the sloping edge of the cliff and disappeared from view.

The whirr sounded again. Something like a hornet brushed past Rosemary's ear. She felt sick, but plainly this was not the moment for standing about and pondering. She flung herself sideways out of the car into a thick clump of heather and rolled past it, mercifully into the slit trench which was about four feet deep. The heather had grown right over the top.

Rosemary lay still, her face on some dusty old dry sand and a weather-beaten cigarette packet. She was terrified of adders and imagined them thudding down on to her back out of the heather, larger than boa constrictors, but even so they seemed preferable to Peterson and his airgun, or whatever it was.

There was no sound from above, however, and after a while she plucked up courage and began inching along on knees and elbows. The going was soft but not pleasant; sharp bits of dead heather pricked her, and once she had to negotiate a dead sheep. After what seemed a mile of crawling, she cautiously put up her head and found she was out of sight of the road. There was no sign of Peterson, and just below was the cliff path, curving temptingly through the heather. She made her way down to it and ran on towards Linhoe.

By this time she was in a considerable rage. It is always a shock when an acquaintance is shot in your presence, even if it is someone you have not known long. Rosemary's knees were knocking together slightly, her heart was beating still more than her steady Guide's trot justified. She certainly intended to see Peterson brought to justice, and that sour-faced blonde too. The first thing would be to visit the police station, before calling up Alan's boss, to make sure the pair were arrested before they left the neighbourhood.

The police station was at the top of Linhoe Hill, opposite the coastguard post. There was a mirror just inside the door, and as she went in Rosemary caught a rather demoralising glimpse of herself — hair like a haystack, a scratched face, and hands stained with sand.

'I want to report a murder,' she said abruptly.

A couple of men were lounging in the little room. One was skilfully darning a sock on an old-fashioned wooden cobble, the other was thoughtfully reading a comic, his tongue laboriously moving from side to side.

'Top Cat's stuck inside the dustbin,' he said. 'Proper job.' Then he raised his head and added, 'Eh? What was that?'

'I've come to report a murder,' said Rosemary crossly.

14

'A man was shot by another man who's just thrown a fifty-pound camera of mine into Polbissick Harbour.'

'Who'd carry a camera weighing fifty pounds?' said the other man.

'Cost, not weight,' snapped Rosemary.

'Where did this happen?'

'On the cliff above Polbissick.'

'Then how could he have thrown the camera into the harbour?'

'We'd gone there afterwards.'

'After what?'

'After he'd thrown the camera in, of course!'

She turned just in time to see the man who had been reading the comic lick his finger and pass it across his forehead with a loud, expressive hiss.

The other policeman looked at her compassionately. 'You've got a touch of the sun, miss,' he said. 'High temperature, I shouldn't wonder. Lay down on that bench for a minute, and we'll make you a nice cupper. Then you can tell us the whole story, at your leisure, like.'

Rosemary looked at them exhaustedly. They did not believe her. People don't shoot one another and throw cameras into harbours. Sunstroke is much more common.

'You'll find his car,' she said, remembering. 'It's at the top of the cliff, and his body'll be somewhere at the bottom, if the tide hasn't washed it away.'

They began to look more intelligent.

'Young Harry could go along on his motorbike when he comes back with the toffee,' the comic-reader suggested. 'That won't do no harm.'

'You wait here in the cool, miss, till he comes,' they told her.

'Could I make a phone call?'

'Surely, surely. It's on the wall behind you.'

'London, Westminster nine thousand,' Rosemary said into

the old-fashioned mouthpiece. There was a long pause while the names of distant towns linked together between her and London; then a snappish female voice was asking her which department she wanted.

All at once Rosemary realised that she didn't know the name of Alan's boss.

'I — I want to speak to someone high up,' she said doubtfully.

'What division?'

'It's a division that a Mr Hawthorne works in.'

'No Mr Hawthorne on our list,' announced the voice after a pause, and Rosemary remembered with a sinking heart that Alan was seconded from some other ministry. 'What did you want to speak about?'

'I — I wanted to leave a message from Mr Hawthorne.'

'What was the message? Perhaps I could identify —?'

'It was a tune.'

'A *tune*? I'm sorry, I can't help you. I think you must have the wrong number.'

'It went like this,' said Rosemary despairingly, and began whistling. A click told her that the operator had hung up.

She turned to see that this conversation had revived all the policemen's doubts. One had brought a jar of aspirin out of a drawer while the other was hastily thumbing through the First-Aid book for Sunstroke.

'The man who did the murder,' Rosemary told them earnestly, 'is tall and dark and rather fat and wears green corduroys and suede shoes.'

'Yes, yes,' they soothed her. 'We'll catch the miscreant, no danger. Soon as Harry gets back with the toffee.'

Rosemary glanced out of the door and her eyes bulged. Walking leisurely down into Linhoe was Peterson himself.

'There he is!' she hissed to the two men. 'Look! He must have left his car behind in the car-park at the top.'

16

Disbelievingly they crossed to the door, but of course by the time they reached it Peterson had turned the corner out of sight. Rosemary darted after him. The two police looked after her for a moment, then returned to their occupations.

'Daft,' said the elder one. 'Daft as my sister Aggie's youngest.'

Rosemary ran down into Linhoe, but to her dismay Peterson had vanished, and though she scoured the High Street, there was no sign of him.

Tired, dispirited, and at a loss, she turned into a snack bar, had a sandwich and some coffee, and tidied herself up. What to do now? Go back to the police? And then, as she stood indecisively in the street, out of a first-floor window came the familiar notes of a tune: 'Pom pom — pom tiddle om pom —' it broke off abruptly and the player switched to the Blue Danube.

Rosemary stopped, as if her head had been pulled up by a string. There was a door beside her, and a flight of outside steps; a notice said that this was Madame Brzofska's Academy of Dancing. Rosemary ran up.

She came to a small lobby, and then to a large bare room, with a polished floor and hard wooden chairs round the walls. Twelve little girls in frilly organdie dresses were dancing with bamboo pipes while a row of parents sat dismally at the end of the room.

Rosemary put on dark glasses, as the best she could do in the way of disguise, and looked about her. The woman who had been playing the piano stood up and glided towards her. She had pale eyes like marbles, a receding chin, and a bun.

'You must be Miss Bugge, our new pianist,' she said with a cross smile. 'You are late. Please sit down and begin.'

If I must I must, Rosemary thought, and she sat down at the piano while Madame Brzofska darted to the little girls, who had been taking a breather.

'A polka now, Miss Bugge, and I want to see some beautifully pointed toes — like *this*.' Rosemary obediently began playing the next piece in the book, *The King Pippin Polka*. Madame Brzofska tripped back and forth, her toes, in their strapped black patent shoes, pointed like daggers, her navy silk skirt held up to reveal chiffon underskirts in puce and cyclamen.

'*Point*, Cecily!' she cried. 'Toes should point *down*, not up. Arms, Prudence — beautifully curved, like a willow. Tum, tum, tara, tum, tum. Nicely, Jacqueline. Cecily, your toes! Again, Miss Bugge.'

As Rosemary began the *King Pippin* again she felt somebody behind her and, turning her head slightly, saw with tightening breath that Peterson had come in.

'Ah, Doctor la Poer', said Madame Brzofska, swimming towards him. 'Delightful to see you here!'

'I have come with your tickets for tonight's concert,' he said affably. 'Seven o'clock in the town hall. But perhaps I may be permitted to stay and watch?'

'Of *course*! Now, children, your pipe dance — *very* beautifully, please, as dear Doctor la Poer is watching. I want to see a row of graceful little fountains, little waterfalls. Miss Bugge, the Windowbox, please.'

Rosemary jumped, flapped over a page, and began playing the Windowbox Waltz while the children once again began skipping round with their bamboo pipes.

I've a bungalow deep in the jungle-oh
For my true love turned out to be false . . .

Something Madame Brzofska had said was fidgeting Rosemary's mind, and it took her a moment or two to realise that the waltz was arranged for four hands and she was playing one part only.

'I will assist you,' announced Peterson, and he drew up a chair beside her and swung into the sugary rhythm of the waltz.

Rosemary was fairly sure he had not recognised her — one mouse-fair girl is very like another — and the glasses helped, but this close proximity made her feel very ill at ease.

All at once, under pressure from her overstrung nerves, perhaps, she remembered what Madame Brzofska's words had recalled. 'A row of little waterfalls,' she had said, and Alan had spoken of his chief as old Waterfalls — of course! If only she could get away to a telephone. Could one ring up a ministry and ask for old Waterfalls?

Her right banged into Peterson's left us they negotiated an arpeggio, and he hit a wrong note. Suddenly she realised that he was staring at her hand, on which she wore an opal ring, set like a silver butterfly. Rosemary cursed inwardly. His eyes met hers.

'Enough, thank you, players,' sang Madame Brzofska, swooping towards them with a toothy smile. 'Rest for a moment, children, and then we will practise our tango.'

A buzz of voices broke out as the children stacked their pipes on the piano.

'They would do for blowpipes, would they not,' said Peterson pleasantly in Rosemary's ear. He picked up one of the pipes and, still smiling, still keeping his eyes on her, he pulled a little case out of his vest pocket, remarking, 'South American poison-arrow darts. No use at long range but invaluable in emergencies like the present and quite undetectable. I never travel without them.'

Rosemary glanced round frantically. Madame Brzofska was at a distance, talking to the parents. Peterson started to open the case.

'Cecily, come here, dear,' called Rosemary. 'Your elastic must have broken.' With a startled look the child obeyed and Rosemary, suddenly springing up, twitched the case from Peterson's hand, dodged behind Cecily, and ran out of the door, slamming it. She turned the key in the lock and flung it and the case of darts into a Corporation garbage lorry that chanced to be passing in the street below, before running down the steps.

She guessed her start would be short. There must be more than one exit to the hall. Peterson would be after her in a moment, so she ducked into the first door she came to.

It was a hatshop with the name Gwendolyn in trailing gilt letters.

'I'd like the pink jersey cap and scarf, please,' Rosemary said boldly, hoping she had enough money.

Looking into the mirror when she had put them on she exclaimed, 'Heavens, I look like the Topless Wonder.'

'It's a lovely colour, isn't it?' the girl said. 'Just suits you.'

It certainly changed Rosemary's appearance.

'Have you a phone I could use?' she asked as she paid the fearful price.

There was one in the little office at the back. As she picked up the receiver Rosemary had the satisfaction of seeing Peterson pound furiously past down the street.

'Westminster nine thousand?' she said into the mouthpiece. 'Which division do I want? Oh,' putting on a high girlish giggle, 'tee hee, could I speak to old Waterfalls, please. Oo, I'm ever so sorry, it slipped out, I *should* say Mr — er —'

'Mr Torrence?' said the switchboard girl. 'I'm putting you through now . . .'

* * * *

The concert in the Town Hall was evidently to be a grand affair. The posters advertised glees and ballads by well-known local artists and — the main attraction — a violin recital by a famous Russian artist accompanied by the High School Parnassus Band (percussion and strings) conducted by Dr J. S. la Poer, who had a string of musical honours after his name.

Old Waterfalls had told Rosemary to keep strictly out of

the way but it was more than flesh and blood could bear; she could not, simply could not resist turning up to see what would happen. After all, didn't she owe it to Alan to see his murderer caught?

She slipped in unobtrusively by a side entrance, bought a cheap ticket, and found herself a little seat overhanging the orchestra platform. The singers and small orchestra were already in position. Rosemary looked round hopefully for signs of Waterfalls' men who, he had promised, would be plentifully there. Perhaps that large man in the front row with his hat on his kness was from the Special Branch?

Peterson appeared, in tails, with his hair slicked down, bowed deeply to the responsive audience, and the concert began.

A large woman (whom Rosemary recognised as one of the dancing-class mothers) advanced to sing some well-loved ballads.

First she sang *Ben Bolt*, drawing out the long notes until the echoes came back from the liver-coloured marble figures of Justice, Plenty, and Civic Pride on the walls, and hit her. The audience throbbed in sympathy.

Then she sang,

> *'The boy I love is up in the gallery*
> *The boy I love is looking down at me*
> *There 'e is, cantcher see, waving of 'is ankerchee,*
> *'Appy as the robin that sings in the tree.'*

Up to this moment Rosemary had not noticed there was a gallery, but now, looking up, she saw another large mass of people overhead. And, surely, wasn't there somebody waving a handkerchief in the shadows?

The next song was ushered in by a resounding clang from the cymbals: the pianist played an introduction that was by now tolerably familiar to Rosemary, and the large woman, taking a hefty breath, proclaimed in her powerful contralto:

'I've a bungalow deep in the jungle-oh
For my true love turned out be false
Though he swore that one day he would fetch me away
As we whirled in the Windowbox Waltz . . .'

Rosemary kept her eyes glued on the gallery. More waving. It must be a code. But who was signalling, and to whom? And were Waterfalls' men in the hall, and had they seen it?

A clang from the cymbals heralded the chorus, and Rosemary's paper bag of sandwiches fell to the floor. She stooped for it.

'But he left me a wallflower from that day to this
And I sit in the jungle and hear the snakes hiss
But as long as I live I'll remember his kiss
As we whirled in the Windowbox Waltz.'

Clang! went the cymbals again, and this time Rosemary's scarf fell off the arm of her seat. Retrieving it, she noticed a neat, slightly scorched hole clean through it. Now she noticed that there was another such hole in the paper bag; in fact, somebody was shooting at her under cover of the noise of the cymbals, and unless she moved before the next clang she was a dead duck.

She slid rapidly to the left, treading on the feet of the whole row.

Gaining the shelter of a pillar she looked back just as the next clang fell due and saw Peterson pointing his baton which, she now observed, was a neat, slender little gun, in her direction. Slam! went the cymbals in a triumphant finale, a chip flew off the pillar, and Rosemary darted out into the passage, to be grabbed by two unmistakable plain-clothes policemen.

'I'm not the one you want!' she snapped. 'The conductor's been shooting at me. And someone's signalling in the gallery.'

They gazed at her doubtfully.

'That's as may be,' said one. 'Someone else'll take care of them. There's one being brought down now.'

And in fact Rosemary saw with consternation that her Aunt Lou was being escorted down by two more burly men.

'I kept waving and waving at you, dear,' said Aunt Lou placidly. 'Didn't you see me?'

'What are you doing here?' Rosemary asked, wondering if she was going mad.

'Oh, that's a long story, dear. However it will have to wait.'

And indeed Aunt Lou disappeared between her guardians before Rosemary could protest, and the only mitigation was the sight of Peterson at the end of the passage in the midst of a mass of dark blue uniforms, complaining and gesturing wildly. Rosemary tried to see more but one of her guides drew her away with a firm hand, saying, 'Mr Torrence said I was to put you on the bus, miss, and see you stayed there, and that you was to go home and not come out again tonight.'

'But my aunt? What about her?'

'I don't know about that, miss. I daresay she'll be along by and by.'

He escorted her to the double-deck bus, and Rosemary took a seat downstairs, with hauteur, but feeling rather like a small child who has been sent home early from a party in disgrace.

The bus had moved off, but was still not at full speed, when there was a sound of running feet and a man flung himself on the platform.

'Single to Polbissick,' he said, and Rosemary's heart sank as she recognised the voice of Peterson. How in Heaven's name had he managed to escape the posse in the Town Hall?

He came and sat behind Rosemary, who felt like Miss Muffet. She said to the conductor, 'I'm going upstairs, I want to see the view, and climbed swayingly to the top deck, which was empty and extremely stuffy. She made her way forward and shoved down one of the side windows to its fullest extent. Then a brilliant and simple plan for escape struck her. The bus was just starting its long, low-gear climb up Linhoe Hill, inching along between twenty-foot banks crowned with a thickset holly hedge. The road was so narrow that every now and then the holly squeaked and rattled on the windows on the left-hand side.

Rosemary acted before she had time to lose her nerve: she stood on the seat, stooped, clutched the sides of the window, wriggled her head and shoulders through, held on tight, and somehow forced the rest of her body out through the narrow space. Turning round and letting go all in one movement she launched herself against the hedge, which was only a foot away. She gasped as she hit it, and shut her eyes; a thousand holly spines seemed to be sticking into her face, neck, arms, stomach, and legs; she wondered if Peterson's blowpipe wouldn't have been preferable.

But she hung on, and heard the bus go up the hill without her, reach the top, and change gear. She thrust painfully through the hedge at a weak point, and came out bleeding, torn, and ravelled, lacking a shoe and the pink hat, her skirt more or less in rags.

Luckily Aunt Lou's bungalow was only ten minutes' run cross the fields. There was no sound as she went through the gate. The place seemed dark, silent, and empty; the curtains were drawn; the key was under the mat.

But when she had let herself into the dark hall she saw a strip of light under the kitchen door.

Rosemary hesitated — could Aunt Lou have got home first? — and then went in.

Alan was sitting snugly in front of the kitchen fire with one leg, heavily bandaged and splinted, stretched before him on a stool.

The sight of him was so totally unexpected that Rosemary

had to steady herself against the doorpost.

'Hi, there, clever girl,' he said grinning.

'Alan! Is it really you?'

'Didn't your aunt tell you?'

'She didn't have a chance. Police were dragging her away.'

'Oh dear, they always make a mess of things. But it'll sort itself out. I rely on your aunt. When I crawled in on knees and elbows she set my leg and treated me for shock like a professional; I needed it, too, after dangling on that cliff under and overhand till Peterson thought I must have been washed away. And then she went off to the concert to see the doings.'

'But how did you know about the concert?'

'Because as soon as I got here I rang my office. You, with remarkable efficiency, had already got on to Torrence, schools of special branch police were streaming down in helicopters, and your aunt, who seems to know your character well, said she'd better go to find you and make sure you weren't getting into trouble. Torrence will bring her along when he comes to collect me. Did they get Peterson?'

'No, that's the awful thing,' said Rosemary, sobering; she told Alan how Peterson had escaped.

'We must phone Torrence at once.'

But when she tried it, the telephone was dead.

Rosemary had become used to the cold clutch of fear, but this time, perhaps bacause she was tired, perhaps because of the presence of Alan, injured and unable to walk fast, she felt numb from head to foot with an awful certainty. The dark fields stretched round the house, the sea washed below, and the nearest help was three miles off.

She imagined the conversation between Peterson and the bus conductor.

'Who's the young lady? Oh, that's Miss Hoylance's niece, staying with her at Moon Cottage, over the fields yonder. This is her stop — funny she don't seem to be coming down...'

She had made a muck of it. How long would it be before Alan was fetched? Where was Peterson now?

Pretending cheerfulness she went back to the kitchen and said, 'The line's engaged. I'll try again in a —'

'*Don't move.*'

Such a quiet voice.

Rosemary's heart gave a violent bang and her fingers clenched the table's edge. Alan's eyes slowly lifted and he looked past her.

'Mr Peterson,' he said gently.

'So I didn't finish you off after all?' Peterson strolled forward to warm himself at the hearth while he continued to keep them covered with his little gun. 'You are an enterprising pair, it is sad that I have to kill you.'

'Why do you?' said Rosemary crossly. 'It won't help you. You've already been identified.'

'Identity is nothing. Dr la Poer will cease to be and Julius Mendes, bass flautist, will take his place.' He smiled complacently. 'No, I am killing you out of revenge, for spoiling my beautiful system. Now: I have only two shots left, so stand quite still, please . . .'

*   *   *   *

Several hours later the police arrived. They had wasted a good deal of time searching for Peterson in the Town Hall after he got away, and were pleased to find him ready for them, neatly bound and trussed. Rosemary said acidly, 'We might have been dead long ago for all your help.'

'How is it you're not?' inquired her aunt interestedly, handing round cups of tea. 'Sugar, Mr Hawthorne? I've given you the invalid's cup.'

'Alan squirted spray furniture polish all over him as he was trying to shoot us. That's why he has a glassy look. And I hit him with a saucepan and we tied him up.'

Aunt Lou looked regretfully at a broken mirror and windowpane.

'That's the lot, then,' the local superintendent said cheerfully, as Peterson was escorted out to the police van.

'I still don't know what it was all about,' Rosemary complained to Alan.

'Shall I tell you a secret?'

'Yes!'

'Nor do I.'

'Oh,' she said. 'Well, do you think your Ministry will give me a new camera?'

'I should think so.'

'Do you know,' she said, starting to laugh, 'I've thought of something. Peterson needn't have chucked it in the harbour. I'd forgotten to wind on the film after the last shot.'

Sure Magic

by MONICA EDWARDS

'When I were eleven I didn't have three pound in my money-box; no, nor I didn't have one.' Old Tim Terrell leaned on his spade for a moment and got his breath while looking at Paul reflectively.

'I've been saving for two years,' Paul pointed out. 'But now I almost think I shall have to give up,' he added sadly. 'It's funny, but when I started I thought I'd only have to save very hard and carefully, and I'd soon have enough to buy a pony. But of course, I was very young then.'

Old Tim took a whetstone out of his pocket, upended his spade and began sharpening the edge of it. 'Thass a thing I wholly do believe in,' he said, 'an edge to a spade.' He suddenly looked up again for a moment, the whetstone poised. 'You could get yourself a real nice nanny goat with that. Chap what sold me mine, he got another up for sale I do know. Now thass a useful animal, is a nanny goat. Usefuller nor what riding a pony would be, I will say. All that milk. Your Mum'd be pleased, I lay.'

'But I don't want a goat.'

'Ah well, that do make a difference,' the old man admitted, resuming the digging, which he was doing for Paul's father. And then he added persistently: 'Some folks do drive 'em in a liddle cart, and that.'

'What I'm in two minds about,' said Paul, 'is spending it on a second-hand air-gun. Roy Boley's got one at Partridge Farm that he said I could have for three pounds. I thought I'd go and look at it this afternoon. Of course I'd much rather have a pony, even if it meant waiting another two or three years, but I'd only have six or seven pounds then, at this rate.

It's pretty hopeless, isn't it, Tim?'

Mr Terrell looked at his watch and then he looked at the heavy sky. 'Thass full of snow,' he said, 'for all it's near the end of March. If you fare to go out to Partridge and back I lay you better start now. That'll get dark early, see, with all that cloud, and your Mum'll worry.'

'If I had a pony,' Paul said, 'I'd be there and back in no time, galloping across the fields.'

'If wishes was horses,' said Tim Terrell, 'beggars would ride. Now mind my pea-rows—troddlin' all over 'em.' He glanced up again at a sky that looked like suspended London fog and shook his head. 'I tell you, spring ain't what it used to be, nor it ain't. I call to mind when I were a tiddler—' but Paul, apologetically waving his hand, was already out of earshot.

Partridge Farm had several attractions for Paul, the air-gun being one of the least. For one thing, there was Roy; a good friend and wonderful company on ferreting expeditions, though quite incredibly disinterested in horses. Oh, the waste of it! Paul thought as he strode across the fields: here was a boy whose father kept and rode such a splendid hunter mare as Calluna was, a boy who could have kept a pony of his own if he had wanted to, but who was much more interested in the two farm tractors and the cowman's motor-cycle.

A further attraction for Paul was the Ayrshire dairy herd. He liked to help in the cowsheds when he could, and Roy often joined him there, though with him the tractors always took first place. But the greatest attraction of all at Partridge was Calluna, and Mr Boley had a special liking for Paul because of this. He would dearly have liked his own son, Roy, to share his interest in horses and hunting, but failing this it was nice to have Paul about the stable, being useful and absorbed in all that happened there.

Calluna was shortly expecting a foal and so had not been

hunted through the winter just finished. The sire was a very fine premium stallion and Calluna herself was an excellent type of hunter mare, so that Paul and Mr Boley expected great things of the foal. In about a fortnight it would be born. Feeling snow suddenly brush his cheeks, Paul wondered what sort of a world it would be born to. Winter, with east winds and snow? Or spring, with mild sunshine? Anything, it seemed could happen in an English spring. This time last year they had been picnicking. Now it looked as if they might be sledging in the morning.

Once started, the snow began to fall fast, like plum petals in a sudden wind, and by the time Paul reached the farm the ground was white. They were already milking in the long cowshed but Paul stopped to look over the loose-box at Calluna, talking to her and offering her the quartered apple he had brought for her. But she was restless, staring past him at the snow and then walking round her box and staring out again. She took the apple politely but crunched it as if her mind was not on it.

'I expect it does look queer to you, old girl,' said Paul, rubbing his hands down the old corduroy shorts that he wore in school holidays, 'when you thought it was spring.' And he went across to the cowshed, shaking the snow from his hair as he hurried inside.

It was the usual thing that, whenever Roy or Paul were at each other's houses around a meal-time, they stayed there for it, unless it was going to be dark before they could get home again. 'And tonight, even with the snowy sky, it ought to be light till half-past six,' Mr Boley said.

'And there's cherry cake for tea,' said Roy, 'and we can look at the air-gun after.'

But somehow, they never did look at the air-gun. At tea, the talk turned to Calluna and her great expectations, and Paul mentioned how restless she had seemed when he had looked in at her.

'That's the snow, I daresay,' said Mr Boley. 'We haven't had much this winter, for all it's been so cold, and I expect it looked strange to her, coming down so fast and swirly. Anyway, we'll have a look at her after tea, and I always go round last thing, too. You never know with mares in foal, though really she ought to go another fortnight.'

'What I'm wondering about,' said Mrs Boley, glancing through the window a little anxiously, 'is Paul getting home safely. I wonder if you ought to start early, Paul? I don't want to hurry you, but it does seem to be getting thicker.'

'It is jolly thick,' said Roy. 'You can't even see where the path is any more.'

'Oh, I'll be all right,' said Paul. 'It can't be really deep before I get home, and I can go back by the road.'

'Tell you what,' said Mr Boley; 'we'll go out and have a look at the old girl, shall we, and then I'll see you back as far as the signpost?'

Mr Boley's hands were deep in his pockets as they trudged through the snow to the stable. 'It's already up to the ankles,' he said. 'Pity the poor wretches who have their dairy herds lying out!'

Because their heads were tucked down against the blizzard they did not notice the open stable door until they were nearly in front of it. Then, for a moment, they stood staring in horrified disbelief at the empty loose-box. Mr Boley swung round, peering through the snow into the corners of the yard. 'She can't be far off,' he muttered in a shocked voice, adding as if to himself, 'in this weather, and growing dusk, and so near to foaling. Did you notice if the door was properly shut when you looked in at her, Paul?' They were hurrying across to the cowshed now.

'It seemed quite firm when I leaned on it,' panted Paul, hurrying too. 'How on earth could she have got out?'

'Heaven only knows,' said Mr Boley, staring into the shadows of the cowshed. But Calluna wasn't there, and the double row of white-splashed cows looked up curiously, clanking their chains. 'She used to be a bit of a devil at getting out when she was younger,' he added. 'Used to pull the bolt back with her lips. But we thought she'd grown out of that, these three years past.'

'How about tracks?' Paul asked anxiously, peering now at the snowy ground. 'No, it's falling too thick for that, son. You can hardly see our own tracks from the house. We'll have to send out searchers. With lanterns, too; it'll be dark in an hour. But I'll get out the car and run you to the signpost before I join them.'

'Oh — couldn't I help to look for Calluna?' Paul's voice went up in an urgent appeal. 'You could telephone Mother: she wouldn't mind, I'm sure. I could get back all right if you lent me a torch.'

'Sorry, old chap.' Mr Boley looked at him regretfully. 'I couldn't have the responsibility. Job enough finding the mare, I daresay — it may take us all night, in this — without keeping an eye on chaps of Roy's and your age. Come along to the house for a minute while I get the search started, and then I'll soon have you on the road. You can come straight out again in the morning,' he added, seeing Paul's forlorn face. 'But we want grown men on this job.'

The next ten minutes for Mr Boley were a whirl of telephoning, and sending one person to fetch another, and someone else to search the farm buildings, until he was satisfied that four were about to set out seeking Calluna, and that the police were on the look out as well. Roy brought out the air-gun, to fill up the time usefully, but Paul hardly felt so interested in it now. He kept looking up, out of the dusky window where snowflakes flew before the wind, and imagining Calluna out in it, probably foaling in it; because, as Mr Boley said, you never knew with mares in foal.

That night the snow fell heavily until dawn. The telegraph wires were down in many places, so that, when Paul got up in the morning, he could not get through to Partridge Farm to inquire about the search. But news came very quickly, of its own accord, on the legs of old Tim Terrell. Tim was postman as well as jobbing gardener in Paul's village, and he stood on the doorstep stamping his feet and sorting letters while Paul looked out past him at the amazing snow of spring. 'Treating you well, this morning,' Tim was saying. 'Five letters, and not a bill among them.'

'Have you heard anything about the Boleys' search party, Tim?'

'I have that. Just been talking to the chap what's driving the snow-plough, and he says their cowman told him as they found the mare in Merlin Wood.' He was talking through the fingers of a glove that he held in his mouth while handling letters.

'Oh, I am glad they found her!' cried Paul, taking the letters. 'Was she all right?'

'Right enough,' said Tim, 'but what do you think? With a foal at foot! In all that snow.'

'Tim! Really? Is the foal all right, too? Oh, Mr Boley will be pleased!'

'The little 'un's good as new, he say,' said Tim. 'Funny, ain't it, the things they'll stand? Sometimes you hear of 'em digging out sheep what have been buried days and days in them deep hill drifts. I reckon they got air and warmth down in that snow — must have, mustn't they? Oh well, this won't do.' Mr Terrell swung his bag round his back again and then set off on his way.

Paul would have thrown his coat and gumboots on and trudged to Partridge Farm at once, if his mother hadn't reminded him that he had not made his bed or dried the breakfast things, which were his holiday tasks, but he was out there before the morning was half over. He found Mr Boley in the loose-box with Calluna, and there, walking experimentally about in the straw on long stilty legs, was the most beautiful but quite the tiniest colt he had ever seen.

'Oh, I say!' Paul stared in rapturous awe. 'Isn't he small?'

'Fortnight premature, of course,' said Mr Boley. 'Lucky to find him when we did. It was close on dawn; we'd been trudging all the countryside. No tracks, you see until the snow began to clear. Still, he seems well enough for all his bitter welcome. It's his mother that worries me.'

'She looks all right to me,' said Paul, studying her anxiously.

'Won't settle,' said Mr Boley. 'She desn't seem to care about the little fellow at all. Seems to want to get out in the snow again. Look at her fretting! I can't make it out. I've been trying to get her to stand for feeding him, off and on, ever since we brought her in. But you can see for yourself how it is.'

Paul could see very easily now, for Calluna fussed around her box with her swinging stride, throwing her head up at the doorway and staring out over the snow with strange restless eyes. And this was the way she went on behaving through all of that day. Paul stayed for lunch, but not for tea because of the snow, and most of his time he spent with Mr Boley in Calluna's box, trying to get the mare to settle quietly with her foal.

'She's always been such a good mother before,' the farmer said in a baffled voice. 'And this little chap — he's so small, being premature, he wants a good start. I don't reckon he's had a proper meal yet. Now, see if she'll stand quietly while you hold her, and I'll help the colt.'

But Calluna swung her quarters this way and that, and stared out at the snow as if it were a green summer meadow and she was starving.

The next morning, with the snow still deep on the ground

and no birds singing, Paul went to the door in answer to Tim Terrell's knock. 'Mouldy old lot I brought you this morning,' said Tim, who always took a great interest in the letters. 'Four circulars and a postcard.'

'How's Calluna, Tim? Have you seen her this morning? Has she settled down yet, do you know?'

'Cor! That's a case, that is,' said Tim shaking his head. 'Rumbusting around her box all night, whinnying and that, so Mr Boley says. Don't know what to do with her, they don't, and that's a fact, 'cept padlock her door. Nice little tiddler too, the colt. But she don't seem to take to him nohow. Just fussing to get out.'

'Oh, Tim!' Paul stared at the letters without seeing them. 'How awful for the colt. I wish — oh, I wish that he were my colt! I think he's quite the loveliest thing I ever saw. So small, and yet so — sort of perfect.'

'You wouldn't be able to ride him now, not for years,' Tim pointed out, straightening his shoulders under the heavy bag.

'I know. But it isn't only riding that's such fun. It's having a horse, and being able to look after it, and all that.'

'Telly what, then,' said Mr Terrell helpfully. 'You wanter find out where the old mare dropped her foal, son; then go there and wish, see. Sure magic, that is — to wish where a foal been newly born. But he must be a colt foal, mind, or it doesn't work out.'

'This one is,' said Tim, his eyes suddenly lighting up with interest. But in a moment they had darkened again. 'Magic, and all that, isn't really true of course,' he said wistfully.

'Telly what parson said in the pulpit, Sunday — since you was at home with your cold —' said Tim Terrell. 'He said: "There's more things in heaven and earth than this world dreams of." Well, this won't do; I must be getting along down the lane, now. Cheerybye, son. So-long.'

36

Paul took the letters in and shut the door. He made his bed
and dried the breakfast things, and then fetched in some logs
for the sitting room fire. Then he put on his gumboots and
coat and set off for Partridge Farm.

Merlin Wood, wasn't it, where Calluna's foal had been born?
It lay between Paul's house and the farm, as near as mattered.
At a pinch, he might say it was almost on his way. Of course,
no one believed in magic in these days, but all the same, it
wouldn't do any harm just to trudge about inside the wood
for a bit. No one need know, least of all Roy Boley, who was
exceedingly practical with his carburettors and magnetos
and overhead drive and the like — good chap though he was.

The snow on the edges of the wood was thicker than in the
fields. It reached nearly to the top of Paul's gumboots in
places, and drifts of it were so deep that he had quickly to step
out of them, though none had fallen since the night of Calluna's
escape. Paul saw her tracks here and there, in sheltered places,
and the tracks of men. Some of the prints were half-hidden
by the snow that had fallen during the search, some stopped
and turned back, and others were criss-crossed and lost in
muddle. Trudging through deep drifts, Paul began to think
he would never find the place. And for how long could one
still consider the colt 'newly born', as Tim had said he must
be? Nearly a day and a half had passed already...

Suddenly Paul stared, opening his eyes wider, hurrying
faster though the snow lipped into his boot-tops. Here, many
tracks came together; the snow was trampled, pawed and
scattered. Hoof-prints and shoe-prints overlapped — and there,
sure enough, was the smoothed hollow in the snow where
the mare had lain down. Paul stopped, puffing from his
struggle through the drifts and flushed with the cold damp of
snowy woods. This was the place. Here was where the small
colt had first opened his eyes; not to daylight but to clouded
starlight.

Oh well, Paul decided to himself in an off-hand manner, now that he was here he might as well make a wish. After all, anything could happen, especially in a wood called Merlin ...

He never could be certain, afterwards, whether he had, in fact, wished at all before, suddenly, he saw the two small brown leaf-things sticking up from the snow. Like leaves, they were, but not quite like leaves; and they stood in the top of a drift against the hedge, not ten yards away. He could almost imagine that one of them had moved. Then something seemed to pull tight in Paul's chest as he floundered forward. He bent and scrabbled at the snow with wet-gloved hands; the small leaf-brown things shook and flickered under his eyes, and — really, yes, there was no doubt whatever about it, but — impossible though it might seem — he knew he was looking at the damp dark ears of a new-born foal.

Gently now, but tense with horrified anxiety, the gloved hands scraped and swept and felt their way. And under them the curled form of the foal was gradually revealed. It looked at him with vague, heavy-lidded eyes, snuffling a little at the snow around its nostrils and shivering at the sudden cold air on wet skin. It was alive — a twin foal of Calluna's! Buried in the snow for a day and a half and still alive — though smaller, even, than the little one already at the farm.

Thinking quickly, Paul pulled off his coat and bent to rub the wet furry coat with the sleeves of it. He rubbed the ears, too, because he knew how important this was from having helped with Calluna after hunting; and he lifted the thin, incredibly long forelegs to rub down the narrow little chest. Then, wrapping his coat carefully round the tiny creature, he lifted it into his arms. The foal took little notice, being weak beyond caring, and accepted all things as it found them. Its weight was quite considerable for an eleven-year-old to carry, small though it was; and through deep snow the task was doubly

Wrapping his coat round the tiny creature, he lifted it into his arms

hard. But Paul trudged on, leaning back to balance the weight. The long legs dangled against his knees as he staggered down the hidden field-paths, and often he had to stop and sit down in the snow to get his breath and stretch his arms, the foal lying across his knees like a big, tired dog, and not moving anything except its small leaf-like ears.

So this was why Calluna swung fretting round her box; why she stared out over the snow across the door that was now padlocked as well as bolted. She knew—though no one else had guessed — that one of her foals lay out in Merlin Wood, desperately needing warmth and milk and dryness.

'I'm bringing it, Calluna. I'm bringing it, Calluna,' Paul was saying over and over in his mind as he stumbled along, as if his thoughts might reach the mare and reassure her.

When at last he came to the farm, and people rushed round him, and the foal was lifted from him, he could hardly straighten his stiff arms.

'Well, bless my soul!' Mr Boley kept saying, as they strode to the stable. 'The old girl knew, all along.'

'It looks pretty far-gone, Dad,' said Roy, in the matter-of-fact tone that Paul could never understand.

'A bit weak,' agreed his father, 'and small wonder. But it's marvellous how they can pull round, sometimes.'

'Listen! She's whinnying,' said Paul, as they came into the yard. 'She knows we've brought him!'

Calluna's lovely head was stretched over the door towards them as they came; and then she was licking the little foal all over its head and ears, and all over Paul's coat, too, wherever it came in her way. Mr Bloey laid the twin in the straw beside her, and Paul thought that he would never see anything in the whole of his life so moving as the mother's reunion with the lost one.

'Another little colt, too,' said Mr Boley. 'Twin sons! Well, I'd sooner it'd been a single: twins don't often do so well. But, bless my soul, Paul, you're a hero if ever I've met one! Look, you can see her settling down already. She knew. My word, it's wonderful what they do know, isn't it?'

But all was not entirely as well as it seemed, for the second twin was very small and weak, and Calluna, proved not to have enough milk to feed both of her foals. The bigger colt took well to mixed feeding, with cows' milk addition, but the small one drowsed in the straw and seemed only to hold on to his frail life by the lightness of a thread. For some days there was much anxiety about him, but no anxiety was greater than Paul's. All kinds of things were tried, such as boiling the milk to make it more digestible, and diluting it with water, and adding fresh yolk of egg, but nothing seemed to make any difference.

Mr Boley tried to comfort Paul with commonsense and praise. 'Well, look at it like this, son; if you've done nothing more than get Calluna to settle, that's enough for anyone to be proud of. I shouldn't set too much store on the little one living, if I were you. He doesn't seem to get on with cows' milk, and—well, even if he does pull through, I doubt if he'll ever be much good, you know.'

'But, in a way, he's almost as if he were my colt,' Paul said wistfully. 'I mean, more especially mine than any other horse ever was. If he died, I don't think I could ever be interested so much in anything, ever again.'

'Tell you what,' said Mr Boley, trying to cheer him up; 'if he pulls through, you shall have him! There, what about that? Mind you, I doubt if he will—or that he'd be a credit to you when he grew up, either. More likely to grow up a weed, the way he's started. But there it is — yours, if you want him!'

Paul simply couldn't find a word to say, except, some minutes later, 'Mine? Really? Oh — I say! Thank you!'

After that, the only thing that mattered to him was the

saving of his colt. He spent most of every day in the box with it, offering small bottles of warm milk mixture after the little that was available from Calluna. But the colt seemed, somehow to grow frailer, more dreamy, more often with the long sweeping lashes lowered over his eyes; though by now his brother was bucking wickedly round the box and biting their mother's tail. In the mornings, Paul talked over these things with old Mr Terrell.

'Well now,' said Tim thoughtfully one day, settling his postman's cap, 'you might try a bit of goats' milk, p'raps. Wonderful, that is, for rearing delicate young things—animal or human, the both. Very digestible, is goats' milk, see.'

Paul stared at him, thinking away backwards. 'Mr Terrell—that nanny goat you told me about—'

Old Tim nodded. 'I reckon she's still available. But Will Fletcher he don't reckon to sell no milk. Says it pays him better to feed it to his pigs. 'Sides, he's a good long way from Partridge Farm, son.'

'I know, I don't want to buy the milk, but the goat,' said Paul. 'I want to have it at the farm, near the colt, so that he can have a little often; and really fresh.'

Tim Terrell looked at him doubtfully for a moment, although it had really been his own idea in the first place. Then he said, 'Well, it's your money, old son. And, after all, as I said before, a goat's a useful thing to have.'

Paul went out to Will Fletcher's smallholding that same morning. The snow had all thawed away now, and blackbirds were singing in softly greening hedges. Will Fletcher fetched out the nanny to show Paul, and expressed himself willing to take three pounds for her, without guarantee (because he was a cautious man) except for his word that she was giving half a gallon a day and was quiet to milk and handle, her name being Milkmaid. She was a nice, intelligent-looking creature with a white coat as white as the snow the colt had been born in, and Paul led her away gratefully, at once, with the promise of sending out his money by Mr Terrell the next day.

He took the nanny straight to Partridge Farm, though it was nearly four miles from Will Fletcher's place, and she trotted along willingly enough on the end of her rope, though plainly much astonished at all this tramping. Mr Boley was quite agreeable to Paul's establishing her in a spare loose-box near Calluna's: and, until he managed to teach himself to hand-milk, the cowman came along and milked a bottleful when needed, as well as supplying a pile of hay and roots and dairy-nuts, which were things Paul had somehow not thought about, in the emergency.

It was even as Tim Terrell had said. Where all else failed, the goat's milk seemed to agree with the small one, and slowly he began to look less dreamy and shadowy, taking a growing interest in the things around him. When, after a day or two, Paul brought his goat right into the loose-box, and taught the colt to suckle properly, the real recovery began. Folding down loosely on his knees to reach the low udder, and wriggling his bushy little tail, the colt took to feeding from Milkmaid at once. As Mr Boley said, from that day you could almost see him growing. Within a week, he also was bucking round the loose-box, and Mr Boley came and watched him one morning when Paul was leading Milkmaid out to her tether in the orchard.

'Bless my soul!' he said, laughing at the twin colts' antics, 'I half regret saying I'd give him to you. Getting on fine, now, isn't he? You'd never credit it.'

'Let me put Milkmaid out,' begged Roy. 'I know about moving her tether.'

'All right,' said Paul happily, handing over the head-rope. He was so happy, now, that he would have agreed to almost anything. Realising this, Roy suddenly said, 'When the colt's weaned, I'll swap you my air-gun for Milkmaid. I think she's rather nice. And I could sell her kids, too.'

'I'll think about it,' said Paul, leaning over the stable door to look at his colt—his very own colt.

'Time you named him, isn't it?' asked Mr Boley.

'I have,' said Paul. 'His name is Sure Magic.'

'Sure what? Magic? Funny name that. Why Magic?'

'Oh well—it just suits him, I think.'

Mr Boley suddenly laughed. 'Oh, I see! Of course—because he was born in Merlin Wood!'

'Well, partly,' said Paul evasively. Then: 'I don't suppose there really is any magic, do you, Mr Boley?' He sounded half doubtful, trying again to remember if he had wished before he saw those leaf-like ears in the snowdrift.

'Well—not quite magic, perhaps,' said Mr Boley thoughtfully.

'Funny thing, though. Parson was talking about it, one Sunday in the snow-time. He was quoting someone, and he said, "There are more things in heaven and earth than this world dreams of." But I took it he was thinking of miracles.'

'I know,' said Paul slowly, remembering old Tim Terrell. And then he added, 'Perhaps that's just what magic means.'

Ashvale Grange

by ELISABETH SHEPPARD-JONES

Linda was on her own, exploring the outskirts of Lympton, when she saw the girl fall. The girl was about her own age, and Linda, who had been walking behind her for some minutes, had particularly noticed her because she had lovely fair wavy hair that fell to her shoulders. Being dark and straight-haired herself, she always envied and admired girls with hair like this.

It had been raining, the pavements were slippery underfoot, and the girl had been hurrying. She gave a little cry of pain as she got up slowly, and was examining her knee when Linda reached her.

'Are you all right? Is there anything I can do?'

'I think I'll live,' replied the girl, grimacing. 'I've grazed my knee rather badly, that's all.'

'May I have a look?' Linda didn't wait for a reply but bent over the girl's leg, which was bleeding badly.

'I'm afraid I haven't anything to tie round it,' said the girl, 'and I don't want to bleed to death.' She smiled.

'I've a big clean hankie in my pocket somewhere,' said Linda. 'Mum's always telling me not to forget to take one with me, and it looks as if, at last, it's going to be of some use. Come and sit down on this wall, and I'll bind up your leg for you.'

There was a low garden wall nearby, and the girl appeared to be glad to have somewhere on which to sit for a minute.

Linda found the handkerchief, and tied it neatly round the girl's knee. 'I think this should be cleaned up properly,' she said, 'you know, with a disinfectant, and then have some ointment put on it. Still I expect your mother will see to it for you when you get home. Have you far to go? Would you like me to come with you?'

'No, it's not far. I'm on my way back there now actually; don't worry about me. I can manage all right on my own, thank you.' The girl's first warm friendliness had gone: she sounded cool and discouraging.

'It wouldn't be any trouble,' said Linda. 'I mean I haven't anything else to do.' She thought the girl needed a helping arm to get her home.

'I live at Ashvale Grange,' said the girl shortly, as if to explain her refusal of the kind offer.

This sounded grand and impressive to Linda, who lived on the council estate, and she supposed it was the reason why the girl didn't want to be accompanied. Perhaps her parents wouldn't like her to appear at their front door with a stranger she had met casually. It was a pity: the girl had seemed nice at first, and Linda had had a feeling that the meeting could have developed into a friendship, and just now she could do with a friend.

'Oh, well,' she said, 'If it's not far, and you're sure you can manage . . .'

'Don't you know Ashvale Grange?' asked the girl, sounding surprised.

'No, I don't,' said Linda. 'We've only just come to live in Lympton, and I don't know anywhere yet.'

'What's your name? Where do you live?' asked the girl. Linda told her.

'I'll return your hankie to you sometime then,' said the girl. 'And thanks a lot; you've been awfully kind.' The warmth had returned to her voice. 'My name's Anne Richards. 'Bye, Linda; see you.'

Linda watched her limp across the road, around a bend and out of sight. Ashvale Grange indeed! The Lady Anne!

Nasty, snobby, haughty girl! Still she did have lovely hair and, Linda had to admit it, a very sweet expression on her face.

A few days later, when Linda was in Woolworth's buying curtain hooks for her mother who still had some curtains to fix in their new house, she saw Anne again. She was with someone Linda took to be her mother, and three small children—two boys and a girl—presumably her brothers and sisters, although they didn't look a bit like her. None of them looked particularly like her idea of landed gentry, but as her knowledge of such people came from the old films on Sunday afternoon television and the magazines she saw in the doctor's waiting room, she did not consider herself an expert.

Linda was determined not to make the first move, so she looked down at the counter and fiddled around with the curtain hooks, while the assistant looked on impatiently at her.

'Hello, Linda.' Anne had put a hand on her arm. 'I was just on my way to see you; you've saved me a journey. Here's your hankie, and thank you again for the loan of it.' She passed over the handkerchief, freshly laundered and ironed—'by one of the many servants,' thought Linda.

Anne turned to the lady with her. 'This is the girl who was so kind when I hurt my knee,' she explained. 'By the way, it's quite all right now,' she said, turning back to Linda.

'That's good.' Linda murmured shyly.

'Anne tells me you've only come to Lympton fairly recently,' said the older woman, 'so I dare say you don't know many people here yet. Still, I expect you'll make lots of friends at school just as soon as you've settled down.' She glanced hesitantly at Anne before speaking again to Linda. 'I wonder if you'd like to come and have tea with Anne one Saturday—perhaps this next Saturday would suit you?'

Linda was taken aback by the sudden invitation, and wasn't

at all sure she wanted to go to tea at a splendid place like Ashvale Grange must be; but she couldn't think of a good excuse and, in a way, she was glad to have something to do on Saturday as she was very much at a loose end. Not that Anne appeared wildly in favour of having her to tea; at least, she didn't say, 'Do come,' or 'We'd love it if you could.' She just looked down at her feet and said nothing.

'Thank you, I'm free on Saturday; I'd like to come to tea,' said Linda politely.

'That's fine; we'll see you at the Grange some time after three then, and I hope we won't all prove too much for you.' Do you know how to get there or shall Anne call for you?'

'Thanks, but I'm sure I can find my way,' replied Linda, wishing to show her independence.

'Oh gracious!' exclaimed the lady at that moment, 'Where *have* the children gone? Come on, Anne, let's find them before they get into too much mischief. Goodbye, Linda; we look forward to seeing you on Saturday then.'

'Goodbye, Mrs Richards,' said Linda. But she and Anne had gone off towards the sweet counter, where the three small children were chattering excitedly in front of a mound of toffees.

When Saturday arrived, Linda confessed to her mother that she wished she had never accepted the invitation to Ashvale Grange.

'I feel quite nervous,' she said. 'I mean, they're just not our sort of people, are they? I'm scared I'll say or do the wrong thing; and I don't know what to wear. I feel I ought to put on my best dress, but I shall look such a fool if the Grange children are in ordinary clothes. And what on earth am I going to talk about?'

'Calm down,' advised her mother. 'You liked the girl, didn't you? Just talk to her as you would talk to any other girl. Living in a big house doesn't make them different people.

Be your natural self and you'll be all right. Keep on the dress you are wearing; it was clean this morning and looks very nice—and do stop fussing. Did you find out how to get there, by the way?'

'Yes, apparently Dad passes it on his way to work; it's a few yards beyond the vicarage. You can't see the house from the road, only the entrance gates. Oh, Mum, I do wish I hadn't said I'd go!'

'Think how thrilled I shall be to hear about it when you come back,' said her mother. 'I shall want to know every little detail; and don't forget to tell me what the garden is like.'

A couple of hours later when Linda was walking up the long, curving drive towards the large, grey stone house she made a mental note to tell her mother that the garden was more neglected than you would expect. There were long stretches of weedy lawn, lots of trees and bushes but, as far as she could see, very few flowers. Halfway up the drive she became aware of the noise of children laughing and playing: glancing about her, she could just see figures moving around in a rough piece of woodland at the side of the house. There appeared to be quite a number of them, and she wondered if the three small ones she had seen in Woolworth's were having a party. The thought of this made her feel less nervous; she wouldn't be noticed so much in the middle of a crowd. Certainly, no one noticed her at this particular moment.

She stood uncertainly in front of the large door which was standing open, not sure if she should ring the bell or walk in. She had just decided to put her finger on the bell when a voice behind her said: 'Did you want someone?'

She turned round to see a boy, aged about nine or ten, dressed as a Red Indian, with a head-dress of feathers perched on top of a thatch of sandy hair.

'I've come to have tea with Anne,' said Linda, wondering

49

if this boy was still another member of the Richards family.

'Oh, I expect she's in her room,' said the boy. But before Linda had time to ask where that was, and if she should go and look for her, the boy, making loud whooping noises, had plunged off in the direction of the little wood.

'Can I help you?'

Linda swung round and faced the door again. This time she was being addressed by a girl in her early twenties. She had a gaily-coloured apron tied around her waist, but she wasn't Linda's idea of a parlourmaid at all, although that was what Linda supposed she was.

'May I see Mrs Richards, please?' asked Linda, thinking perhaps it would be better to ask for Anne's mother instead of Anne herself.

'Mrs Richards?' The girl looked puzzled.

'Yes, Anne's mother.'

'Oh, you're the girl who's come to have tea with Anne Richards; I'd quite forgotten. I'm awfully sorry.' She held out her hand. 'My name's Sally Hill. The children call me Auntie Sally, so please do the same. I'm a student here.'

It was Linda's turn to look puzzled.

'Anne doesn't have a mother, you know,' went on this girl. 'That's why I didn't cotton on immediately. Your name's Linda, isn't it? Anne's talked a lot about you; you made quite an impression on her, it seems. I'll call her now; she'll be delighted you're here; Ever since dinner time she's been counting the minutes till you came.'

Linda was in a complete whirl—so many different people, and the lady she met in Woolworth's not Anne's mother at all! And what was a student doing here?

When Auntie Sally called her, Anne came running across the hall, which Linda could just see through the open door. They smiled at each other a little shyly, and said 'Hullo.'

'Do you play tennis, Linda?' asked Auntie Sally. Linda said

she did. 'Then why don't the two of you have a quiet game? The other kids are having some wild romp in the wood, so it's nice and peaceful on the court. You'll find the rackets in the shed, Anne. Here's they key, and don't forget to lock up and let me have it back, or we shall find all the sports equipment scattered to the four winds next time we want to use any of it.'

'How very strange,' thought Linda. 'Was Ashvale Grange some sort of mixed boarding school and not a private home at all?'

She followed Anne along the edge of the wood towards the bottom of the garden, making a few comments about the size of the grounds and the age of the house, which looked early Victorian and was very big. The tennis court was not clearly marked out, the net was torn and not quite the right height, and the rackets—which Anne fetched from the garden shed nearby—had a few broken strings.

'It'll be more a sort of knock-up than a real game,' apologised Anne.

'That doesn't matter, said Linda. 'In fact, I like it better that way: I'm not very good at tennis; swimming's more in my line.'

'I love swimming, too; you must come to the baths with us some time. Mrs Ford is a wonderful swimmer and a jolly good instructor; she's even managed to teach Betty to swim, and she's our youngest—only five.'

'I don't quite understand all this,' said Linda. 'You have an awful lot of brothers an sisters, haven't you? And who is Mrs Ford?'

'They're not my brothers and sisters,' laughed Anne, tossing back her hair. 'And you met Mrs Ford in Woolworth's; she's Matron here. We like her a lot; she's much nicer than the last one. I wish you could see your face, Linda! What's wrong? Is there something you want to know about?'

51

Linda plucked up her courage, especially as Anne was now being so friendly and approachable. 'Yes, lots of things actually. First, I thought Mrs Ford was your mother'—Anne's face clouded. 'Oh, I'm sorry,' went on Linda, 'that student girl told me you had no mother—'

'Yes, that's right,' said Anne.

'Then I thought this must be some sort of school,' said Linda hurriedly, 'because there are so many children about; and now you talk about a matron as if it were some sort of hospital. So, if I look puzzled, it's jolly well because I feel puzzled. What exactly is this place anyway?'

'You know, I just can't understand it!' cried Anne, twirling her racket into the air and catching it again. 'I thought everyone in Lympton knew about Ashvale Grange. I got the idea you never knew when I first met you, but I was sure someone would have told you by now. It's a Children's Home.' She said it with an air of defiance, as if daring Linda to be sorry for her.

'You mean you're all orphans here!'

'Not necessarily. Most of the kids have people of some sort, maybe a mother and no father or the other way round. A few haven't any parents at all, and some have got mothers in hospital—but they don't stay here very long, of course.'

Linda longed to know about Anne herself but, since she offered no information, she asked only how long Anne had been at Ashvale Grange.

'About as long as I can remember,' replied Anne. Then, as if to ward off any further questions of this nature, she said, 'Come on, how about this game of tennis?'

They knocked the ball about for an hour or so, until a bell sounded calling them in to tea. Children came running to the house from all parts of the garden. Linda estimated there were nearly twenty of them, the youngest the five-year-old Betty and the eldest a tall boy of about sixteen. Anne appeared to be about the oldest girl.

The dining-room was large, and the children sat at small tables, an older child in charge of each table. At a top table sat Mrs Ford, another middle-aged woman, Auntie Sally, and a middle-aged man. Mrs Ford welcomed Linda and told her to sit at Anne's table.

'The woman sitting next to Mrs Ford is the assistant,' explained Anne. 'Auntie Sally you've met, and the man is Mr Ford. He works at the Town Hall but lives here, of course, and helps out when necessary. He's particularly popular with the boys because he's a wizard at carpentry; also, he's got a super voice and can play the guitar. We all tease him and say he could make his fortune with a good agent, but he always comes back with "Who ever heard of a middle-aged pop singer?"'

'Well, there *is* Frank Sinatra,' said Linda.

'Mm, I must remember to tell him that,' said Anne.

The meal—baked beans on toast, lots of bread and butter and honey ('from our own hives,' said Anne) and cake—was eaten amidst a babble of chatter. The children appeared healthy, happy and very lively. Linda, who was an only child, could not remember when she had enjoyed herself so much. After tea, many of the children crowded round her, anxious to know who she was and where she lived. Then Mrs Ford detailed three of them to clear the tables and to the washing-up; some of the others went into the sitting-room to watch television and the rest went back into the garden.

Anne took Linda upstairs to her bedroom. It was a little shabby and needed re-decorating, but it was comfortable and there were gay chintz curtains at the windows, with matching bedspreads on the three single beds.

'Do you mind sharing a room?' asked Linda.

'Not really,' said Anne. 'The other two here are sisters; they don't bother me much, and they get on well together.

The smaller one sometimes cries for her mother at night, and this used to stop me getting to sleep, but either I've got used to it, or she doesn't do it as often as she did. The eldest boy or girl here has a single room, and when Peter leaves next year, I'll have his room and I must say I'm quite looking forward to it. Lots of the kids prefer sharing a room; they'd be frightened on their own. I don't think I'll be scared though; I shall be only too glad of a spot of peace and quiet. This isn't a bad place, but it's awfully difficult to get away from everyone when you want to. There's a tree in the garden, and I'm the only one who can climb it: when I'm feeling really sorry for myself, I go to the top of that—it's wonderful! If I put up my hand, I can nearly touch the sky.'

Linda had a lump in her throat and, listening to Anne, she realised, for the first time in her life, that there were some children not as well off as she was. It was ironic to recollect that she had thought she was coming to tea with the favoured, spoilt daughter of the Lady of the Manor!

Later, Anne took Linda on a tour of the grounds, showed her the out-buildings where the bicycles, the coats and the gardening tools were kept and the stable which housed the various pet animals; let her admire the little patches of garden some of the children tended and the beehives which were Mr Ford's pride and joy; and joined her in a hilarious trip down a home-made slide. Then they made their way back into the sitting-room where Mrs Ford was gathering together the smallest children to take them up to bed. Linda said that it was probably time for her to go.

'Don't go unless you feel you must,' said Mrs Ford. 'There's no hurry from our point of view. I'd be glad for Anne to lend me a hand with bathing the little ones—she's so good with them—but I'm sure Auntie Sally will find something for you to do while Anne's upstairs. I think she's in the kitchen, getting suppers ready.'

Linda needed no further persuasion: she was delighted she could be useful and was being accepted into this cheerful community. In the kitchen, Auntie Sally explained that the children came downstairs, after their baths, to have their milk and biscuits. She gave Linda a tray of plastic mugs and some bottles of milk, and told her to fill them up.

'What sort of student are you?' asked Linda, her shyness completely leaving her now that she had a job of work to do.

'An ordinary University student, from London: I'm doing my practical at Ashvale Grange.'

'What exactly does that mean?'

'Well, I'm taking a degree in Social Studies; I want to work with children when I've graduated at college. Every now and again, each student has to do a month at various places like this one. It's to give us an idea of the practical side of the job. Back at college, of course, I carry on with my studies, and take my exams.'

'It must be awfully interesting,' said Linda.

'If you like children and you've a lot of patience, it is,' said Auntie Sally. 'There's never a dull moment.'

'Will you have a job like Mrs Ford's when you've finished?'

'Well, no, not really; you see, on the whole, matrons of homes like this one don't have any particular training. They just need to be warm-hearted and sensible like Mrs Ford is. No, I hope to be a Probation Officer or a Children's Officer; something like that you see. Maybe I will be able to help families who can't quite cope with life and need help and guidance over their problems.'

'They're worthwhile sorts of jobs, aren't they?' said Linda thoughtfully. 'I mean, you're helping people who badly need help. Until I met Anne, I'd never thought about girls like her before; at least, I'd never thought about them as real people, if you know what I mean. All my other friends have a mother and a father and a nice home, like me.'

Auntie Sally smiled at her. 'I hope you and Anne are going to be real friends. You know, there isn't really another girl of her age here, and it's super her having a friend who doesn't live at the Grange. Now let's have less talk and a little more work. Put these biscuits on the plates you'll find on the dresser over there.'

It wasn't long before Anne joined them, and together they handed out the supper to the children as they came downstairs in their pyjamas and dressing-gowns after having their baths. They looked very rosy-cheeked and very angelic.

'They look so sweet, don't they? Who would think they could be such little devils during the day!' teased Auntie Sally.

Reluctantly, Linda said that she really must go now; her mother would be wondering what had happened to her. She found Mrs Ford upstairs, and thanked her for the lovely time she had had. Mrs Ford told her to come whenever she felt like it.

'One extra never makes any difference here; you'll always be welcome, so don't wait for an invitation. The children love visitors—and we can always find you something to do, you know.'

Anne walked down to the gates with her, chatting casually about this and that. She seemed more at her ease now that Linda knew a bit about her, and about Ashvale Grange.

'I hope to see lots more of you,' she said, as they parted.

And they did see lots more of each other, in spite of the fact that, living in different areas of the town, they didn't go to the same school. They visited each other often. And if Linda found the noise and bustle and company of the Grange an exciting change, Anne found the homely, quiet atmosphere of the little council house an equally exciting change. But Linda could always tell she had the best side of the bargain.

They handed out supper to the children as they came downstairs

The Fords did not belong to Anne as Linda's mother and father belonged to Linda.

As time went on, Linda gradually found out something of Anne's history. Bit by bit, as Anne learnt to know and trust her new friend, it all came out. Her mother had died when Anne was very small. There were no relations who could care for her, and she had had to be sent to Ashvale Grange. Her father was a seaman, and she saw him only once or twice a year when he was home from his long trips to the Far East.

'Sometimes,' Anne said, 'I feel almost entirely alone, and it seems more than I can bear until I remind myself that I do have Dad, and that's more than some of the kids have; and I get lots of letters and presents from him. I don't want you to get the idea that I'm unhappy here because, most of the time, I'm not.'

In spite of what she said, as the end of the school term got nearer and the long summer holiday became almost a reality, Anne began to look more and more unhappy. She lost a lot of her sparkle and was often snappy and sulky. Linda was too loyal and understanding a friend to be put off by this, and she continued to see her as often as possible; but, one Saturday afternoon, when she called at the Grange, Anne was nowhere to be found.

'Did she know you were coming?' asked Auntie Sally, who was mending a pile of clothes in the sewing-room.

'Yes, I think so' replied Linda, 'and I've asked some of the children; apparently no one's seen her since dinner.'

'I think I can guess where she is,' said Auntie Sally, 'but I don't think I'd go and look for her if I were you.'

'Well, where is she? And why shouldn't I go and find her?' Linda felt cross.

'She's probably in her tree; she's been crying and she's gone there to get over it—that's my guess.'

'But what's she been crying about?' asked Linda.

'Mrs Ford was talking to the children about summer holidays this morning. This place closes down for the month of August; the children go to their homes or to friends or relations. Anne had a faint hope that her father might be back from a trip and be able to take her somewhere for a holiday, but it seems his ship has been delayed. Mrs Ford had to break the news to her this morning, although I think Anne has suspected this would happen. She can stay here during other holidays but not during August; arrangements always have to be made for her to spend the time at another Home. I don't think she minds so much when she can stay here, but she hates going off to another Institution. It's very bad luck on her, and everyone feels enormously sorry about it, but there really isn't any alternative. Mr and Mrs Ford must have a holiday themselves; they work terribly hard during the rest of the year and, if they didn't get right away for a few weeks, they wouldn't be able to do their job properly. You see how it is.'

Linda saw only too well. She was tempted to go and find Anne to try and comfort her, but decided against it. Anne was a proud sort of girl, and would prefer to be left alone while she was still feeling upset; she wouldn't want Linda to see her crying. So, Linda made her way slowly home and, as she did so, she thought hard about her friend's situation and, finally, she had an idea. It was a good idea but how to get it successfully across to her mother was another matter.

She needn't have worried. Her mother listened to her first few stumbling words and immediately agreed, without any sort of pressure being put on her.

'It's a splendid plan,' she said. 'I'm all for it, and I know Dad will be, too. Why don't you go back to the Grange after tea, and see what Anne herself thinks about it?' Then she added an idea of her own, with which Linda was equally delighted.

As soon as she could, Linda raced back to the Grange. This

time Anne was easily found: she was washing up the tea things with a couple of other children. She looked very red-eyed, and greeted Linda quietly and without a smile.

'Can I see you privately somewhere?' asked Linda. 'It's frightfully important.'

'I suppose so,' said Anne dully. 'Just give me a hand with the rest of these dishes; then you can come with me to feed the guinea pigs and rabbits. No one will be around outside; they'll all be watching television.'

'I've heard about your disappointment,' said Linda, when they reached the stable.

'Who told you?'

'Auntie Sally.'

'She had no right to talk to you about my business.'

'I don't know why not. We're friends, aren't we? I suppose you would have told me yourself sooner or later.'

'I suppose I would,' admitted Anne. 'Anyway, I'd rather not talk about it right now, if you don't mind.'

'Well, I do mind, because I want to talk about it,' said Linda determinedly. She pushed a lettuce leaf at a fat, little rabbit. 'Mum, Dad and I are going to Cornwall for the first fortnight of August—'

'Some people have all the luck, don't they?' said Anne, sighing.

'Stop interrupting and listen to me. We've taken a caravan; it's a four-berth one, and we hate the thought of wasting a bunk. I thought, and Mum agreed, that is, if you'd like it, well, that you could come with us. Oh, do say yes; it would be just heaven for me to have company—you'd be doing me a favour really—and it's a gorgeous place we're going to. You'd just love it. We went there the year before last, and there's a lovely beach only a few minutes away, and a dear little village, and lots to do and, of course, we explore for miles around and go for trips in the car. Oh, Anne, please,

please say you'd like to come!' Linda scarcely paused for breath. 'And when we come back, Mum says, will you stay with us for the other fortnight?'

She stopped and waited for Anne to reply. Anne stared at her, open-mouthed and unspeaking, for what seemed an eternity. Then her blue eyes filled with tears; yet, at the same time, she smiled. Linda thought it was the most beautiful smile she had ever seen.

'This is one of the best things that could have happened to me,' said Anne simply. 'It's like a dream come true.'

'Then you'll come?'

'Of course,' Anne shouted the words which echoed up to the rafters of the old stable. She grabbed Linda's hand. 'Come on!' she cried, 'let's go and tell Mrs Ford; she'll be nearly as happy about it as I am.'

And the two girls ran out of the stable, hand in hand, laughing and chattering, and leaving behind them a few hungry guineapigs and some very startled rabbits.

The Leopard

by ROSEMARY WEIR

Judy was halfway across the farmyard before she saw the leopard. He was crouching down in the shadow of the barn, licking his paws. Feathers scattered around him explained the commotion in the fowl house which had brought Judy out to investigate.

She stopped dead, her heart thumping wildly, hardly able to believe the evidence of her own eyes. A leopard on an isolated Welsh farm! It wasn't possible; and yet there the beast was, sleek, sinuous, deadly. He yawned widely, wrinkling back his lips, stretched, then lay down again, his great head lowered on to his paws, blinking sleepily in the afternoon sun. He had not scented the girl; the wind was blowing her way.

Slowly, a step at a time, hardly moving, Judy edged her way back to the house, her feet in light, rubber-soled shoes making no sound. The leopard yawned again and rolled over on to his side like a cat and lay outstretched with closed eyes, sleeping after his recent meal.

Judy's foot caught on a stone, which clinked. Instantly the leopard was awake. For one horrifying second the golden eyes glared into her own and then the beast had gone, melting into the shadows behind the barn.

Judy ran then, her heart thumping, her head dizzy with fright. She reached the farmhouse and slammed the stout door behind her. Her legs gave way and she slid to the floor.

'Judy—is that you?' called an anxious voice from upstairs. 'Is anything the matter? Why were you running?'

Slowly Judy got to her feet. Her heart was steadier now and her legs felt stronger. She peeped through the window before replying, but of the leopard she saw no sign.

'Judy!' the voice called again more urgently, and she ran upstairs to where her mother lay in bed.

'Mother—there's a leopard in the yard!'

'A leopard? Oh, Judy, this is no time to make up your stories. It's time for my medicine, dear. Would you get it for me, please?'

'But, Mother, there *is* a leopard!'

The invalid moved her head irritably on the pillows.

'Judy, *please*. You know I enjoy listening to your stories when I'm well, but sometimes I really think you hardly know invention from truth. You must be careful, dear. Some people who didn't know you might consider you were telling lies.'

Judy thought desperately. It was obvious that her mother was never going to believe in the leopard unless she saw it with her own eyes, and that she couldn't do, for she was too ill to get out of bed. If only Dad was at home! But Dad had gone to market, fifteen miles away over the mountains, and would not be back until milking time at six. The two younger children, David and Gwennie, had gone to school, but Judy had had to stay at home to look after her mother. There was no one else to do it. The nearest neighbour to this isolated farm was a mile away, and the village where the children went to school was two.

Judy gave her mother the medicine, then crossed over to the window and looked out. It was a day in early spring when the greenness was just beginning to spread over the grey, rocky landscape like a soft gauzy veil. It had been wet weather lately and the face of the mountains was streaked with waterfalls shining in the sun, and the air was full of the sound of running water and cries of sheep. The lambs were arriving thick and fast now, and the farmers had to be on the alert all the time to guard them from the strong, cunning mountain foxes. They had never had to contend with a leopard before.

Where had it come from? Judy had never been further away

from home than the county town of Caernarvon but she knew enough to realise that leopards don't normally roam wild in the Welsh countryside. Could it have escaped from a circus or a zoo? If only the wireless was working they might have heard something on it, but the battery had been flat for the last week, and Dad was bringing the new one out from town today. Newspapers hardly ever found their way to the farm, unless they arrived wrapped round the fish or meat and then they were generally weeks old. It would be hard to find a more isolated farm in all the British Isles than Cwm Llwyn.

It was because of the loneliness that Judy had begun making up her stories. They seemed to come easily to her, long, complicated, exciting stories which she told to her younger brother and sister and to the other children at school. Even her father and mother listened sometimes, and her father teased her, saying she must be a descendant of the old story-tellers who used to go round the country in the olden days, telling their tales in castles and farms and earning their living by it. Secretly, Judy planned to write books when she grew up. Then she would be rich and she would buy a better farm for her father, and pedigree rams to improve his flock. Her mother should have an electric stove and a washing machine, and they would have a telephone.

A sudden movement over by the barn brought Judy out of her dreams and again her heart gave a great thud and seemed to jump into her throat. One of the farm cats, a half wild black tom, sped across the yard, the fur on his back standing erect, his green eyes terror-stricken. He disappeared behind the pigsties and, in the same moment, a pig grunted and the flat, broad head of the leopard was thrust round the corner of the barn, followed by his whole body, low to ground, crouching, creeping towards the pig.

'Oh, no! Oh, he mustn't,' cried Judy wildly. Opening the small window she leant out and shouted:

'Shoo — go away, you! Get out of here!'

The leopard looked up and caught her eye. He stopped in mid-stride and again Judy shouted:

'Get out! Get away!'

'What *is* it?' asked her mother anxiously from the bed. 'Don't tell me there's a fox come in broad daylight?'

'I tell you it's a *leopard!*' said Judy desperately and her mother sighed.

'Have it your own way,' she said wearily. 'I'm too tired to argue. Better go down and let the dog out.'

'He's not here. Dad took him to market in case he had sheep to bring home,' Judy reminded her, and felt relief. If Fron had been at home he would undoubtedly have attacked the leopard and been torn to pieces. She shuddered as she looked down at the retreating form of the great beast. He had gone back to the shelter of the bushes which grew beside the barn, but he was still on the alert, and when the pig grunted again he gave a low snarl, twisting his head sideways and showing all his white teeth.

Downstairs in the kitchen the old wall clock whirred and struck four with ponderous, deliberate strokes.

'I could do with a cup of tea,' said the invalid longingly. 'Make me one now, will you, dear? I won't wait for the children to get home.'

A cold chill ran down Judy's spine and again her legs went weak. The children came out of school at four. Now, at this very moment, they would be starting for home. They would come shouting up the glen, talking and laughing and kicking stones and the leopard would be waiting for them in the bushes by the barn, his eyes glittering as they had glittered when he heard the pig!

'Mother! The leopard! It'll get them when they come home! Oh, Mother, what shall I do?'

The sick woman spoke decisively.

'Judy, you don't want to make me angry, do you? Then stop this nonsense and go and get the tea. A girl of eleven is old enough to know when to stop play-acting and behave like a reasonable person. Now, I don't want to hear another word.'

Judy went downstairs, filled the kettle from the tap and put it on the stove. She fed the fire with chunks of wood and raked out the ash. Her mind seemed to have stopped working and she could only move mechanically, doing the familiar jobs as if she were in a dream.

Suddenly a chicken squawked, loudly, desperately. Judy, running to the window, saw the bushes move, and a small cloud of white feathers rose into the air, then sank to the cobble-stones. The bushes rustled again and a yellow head looked out. The clock struck the quarter and Judy came back to life.

The children would be out of the village now and climbing the long ascent which led over the foothills of the mountains to the farm. Somehow she had got to stop them, and that meant leaving the safety of the house and crossing the yard to reach the only track which led to the valley below. At the foot of the track stood their nearest neighbour's house. If she could reach this before the children got there they could all take shelter, and Mr Jones had a telephone, and a gun.

The kettle boiled over with a splutter and hiss. Hastily she poured the water into the teapot and carried the tray upstairs.

'I'm going to meet the kids, Mother,' she said. 'I'll have my tea with them when I get back.' Quickly, before her mother could detain her, she ran downstairs and let herself out of the door into the unbroken quiet of the yard.

Everything was still. No sound came from the pigs or the poultry and the bushes were unmoved by any breath of wind or stirring of the beast they sheltered. *Was* the leopard still there or had it slunk away among the rocks which bordered the track? Was it lying stretched out on the warmth of a flat rock, resting after its second meal, replete and satisfied? Was it asleep, so fast asleep that she could creep past it unheard and then run, run for her life, down to the valley below?

Very cautiously she took a step forward, then another, her eyes glued to the bushes by the barn. To get to the head of the track without passing the leopard she must cross the yard to the other end of the barn, skirt round it to the back and then slide or scramble down a steep bank where tree roots, washed clear of earth by winter rains, made traps for unwary feet.

She had taken a dozen steps before the leopard stirred. Again the flat head was pushed out from the bushes, again it twisted sideways in a wide-mouthed snarl. Judy shot back to the house like a bullet from a gun and again the door slammed behind her.

'What is it?' called her mother. 'Why have you come back?'

'Forgot something,' gasped Judy. What use was it to waste time trying to convince her mother of the danger? There was nothing she could do even if she believed in the leopard. There was nothing anyone could do — except Judy.

The clock on the wall said twenty-one minutes past four. The children never got home until at least a quarter to five. They were inclined to loiter and play, especially by the stream in the valley. When Judy was with them she would make them hurry up, but today they were alone and with any luck they would take advantage of Judy's absence to stop on the wooden bridge and drop sticks into the water, to watch them swirl and glide, become caught up in whirlpools and eddies, and finally slip over the falls into the deep pool below. Once over the bridge there was Mr Jones's black pony to talk to, if she was in her usual field, flicking flies off her back with her long tail in the shade of the rowan tree. After the rowan tree the farm track began, and there was every excuse to loiter, for it was long and steep and small legs easily grow tired.

The clock ticked on, while up above the invalid poured herself another cup of tea, thinking with half impatient amusement of Judy's latest invention, and downstairs Judy herself hovered wretchedly, her hand on the latch of the door.

Suddenly a thought jumped into her head and she felt such relief that she nearly cried. The little window in the dairy at the back! If she squeezed through that it would bring her out in the home field and she could cut across there to come out on the track more than halfway down! If the leopard remained where he was now she would be safe.

The shadows were lengthening. Another half hour and the sun would sink behind the mountains and the evening chill would be in the air. Where would the leopard go then? Down into the valley perhaps, where the air was less keen than on this upland farm. There was no time to lose. The clock showed four, twenty-eight.

The dairy window was narrow and the drop outside was deep. Judy landed with a jolt on the hard ground where only the thinnest layer of turf covered the living rock of the mountains. She was bruised and shaken but there was no time to think of such things now, and picking herself up she ran round the back of the house to a point where a low stone wall divided field from farmyard.

The leopard was still in the bushes. Judy heard him yawn, a deep, satisfied, sleepy sound which ended in a little yowl, like a cat. One long golden foreleg stuck out from under the bushes and the claws were extended and flexed as the leopard stretched. The cat appeared again, his eyes slits of suspicion, his tail like a bottle-brush, every hair on his body quivering with the fear that was in him. Opening his mouth so wide that it showed pink he howled his defiance to the other male creature which had dared to enter his domain. The bushes waved wildly as the leopard sprang, and Judy, shuddering, closed her eyes, but when she ventured to peep over the wall again the cat was spitting defiance from the top of the ash tree by the house, and the leopard, too lazy and disinterested to pursue the matter further, had laid itself down in the last patch of sun to bring warmth to the rapidly shading yard.

Judy crept on. Very faintly came the sound of the church clock in the village striking the half hour. The children must be on the track now; however much they lingered they would not dare to get home too late or there would be trouble. A quarter to five was their limit. Time was racing on.

The sun disappeared behind the mountains, taking with it the deep shadow of the rocks by the track and leaving everything bathed in a soft luminous grey. Twilight was creeping on, and after twilight came the dark, when the great animals woke from their day-time drowsiness and stalked their prey. In the hours of darkness the leopard would hunt for food, hunt seriously, savagely, and two small children were coming his way!

Now it was time to leave the shelter of the wall and cut across the open field to the point where it was possible to slide down the bank on to the track. Judy hesitated, and then ran, the small hairs rising on the nape of her neck as she imagined the leopard leaping the wall from the yard and silently padding after her through the grass. Something moved behind her and she stifled a scream, forcing herself to look over her shoulder as she ran. It was only an old sheep disturbed by her passing and she gave a sob of relief.

Now she was at the top of the bank, clinging to a tree, gasping for breath. It was darker under the trees even though they were still only in young leaf, and the track down below seemed darker still between the high banks. If she met the leopard down there on the track there would be no way of escape, she would be trapped. Suppose it had tired of lying up in the bushes and was making its way down the track to the stream at the bottom to drink? Suppose, as she stumbled over the loose surface, it came up behind her, stealthy in the growing dusk? She shivered and clung to the tree and then heard, faint and far away, the voices of the children as they came up the track!

Now there was no time to be afraid. Frantically she slipped and slithered down the muddy bank, clutching at roots to steady herself, and landing in a heap at the bottom with grazed and bleeding knees. Picking herself up she began to run and as she did so she heard David's voice, much nearer now, 'Hurry up, slowcoach! We'll be late for tea!'

'David!' she shouted. 'Go back — go back!' And the echo they always heard in that valley mocked her: 'Go back — go back!'

A rattle of stones behind her made her heart jump, and she swung round, one arm up as if to defend herself from the leopard's spring. It was a sheep, and it was followed by other sheep until the track was full of them, baa-ing, bleating, hesitating, then coming on again as if uneasy and bewildered; afraid of something they did not understand.

Suddenly they were all around her, fleeing in panic, and she fled too, for behind them, padding silently over the rough stones, came the leopard! He made no effort to molest the sheep, he just kept them on the move, creeping along like a great golden shadow behind them, amusing himself and biding his time before he killed.

David's voice came again. 'Hey, Gwennie, mind the sheep!' And then the panic-stricken flock were all around the children and Judy had them by the hands and they were all three running, running with the sheep, driven by the beautiful, lithe, golden killer on the track above.

Then small Gwennie fell, dragging David down with her, and as Judy bent to help them up the sheep poured round them and over them and away, leaving them alone on the track with the leopard. Gwennie gave a thin wail of terror and Judy felt as if she had turned to ice. All fear, all feeling of any kind left her and she stood like a statue between the younger children and the great spotted beast, staring into the slitted, golden eyes.

'Get out!' she shouted. 'Get out of here!' and bending down she picked up a stone and threw it feebly, in the direction of the leopard, who blinked, and turned his head sideways as he snarled.

Behind Judy, David moved suddenly; the leopard, startled, crouched to spring, Judy saw him gather his legs under him, saw him leave the ground, and then a shot cracked out and the great golden body dropped lifeless at her feet.

Men came running, strange men with guns. They picked the children up and comforted them, but Judy they could not comfort; she was crying as if her heart would break for the glorious golden beast which now lay dead.

'H-how did you know he was here!' she asked the strange man with the gun. 'Where did he come from? Was he yours?'

'No, he wasn't mine,' said the man soberly. 'He came from a lorry which was taking him to join a circus near Caernarvon. The lorry was involved in an accident, three days ago, and the leopard's cage was damaged. He escaped, and for three days and nights we've been hunting him through the hills. As for how we knew he was here, half an hour ago someone saw him through binoculars. They saw you come out of the house and they saw him in the farmyard and we've been speeding to get here ever since.' He mopped his forehead with a handkerchief. 'I never want to live through another half hour like than again!'

'If it hadn't been for you kids we might have been able to catch him alive,' grumbled the second man. He looked pale and shaken and was obviously in a bad temper. 'He cost me a small fortune, that animal did, and now he's had to be shot.' He turned and went down the hill without another word

'Get out of here!' Judy shouted at the leopard

and the first man looked after him thoughtfully.

'That's the circus proprietor,' he said. 'He's angry and disappointed and I suppose one can't wonder. But for myself— well — I'm glad the leopard's dead.'

'*Glad?*' cried Judy. 'How can you be glad? He was so beautiful when he was alive.' She choked, and blinked back the tears that filled her eyes.

'Look at it like this,' said the strange man gently. 'That leopard was going back to life imprisonment in a circus. He was going to be taught shabby little tricks—sitting on a barrel — jumping through a hoop. That would have been his life until he died, a life without hope or dignity. You've seen him as few people in this country have ever seen a wild animal, in all the glory of his freedom; cruel perhaps in our eyes, a killer; but don't *we* kill for food? He has had one last taste of freedom after weeks in captivity, shut in a small travelling cage, and he died quickly and cleanly, in the prime of his health and beauty and strength.' He sighed, and looked kindly at Judy. 'You'd better go home, you've had a great shock and you must rest.'

Slowly, every step an effort, Judy climbed the steep track towards the house. Once she looked back, but the day was dying fast and she could only dimly see the great spotted body sprawled on the stones and the tall man standing beside it, leaning on his gun.

The younger children had arrived home when Judy got there. They were upstairs in the bedroom pouring out an excited, incoherent tale. As Judy came in her mother said wearily:

'Really, Judy, you've made David and Gwennie as silly as yourself. *They* can talk about nothing but a leopard now.'

'I'm sorry, Mother,' said Judy quietly. 'We won't talk about it again. There isn't a leopard any more.'

Being Witches

by LORNA WOOD

On my tenth birthday, I was given the old henshed at the bottom of the garden, to do as I liked with. My friends, Daisy and Edna, who appeared after breakfast with small parcels wrapped in tissue-paper, took varying views of this present.

'What I mean is,' said Edna, screwing up her small, freckled face doubtfully, 'a henshed is kind of odd. I don't mean it isn't a nice one — it's like a little house — but it's... well, it's sort of funny.'

My heart sank but I said loftily that just because no one had ever thought of giving *her* a henshed that didn't mean it wasn't a perfectly lovely present to have. I should have thought that absolutely anybody would have been glad of one.

'I bet you,' said Edna stubbornly, 'that if you'd've been a queen or a princess you wouldn't have had one. I bet you...'

I turned to Daisy for comfort. Her eyes were shining, they had that faraway look that always meant she had had an idea.

'But Prue, it's marvellous! In a beautiful henshed like this, just anything could happen!'

'What?' asked Edna scornfully. Daisy pressed on.

'We can scrub it out and put pictures on the wall and... I tell you what, we can be witches!'

Edna snorted and asked what you did to become a witch. Daisy tossed her head impatiently.

'You just let people know you are and then they come to you for spells and potions and things. And you have a bonfire and you mix things in a cauldron and nobody knows what they are...'

Edna looked thoughtful. She too had taken part in the school performance of 'Macbeth'.

'Would we? I mean it's daft just to go on mixing unless you're making a pudding or something. What *good* does it do?'

I suggested that people might be made to pay for spells and potions.

'But how do we let them know we make them? And I shouldn't think they'd come to us, they'd go to the chemist...'

'What we must do,' said Daisy, 'is to make things to make people beautiful. They'll always have a try at something like that.' Her expression grew dreamy. 'We could start with shampoos. We wouldn't poison anybody that way and shampoos are jolly easy, you just get soapflakes and shake them up in little bottles of rainwater and there you are. We would call them something interesting like pearl-water and...'

'They'd know that if we had some pearls we wouldn't go mashing them up for shampoos, we'd wear them or sell them.' objected Edna.

Daisy gave her a withering look.

'We'll start on Lizzie,' she said firmly. 'She's going out with her young man the day after tomorrow and you never know — why, twopennyworth of pearl-water might make a difference to her whole life. I mean her hair's so sort of streaky it's no wonder he doesn't propose...'

'How do you know he hasn't?'

'Because she keeps getting her fortune told. If you're engaged you just know you're going to be married and live happily ever after, you don't need anybody to tell you. And she never asks how many children she's going to have, she just asks Cook whether she can see a wedding-ring.'

'Has she seen one yet?'

'I don't know, it's mostly things like meeting a dark stranger and being in his thoughts and having to beware of a false friend.'

Edna started to say something about how could you beware if you didn't know which friend, but Daisy and I set off for a brush and a bucket of water and soon we had her resignedly scrubbing. I collected lots of little bottles from the larder and bathroom and Daisy went home for some soapflakes and soon we had the first consignment of pearl-water ready for sale. From inside the shed came Edna's grumbles about needing yellow soap and disinfectant but we paid no attention.

'Just think, Prue,' said Daisy, staring at me as though she saw a vision, 'if this is successful we might have the whole village coming to this shed to be made beautiful!'

My good sense told me that most village people were quite satisfied with the way they looked already but I recklessly smothered it. For perhaps thirty seconds we were happy and then Edna came to the door of the shed and said that it was scrubbed out and after she had washed her hands and knees she would have to go home. Should she, she demanded, let her mother know that she had become a witch? Daisy hastily said no, she must just look rather mysterious and by and by the rumour of the pearl-water would spread round the village and then Edna's mother would guess . . .

Of course she did not guess right and for a couple of days Edna did not reappear. ('She never could act,' Daisy said disgustedly.) An epidemic of measles was sweeping the village and Edna had been kept at home to be on the safe side. In her absence, the pearl-water was launched — Daisy used a cunning line of sales-talk on Lizzie and collected threepence — and proved astonishingly successful.

'Of course,' said Daisy afterwards, 'I told her to use three rinsing waters afterwards, and there's always soap in her hair. But I should think it's really the pearl-water, shouldn't you? Honestly, her hair looked jolly nice, she's a terrific advertise-ment for us. But if that Olive Tomkinson comes round and asks for any, we must say it's all ordered.'

I pointed out that Daisy had visualised the whole village coming to the hut and asked why.

'Because she's the false friend. She's the only one Lizzie can think of, anyway. She deliberately took Bert in the 'Excuse Me' waltz last Saturday night and Lizzie said she saw her game right away. Anyway, we're not going to help her, we're on Lizzie's side.'

We had a happy couple of days, pottering about the henshed and dreaming about all the things we might do. But Edna's return broke up all this happiness. For one thing, she jeered at the bottles of pearl-water that stood there unsold and for another, having presumably had plenty of time for thinking, she said she thought this witchery business was a silly game and she did not think she would play any more. Could we not, perhaps, play something sensible in the henshed like 'House'?

Daisy and I restrained our tempers and said we thought Edna would get to like it in time.

'But it's not as if we really *know* any spells and if we pretend we do, that's telling lies.'

I looked from her flushed, bulldoggy little face to Daisy's pale, romantic one. Daisy did not fail me. She said loftily:

'You don't know what Prue and I have been doing while you've been away. What'd you say if we'd learnt to turn people into toads? What'd you say if we could turn Miss Williams into a toad?'

'I'd say you were both telling lies, so there!' Edna looked at me suspiciously but I was too full of dismay to utter a word. 'Besides, I don't see why it should be Miss Williams. Why not Miss Adams?'

'Because Prue and I both like English and can't do arithmetic like you, so that's two to one. Anyway, Miss Williams won't be in school tomorrow morning, you'll see!'

Edna went home jeering but her laughter sounded a little bit hollow. Daisy beamed at me.

'The whole village may come to us for a beauty potion!'

'I just heard Miss Williams's landlady telling someone she wouldn't be in tomorrow. They think she might have measles.'

'Then we needn't do our homework sums?'

'Of course not. If you've got a box, I know where there's a marvellous toad and we can go and get it — it lives in our rockery.' She gave a self-satisfied chuckle. 'It will serve Edna jolly well right for being such a prig.'

Edna was visibly shaken when there was no Miss Williams in school the next day. She went so far as to make enquiries but was given guarded answers: presumably the headmistress knew that some of the parents might bring up the question of closing the school and did not intend to say anything until Miss Williams actually came out in spots.

That evening we went to Brownies and by the time we were walking home, twilight had come. The remains of a brilliant sunset still showed blood-red and bonfire-smoke came to our nostrils. I said carelessly:

'Like to come and have a look at Miss Williams?'

Edna said defiantly that we were both dreadful liars and people who told lies went to hell. But she turned in at our gate and presently we were outside the henshed.

I brought out Miss Williams in her box. Daisy had persuaded her into it with a shovel, to my great admiration. I could not really like toads, there was something uncanny about the way they never gave any clue about the way they were going to leap.

An owl screeched and swooped close to our heads. Did it know we were witches?

'Raise the lid, Prue,' said Daisy, in what we called her 'Macbeth' voice.

I did so and Edna switched on her electric torch, the better to see. For a few seconds we gazed on the baleful face, the fixed eyes, the little pulse working up and down. It might have been unkind to say so but it *was* exactly like Miss Williams when you gave a wrong answer. And then, Miss Williams, obviously bored to death with being shut up, leaped out. All three of us fled, screaming.

I was breathless when I went into the drawing-room. I sat down at the piano and started to practise my scales but they didn't go very well. My mother asked where Daisy and Edna were. I said they had gone home — and so they had, quicker than they ever had before.

When it was nearly bedtime, I offered to sleep in the spare bed in my little brother's room. I said I was sure he was afraid of the dark.

The following day, Miss Williams was in school, as usual. We managed to avoid Edna at the breaks but at four o'clock she caught me up on the road.

'You two are liars,' she said doggedly, 'and I'm not playing witches any more.'

We did not reply for some time but neither were we! Somehow we were tired of that game. Then Daisy said: 'Bert's jilted Lizzie. And he took Olive Tomkinson to the pictures last night.'

There did not seem anything left for me to say. Silently, I led the way to the henshed.

'People who tell lies *do* go to hell,' nagged Edna, but Daisy was not listening. The faraway look was in her eyes again. She halted and pointed to the henshed.

'Prue! What does it remind you of?'

I looked and tried to think of something clever but all I could see was just a henshed. But Daisy did not wait for my reply.

'A missionary's hut, she said impressively, 'That's what we can be — missionaries. Why . . .' she looked at us both beaming but unseeingly, 'just suppose we were so good we converted the whole village. She became suddenly brisk. 'I know how to begin. We'll convert Lizzie. It'll cheer her up for losing Bert.

Lucinda's Long Afternoon

by Margaret Biggs

At the bottom of Lucinda's garden, and backing all the houses on her side of the road, was a small, bumpy field. Nobody seemed to bother about it, and all the children in the road congregated there, when their long-suffering parents had tired of them whooping over their flower-beds. It was an ideal place to go if you didn't want to be bothered by grownups. There was a muddy pond in one corner, surrounded by tall chestnut-trees. You could wade in the pond, or even fish, if you felt optimistic, and slither about in the trees. In the autumn, of course, there were conkers to be squabbled over. You could run races all over the field, play ball games, construct a den with cardboard boxes surreptitiously brought from home . . . The field provided scope for everybody, and most tastes.

On a windy Saturday afternoon, just after she had eaten her lunch, eleven-year-old Lucinda sat swinging her legs on the fence at the bottom of her garden, and eyeing the gang of children sitting beneath the trees. They had not seen her, and she was wondering whether to go boldly over and join them, or wait until Ann Drake, who lived next-door, put in an appearance. Ann knew everybody in the road, and was liked by them all, but thin, dark-faced Lucinda had only moved here from Kent four months ago, and was not yet accepted as one of the gang. She yearned to be popular with them all, and made desperate attempts in that direction, but so far the only friend she had really managed to make was quiet, kindhearted Ann. Ann was all right, Lucinda admitted grudgingly, but a bit dull and uninteresting. Lucinda wanted the others, all of them, to like her, and realise how much more interesting *she* was.

From the garden behind her came a gurgling chuckle. Lucinda looked round impatiently, and scowled at the sight of her baby brother, Graham, crawling round the lawn after his beloved yellow ball. From the open French windows she could see her mother waving to the baby, and from the apple-tree, which he was pruning, her father glancing up with a smile. Lucinda began to bite her nails resentfully. Since Graham had been born, what an absurd fuss her parents made of him! There never seemed any peace from him. Lucinda never took much notice of him. She thought they had been much happier without him. Now they always had to pack his push-chair into the boot of the car, take strained foods for him on a day out and a pile of snowy nappies, and come home early just because he had to be in bed by six. Life was boring with a baby brother, Lucinda thought. It had been much more fun to be an only child, with her parents' undivided attention. She just didn't know what they saw in Graham . . .

She slid off the fence into the field, and walked quickly over to the others. They looked up and stared as she came nearer. Nobody looked particularly welcoming. What a mouldy lot they were, thought Lucinda. But somehow she would make them like her, whatever happened!

'Hello,' she said, halting a few yards away.

After a pause Paul Scott, who lived in the house opposite, said 'What do *you* want?'

Lucinda flushed indignantly. 'What do you mean, what do I want? I can come in this field if I want to, can't I?'

'We can't stop you,' said Paul, sounding resigned.

'You'd like to stop me, I suppose?' said Lucinda truculently.

'Oh, don't let's start arguing,' said Jill Scott, who was a year older than Lucinda. 'You can join in if you like, Lucinda, but for goodness sake don't keep interrupting and boasting all the time, like you usually do.'

'I don't — I think you're awfully rude!' said Lucinda, her cheeks blazing.

'Yes, you do,' said Audrey Carter, who was in Lucinda's class at school. She looked earnestly through her glasses. 'I'm tired of hearing what a good swimmer you are, and how well you can play tennis, and how you used to be in your school team where you lived before, and all the rest of it.'

There was a murmur of agreement. Lucinda stood stock still, glaring at them. They didn't like her, and whatever she did they were beastly to her. 'You're not fair,' she muttered. 'I don't boast — I only just tell you things . . .'

'Why don't you wait until we ask you?' said Jill reasonably. She liked Lucinda sometimes, but honestly, *nobody* could put up with her for long. She wanted all the limelight and attention all the time — she grumbled about her little brother, who was much nicer than she was, Jill thought — and whenever she joined a group there was bound to be trouble. Jill had overheard her mother sighing, 'Oh, that child — I know what she needs!'

Poor Lucinda, instead of sitting down and listening quietly, which would have been the best thing to do, burst out 'You're all stupid, and I don't want to do things with you, anyhow!' She turned and went running off acrosss the field, with her black hair glinting in the October sunshine.

'Good,' said Paul with blatant satisfaction.

'Here comes Ann,' said Jill. 'I expect she'll stick up for Lucinda, as usual.'

Ann, who was plump and round-faced and cheerful, came hurrying up. What's up with Lucinda?' she asked anxiously.

'Nothing. Jill told her she boasted, which is quite true, and she didn't like it,' said Audrey.

'I wish you'd all be nicer to her,' said Ann, wrinkling her brow.

'She's not nice to anybody else,' said Jill defensively. Her conscience was stirring.

'Do her good. She's the most conceited girl I've ever met,' said Paul. 'I wish she hadn't come to live in our road. She just doesn't fit in.'

Ann sighed. She genuinely liked Lucinda, though she saw the others' point of view. But sometimes, when Lucinda forgot to try to impress you, she was really nice! 'I don't think she's very happy,' Ann remarked regretfully.

'I'm not surprised,' said the implacable Paul. He was thirteen, and the acknowledged leader of the group. He intended to keep Lucinda firmly in her place, whether she objected or not.

Seeing Ann opening her mouth again, Jill put in hastily, 'Oh, let's forget Lucinda for a bit. I'm tired of the subject. Ann, we were talking about having a climbing competition this afternoon. If we go home and get our gymshoes..'

Ann listened, but glanced over towards Lucinda, who was standing staring into the pond. 'It sounds fun,' she broke in, as soon as Jill paused, 'but do let's have Lucinda in on it. She looks terribly lonely.'

The others exchanged wry glances. Ann looked at Paul. 'Do you mind if I go and ask her to join in, Paul?'

Paul was kind-hearted, though he always did his best to conceal it. 'Oh, all right,' he said. 'Go and have a word with her. But make her understand she's got to do as we tell her, and not try and run everything, as she usually does.'

Ann was on her feet in a flash. 'Thanks, Paul. She's all right really, you know — she just doesn't realise!' She went darting off before Paul could change his mind.

Lucinda saw Ann coming, but pretended not to. She felt

sore and miserable, as she so often did nowadays. Everybody seemed to be against her, no matter what she did!

'Hello,' said Ann breathlessly coming up. 'Want to join us for some tree-climbing, Lucinda?'

'I don't know,' said Lucinda sulkily.

Ann sighed. Really, Lucinda did make things difficult! 'Oh, come on,' she said with a tinge of impatience. 'You don't want to stand here moping all afternoon, do you?'

'They were horrible to me,' muttered Lucinda. She longed to ask Ann if *she* thought she boasted, but was too proud to confide in her. It was all rubbish, anyhow, she thought, not realising that in her eagerness to make the others like her, she *did* exaggerate her own prowess, piling it on to try to impress them.

'They didn't mean to be, I'm sure,' said Ann.

'Paul's so bossy,' muttered Lucinda. But she fell into step beside Ann and felt better with an ally. Ann was eminently reassuring and reliable.

Once they reached the others she kept silent, in the background. They were discussing tree-climbing. Lucinda was not very keen on it, as she hated heights, but she vowed to show them how fearless she was. They wouldn't think she was just a boaster if she climbed higher than any of them! Dreamily she imagined them all crowding round her praising her, saying, 'You were terrific, Lucinda — nobody else dared go as high as you!' It was a pleasing picture, and cheered Lucinda. She shook her dark lock impatiently off her face, and listened to the details.

'We'll divide into two teams, to make it more interesting,' Paul was announcing in lordly fashion. 'I'll pick one team and Ann can pick the other. We'll have to go home and put on gymshoes, as we were saying just now. Each team can choose a tree, and the team that gets up and down first wins, of course.'

'We ought to have a prize,' said Audrey.

'Losers buy ice-cream all round — how about that?' said Paul.

Everybody nodded, and Jill, feeling hungry already, said, 'Let's start straight away, then!'

'Shall we have to go right to the top of the tree?' said Lucinda.

'Yes. Don't tell me you can't climb,' said Paul with a touch of sarcasm.

'Of course I can,' said Lucinda, jutting out her chin. 'I just wanted to know, that's all.'

'Shall we pick the teams, then go and get our shoes?' suggested Ann quickly, before another disagreement could blow up.

This was done. Ann hastened to choose Lucinda first, knowing that her feelings would be hurt if nobody seemed to want her. Lucinda felt grateful, but did not show it. There were four of them in each team. They all split up then to rush home to change their shoes. Lucinda scrambled over her garden fence and raced into the kitchen like a tornado.

'My gym-shoes, Mum, do you know where I left them?' she cried impatiently, eager to get back and show them how brilliant she was.

'Still in your satchel on the hall-stand, I think,' said Mrs York. 'What do you want them for?'

'We're going climbing in the field,' said Lucinda briefly, rushing into the hall and nearly cannoning into her father. 'Sorry, Dad, I'm in a hurry —'

'I can see that,' said her father.

'Be careful, won't you?' said Mrs York.

Lucinda was sitting on the bottom stair, pulling the gym-shoes on. 'Oh yes, of course,' she said vaguely. She tied the laces and jumped up. 'Bye!' The kitchen door slammed behind her.

'Makes you feel breathless to watch, doesn't it?' said her father, smiling.

'I'm glad she's starting to get on better with the other children,' said Mrs York, looking out of the kitchen window where Ann stood at the fence waiting for Lucinda. 'She's had rather a tough time lately, I'm afraid.'

'Won't do her any harm,' said her father hard-heartedly. 'She was getting painfully spoilt before Graham was born.'

'Oh no! — well, perhaps just a little,' admitted Mrs York. 'I wish she took more interest in the baby,' she added wistfully.

Her husband nodded. 'Poor kid, if he was left to *her* tender mercies! Still, I expect she'll come round to him eventually.'

'I do hope so. I thought she'd be so thrilled with him,' sighed Mrs York.

'I suppose she was bound to feel jealous,' said Mr York. 'Still, don't blame yourself, darling. You've fallen over backwards to make a fuss of her, and she's just sulked. She'll have to learn the hard way that she's not the most important person in the world.'

Mrs York sighed again. She had a tender heart, and loved her family all to be happy and contented. Oh well, she hoped Lucinda would feel better once the other children took to her . . .

The two teams lined up in front of the chosen two trees. Lucinda eyed hers dubiously. The top looked very far away, and a faint sick feeling stirred in her stomach. She wished rounders, or marbles, or racing had been chosen. Oh well! She swallowed and clenched her fists inside her shorts pockets.

'Ready — steady — *go!*' piped Bill Franklin, a seven-year-old who was too little to join in but had been delighted when Paul said he could start them off.

Lucinda watched. Ann swarmed up the tree like a monkey, hanging on tight and swinging up from branch to branch. Lucinda's sick feeling increased. But they would have laughed at her if she had said that she hated climbing. She must do it, she must!

Ann landed with a bump on the ground. 'Come on, Audrey!' she called encouragingly. 'Lucinda, you're after Audrey, aren't you? Be ready to start as soon as she's down. The others are ahead a bit already.'

'All right, I know what to do, don't fuss,' said Lucinda.

Audrey was a slower, more painstaking climber than Ann. She selected her hand-holds with care, and would not be rushed. 'Oh, get a move on!' Ann shrieked. 'Oh good, she, got to the top — here she comes down — now, Lucinda, up you go. You're all right, aren't you?' she added suddenly, catching a glimpse of Lucinda's white face.

'Yes,' said Lucinda grimly. Audrey jumped down to the grass, and Lucinda leapt up. As soon as she was beginning to climb, she knew she would never succeed. Gritting her teeth, her face set in a ferocious, determined expression, she pulled herself up, hanging on as tight as possible. She knew she was climbing slowly, but at least she was managing. From below she heard Ann call 'Jolly good, Lucinda! You're nearly at the top!' Lucinda hauled herself up further. It was difficult finding a foothold near the top, but she managed somehow, and her hands, rather scratched now, pulled herself up on to the top bough. The tree swayed, and Lucinda hated the sensation. 'That's it — start down now!' called Ann encouragingly.

Lucinda drew a deep breath and glanced down. Terrifyingly far below the others stood on the grass, tiny, distant figures. If she fell that far she'd break a leg at the very least! Waves of panic began to rush over Lucinda. Her hands were slippery with sweat, and when she tried to move downwards her leg shook. It was no good, she was stuck. She dared not move an inch. She stayed motionless, gulping.

Paul was gazing up at her, like everyone else. Jill had just slid down from the other tree, but now the race was forgotten as they all stared at Lucinda.

'I might have known,' said Paul. 'She's lost her nerve. Oh heavens, *now* what do we do?'

'Oh dear, this is awful,' said Ann, nibbling at her lip. Trying to make her voice sound reassuring, 'Lucinda, take it very slowly and steadily, I should,' she called. 'It's much easier coming down. Just don't try to rush it.'

'I c-c-can't!' floated down Lucinda's voice, after a long pause.

'Come on, don't be a little fool!' called up Paul in an encouraging bellow. 'It's not difficult. Just keep calm.'

Keep calm! Lucinda's heart was pounding like thunder, and her hands were shaking now. She tried to move, one of her feet slipped a few inches, and with a gasp of fright she clung against the tree. Everything began sliding up and down, sickeningly, in front of her eyes. 'I want to get down,' she wailed, giving up all pretence. 'Please get me down!'

Paul and Ann exchanged anxious glances. 'It's not going to be easy,' said Paul, 'Still — I'll have a try. Poor kid, why did she go up if she hated it?'

'She wanted to show us she could, I suppose. Oh dear, what if she falls? Do hurry up, Paul. Or shall I run and get her father, or somebody?' said Ann, perplexed.

'No, don't get an adult yet. You know what a fuss they'll create over a thing like this. If we have to get somebody older, well, we'll just have to, but I'll go up first,' said Paul.

'Get a move on, then,' said Jill. 'She might let go. She sounds awful to me!' Jill felt a stab of sympathy for Lucinda, for whom she had never cared twopence before.

Anxiously they all stood watching, as Paul with infinite care began to climb up to Lucinda. Paul was the best climber, but Ann gnawed her lip as she watched. What if Lucinda was too petrified to move even when Paul got to her?

Lucinda saw Paul was coming, and felt a degree better. Her

'Please get me down!' Lucinda wailed

heart beat less frighteningly, but she still stayed tense and still, unable to move an inch.

'Now, Lucinda, here I am,' said Paul's breathless voice; he was only a foot below her. 'Take a few deep breaths, that always helps. You can hear me, can't you?'

'Y-y-yes,' said Lucinda, her voice wobbling. Oh, what a fool he must think her!

'Now, take it easy. We'll be O.K., I know we will.'

'I can't move!' said Lucinda shakily.

'Of course you can. Now, begin. Move your hands first, then your feet when you've found a good hand-hold. This tree's simple to climb if you don't get worried. Right?' Paul's voice sounded firm but kind. Lucinda decided she must do what he said, though she was convinced she was going to fall. Her legs felt like jelly. Gasping and shivering, inch by inch she came down. Just below her all the time Paul moved when she did, constantly encouraging her. 'That's it. Move your right foot down to the next branch, it's firm as a rock. Good — now wait while I get a bit further, out of your way ... We're nearly halfway, jolly good! Take a breather, then we'll carry on. It's much easier here, and if you fall it's not far enough to hurt you.' (Paul crossed his fingers mentally as he said this.)

Lucinda never remembered how she got down, only the way Paul kept talking all the time. Every time the faltered he reassured her. The others stood still, watching intently. Ann let out her breath in a long, long sigh of relief as first Paul, then Lucinda, reached the ground.

'Oh, thank goodness!' she burst out, rushing forward. 'Are you all right, Lucinda?'

'Do you feel O.K.?' 'You look terrible, Lucinda!' 'Are you all right, Lucinda?' 'What happened, did you get giddy?' Everybody crowded round Lucinda, who stood, swaying a little, unable to say a word.

'Come on, Lucinda, I'll take you home,' said Paul.

He sounded kind, and so did the others, but Lucinda was sure they must really despise her. What a coward they must think her! They would never, never like her now, after she had let them all down like this. She felt she could never face them again, even Ann.

'Don't come with me. I'm all right,' she said. 'Thanks, Paul.' She had to thank him, but she could not look at him. She pulled herself between them and began to run for her garden. She pulled herself over the fence and lay down on the lawn. It was all finished now. Of course they would never be her friends, and no doubt even Ann, the tender-hearted, despised her. Lucinda fought back her tears, and buried her face on her arms. Everything was hopeless and miserable, and she would never feel happy again.

Her father, a few minutes later, came down the garden carrying the baby. Lucinda saw him coming, and sat up, brushing grassblades off her, and trying to look unconcerned.

'Hello, Dad,' she said, and was surprised at how normal her voice sounded.

'Hello. Not playing with the others now?' said her father, scrutinising her more closely than she cared for.

'No, not now.' Lucinda smiled as well as she could.

Something's up, thought her father. But he merely said, 'We wondered if you'd keep an eye on Graham for twenty minutes. Your mother's got some things to take down to the Oxfam Jumble Sale, and I've promised to drive her down to the High Street. We're just going to drop them in at the hall — we shan't stop. Can we leave Graham with you? It's not worth taking him.'

'I suppose so,' said Lucinda slowly. The last thing she wanted was to look after Graham, but she didn't see how she could get out of it.

'He's just had his nap, so he's full of beans. Here you are, old chap, here's Lucinda to look after you!' Mr York passed the baby over. Lucinda took him reluctantly, and sat him beside her on the grass. Graham gurgled at her, and reached up a hand to pull her dark hair. When Lucinda said 'Ouch!' he repeated an experimental 'Ouch!' himself, and tugged again.

'Shan't be long,' said Mr York, and walked swiftly back towards the house. He hoped Lucinda could be trusted. His wife thought so, but he had uneasy doubts.

Lucinda heard the car move off down the road. She sat and looked at her brother, who had lost interest in her hair and begun to crawl at top speed across the grass. A daisy tickled his chin, and he stopped to stuff it into his mouth. 'No,' said Lucinda firmly, removing it.

'He is rather sweet,' flashed through her mind, followed instantly by, 'Oh no, he's not he's just a nuisance!'

Yes, he really *was*, she thought in exasperation a few minutes later, after three times retrieving him from some prickly rose-bushes. She picked him up and peered cautiously over the fence. If she took him in the field a few minutes he could crawl about there without being such a bother. There was so much more room there. The only thing was, she didn't want to meet the others. But she couldn't see any of them, so, after hesitating a few seconds, she lifted him over the fence and followed. Graham babbled to himself as the wind blew his hair about, sucked his thumb thoughtfully, and then, as Lucinda put him down on the grass, set off purposefully to explore this new, fascinating place. Lucinda stayed near the fence, her gloomy thoughts coming over her again, abstractedly watching his blue rompers, and his small bare feet, getting rapidly smaller. 'It wouldn't be so bad if he were nearer my age,' she thought. 'At least I'd have someone to talk to. The others will just ignore me now, I suppose. They were rude enough before. Ann might be nice, but only because she's sorry for me, and I do hate people being sorry for me!'

She wondered where they had all gone. Probably off on

their bikes somewhere, to buy ice-cream and joke about *her*. Lucinda writhed at the thought. She wouldn't think about them, she didn't care a straw *what* they did!

Suddenly she jumped. A dog was growling somewhere not far away. And where was Graham? Deep in her gloom, she had forgotten him. She ran forward, calling his name, looking everywhere for a gleam of blue. He couldn't be far, she'd seen him only a few seconds ago ... 'Graham! Graham!' she called, and began to feel worried and uncomfortable. But it was silly to feel like that, he could only be a few yards away, hidden in some of the long grass. 'Graham!' she called again, louder. 'Oh, why don't you answer?' But of course he was too little. She was sure he had gone this way, she had been watching him only a few moments ago ... The dog, wherever he was, was growling again. A shivery feeling came over Lucinda. Could the dog be growling at Graham? She ran frantically towards where the noise was coming from, dreadfully apprehensive. And then she saw the baby, very small about a hundred yards ahead, and near him, still looking and sounding menacing, Major Kennedy's Labrador, a large formidable dog Lucinda always gave a wide berth. The dog was often roaming about on its own, and Lucinda never liked the look of it. It had a habit of stopping dead, and staring fixedly at her, as if it might spring at any moment. And now there it was, making ominous noises in its throat, with Graham crawling right up to it.

Lucinda felt exactly as she had felt at the top of the tree. She could not move, and her heart thudded loudly.

'Graham!' she called in terror.

The baby heard her and turned his head. Seeing his big sister he cooed and chuckled, beaming at her. The dog saw her too, and stiffened. Gulping, Lucinda began to walk slowly steadily forwards. Whatever happened she must get to Graham and pick him up. Why, that horrible dog might snap at his face at any second!

'Good boy, good old boy,' she said tremulously, trying to sound confident, as she reached Graham.

The dog remained immovable and went on growling. Lucinda wanted to turn and run as fast as she could. Instead she went on and at last, very slowly and gently, picked Graham up, facing the dog all the time, with some dim memory of a book telling you always to face a fierce animal and keep looking at it. She felt Graham's fat arms against her shoulder with unspeakable relief, and squeezed him tightly against her. 'Oh, Graham, thank goodness!' she muttered against his soft hair, very shakily.

At least now if he goes for us, he won't be able to get at Graham so easily, she thought. He might snap at my legs, but that won't matter so much.

To her horror the Labrador began to advance on her, tail quivering. Lucinda clutched the baby to her, and stared grimly back at the dog.

'Good boy, all right, then,' she said, trying to sound friendly but firm.

'Get away, Butch. Go on—get off with you!'

At the sound of Paul's authoritative voice behind her Lucinda jumped, and the Labrador halted, and immediately looked much less frightening. His tail even began to wag slowly.

'He tries it on sometimes. He's old and crotchety, that's his trouble,' said Paul aside to Lucinda. Lucinda saw that several of the gang had come up behind with him. 'Off you go, Butch—home, boy!' he added commandingly.

Butch trotted rather reluctantly off across the field towards his master's house.

'Oh, thank goodness!' sighed out Lucinda, overcome with relief.

'We were all in Ann's garden,' said Paul. 'We heard you calling Graham, and when I looked over the fence I saw

Butch, and the baby, and you coming like the wind. I thought you might need a bit of help. Butch might easily have snapped at Graham, if he'd pulled his tail or something like that.'

'It was jolly brave of you to go right up to him and pick Graham up, Lucinda,' said Jill—Jill, of all people, 'I don't like that dog one bit. He bit my ankle once, when I was small.'

They were all standing round her now, Lucinda realised rather dazedly, and they all looked friendlier than she had ever seen them look before. They thought she was brave! Lucinda, going red, stammered, 'I was awfully scared, but—but I had to pick up Graham. I nearly ran away.'

'You didn't, though, did you?' said Paul, smiling at her. 'Good for you, Lucinda.'

'We've got some spare ice-cream left in my fridge,' said Ann. 'I was going to bring it round to you anyhow. Will you come and eat it now with us? Perhaps Graham could have a little, too.'

'Well, I . . .' Lucinda was so flummoxed she hardly knew what to say.

'Oh come on,' said Paul. 'Come and bury the hatchet.' He smiled, and did not look a bit superior or condescending. Lucinda began to smile back, to smile at them all in dawning delight. They really seemed to like her! How funny, just when she had given up all hope!

'I'd love to,' she said. Then, nerving herself, she went on, 'I never thanked you for helping me down that tree, Paul . . .'

'Forget it. I have,' said Paul. 'I'll show you a cast-iron way up it sometime, if you like, though.'

'You only need a bit of practice, I expect,' said Ann. 'But come on, or the ice-cream will have melted!'

As they neared Ann's fence Mr and Mrs York, looking for their children, appeared in the next-door garden. Seeing the group with Lucinda in their midst, they felt—and indeed looked—staggered. Lucinda saw them, waved eagerly, and called, 'Can I take Graham into Ann's house for some ice-cream? I'll look after him, and we'll only be a few minutes. Is that all right?'

'Yes, of course it is,' called back her mother, bewildered but deeply pleased. It was the first time Lucinda had ever offered to take Graham anywhere.

'You are lucky, Lucinda. I do wish *we'd* got a baby,' said Ann longingly.

'He's a bit of a nuisance at times—but he's a darling,' said Lucinda, suddenly realising she really did think so.

In a noisy, laughing bunch, with Graham cooing and thoroughly enjoying all the attention, they surged into Ann's house.

Lucinda never needed to boast again.

A Wood by Moonlight

by GEOFFREY TREASE

'All right,' said Peg, 'then I shall be the Devil.'

'You can't,' piped young Timothy.

'Why the devil can't I?' his sister demanded. They could speak freely in the safety of the beech-wood, but even grown-ups had to guard their tongues in the village. If one of those real Puritans had his long ears within range, a wrong word was enough to land you in the stocks. It was as bad as playing football, or keeping Christmas, or any of the other wickedness forbidden by Parliament.

'Course you can't,' Timothy repeated scornfully. 'A girl can't! Who ever heard of a female devil?'

'By all accounts,' said Anthony Sackville lazily, with the indulgent grin of an elder brother, 'I should think the most devilish devils *would* be female. When Tim's older, he'll learn.'

'That's settled then,' said Peg, ignoring the slur on her sex. 'You're Doctor Faustus, and Tim can do all the small parts—those we leave in. Only we'd better share out the Seven Deadly Sins between us, and *I'll* look more like Helen of Troy than Tim will, though it's a shame she hasn't any lines.'

'It's a good play for us, you know.'

'Yes, only two big parts. Tim can't do much harm to what's left,' she added cheerfully.

'Any singing?' Timothy inquired.

'Not a note,' said Tony.

'Pity. I can't *act*, I know,' the smaller boy admitted philosophically, 'but I like it when there's songs.'

Peg glanced at her elder brother. He nodded. 'We might work in a song,' he offered. 'We'll see how keen you are at rehearsals.'

101

They were standing in the hollow which they called the Playhouse. It was not much like a Playhouse, but that did not matter because they had never seen one. Nor had any one else of their age, in the whole of England. The Puritans had closed all theatres in the Civil War, and not even Tony could remember so far back.

Still, the hollow in the wood did well enough. Its steep sides contained the sound, so that their voices were not lost, thin and small, in the vastness of the open air. There was a most convenient stump for a throne, and in one place the trees sent groping roots half out of the chalky slope, making a twisty staircase which was very useful in *Macbeth* and *Hamlet.*

Tony had the book, not only because he was the eldest but because he had the longest part and it looked all right for a scholarly magician to be peeping into it all the time. Anyhow it was a heavy volume, borrowed from the shelf of play-books their father had collected in happier days. Tim could hardly have held it, and Peg liked her hands free so that she could sweep about and make dramatic gestures. She was wonderfully quick, and had already learnt most of Mephistopheles' speeches during the past week of snow and rain—she had privately made up her mind from the beginning that she would act the Devil's part.

Now the bad weather was forgotten and it was a soft spring day, the first time for ages that they had been able to use the Playhouse. They began to act without further waste of time, and with the same intense seriousness as thought they had an audience of critical lords and ladies, not silent grey trunks standing round them on a golden carpet of leaves.

Tony and Peg, of course, were acting mad, and always had been. Timothy was young enough to do as he was told. He was almost as wooden as the trees about him, but at least he tried.

They skipped some of the duller opening scenes and hurried on to the place where Faustus went into the solitary grove at midnight to conjure up the Devil.

Even Peg, though dancing with impatience to make her first entrance (she had been practising a demoniac laugh in private) had to admit to herself that Tony was good, really good. She forgot the sunshine spangling the leaves underfoot. It was as though the sky had changed from pale blue silk to deathly black velvet, and the friendly wood she had always known into a haunted moonlit grove near Wertenberg. Her skin crept as Tony declaimed in a marrow-freezing voice:

> '*Now that the gloomy shadow of the earth,*
> *Longing to view Orion's drizzling look,*
> *Leaps from th' antarctic world unto the sky,*
> *And dims the welkin with her pitchy breath,*
> *Faustus, begin thine incantations—*'

Tony was no longer a snub-nosed schoolboy in a darned grey coat with mud-splashed shoes and stocking. He felt himself—and she could almost see him as—the skullcapped, long-robed magician, with fanatical eyes bent greedily upon a volume of ancient and forbidden secrets. When it came to the climax of the speech, seven lines of terrifying mumbo-jumbo, all in Latin, his voice rose to a scream and Peg was so shaken that, for a moment, she forgot it was her cue.

'Excellent,' pronounced a sepulchral voice behind her.

The three young actors spun round as one.

A tall figure, swathed in a black cloak with a broad-brimmed hat pulled down so as to show no more than two black, twinkling eyes and the top of a long nose, was standing completely motionless among the trees.

Peg smothered a scream, Tony paled visibly, and nobody noticed how Timothy looked, because he had promptly moved to a safer position in the background.

For a few moments it looked as though the magic words

It looked as though the magic words had produced the Devil

had really worked and produced the Devil in person. Then the stranger spoke again and his words, though delivered with a kind of graveyard magnificence, belonged strictly to the world of everyday.

'Excellent, my boy. Well delivered. A most promising performance.'

Tony grinned foolishly. He felt rather as he did at the grammar school, when the master praised his Latin recitation. The three Sackvilles glanced at one another uneasily, wondering what to say, but the man took command of the situation. He strode forward with an easy natural dignity, and peered at the book in Tony's hands.

'I thought as much—a mighty old playbook, and a piece that was long out of fashion even in my time. But it has life still, on *your* lips, my boy. You might have a great future on the boards. If only,' he added lugubriously, 'the boards themselves had any future. But they have no more future, I fear, than present—only a past, a glorious heart-swelling past. All the more pleasure, my boy, to hear lines well delivered in these joyless days.'

'You ought to hear my sister, sir.'

'Oh, *sh!*' Peg began to protest, her face scarlet. But half of her was aching to perform.

The stranger swung round and eyed her with some surprise. 'A young lady? Acting?'

'Why not?' she demanded.

'Only,' said the stranger with a sweeping gesture, 'that it would be clean contrary to the great tradition of the English stage. In a court masque, of course, in the good old days, the highest ladies in the land were wont to amuse themselves—if no one else—by posing and reciting. But in the public playhouse, my dear ...' he dwelt on the phrase with all the age-old contempt of the professional for the amateur, 'all female parts were played by pretty boys, like your brother.'

105

Tony scowled and Timothy sniggered at this description. Peg was too indignant on her own account to notice it.

'I don't just play female parts. I was about to make my entrance as Mephistopheles, when you—when you—'

'When I so rudely interrupted? A thousand pardons, young lady!' He swept off his hat and bowed. His black eyes twinkled with mischief. 'I perceive that you have got well inside your part—you are all but breathing fire in my direction. Pray continue, but permit me the rare pleasure of playing audience.'

He moved aside, and seated himself on a fallen log. The three children looked at one another again. It was embarrassing, but they could hardly ask the man to go away. Peg took a deep breath and released the demoniac laugh she had prepared for her entrance. The play continued. But it was not fated to get far without interruption. They had just reached the scene in which Doctor Faustus sold his soul to the Devil, writing the contract in his own blood, when a thunderous voice from the top of the bank cried:

'*Stop!*'

The three Sackvilles looked up in alarm. The boys pulled off their caps, Peg bobbed a rebellious curtsy. Only the cloaked stranger remained unmoved.

'Stop this ungodly wickedness this instant,' ordered the newcomer. He came slithering heavily down the bank, a portly, passionate-looking fellow, all white collar and cuffs above, and huge riding boots like leather buckets below.

'Please, Colonel, we weren't doing any harm—' Tony began nervously.

'No harm? When you make the woods ring with your blasphemy!'

'It is a most moral piece, sir,' said the man in the black cloak, rising from his seat on the log. 'It shows how the sin of Faustus is punished—'

'I don't care what it shows. It reeks of the playhouse and

all the wickedness which went with it, wickedness which today we have nearly stamped out of the Commonwealth. And who, sir, may I ask are you? Encouraging these children in such things!'

The twinkling black eyes met the angry blue ones of the Colonel. Again the stranger swept off his hat and bowed.

'Just a little part, sir, of the wickedness you and your friends have come so near to stamping out! Francis Coverley, sometime master of the strolling players—but these many years out of his proper employment.'

'So I should hope! Then, if you are out of employment, beware, Master Coverley, that you are not taken up as a rogue and vagabond. We want none of your sort in the parish.' The Colonel puffed out his crimson cheeks. 'You will be looked for in the morning—so, if you do not fancy a day in the stocks, take care you are not found.' He swung round upon the children.

'As for you Sackville brats, it is clear you lack a father's hand. I shall speak to the schoolmaster. You boys, at least, can have some righteousness trashed into you!'

With this Christian sentiment the Colonel continued his woodland stroll. The children looked at one another, white-faced.

'And who,' inquired the stranger softly, 'was that gentleman?'

'Colonel Elijah Clegg,' said Tony in a voice of venomous scorn.

'A personage of some importance in these parts?'

'He thinks so,' said Peg.

'He *is*,' Tony admitted. 'He just about rules this district. He spends all his time nosing out people who break the new laws. He can see a pack of cards a mile off—'

'Or a maypole,' said Peg bitterly.

'You daren't kick a football—'

'Or sing one of the old Christmas carols—'

'A man played the organ once in our church,' said Tim, round-eyed at the memory. 'It was the most wonderful thing I ever heard! But of course *he* got to know of it, and there was trouble.'

'He could make things very unpleasant for you, sir,' Tony ventured a little awkwardly. 'I mean—I don't suppose you would count as a "rogue and vagabond"—'

'What else?' said the old actor with a bitter chuckle, 'I have very little notion where I shall sleep tonight, and none at all where I shall sup.'

'You mean, you've nowhere to go?' Peg demanded, horrified.

'The world is wide, young lady. And my choice is... completely free.'

'Oh, but that's terrible! At this time of year, too! Oh, Tony, do you think...?' She turned to her brother.

Tony hesitated for a moment, then flung caution to the winds. 'Yes, I'm sure Mother wouldn't mind! The Bible says we ought to shelter strangers within our gates. And he wouldn't be a rogue and vagabond if he stayed with us, so the Colonel couldn't touch him!'

'Oh, *do* come!' begged Tim.

Mr Coverley looked round their excited faces. 'Perhaps the matter might at least be discussed with your good mother. The nights are cold,' he added thoughtfully, 'especially in the woods.'

* * * *

Mrs Sackville was small, bright as a robin, and quite as spirited. Her husband had died young, from the delayed effects of a wound received as a boy, fighting on the King's side at Naseby. Times had been hard ever since, but somehow she had brought up the family in the old cottage which faced across the village green to the church, and neither poverty nor Puritans had quenched her courage.

All the same, she seemed a little daunted when Mr Coverley

bowed over her hand in the fire-lit parlour, and was intro-
duced by Tony as a candidate for the spare bed.

Peg was quicker than her brothers to detect the faint hesitat-
ion in their mother's welcome. Leaving the boys to entertain
their visitor—or more likely, as it seemed, to be entertained by
him with an endless flow of adventures and experiences on and
off the stage—she flew after her mother into the kitchen.

'Mother! It *is* all right? Bringing him, I mean? He's nowhere
else to go—I don't think he's any money, or anything—'

'It's quite all right, dear.' But Mrs Sackville's brow remained
furrowed as she took down the pewter plates.

'I knew we had that rabbit Mr Oakley gave us, and there's
cheese and cold bacon, and he won't mind drinking small
beer—'

'Oh, we can feed him.' Mrs Sackville smiled.

'He's rather *long* for the truckle-bed—'

'He looks as though he has slept in worse places before now.'
Mrs Sackville flitted busily about the kitchen as she talked.
'We'll make him comfortable enough, never fear. Get the
clean sheets aired, there's a good girl, and then lend a hand
with the table.'

Peg was back in a minute with an armful of lavender-
scented bed-linen which she hung up where the firelight
could play on it. She was still not reassured by her mother's
brisk cheerfulness. Something was wrong. But what?

She had to restrain her curiosity for the time being. Only
when the table was set, and Mr Coverley had been shown
upstairs with a great jug of warm water to remove the stains
of travel, did Mrs Sackville reveal what was in her mind.
Softly closing the door at the foot of the stairs, she motioned
the children around her and laid a warning finger on her
lips.

'Listen, all of you! I am quite sure poor Mr Coverley
is an honest man and the very last person to spy on us...'

'Of *course*, Mother!' Tim began indignantly, but his mother silenced him with a look.

'None the less,' she went on in a brisk undertone, 'these are troubled times and we must not add to our dangers. Mr Coverley is very welcome to stay here tonight, but he must be gone by tomorrow evening. So, please, none of you start pressing him to remain any longer, or it may be serious—not only for ourselves, but for other people we have no right to endanger.'

'All right, Mother.' Tony spoke for them all. 'But... mayn't we know what this is all about?'

Mrs Sackville hesitated. 'I would be better not—so long as he is in the house. The fewer who know, the less risk. But—I hardly know. What is to happen tomorrow night concerns you all three very closely. Perhaps you *should* be told. It is something that should be prepared for, not something that should come on you as a surprise.'

Despite the seriousness of her tone, Peg could not check a laugh. 'Well, Mother, you *must* tell us, after all that. We can keep secrets.'

'I hope so. Very well. You know that the Puritans have made great changes—forbidden many things that your father and I were brought up to believe were right? It is not only that they have done away with choirs and surplices and weddings in church, but they will not have bishops, any more than they will have a king—'

'They say there are some bishops, still,' Tim broke in excitedly, 'but they live in hiding, and go about in disguise ...'

'That is true,' agreed Mrs Sackville. 'That is what our own bishop has done. Otherwise he could not do his work.'

'What *is* his work?'

'Two things in particular, Tim, so that the Church will survive our present troubles. He ordains new ministers—because we believe that only a bishop can do that. And he

110

confirms the children whose parents want them to be brought up in the old way.'

'I say, Mother—have you ever *seen* him?' Tony demanded with growing interest.

His mother looked at him steadily. 'No. But I hope that we shall all see him tomorrow night.'

There was a brief silence, which Peg was first to break. 'I understand, Mother,' she whispered. 'That's why you've spent all these winter evenings explaining about the old prayer-book and —and everything? You were preparing us. You want us to be confirmed.'

Mrs Sackville nodded. 'If *you* do, my dears. Of course, it should be done openly in church, it should be an occasion of rejoicing. But that's impossible. The Bishop will come like a thief in the night, and no one in the village must know. But at least it can be done in church, in front of where the altar used to stand.' She laughed softly. 'I have borrowed the key to the side door.'

'How wonderful! Oh, Mother, I *am* glad—'

Swoosh!

'What on earth...' began Tony, dashing across to the uncurtained window and peering out into the darkness. 'There was someone there. I saw him bolting away.'

'But the noise?' exclaimed his mother, pale to the lips. 'It was like somebody emptying a bucket of water.'

'It was, madam. Or a basin, to be precise.' The door at the foot of the staircase stood open, and Mr Coverley stood gravely regarding them. 'I looked out and saw some fellow crouched listening at your window—an act useful in a play, but contemptible in real life. So I thought fit to empty my basin on his head. I trust that no harm has been done?'

* * * *

It seemed all too obvious that a great deal of harm had been done. Not by Mr Coverley's prompt and well-justified action, but by the presence of an eavesdropper at all.

In for a penny, in for a pound, thought Mrs Sackville with a sigh; and, being a fair judge of character, she took a chance and explained the whole situation to the actor. 'That man outside would be one of Colonel Clegg's faithful followers,' she concluded bitterly. 'He'll be off to the Colonel now with a fine tale.'

'We must do something, Mother,' urged Tony.

'Of course. We must get word to the Bishop—somehow. If he comes here tomorrow night he'll probably walk straight into a trap. But *how* to get word to him, I'm not so sure. I know where we could send a message, but it's a terrible long tramp, and I don't know if you'd manage it...' She smoothed back her hair with a worried gesture.

'Perhaps I...?' suggested Mr Coverley gently. 'That is madam, if you will trust me further still?' As she still hesitated he went on: 'After all, I am to blame. If I had not come to your cottage there would have been no spy sent to listen under your window. I have not the honour of the Bishop's acquaintance but I have met Colonel Clegg—and any triumph *he* achieved would distress me in the extreme!'

There really seemed nothing else for it. Mrs Sackville told him the name of the inn, in a town ten miles distant, where a sympathetic landlord would see that the warning was passed on to the Bishop in time. It was agreed that Mr Coverley should start out a good two hours before dawn, and as the children might be still fast asleep then, in spite of all the excitement, they made their farewells after supper.

'Do ask them to tell the Bishop how disappointed we are,' said Peg dolefully, 'for goodness knows when we shall ever get confirmed *now*.'

'And I wish *you* hadn't to go so early,' Tony added. 'I

suppose we shall never see you again, either?'

'This is an uncertain world, said the actor with a hollow chuckle. 'Good-night, sweet prince.' Reluctantly, the three children filed upstairs.

* * * *

In the morning it was hard to believe that any of it had happened. Their romantic visitor had gone, and the Bishop was not coming. Life would go back to what it had been twenty-four hours before. Only a sodden patch under the window outside, and two or three footprints, showed that they had not imagined it all.

No, there was one other memento of their visitor. A scrap of paper had been thrust under the boys' door. On it was written, in a flourishing hand: *'Come to the grove near Wertenberg an hour after sunset, but see that you are not followed. It may be possible to play another scene.'*

'I don't understand,' said Tim. 'We can't act there in the dark, and it'll be so cold...'

'Don't be a fool,' Tony told him. 'He only means that he's coming back to tell us how he got on. We shall see him again, that's the main thing.'

In that, however, Tony was mistaken.

True, when they crept stealthily through the rustling wood that evening, there was a figure standing motionless in the centre of the Playhouse; but the moonbeams, slating down through the treetops, showed a much shorter man than Mr Coverley, and, when the broad-brimmed hat was swept off to greet them, the head beneath gleamed silver.

'Good evening, my children, said the Bishop quietly.

They all gasped. Peg was the first to find words. 'But, sir—where is Mr Coverley?'

The Bishop laughed. Old though he was, his voice was musical. 'Your friend begged to be excused, my dear. Much

113

as he would have liked to be with us, he has to make an appearance elsewhere. As he remarked—a shade irreverently, I fear, but we must forgive a man of his profession!—he would have had no lines to speak, only what he termed a—er—"walk-on" part.'

'We did hope we should see him again,' said Tim in a flat little voice.

'You will, my boy. In an hour's time, he said, be at the side door of the church. That is where I should have met you, according to the original plan, but by that time I must be over the hills and far away. There, in your own church, I should have confirmed you, but what does the place signify, after all?'

What indeed, thought Peg, looking round her? Yet in after years she was glad to think it had happened in their own beechwoods, with the moonlight shining down and turning the ranks of silvery tree-trunks into the innumerable aisles of a vast cathedral.

The Bishop talked for a few moments longer, reminding them of the solemnity of the occasion; asked them a question or two and said their mother could not have prepared them better had she been a Doctor of Divinity; and then, bidding them kneel on the carpet of leaves, he laid his hands on each in turn and pronounced the words printed in the prayer-book.

'And now I must be gone,' he said in his normal tone when they stood up again. 'I have an hour's start before a wrathful Colonel Clegg rouses the countryside in search of me. Good-bye, my young friends. May we meet again in happier times.'

He hurried away, and was lost among the thousand shadows of the wood. They stared after him and then, rather silently because they were still awed by what had happened, made their way back to the village.

* * * *

Clouds were drifting across the moon. The village green darkened and silvered alternately. The churchyard was a place of nodding shadows. They stationed themselves in the lee of a great buttress by the side door, and waited for the hour to strike. At one moment they were alone at the next, as the bells chimed in the tower above, a tall cloaked figure was beside them.

'Mr Coverley?' said Peg softly, but her voice was drowned in the chiming of the bells. Then, as the echoes of the last stroke faded, making conversation possible, a fresh voice rang out, rasping from the darkness in triumph:

'Good evening, my lord Bishop!'

Colonel Clegg swaggered forward from the shelter of a yew tree. Several other men closed in, dim shapes against the gloom. A lantern was unmasked, and a beam of yellow light lit up the little group in the doorway.

'A tedious cold wait you have given us,' said the Colonel. Then his voice changed. He let fly a word which would have brought him into sad trouble in the higher Puritan circles. 'You're not the Bishop!' he snarled. 'You're that—that—actor fellow...'

'I have never denied it,' said Mr Coverley with magnificent dignity.

'You think yourself mighty clever, no doubt, leading us on this wild-goose chase! But you shall pay for this, my fine fellow. My name counts for something in this part of the country. I shall find ways of making things warm for you...'

'Then you had better be quick, my dear Colonel. For I fancy your reign as a petty tyrant is drawing near its end.'

'W-what do you mean, y-you insolent ruffian?'

'I was in the town this morning. The talk is all of great changes in the state of England. The Army is going to take a hand. There is a new song from London, and everyone is singing it. It goes thus.' The old actor sang mockingly:

'Ding-a-ding, ding, I heard a bird sing—
The Parliament soldiers are gone to the King!'

'What does it mean?' demanded Tony excitedly.

'It means, said Mr Coverley exultantly, 'that before this year is out we shall see Charles the Second crowned in Westminster! It will mean a quieter life for our friend the Colonel here, but a gayer one for the rest of us! We shall see the Bishop back in his cathedral, and maybe young Timothy singing his head off in the choir ... Who knows?' He turned and hugged the three children, unable any longer to restrain his delight. They were alone again in the churchyard, for Colonel Clegg and his men had moved away, muttering anxiously together. 'Who knows?' he repeated. 'When the theatres re-open, perhaps I can re-form my company! What do you say, Anthony—does the actor's life appeal?'

'*Oh* ... would you really have me, sir?'

'Of course!'

'Me, too?' Peg demanded.

'A girl actor?'

'An actress!' she corrected him, her eyes shining. 'They have them in France. And they say the Prince—the King, I mean—likes everything French!'

'I must consider it,' said Mr Coverley grandly. But, as they took his hands and ran him across the green towards the lighted window of their cottage, Peg felt sure that all was going to be well.

The Beach Hut

by Elizabeth Stucley

Do you know Westinghoe? It is a seaside town in Devonshire, and rather a queer place. When it was first thought of, about a hundred years ago, a grand design was drawn up of a wide promenade with towering hotels and a long pier. It was to be the Brighton of the west. Yes, it was all beautifully designed on the plan, and then the sea spoilt it all.

For hardly had the first legs of the pier been sunk into the rocks, or the first of the lodging houses built, than a huge tidal wave came rolling in across the bay. When it rolled out again, the pier was a jumble of wrecked spars, and a few of the new houses had been washed into rubble. This wave so frightened the builders, that although the new little town was shoved a mile back, up against the cliff, it never became a grand watering place, and stayed cheap and unknown.

It was because of the cheapness that the Martin family went to Westinghoe for their holiday every year. Mr Martin was a clerk in an office and earned a small salary because he was a timid man who could not take risks. His wife was a mousy little woman, very nervous and anxious, and the boy, Newton, who was twelve, had dark curling hair and looked thin and frail. But at the end of this quiet, rather dim family, there leapt up Alice. At ten, she was violent, gay and full of energy, tall, with thick brown hair and pink cheeks. Her hazel eyes shone. She laughed and cried louder than other people and always banged doors. The only quality she seemed to share with the rest of her family was a too vivid imagination.

And so the Martins went to Westinghoe every year, even though a great cliff loomed above the town, cutting off all the afternoon sun, and although the streets were full of hideous mid-Victorian houses and there were no flowers in the gardens because the salt west winds killed them all. The Martins went to Westinghoe because they felt safe there. They knew where the post office was, and the deck-chair man touched his hat to them and made them feel "Somebody". The wrecked pier and the washed-away houses that had never been rebuilt, did not frighten them, because they felt another tidal wave might never come.

Their courage about the tidal wave was odd, because as a family they had very little hope. If the sun shone, Mr Martin would be sure to remark, 'We'll pay for this fine weather later'. If the children boasted, they were at once reproved and everybody touched wood. If someone praised the children, the Martins would brush off the compliments with a phrase such as, 'Up like a rocket and down like a stick'. It was only Alice who went forward boldly, but even she did not walk under ladders or turn the mattress on a Friday. When they were at home in their London suburb, the Martins went to church every Sunday morning, and the preacher was a stern man who was not very hopeful either, and was always warning his congregation about the wrath to come.

Every first week in August, the Martins arrived at Bay View, which was one in a row of hideous yellow brick houses that ran end on to the sea. A stone wall with a coping of whitewashed pebbles protected the house from the road. Inside, the rooms were shabby and filled with flying sand that had crept in through the ill-fitting windows or had walked in on the lodger's shoes. Mrs Maundy, the landlady, produced fair sized helpings of tasteless food that the Martins ate quite happily. They would have suspected really tasty food as dangerous.

During their fortnight's holiday, the parents allowed themselves one luxury. Mr Martin enjoyed visiting churches and old buildings, and so to give himself and his wife freedom, and to quiet Mrs Martin's fussy fears, he hired Mrs Maundy's spinster sister, Miss Newcombe, to look after the children on certain afternoons.

Miss Newcombe was a tall, gaunt woman, who, for many years, had worn a large, black, felt hat, skewered to her bun with a long hatpin. She was so thin, she looked like a shut-up umbrella as she padded along on her immense, flat feet. From perpetually walking against the western gales, her body had become as bent as the trees in the municipal gardens. Her face was yellow and she spoke in a mincing voice. No more dreary companion could have been found with whom to walk the yellow brick streets.

Yet, oddly enough, the children liked Miss Newcombe. She was a great gossip and she talked freely to them. She would walk along the hardy hedges of veronica and aucuba, pointing out the houses and describing their inhabitants. All her stories started ominously in the middle. 'When I saw the book on the hall table ... I knew ...' or, 'They turned off the lights on the Friday and they never came up again.' So then the children would implore her to finish the rest of the horrific tale. Miss Newcombe would protest that it was not suitable and that they must not pass it on to Mamma, but she always finished the story. After years of taking children for walks, she had learnt to amuse herself.

The other advantage of Miss Newcombe was that she really knew the town. She knew where the best humbugs might be bought, and the pools where the largest prawns lurked. She could tell Newton all about the buried forest under the sands that peeped out here and there looking like green clay. She also told him all about the strange pebble ridge, that great, five-mile shifting wall of stone that travelled along the coast to pile up and protect Westinghoe from the sea.

But although Miss Newcombe was a professional looker-

after of children she did not like walking because she had
bunions on her feet. She preferred to sit in the shelters on the
front, or go along to the beach huts that lined the west side
of the bay.

'This is where the best people come,' she told the children.
'All the nicest families rent a beach hut. Why when I was
looking after the Basset children last summer, we had the best
hut of all. That blue one, "Kumonova" it's called. I could
make a nice cup of tea there, and put my feet up for a bit.'

Alice loved to walk along the beach hut path. She found all
the little chalets as entrancing as a set of dolls' houses. Each
one was brightly painted, and if Alice paused and stared
rudely, she could just make out the cupboards inside. There
might even be a table and a couch. Some of the huts had
grassy strips where clothes lines carried towels and bathing-
suits. Alice soon learned the names of all the huts: "Uandme",
"Fish Hall", "Seatop".

The people who owned the huts seemed a special race,
wonderful and set apart. Each hut had a sunburnt Mum who
kept running in and out bringing pots of tea, glasses of squash
or bottles for the baby. On the grassy strip a Dad sprawled
in a deck-chair, and children lay on lilos. Best of all there
might be a baby in a pram. Alice soon felt she knew these
people as well as the puppets in her own doll's house.

She soon found out that the beach hut people lived very
regular lives. They would arrive about ten and set out their
deck-chairs and table, before they changed into bathing-suits
for the first dip of the day. After swimming, they played
cricket to get warm, and there were hot drinks brewed by
Mum. After that came lunch, a short rest, another swim,
perhaps a walk up the sands, and at about half past five, the
great pack up; the folding of chairs, rolling up of sandy
towels, closing of shutters and doors before the nightly trek
home to high tea.

The odd thing about these people was that they never did anything but camp outside their huts. They did not go on expeditions. They just stayed in one tight family party. Yet, there was a snugness about it all that pleased Alice. She was a domestic character and longed to brew tea or feed the baby. She began to wish for a beach hut more than anything else in the world, and Miss Newcombe egged her on. 'If we had a hut, you wouldn't know your own comfort, dear. You drop a word to your mummy and I'm sure she'd get one. There's "Cockleside", now. That's not taken. The Thompsons had it last year, and after they left there was such a pile of bottles—still, I shouldn't tell you that. But you just get round your mum.'

Alice did not dare to ask her parents for a day or two, but she went on watching the "Hutters" as she called them. To her, even the children seemed specially grand and set apart. Having a headquarters, they could have more beach equipment such as kites, frogmen suits, wind yachts and inflatable canoes. Even when they went down on the common sands, they stuck together. After their bathe, they hurried back to the huts, because it was more comfortable to sunbathe there on a lilo with a glass of squash. The hutters never seemed inclined to go and scramble on the rocks or visit other coves. There was one particular family that Alice longed to know. The eldest boy, who must have been about thirteen, was really beautiful. He had dark red hair and was called Andrew. His two younger sisters were very pretty too and wore lovely, bright clothes. Alice really loved this family. Everything they did seemed exciting to her. She asked Newton if he wouldn't like to know Andrew, but Newton was only interested in his collection of shells and was too shy to be sociable. When Alice tried to scrape acquaintance with one of the lovely little girls, the child just smiled vaguely and hurried away.

'If we had a beach hut, they'd be my friends,' thought Alice

121

bitterly, and she went straight home and implored her mother to rent Cockleside, but Mrs Martin only told her not to be silly.

The weather that summer was enough to make a beach hut necessary. Miss Newcombe even began to prophesy a new tidal wave. 'Mark my words, what's happened once, could happen again,' she said. 'If you just had my bunions, dear! I can feel the weather in every toe!' If it did not rain, it blew, and the wind seemed to pick up the spray and fling it against the houses. There was nothing to do in the lodgings. Every room smelt of hot vinegar because Mrs Maundy was making pickles.

Delicate Newton was forced to stay in, but Alice insisted on going out, if only to get an appetite for the next dull meal. So Miss Newcombe, in a flapping mackintosh, trailed after her up Church Street, along by the shops and down the Avenue where the wet evergreens smelt vilely in the rain. If the wind dropped for a moment, the walkers could go out on the cliffs to pick sea thrift and bladder campion. Sometimes, Alice would persuade Miss Newcombe to pass the beach huts. Even in the worst weather, the hutters were there, having their money's worth, although they must sit in semi-darkness with the doors and shutters half closed to keep out the rain and spray. Alice could see they were playing dominoes or cards and she longed to play with them.

Every day she badgered her mother to rent a hut.

'You couldn't use it in this weather, dear.'

'Oh, Mum, we could! We could go down there and pop out if it cleared up for a minute. Besides, we could boil a kettle and put up our legs for a bit.'

'It would be just a waste of money,' said Mrs Martin. 'We couldn't really afford a holiday this year, but Newton needed one. It's such a big expense.'

'Everyone else has a hut and makes friends,' whined Alice.

Alice wished for a beach hut more than anything else in the world

'We aren't everyone,' sighed Mrs Martin. 'And you don't deserve a nice holiday, if you grumble so.'

Alice could not find the words to explain how bored she was. Besides, she knew it was wrong to be bored on an expensive holiday. Nor could she make her mother understand how much she wanted to be friends with Andrew and the other hutter children. In the first break in the rain, she ran off secretly and walked round and round Cockleside, pretending that it belonged to her.

On the first fine morning after the storm, Alice and Newton went to play on the beach. All the hutter children were there, having a cricket match. Alice stood about feeling odd man out. Andrew was very good at cricket and made the most runs. His two sisters were fielding. They paid no more heed to Alice than if she had been a pebble on the beach. She was not in their set.

'If only I were a hutter,' she thought.

At that very moment, a tall, cheerful young man wearing a bright blue shirt and carrying a large spade came hurrying across the sand.

'Come and help me,' he shouted to the children. 'I'm going to dig a sand church.' With the blade of his spade, he started to draw out the design of a church interior on the sand: an oblong for the altar, a square for the pulpit and long rows for choir stalls and pews. 'Come and dig!' he shouted again. 'Bring your spades! Quick, before the tide turns'.

All the children stopped playing and began to gather around. The young man himself was already digging frantically, throwing up great lumps of sand, patting it down, squaring it off. Soon the children began to dig too, and the young man allotted each of them a job. They all dug with a will because it was fun to make something definite after long wet days of cowering under shelter.

The sun shone. Newton and Alice worked together, digging

124

a beautiful pew that had a proper shelf for hymn books and gloves, and sand hassocks on which to kneel. More and more children came to help, and even some fathers got interested and joined in. Two girls made a beautiful crucifix of drift-wood and shells to place upon the altar, and they ornamented the pulpit with stones of shining quartz. The sun grew hotter and hotter but the builders were so busy they did not notice, for the sand church was growing in a miraculous way. At the end of an hour, it was finished ... alter, pulpit, choir stalls and pews.

'It's the best church I've ever seen!' shouted the young man in the blue shirt as he mopped his face with a handkerchief. 'Now what about holding a service in it? Here are the hymn sheets.' He pulled them out of his trouser pocket. 'We want a choir. Anybody sing? You? And you? Jolly good. Go and sit in the choir stalls. Bill, you dish out the hymn sheets. Andrew read the lessons. Alice, you take round the bag. We'll have a collection for poor children who never go to the sea.'

'What shall I use for the bag?' asked Alice, very proud at being chosen.

'Borrow a hat!' shouted the young man, laughing. 'Now I'm off to the vestry to change. You all be ready by the time I get back.' He strode off to a rock where he had left his cassock and dog collar, because he was, in fact, the curate of Westinghoe.

Alice borrowed an old panama from one of the fathers. He gave it to her, saying: 'Well if I get sunstroke, it's in a good cause. Here's fifty pence to start the collection.'

There was a great deal of excitement as the congregation got itself seated. Pews got a little damaged and had to be patched up. Mums and Dads dragged up their deck chairs and made another row behind the pews. But by the time the young priest came walking back in his cassock, everyone was in place. If the children had been asked to join in a religious service on the beach, they would have been embarrassed and walked away, but now they were only too anxious to have a service in the church they had built.

The young man in the blue shirt had changed into a priest, and he walked up the sandy aisle and took his place beside the choir. 'Hymn 24 on the sheet,' he announced. Suddenly all the children were singing.

Alice sang with all her might, if rather out of tune. One boy had a recorder and another a mouth-organ, so there was some other accompaniment besides the murmuring song of the sea. The tide was still very low and the waves were a long way off.

Suddenly, Alice wanted to cry. She did not know why; but there was something exciting and wonderful to be singing by the sea, under a hot sun, in company with all these children. They had worked hard together to make the church. It was theirs. Usually, she hated going to church, but this was different. When Andrew went up to read the lesson, and he read it very well, she really listened to the story about how Jesus had preached from a ship to a multitude on the shore.

At last, the curate went into the sand pulpit to preach. It was rather a short pulpit, coming barely to his waist, but its builders looked on with pride for all the quartz stones shone in the sun.

'I'm not going to preach you a long sermon, because very soon the sea will come galloping over the sand to wash our church away. I expect you often wish in church that a sea would arrive to shorten up the sermon.' Everybody laughed and looked at the sea. It was true that the waves did seem to be a little nearer. The life of the sand church would be very short. 'You heard in the lesson about how Jesus preached out of doors standing in a ship. Sermons can be preached anywhere for God is omnipresent, which means he is every-where, all at the same time. Lots of famous preachers have held services under the sky, but none of them had a church of sand like ours. Our church is only going to be used once. It will only stand for about an hour more, but what happens in this church may be important to you. In this sand church you may find it easier to recognise the presence of God, easier even than in a church of stone; because here, in this roofless tabernacle you can see the whole beautiful world, the sky, the sea and the cliffs...'

Alice looked at the sky, so blue and far above and she felt happy. For a few moments she did not listen to the sermon, but just sat and thought about her sudden happiness. When she did listen again, the curate was talking about prayer. 'You must all pray,' he was saying. 'You may ask God for what you want. He may not give you what you ask, because he knows, better than you do, what you really need. But if you pray for what is good and right, if you pray for others and not only for yourself, if you pray with faith, God will answer your prayers, even if not always in the way you expect. Now let us all say one last prayer together in our sand church.'

At that moment, Alice knew what she must pray for. She shut her eyes tightly and put her request in the plainest, clearest words. 'Please, God, could I have the beach hut, just for this one last week of our holiday. Cockleside is still empty. Please, please let me have Cockleside. I will be good. I will do anything, anything, just to have a beach hut. Amen.'

The hot sun on her bare shoulders made her feel that her prayer was heard. When she opened her eyes, she saw that all the children had prayed for something they wanted very much, and they were now scrambling up to sing the last hymn.

Feeling very happy and proud, Alice took round the hat, and the children put in their pennies, while some of the grown-ups even gave a few pound notes. Alice carried the heavy panama hat up to the curate who now stood in front of the altar and he raised it to the cross made of driftwood and stone.

After the service, the hutters went back to their huts, most of the children ran off, and only a few stayed to see the first waves wash down the altar and the pulpit.

The last week of the holiday soon passed, and each morning Alice expected her mother to say, 'Well, I've got the hut for you, just for these last days,' but she never did. At first, Alice could not believe her prayer was to remain unanswered. On the very last evening, the Friday, she went down to the huts and there was a new family at Cockleside, just starting on the shutting up for the night. Alice walked home, kicking the pebbles in her way, and determining not to pray again. It was all no use.

On Saturday morning, Mrs Maundy stood by her front gate waving to the Martins as they drove away and crying, 'Come back next year,' before bustling upstairs to make beds and sweep out the sand, ready for her next tenants.

In January, the Martins thought that Newton would never go to Westinghoe again. He caught pneumonia and nearly died because he had always been so delicate. Alice was never to forget those awful days when she scarcely dared to come home from school. She would stand by the garden gate and wonder if Newton was still in the house or if he had gone away for ever. She would creep in quietly and call softly, 'Mum?' At the sight of her mother's face she would know Newton was still alive.

By May, there was some hope he would live, although he still lay on the sofa, looking white and lifeless. And he kept on coughing. His legs were so weak, he sould not walk across the room, and Alice almost cried to look at him. Each day, Mrs Martin asked, 'You are better, darling, aren't you?' and Newton always nodded. Yet if he was better every day, he did not seem greatly improved by the end of each week.

'I think we should take our holidays now,' said Mr Martin

at the end of May.

'Now?' asked Mrs Martin very much surprised. 'But it's not August.'

'I think we won't wait for August this year,' he replied. 'I will write to Mrs Maundy at once.' Alice stared at her parents with astonishment and fear. To go for a holiday in June, during term time was staggering. She guessed that they must go now because Newton might not be there in August.

It seemed very odd indeed to arrive at Westinghoe in June. It was not like an ordinary holiday at all. The little town looked empty and felt different. When the taxi drove up at Bay View, Newton was almost whimpering with exhaustion. His head flopped against his father's shoulder when Mr Martin carried him into the house and laid him on the bed upstairs. Mrs Maundy had run out crying; 'The poor little lad! Still the air at Westinghoe is as good as a tonic. Everyone says so. You'll see. He'll pick up in no time. Shall I wet the tea, Mrs Martin?'

But Newton did not pick up, although a bath chair was found to carry him to the beach. He just laid there and showed no interest in the sea or the crabs that Alice brought him. Sometimes he rolled his head away from the sight of the other children who were well, and ran about and screamed. Old ladies came up and asked pitying questions. It was terrible — a nightmare of a holiday.

On the fourth evening at supper, Mr Martin suddenly announced: 'I've booked us a beach hut. I think it will be better for Newton, more sheltered; and, Mummy, you can boil up hot drinks for him there. It's even got a couch inside.'

His words went through Alice like a sharp sword. The beach hut! God had answered her prayer at last, but in what a fearful way! She had said she would give anything for a beach hut, and He had taken her at her word, and would take Newton. She had exchanged the brother she loved for a beach hut!

She wanted to shout out, 'No, no. Don't get it! I didn't mean, it. I love Newton. I don't want the hut. I don't want it.' But her lips wouldn't move. If she had spoken, her parents would have thought her mad, they would have imagined that she did not want Newton to get well. They would never understand her explanations.

She got up and went over to the window, but she was shaking with fear. She knew now that her prayer had been a selfish one, and the curate had said it was dangerous to pray selfishly. She knew that she had pretended to God that the beach hut was for the pleasure of the whole family, but that, in fact, neither her parents nor Newton had wanted it last year.

'Well,' said Mr Martin as brightly as possible. 'It's an ill wind that blows nobody any good. Alice, you kept on badgering me for a hut last year, and now you've got it! Now you'll be able to boil up kettles and keep house.'

'What's the hut called?' Alice heard her own voice like a husky squeak. She had to ask this question, even though she was afraid to hear the answer.

'I've got the key here,' said Mr Martin. 'There were plenty of huts free at this time of year, so I picked the best. It's —' he pulled out the key and looked at the label. 'It's Cockleside.'

Without another word, Alice ran from the room. She had indeed got her wish.

It was terrible to have to sit in the hut and watch Newton lying on the couch, eyes half closed, his white hands limp. The hut was very quiet because most of its neighbours were empty. Alice loathed the place. To her it was a prison, a punishment. She had got what she had asked for and she had got it at a terrible price. All day long she had to listen to her parents congratulating themselves on the convenience of Cockleside, and even congratulating her, Alice, for thinking of it.

She could not bear it. She would run down on to the sands

so as to escape the sight of Newton lying there, from the sight of her mother making tea, and her father sprawling in a deck chair. The picture was so exactly what she had imagined, but just twisted and spoilt. She felt deeply guilty and she did not know how to tell anyone about the misery she endured. As she walked on the sands, she longed to pray again that Newton might get well, that she should be forgiven her first selfish prayer; but she dared not pray. She might make another mistake.

Alice could not sleep at night, she did not want to eat, and her parents began to look at her anxiously, fearing that she too might be falling ill.

At last, one afternoon while Newton and his parents dozed after lunch, Alice could bear her unhappiness no longer. She muttered something about buying sweets, and dragged her sandshoes along the rocky lane that led to the main road and the church. She had a dim idea of finding a prayer book and looking in it to find some formula for cancelling a prayer. If the words were written in the prayer book, they could not be wrong.

The fuchsias in the hedge around the church were still in bud. It was an ugly little building filled with pitch pine seats varnished a bright yellow. She tiptoed into the coolness and was relieved to find the place empty. Picking up a prayer book, she sat down in a pew. Now that she was in the quiet of the church, she felt calmer. It was easier to think, out of the glare of the sun. She began to look through the prayer book, until she came to the special prayers. She found some for time of war and pestilence and some for illness and famine, but nothing that suited her need. She did not want to pray a new prayer, but just to unpray one. The prayer book makers had not thought of that.

'I shall have killed Newton, if he dies—' she thought and the tears began to trickle slowly down her cheeks. She covered her face with her hands and whispered. 'Please, I love Newton. Don't take him away.'

When the young curate came into the church, he was surprised to see a little girl weeping in a pew. He stopped in the aisle, afraid to intrude upon her grief, but wanting to help if he could. When Alice heard footsteps, she tried to hide her face, and then she heard a deep voice ask, 'What is it? What's the matter?'

Alice started. She remembered that voice. It was the young curate of the sand church; but she wanted nothing to do with him. In the nightmare of the last week he had become the cause of all her misery. She brushed the tears off her face. 'It's all right,' she said and tried to get up with dignity. 'I — I've fixed it — I hope.' She would have slipped by him, but he blocked the entrance to the pew.

'I'm glad you've fixed it ...' he said, looking at her in a puzzled way. She nodded, biting her lip, and keeping her eyes on the east window.

'You are sure it's all right?' he asked and his blue eyes were very kind. 'Because you still seem to be pretty miserable.'

She turned and faced him defiantly. 'Let me go. Let me pass, please. Anyhow, it's all your fault —'

'My fault?' he was amazed. He pushed her up the pew and sat down beside her. 'What's my fault?'

'You told us to pray for what we wanted. Well, I did. It was a flop.'

'Oh! I say. I'm so sorry. But what was it I said?'

'Don't you remember? Last year, in the sand church. The one we built. You told us to pray for what we wanted.'

'Yes?'

'Well, I prayed for a beach hut. I said in my prayer that I would give anything for a beach hut ... and now, we've got one!' She began to sob, her whole body shaking. 'God gave it me.'

'Listen, don't cry. I don't understand ... Could you .. ?' he put his hand on her shoulder, but she shook him off, and faced him defiantly.

'Newton's going to die. They pretend he isn't, but he is. That's all. He's my brother. I told God that I would give anything for a beach hut. Now my parents have hired one — because Newton's so ill. Now do you see? It's me who's killed him!'

The curate caught at her hand and held it tightly. 'Alice, listen to me. You must.'

'It's no good,' she was crying again. 'There's nothing you can do.'

'Alice, what you want is a new God. The one you've got is a nasty, mean revengeful sort of person. You must find yourself a new God.'

She stopped crying and stared at him.

'Suppose you were God,' said the young man 'and a child prayed to you for a beach hut. Would you be so cruel as to give her the beach hut and take away the brother she loved? Would you do that?'

'No. I wouldn't be so mean.'

'And you would willingly give up the beach hut if you could keep Newton?'

'Of course, of course I would. I hate the hut, I hate it, and Newton is my best friend. I love him so terribly.'

'Then if you love him, that's all right. You see human beings are a bit ignorant and they do invent nasty mean little gods for themselves. All you need, Alice, is to find and love the real God, the great, tremendous, wonderful God who created the Universe and who is Love. If you pray to that God, everything will be all right. Yes, even if Newton does die, though that may be difficult for you to understand. You mustn't feel guilty, Alice honestly you mustn't. Getting the beach hut might just be an accident, or one of those queer things that do happen. Or perhaps the beach hut you prayed for was really sent to make Newton well. You may have prayed better than you knew. Perhaps, at this very moment, the sun and the sea, and even the beach hut, are curing Newton. If they aren't, I promise you, Alice, that it's not your fault. It's only superstitious, ignorant people who believe in a cruel vindictive god. All you've got to do is get in touch with the God who is Love itself.'

They talked together for a little longer, and presently they left the church. Alice walked down the pathway like a person released from prison.

Something, perhaps the sea, the sun or the beach hut, or perhaps some Power that was greater still, did work a magical cure on Newton. By the end of a fortnight, he was beginning to smile again, to eat his food, to look at the crabs and shells Alice brought him. The Martins decided to stay on yet another week at Bay View, and before they went home, the boy was playing on the beach with the other children.

'There, what did I tell you?' cried Mrs Maundy. 'The air here is like a tonic. I knew he'd soon pick up.'

'There's nowhere in the world better than Westinghoe, said Mrs Martin. 'We'd like to book our rooms for August next year, Mrs Maundy.'

The Stolen Ponies

by JOHN DAVIES

The top of a white sail was fluttering above the harbour wall. Sue said, 'I'm sure that's David, getting ready to go without us. The beast!'

She and Jo hurried on along the road, and when they got to the harbour, they found that Sue had been right. David and his friend Peter were just getting into *Windsong*, David's little sailing dinghy.

'Sorry we can't take you with us,' David said, 'but we must get in some practice for the race on Saturday.'

He pushed the boat off from the harbour side. The wind filled its sails and it sped away. After it had gone a short distance, the two boys turned and waved.

Jo waved back, but Sue didn't.

'It's not fair!' she protested. 'Just because we're girls! And I'm sure you would have loved to go, Jo.'

Jo didn't mind. Of course she would have liked to have gone out in the little boat, but there were plenty of other wonderful things to do. She was still only in the first week of her stay with Sue and David, her Devonshire cousins, in the little seaside town of Westhampton. Jo's own home was in London, and to her Westhampton, with its cliffs and beaches and wide, rolling moors, was a heavenly place.

'Oh, well,' Sue said, 'we can get on all right without them!' She looked at the little boat again for a moment, then turned to Jo. 'I know! Let's have a picnic up the moors. We could go up to Heath Tor and see if there are any ponies there.'

'Oh, yes — do let's!' Jo said at once. She was thrilled at the idea. She was having riding lessons at stables in London, and she was crazy about horses and ponies.

'We can go on the bikes,' Sue said. 'I can ride David's, and you can have mine.'

They hurried home. Mrs Marsh was in the kitchen, and, as soon as the girls told her what they wanted to do, she bustled about getting a picnic lunch for them. Sue and Jo helped, so it didn't take long.

A few minutes later they were on their way, with Sue riding David's racing bike. Sue was a real tomboy, very sunburnt, with fair, tousled hair, and quite big for her thirteen years. Jo, who was a year younger, was slightly built and dark. She was quiet and rather shy.

They cycled through the town and then up the narrow, winding moorland road. They soon left the last houses behind, and the wild loneliness of the moors lay all about them.

After a while they turned off the road, and had to push their bikes up the rough, steep track which led to the top of Heath Tor. They arrived at the top laughing and gasping for breath and, dropping their bicycles, flung themselves thankfully down on the sweet-smelling heather.

Heath Tor was a marvellous spot, breezy, lonely, the highest point for miles around. There was a terrific view in all directions: inland were the purple folds of the moors, stretching on and on into the hazy distance. Far away in the east, a long way below them, was the silver thread of the River Tamar. To the west lay the little town they had just cycled up from. And to the south lay the glittering sea.

There was a solitary little boat with white sails out on the sea.

'Do you think that is David's?' Jo asked.

'I don't know,' Sue said. 'And certainly don't care!'

There was only one thing wrong with Heath Tor. There were no ponies.

'Let's move on a bit,' Sue said, when they had had their

picnic. 'There may be some drinking at the stream on the other side.'

They got to their feet and walked along the crest of the Tor, leaving the bicycles where they were. After a little way a bubbling little moorland stream came into view.

There were no ponies there either, but Sue scarcely noticed that.

'Look!' she said. 'Down there — behind the old farm!'

Jo looked in the direction in which Sue was pointing. There, about a quarter of a mile away and some hundreds of feet below them, lay Tor Farm. Tor Farm had been deserted for years and was in ruins. It looked so lonely and lifeless that even on such a lovely, sunny day it gave Jo a shivery feeling.

But what Sue was really pointing at was the small field behind the farm. In that field, which had a rough stone wall round it, were seven or eight ponies.

'What are they doing there?' Sue asked, speaking more to herself than to Jo. 'The ponies always run wild on the moor — no one's supposed to shut them up like that.' She stared hard at the field. 'And someone's built the wall up specially to keep them in. The last time I saw it, there were gaps in it where it had fallen down.'

Now it was Jo's turn to exclaim.

'Look — over there!' she cried. 'There's something driving up to the farm. It's a horse-box!'

She was right. A horse-box, a very shabby and dilapidated one, was lurching slowly along the overgrown track which led to the farm.

The two girls watched breathlessly. The horse-box lumbered on until it came to the gate of the field behind the farm. It stopped there and three men got out. Two of them went into the field, while the third let down the tailboard. The two men in the field began driving the ponies towards the gate.

'They're going to take them away!' Sue said. 'But they're

The men in the field drove the ponies towards the gate

not allowed to do that!'

There was nothing at all they could do except watch. The men drove the ponies out of the field and into the horse-box. They shut the ponies in and then climbed up into the driving seat. The horse-box lurched round and started off back by the way it had come.

So far Sue had been too horrified to move. Now she suddenly came to life.

'They're stealing them!' she exclaimed. 'They're not supposed to take the ponies off the moor!' She grabbed Jo's arm. 'I know! If we hurry back to the road, we may be in time to see them go by!'

Jo didn't need any urging. She was just as anxious about the ponies as Sue was. The two girls dashed back to their picnic place, snatched up the things they had left there and stuffed them into their saddlebags and pedalled off as hard as they could.

They didn't have to pedal far. In a few yards they reached the edge the flat expanse of turf and heather on the top of the Tor. The rough path by which they had come up fell away steeply below them. At any ordinary time even Sue wouldn't have dared to ride any further, but now she went flying down the path, bumping and skidding over the grassy tufts and the ruts. And Jo was close behind her.

It didn't seem that they could possibly stay on, but they did. In only a minute or two they had reached the road. They fell off then rather than got off, and, leaving the bicycles lying on the grass verge, stood staring in the direction from which the horse-box must come.

'It's got to come this way,' Sue said. 'It's the only road.' She gave a sort of little gasp. 'It's coming now! I can hear it!'

Jo could hear it too. Its engine was whining loudly as it came up one of the many steep hills on the moorland road. Soon it would come round the corner a few yards away...

And go roaring past.

Jo thought of the ponies again, and felt terribly helpless.

'Oh, Sue!' she breathed, 'What can we do? We can't stop it. What can we *do*?'

Sue spoke quickly. The sound of the horse-box's engine was louder now.

'There's only one thing we *can* do,' she said. 'Try to get a look at the men in it. Then, when we get back to Westhampton, we can tell someone — the police or somebody — what they look like.' She draw in her breath sharply. 'Here it is! Try not to look too interested.'

As she spoke, the horse-box came swaying round the corner. It seemed to fill the whole road. It bore down upon the two girls and they glanced quickly up at it as it passed.

A dark-haired man who looked like a gypsy was driving, and he stared at them as the horse-box roared past. Next to him was a big man with close-cropped ginger hair. Neither Sue nor Jo got a clear look at the third man.

In a few moments the horse-box had disappeared from sight. 'Come on!' Sue exclaimed.

She and Jo jumped on their bikes again and pedalled hard towards Westhampton. But it was a hot day, the road was very hilly, and they had more than two miles to go. When they had covered about half the distance, they came to a hill so steep that they had to get off and walk. They pushed their bicycles up it as fast as they could. Their legs were aching and they were gasping for breath.

They simply had to stop at the top.

'I can see it again!' Jo exclaimed. 'There it is — down there!'

There was the horse-box, far below them and a long way ahead. They stood and watched it. They had an awful, helpless feeling that by the time they got into Westhampton it would be miles and miles away.

But then something unexpected happened. The horse-box

turned off on to an old, overgrown side road which led down to the sea.

At the end of this road there was a crumbling jetty where ships had once come in to load clay from the pits nearby. It was a desolate, ugly bit of the coast, and no one ever went there nowadays. The clay pits had been worked out long ago, and there hadn't been a ship there for years.

But there was one there now. Sue had been too intent on the horse-box to notice it at first. When she did spot it, she couldn't imagine why it was there.

Then the answer suddenly came to her. The ship was going to take the ponies away.

Her heart sank as she realised what that might mean. She was sure something dreadful would happen to them. She had heard terrible stories of horses and ponies being shipped across the Channel to be slaughtered for horseflesh.

Quickly she told Jo her fears and Jo's eyes widened in horror.

'Oh, how awful!' she exclaimed. 'We *mustn't* let that happen!' She jumped on her bicycle and pedalled off as hard as she could.

At last they reached Westhampton, and, as they rode through the outskirts, they began to wonder what they were going to do now. So far it had all been very simple — they'd just had to get back to the town as quickly as possible. But now?

Sue didn't think they could go straight to the police — they might not take much notice of two breathless and untidy girls on bikes with a rather unbelievable story to tell. She thought: *If only Daddy were home!* But he wasn't. He was at work. Perhaps the next best thing would be to tell her mother?

But then, as they were riding past the harbour, they saw David and Peter, who had just come back from their sail. They were tidying up the little boat before leaving it. And Sue thought: Why not tell them? They were a bit older, and they were boys. They might know what to do.

She and Jo stopped by the boat and poured out the story of the horse-box, and the men who had driven the ponies down to the old jetty.

At first the boys just didn't believe them.

'You must have been seeing things,' David said.

'Sounds like a touch of sunstroke,' Peter added, grinning.

'But you *must* believe us!' Jo broke in, passionately. 'You must, you *must*, because it's true! And we've got to do something!'

David looked at her. He was beginning to think there might be something in this after all.

'Well,' he said. 'I don't know. It's certainly odd if there really is a ship at the old jetty.' He turned to Peter. 'It wouldn't hurt to sail over there and have a look.'

'I'm game,' Peter said.

'And so are we,' Sue said quickly. 'You're not going to leave us behind this time!' And, to make sure of that, she climbed down into the boat.

David opened his mouth to tell her to get out again, but then he shrugged instead. He knew his sister. When she'd really made up her mind, there wasn't much anyone could do about it.

'O.K.,' he said. 'You'd better get in too, Jo. Just see you don't get in the way, that's all.'

A minute or so later the dinghy was on its way out of the harbour with the four of them aboard.

The jetty was on the other side of Westhampton Bay. The little boat sped across the sparkling sea. Everything seemed unreal to Jo as she watched the clear water rushing past. This was the first time she had ever been in a sailing boat, and it was a great thrill. But at the same time she was so worried about the ponies that she couldn't really think about anything else.

Slowly the old jetty came into view. And there *was* a ship there.

'Well — you were right, after all,' David told the girls.

'Of course we were,' Sue said. 'We were right about all of it!'

The ship was quite small and very shabby, with rusty sides. The jetty it was moored to was deserted. There was no sign of the horse-box.

'Perhaps they've got the ponies on board already,' Jo said.

'I wonder,' Peter said. 'If they're down in the hold, how shall we know they're there?'

'If we go close enough, I should think we'd hear them moving about,' Sue said, but she said it rather uncertainly.

They were now getting closer to the ship and they could see two men leaning over the side, watching them as they approached. One of them disappeared, but the other stayed where he was.

'Is that one of the men with the horse-box?' David asked his sister.

'No,' Sue said. 'At least, I don't think so.'

At that moment the man waved, then cupped his hands and called out 'Ahoy, there!'

'Ahoy!' David called back.

'Would you do us a favour?'

'What?'

'We can't get into the town — we're leaving soon. Would you post some letters for us?'

David hesitated before replying. He had a sudden sense of danger. On the other hand the crews of ships quite often did ask people passing in boats to post letters for them.

'Say yes!' Jo whispered, fiercely. 'Then perhaps we can get on the ship and find out if the ponies are there.'

David gave Jo a quick look of surprise. Until now she'd seemed to him to be so quiet and shy. She really must be worried about those ponies!

He suddenly made up his mind.

'O.K.,' he called out to the man on the ship.

143

He steered *Windsong* alongside the ship. Peter threw a rope, and the man caught it and tied it to the ship's rail. Then he began letting down a rope ladder.

'You might as well come on board for a minute,' he said.

Again David, hesitated, but Jo was already climbing the ladder. Sue was close behind her. The boys followed, and a moment or two later all four of them were standing on the ship's deck.

The man was big and weatherbeaten. He was wearing seaboots and his strong brown arms were heavily tattooed. He was quite obviously a sailor. He grinned at his four visitors, but somehow it wasn't a very nice grin.

'Come down and see the captain,' he said. 'The letters are in his cabin.'

He turned away and they all went in through a door and along a narrow passage lit by a naked electric light bulb. It seemed dark in there after the bright sunshine outside, and there was a smell of oil and stale food. Jo had been hoping that, once they got inside the ship, they might be able to hear whether the ponies were there or not, but there was some sort of engine running which drowned most other sounds.

The sailor stopped at a door, knocked on it and opened it. 'In here,' he said.

David and Peter went in first. Sue and Jo followed — and stopped dead just inside the door.

There were three men in the cabin. One of them, who was wearing a reefer jacket, looked like the captain. The other two the girls had seen before — in the driving cab of the horse-box!

'So it's you, eh?' the gypsy-like man said. He jerked his head at the sailor, who had brought up the rear. 'You'd better shut the door.'

The door slammed to with a heavy thud.

'Here!' David protested. 'What — ?'

The black-haired man interrupted him roughly. 'I'll ask the

questions,' he said. He looked at Sue and Jo again. 'It was you two we saw on the raod, wasn't it — and now here you are again. What's your little game?'

'You mean, what is your g-game,' Sue said. She said it bravely, but she couldn't help her voice shaking a little.

'You stole the ponies,' Jo said. 'You're taking them away.'

David said, 'Don't you think you're being very silly? There's a law against —'

The man growled angrily.

'I've had about enough of this,' he said. He turned to his companions. 'It's like I said — they know too much. We'd better make sure they keep quiet —'

'You'd better not touch us!' Peter said sharply.

The man got slowly to his feet.

'Is that so?' he said with a sneer. And all at once he gestured abruptly to the other men. 'Grab them!' he snarled.

* * * *

The girls were in another cabin. They had been separated from the boys and brought here and locked in. That had been ages ago, or so it seemed, and no one had been near them since.

The cabin was very small. There was a single bunk, with drawers built in underneath it, a wash-basin, one shabby wooden chair, and a sort of alcove to hang clothes in. There was one porthole, over the bunk. Sue had already climbed on the bunk to look out through it. But the cabin was on the side of the ship next to the jetty and all she could see was some rough stone-work. She had hoped that, if the could see out, she might be able to call for help, but of course she couldn't. Even if she could have seen along the jetty, it wouldn't have been any good, because no one ever came that way any more.

Now she was sitting helplessly in the bunk, while Jo wandered about the cabin. Unlike Sue, Jo simply couldn't keep still.

They had no idea how long they had been in the cabin,

because neither of them had a watch. But it must have been a long time, because it was beginning to get dark.

Suddenly a throbbing began under their feet. A glass on the wash-basin started to rattle. Jo stopped in her prowling.

'What's that?' she asked.

'It's the engine,' Sue said. 'It means the ship will be going soon.'

They looked at each other. Both of them were thinking: What is going to happen to us now? And Sue gave a sudden shudder as she remembered what the gypsy had said: 'We'd better make sure they keep quiet.' What had he meant? What was he going to do with them?

The throbbing continued, and Jo started her pacing again. She paused at the door and tried the handle, but of course it was locked.

A minute or so later she stopped again, this time by the alcove where the clothes were hanging. She was listening. She could hear something. What was it? The ship's vibration was causing a faint clinking sound somewhere there.

Without knowing quite why she was doing it, she felt along the row of clothes, and then put her hand in a pocket of a rough blue serge coat. She took something out of the pocket and stared at it.

It was a bunch of keys.

Sue and Jo looked at each other, feeling a sudden, wild hope. Could one of these be a duplicate key to the cabin door?

Sue jumped off the bunk and together they went over to the door. With a trembling hand Jo tried the keys in the lock, one after the other.

And — yes! One of them fitted, It turned smoothly in the lock.

Jo paused, with her hand still on the key.

'It's open!' she whispered. 'But — what can we do now?'

'There's only one thing we *can* do,' Sue whispered back. 'We

146

must get off the ship?'

'What about the boys?'

'We can't do anything about them. We don't know where they are or anything.' Sue clenched her fists. 'The only thing we can do is get away and fetch help!'

Jo drew a deep breath.

'All right,' she said.

'Go on then!' Sue said fiercely. 'But be careful!'

Very slowly and cautiously, Jo opened the door of the cabin and looked out. The passage outside was deserted. She slipped out and Sue followed her. They hurried along the passage through a doorway, and found themselves on the deck of the ship. It was dark out there. Instinctively they turned towards the jetty, but they had only gone a step or two when the figure of a man loomed up in the night.

Sue stopped dead, then tip-toed across to the other side of the ship.

Jo was there at her side.

'We can't get off if he's there,' Sue whispered. Then she put a hand quickly on Jo's arm. 'I know! David's boat!'

They both turned and looked over the ship's side. They could just see the little boat in the darkness a few yards further along. They crept along the deck until they were right above it. And they were in luck! The rope ladder was still there too. Perhaps the men had forgotten it.

'You go first,' Sue hissed in Jo's ear.

Jo climbed down the ladder while Sue undid the rope by which the dinghy was tied to the ship's rail. With the end of the rope in her hand, she went down the ladder after Jo and scrambled into the dinghy. As she did so, the little boat began to drift away from the ship on the tide.

'We'll have to row for a bit,' Sue said. 'They might see the white sails.'

She got out the oars and rowed. After a little while the ship was lost in the darkness.

Sue stopped rowing.

'I think we can hoist the sails now,' she said.

'Do you know how to?' Jo asked.

'Of course!' Sue said. 'I've been sailing with David a lot of times. He's not the only one who knows how to do it.' Then she remembered where her brother still was. 'Poor David!' she said, with a choke in her voice. 'And Peter. We *must* get help as soon as we can!'

In a minute or two the sails were up. Perhaps they weren't up quite properly, but that didn't matter. There was a fresh breeze, and *Windsong* began to skim swiftly over the water.

Sue steered for the red light at the entrance to Westhampton harbour. It seemed to take them years to get there, but they reached it at last and tied up the boat. Luckily their bicycles were still where they had left them, and they jumped on and pedalled off furiously through the town. They hadn't any lights, but they couldn't worry about that.

When they got home, they found Sue's father and mother standing at the front door, looking very worried.

'Good heavens!' Mr Marsh exclaimed. 'Where have you two been? And David's not home either —'

Sue broke in.

'Daddy — listen!' she said. 'Don't ask questions — just listen!'

They went into the house and Sue poured out the whole story. Her father looked more and more worried as she did so, and as soon as she had finished he got up and went to the telephone.

'We must stop that ship!' he said as he picked up the receiver.

After that things began to happen. Mr Marsh telephoned the police, and the coastguards. A quarter of an hour later a police car screeched up outside the house and a police constable came dashing in.

148

'We've been out to the old jetty, sir,' he told Mr Marsh, 'but we were too late. The ship's gone.'

Sue's father nodded quickly.

'All right,' he said, 'then we'll have to go after it.' And then he did a surprising thing. He turned to Sue and Jo and added, 'Come along, you two!'

Almost before they knew what was happening, they were all in the police car, speeding down to the harbour.

'We'll need you with us to identify the ship,' Mr Marsh explained on the way. 'You're the only ones who know what it looks like.'

There was a coastguard ship in the harbour. The police car drew up beside it, and Mr Marsh and the two girls dashed on board. Sailors were bustling about the deck, and a minute or two later the ship was steaming out of the harbour.

Mr Marsh had taken Sue and Jo up to the bridge. He was talking to the captain now, while they stood staring ahead. It was quite late at night by this time and they were wondering how it would be possible to find another ship in all that vast, dark expanse of sea.

But wireless messages were coming in. Then the captain spoke to someone on the ship's telephone, and all the men on the bridge seemed to get excited.

A few minutes later the reason for the excitement appeared ahead. A dark shape. A ship. It wasn't possible to see what sort of ship it was. But then the captain of the coastguard ship gave an order, and a powerful searchlight suddenly blazed out, lighting up the other vessel.

Mr Marsh turned to Sue and Jo.

'Is that the ship?' he asked quickly.

'Yes!' Sue said. And Jo added, 'Yes, I'm sure it is!'

The coastguard ship drew nearer to the other, and then the captain picked up a microphone and spoke into it. A great, loud voice boomed out, telling the other ship to stop.

149

For a little while it looked as though the men on the other ship weren't going to take any notice. But then it slowed down, until finally it was lying motionless on the sea.

The coastguard ship came up beside the other one and some of the coastguard men jumped on to it. Mr Marsh went with them. Sue and Jo knew why. He was anxious to make sure David and Peter were safe.

They waited, expecting that Mr Marsh would bring the boys back with him. But when, after what seemed a long time he came back, he was alone. And he was looking more worried than ever.

'The ponies are on board all right,' he said, 'but the boys aren't. And those brutes won't say what they've done with them. They say they've never seen them.'

The other ship was turning round now. The coastguard ship turned too. They were both heading back for Westhampton harbour. The hunt had been successful. But Mr Marsh and the two girls were desperately worried now about the boys. What could have happened to them?

They got their next surprise when the coastguard ship came into the harbour — and there were David and Peter, waiting on the quay! They looked all right, except that their clothes were very dirty.

'But — what happened?' Mr Marsh asked, as soon as he and the girls had got off the ship.

'They turned us off just before they sailed,' David said. 'They knew it would take us a long time to walk back to Westhampton.'

'We were trying to take a short cut across the marshes when we heard the police car,' Peter said. 'We tried to run to the road to stop it, but I'm afraid —'

'It was dark, and we fell in a ditch,' David said.

Sue giggled. She couldn't help it.

'So we didn't save them from a watery grave after all,' she

said to Jo.

'No,' Jo said. She was grinning. 'But we saved the ponies, and they're much more important than two boys.'

David shook his fist at her.

'You wait!' he said. He turned to Peter. 'Shall we take them sailing tomorrow and drop them overboard?' Then he said to his father, 'Incidentally, how did my boat get back here?'

'You'd better ask Sue,' Mr Marsh said.

'Perhaps *we'll* take *you* sailing tomorrow,' Sue said.

'Then they can tell you all about it,' Mr Marsh told David. 'It's much too late now.'

And that is more or less what happened. The four of them went sailing together next day, and talked nineteen to the dozen about their adventure.

In fact, they never stopped sailing and talking for the rest of the holiday.

No Country Holiday?

by Lois Lamplugh

Whenever Maggie stood in the middle of the supermarket and tried to remember what it was that she had been sent to buy, she usually remembered instead that a farm had once stood here. And not so very long ago, either; her grandmother had often fetched eggs and milk from the farmhouse door, when she was a girl, and there had been fields then where all the housing estates stood now. There were times when Maggie wished she could go back and live in those days, so that she could have country all round her, instead of a London suburb with row upon row of semi-detached houses, and shops and petrol stations and traffic lights.

On a hot cloudy July afternoon, with grit and bits of paper blowing about in the High Road, Maggie went down to the supermarket after school to get herself an ice lolly with the last fivepence of her pocket money. She was by herself, because Marcia, her elder sister, was playing tennis, Joe, her younger brother, would be going to the swimming baths, and her best friend had gone to the dentist. She had almost decided to go to the swimming baths too, but she knew how crowded they would be on an afternoon like this. Joe was quite content to spend an hour or two jumping into the shallow end and scrambling out again, and splashing his friends and yelling with excitement, but Maggie liked to go in the early morning, when it was quiet and you could swim. But in the baths she longed for the real sea, as she had known it on holidays. Nothing was as good as that. Sometimes she felt as though her whole skin was thirsty for it. And even more, on hot gritty days like today, she felt thirsty for the green country. What made it worse this year was knowing that her family could not afford to go away for a holiday. Her father was a nursery gardener, and in the winter he had slipped on a patch of ice and fractured his thigh. Having to spend a long time on sick pay had meant no saving up for a country holiday.

In the supermarket, Maggie walked slowly along an aisle between racks of tinned soup and sauces and pickles. Over the butter and cheese section was a large coloured cardboard cow, with rolling eyes in a head that waggled from side to side. Forty years ago, she thought, there had been live cows in byres outside, instead of cars in a cindery car park. When the farm was sold, and pulled down, a cinema had been built in the place where it had stood. Maggie could remember the cinema, and the day it had shut because it didn't pay any longer, and the two years it had stood empty before it was turned into a supermarket. A white elephant, people had called it then.

Her grandmother had said, '*That* didn't last long, did it? The farm had been here for three hundred years, I've been told, but the cinema went out of business after thirty.'

Maggie took an ice lolly out of the freezer near the waggle-headed cow and wandered back to the cash desk. She handed over her fivepence and went out into the dusty High Road.

She tried to think of something to do to fill in the time before tea. It was Wednesday, and on Wednesday afternoon her mother did the ironing, with the radio on and didn't expect her family to come home early if the weather was fine.

She passed the radio shop, with its row of television sets all showing the test card in different shades of grey, and the tobacconist, and the co-op grocery. At the pet shop she paused, but even the pet shop was dull today; no puppies, kittens or rabbits in the window, only a tank of goldfish.

Soon term would be over, and then, it seemed to her there would be six weeks of afternoons, or whole days, like this, with nowhere to go and nothing to do, and only thoughts of the country and the sea to tantalise her.

She turned the corner into Washington Avenue, and left the High Road and its traffic behind. Not long ago, Washington Avenue had been a road of semi-detached houses, all about fifty years old. Now one side was lined with new maisonettes and blocks of flats; in places building was still going on. A development company had bought all the houses that side and koncked them down, to use the sites for rebuilding.

Maggie turned into an alley between garden fences. It brought her out near her grandmother's house. It was a small house standing alone, and in a wider garden than most of its neighbours. Once Maggie had been told that it had been built the year the old Queen died. At first she had not understood who the old Queen was, but her grandmother had said 'Why, Queen Victoria, of course. I was only a little girl when she died.'

To Maggie, Queen Victoria seemed far back in history; she found it strange to think she had been ruling England when her grandmother was born.

She went round the side of the house. As she had expected, her grandfather was working on his vegetable plot, which took up more than half the garden. Her grandmother was sitting in a deck chair, knitting.

'Hello, duck, come and sit down,' she said. 'You look as though you'd lost a sixpence and found a bad halfpenny.'

'Do I? I didn't know I did,' Maggie said. She smiled, but it felt much too bright and unreal.

'What's wrong? Wishing you were in the country again? It seems to me you were born in the wrong place.'

'Do you miss the country, ever, Gran? I mean, did you feel sad when you saw it all going, when all the houses were built round here?'

'Of course I did. We both did, your Grandpa and me. But we were grown up then, you see — we got used to it. It came gradually, too, a few fields here and a few there. But talking of things like that, I was going to slip over to see your mum this evening. We've had a letter — well, Grandpa has. We don't know quite what to make of it. They're making us an offer, you see, to buy this house.'

She broke off and looked closely at her knitting. 'Oh, I've made a mistake. That's what comes of talking.' She began to count stitches.

Maggie said, 'Who's made you an offer?' but she knew she would have to wait. She was used to this sort of thing. When she had been very small, her grandmother had knitted while she told her stories, and always seemed to have to stop at the most exciting part to check her pattern.

'There, that's got it,' her grandmother said, and her needles began to click again. 'What was I saying? Oh yes, we had a letter from these building people. It came from some posh address up in the West End. Mrs Nash next door had one, too, and several others along the road. They want to do the same as they've done is Washington Avenue — buy up our houses and knock them down.'

'Knock down your house!' Maggie exclaimed. She looked up at her grandfather, who came over to join them, carrying a basket of broad beans he had just picked.

'Take some of these home with you,' he said, putting the basket down beside her. 'Well, have you been telling her all about us going to make our fortune selling houses, Gran?'

'I've told her about those people wanting to buy our house. But it's not likely to make our fortune, even if we do sell. We'd have to find somewhere else to live, and with houses round here the price they are, we'd be no better off.'

The old man fetched a wooden box from the shed nearby and sat down on it.

'It's a lot of money, what they're offering,' he said. 'Of course, this is what's called a double plot — it's twice as wide as most of the ones along here. That's why they're willing to pay more.'

'It's silly, really, when you think that these houses only cost a few hundred pounds all those years ago, when we bought ours,' Maggie's grandmother said. 'Now they offer thousands, just so that they can use the ground they're built on for blocks of flats, and these maisonette things that are only flats too, when you come to look at it. But anyway, what would be the point of us moving? We're comfortable here.' She paused again to consult her pattern, then added, 'All the same, Maggie, I'll slip along and tell your mum about this, and see what she thinks. I made a few buns this morning that might come in handy for tea.'

So a little later Maggie walked home with her grandmother, carrying the beans, and the buns, and at tea time there was much talk between the grown-ups about the price of houses and land, and buying and selling. Maggie and Joe, who had come back from the swimming baths with his hair sleek as a seal, found it all rather dull. (Marcia was not there; she was having tea with the friends whom she had been playing tennis with.) The upshot seemed to be that their grandmother thought it best that they should stay where they were.

After tea Joe said he was going down to the library to look for a new book on space flight. Maggie decided to go with him to see if she could find a pony book she hadn't read. Riding was one of the things she would have liked to do if she had lived in the country.

On the way to the library they passed the station, from which Southern Electric trains ran up to Waterloo and down to the coast. On the walls outside, posters advertised cheap day tickets for ramblers to places in Kent and Hampshire and Sussex.

Maggie stopped and stared at a picture of a hillside with cows grazing under tall trees and a stream flowing along the

157

foot of the hill.

'I wish we could go down there for a day in the holidays,' she said. 'But even a cheap ticket costs a lot.'

Joe nodded. He liked the country, too, though not quite as much as his sister.

'We might get Gran to take us, just once,' he said. 'Look, this place in Sussex doesn't cost all that much. It's straight down the line from here.' He pointed to a picture of a little square of cottages and a church with a pointed spire. Maggie gazed at it intently.

'Fancy being able to *live* there,' she said, and sighed with longing.

'Well, we can't,' said Joe practically, and began to move away. Suddenly he turned to look at the poster again. 'But Gran could, and Grandpa, if they sold their house. Or somewhere like that. And cottages in the country don't cost as much as houses round here, so they'd have money to spare.'

'But they don't want to move.'

'Perhaps they haven't thought about moving to the country. Grandpa would like it. He would have a proper village garden then.'

'Yes, and they both like the country. They grew up in it. They were saying this afternoon —'

'Come on, hurry up, or the library will be shut before we get there,' Joe broke in.

To him, it was just a casual idea. To Maggie, it was like a glimpse of a promised land. But what use was it if their grandparents made up their minds not to move? Supposing they wrote straight away, tonight, and told the building company that they didn't want to sell their house?

She stood still. 'I won't come to the library, Joe, after all,' she said. 'I'm going back to speak to Gran.'

He grinned. He didn't need to ask why; he could guess. 'See you later,' he said, and waved, and ran off towards the library.

At home, her grandmother was still chatting to her parents. Maggie opened the library book she had been meaning to change and pretended to read it, but inside she was bubbling with impatience.

She wanted to speak to her grandmother alone, and when she was ready to leave she said, 'Shall I come down the road with you?'

'That'll be nice, duck. Come along then.'

But when they were walking along together, Maggie found it difficult to begin. Presently she said, 'Gran, do you think Grandpa will write to those building people tonight about not selling the house?'

'Not selling it? Who said we weren't going to sell it?'

'Well — just now when you were talking, you didn't seem to want to.'

'Oh, that was just talking. And Grandpa and I will talk about it a lot more before we make up our minds, I expect. You can't get away from it, it's a very good offer. And with no trouble — no lawyer's fees and house agents' fees or anything.'

Maggie had heard a good deal about lawyer's fees and house agents' fees at tea, but they still didn't mean much to her. She plunged on with her own idea. 'Gran, this afternoon, you said you felt sad when you saw the houses being built round here, and the farms going. Wouldn't you like to go and live in the real country again?'

Her grandmother slowed her step for a moment, as though taken aback by this. 'What, do you want me to go away from here, so that I hardly ever see you all?'

Maggie simply hadn't thought of it like that. Somehow she had pictured her grandparents still living near at hand. Then she remembered what Joe had said.

'You needn't be very far away. There are places you can get to by train in less than an hour. And if you got a lot of money for your house, and bought one that didn't cost so much —'

159

Her grandmother smiled. 'You've been planning everything out for us, I can see. It would be nice to have a little money of our own, that's true enough. Since Grandpa retired, we've only had the pension, and it doesn't go far.' She gazed at the crowded pavements of the High Road, and the queue of traffic crawling along the road, and sighed. 'It would be lovely to look out on fields again, or just a village street. But mind you I don't want some damp little poky place with no drains and no electric light. Still, we'll think about it.'

That evening, out of earshot of their parents, Joe said to Maggie, 'I looked at a paper while I was in the library.'

'What sort of paper?' she asked, puzzled by his air of triumph.

'The sort that has nothing in it except advertisements of houses for sale and to let and all that. I knew about it, because when Johnny Willis's family was going to move from here, Mr Willis bought it every week. Johnny used to call at the shop to fetch it for him.' He produced a piece of paper from his pocket. 'The advertisements are put in county by county. I saw some in Kent, and Sussex, and Surrey, father out than this. I asked the librarian for a pencil and wrote a few down. But there's lots more. We need a map to find out where all the places are.'

'Let's see,' said Maggie eagerly.

'You can look,' her brother told her. 'But it's my list and I'm going to show it to Gran.'

'Let's go and show her now.'

'No use. She and Grandpa are going out to the Darby and Joan Club. She said so at tea. You were in a dream.'

'I wasn't,' Maggie protested. But she knew she had been thinking of buttercup fields and high banks grown with foxgloves, and honeysuckle in creamy garlands along the tops of hedges. 'When will you show her, then?'

'Tomorrow, after school.'

'I'll come too.'

'All right. But *I'll* tell her about the paper.'

The next day Maggie got into trouble at school for not paying attention. The hours seemed endless. As soon as she was free in the afternoon she ran out to meet Joe.

He said, 'I've just thought. It's Thursday, and that's the day that paper comes out. We could get a new copy. Have you got any money?'

Maggie shook her head. She wished she hadn't eaten that ice lolly yesterday.

'I haven't got any at all, so it's no good,' Joe said. 'Come on then, I'll just have to show them what I copied down.'

It was another hot day, and sunnier than the day before. Their grandparents were in the garden again. Joe burst in and began to explain about the houses he had seen advertised, waving his piece of paper and talking so fast that it was some time before they could understand what he meant. His grandfather grasped it first. 'That's an idea,' he said. 'Let's have a look, Joe.'

He took the list and began to read it to himself, murmuring words aloud.

'Well, let me look too,' his wife said. 'Mm, "Cottage, two bedrooms, all mains". Doesn't say if there's a bathroom. "Attractive thatched cottage" — that sounds lovely, but I expect it's very old and probably needs rethatching. But the prices aren't bad. A good bit less than houses cost round here.'

Joe said eagerly, 'Those are all from last week's paper. It comes out today, but I haven't any money left.'

His grandfather chuckled. 'I can take a hint,' he said, and pulled some coins from his pocket. 'Run down to the shop and fetch a copy. It there's any change, buy yourself a lolly. And one for Maggie, if she'd like one.'

In ten minutes Joe was back, with the paper in one hand and two lollies in the other. Meanwhile his grandfather had gone

161

into the house, muttering something about a map. Joe dumped the paper in his grandmother's lap; she thanked him and laid aside her knitting. Maggie leaned over one shoulder, and her grandfather, coming out again at that moment, leaned over the other. Joe squeezed himself in beside Maggie.

'Come on, Gran, open it,' he said.

For the next half-hour they read out descriptions of houses and cottages and even what were called chalet-type bungalows. Joe spread open the map his grandfather had found — it was a cyclist's map, many years old — on the grass, searched for places where the houses were, and pointed them out to the others. To Maggie, they all sounded perfect, but her grandparents frowned or shook their heads over several. At last her grandfather said, 'Well, it seems to me there's only one thing to do. We'd better go and see over some of them.' He looked at the hopeful but uncertain faces of Maggie and Joe. 'All four of us. It would never do if we chose a place you two didn't approve of.'

And so the next Saturday morning they set off by train for a village in Sussex. They looked at a house there, and then took a bus to a cottage out in the country. Finally, after a picnic lunch in a field by the roadside, they caught another bus to a second village, and an agent showed them an empty cottage.

Coming back in the train that evening, Maggie felt flat and disappointed. It had been a lovely day out — it had been the very thing she had been longing for. And yet even she could see that none of the places they had seen would do. One cottage had smelled of the damp that showed in patchy stains on its walls; another was dark and low-ceilinged with hardly any garden, and the third had an old, sagging, leaking roof. She looked longingly out of the train window at the golden summer evening landscape. All this — and yet how difficult it was to *live* in it.

'Cheer up, duck,' her grandmother said. 'Nobody expects to

buy a house in a day. We haven't even had time to see all the ones that sounded likely. This has just whetted my appetite. I'm really looking forward to doing it again.'

'Then you'll go on looking?'

'I think we will, don't you, Grandpa?'

He nodded. 'Why, we've only just started. I'd better write to some house agents. You wait till next Saturday.'

Maggie found it hard to wait. But next Saturday, too, was a disappointment. For one thing, it rained; heavy slashing showers all day. They travelled by Green Line bus to a town called Hurston Green, where a house agent met them and took them by car to look at several cottages and small houses. But again none of them looked as Maggie had imagined from the descriptions, and she could not picture her grandparents living in any of them. Evidently they couldn't, either, and in the bus on the way home they seemed thoughtful and a little depressed.

Maggie dared not ask if they were going to give up house-hunting, in case they said yes. But when they got off the bus in the High Road, her grandfather said 'Well, I didn't care for that house agent much. But there's others. There's plenty of time.'

Maggie's heart jumped with hope. 'But what about the building company?' she asked. 'Will they go on waiting for you to answer?'

'Oh, I'll write to them. I'll say we think we might accept their offer, but we want a bit longer to think about it. We're not the only ones who haven't made up our minds yet, don't worry.'

It was the last full week of term, with tests and a sports day and a concert, and Maggie went through them all somehow, but without doing anything very well.

When she came out of school on Thursday afternoon, she was surprised to see her grandfather waiting by the gate. This was so unusual that for a moment she felt frightened. 'Is anything wrong?' she asked. 'Is Gran all right?'

'Everything's fine. There's Gran.' He pointed to a car drawn up at the kerb. Maggie stared. Her father was at the wheel. But it wasn't his car. He had had a second-hand one a few years ago, but it had always been going wrong, and had cost so much for repairs that he had sold it, and somehow never managed to buy another.

'We're going for a drive. Your father borrowed a car for the afternoon,' her grandfather said. 'Has Joe come out yet — oh, here he is. Jump in, both of you.'

'Where to? Where's Mum and Marcia?' Joe asked, gazing at the car as Maggie had done.

'There isn't room for all of us, so they'll come another day. As for where we're going, you'll see.'

'Tell us now, tell us,' they pleaded together, as they climbed into the back seat. Their father looked over his shoulder. 'All ready? Off we go then.'

'But where *to*?' Joe insisted.

His grandmother, sitting in front, said over her shoulder, 'Tell them Grandpa, or we'll have no peace.'

'Well, it's Thursday, you see, and I've been busy,' the old man said, as they slid into the traffic of the High Road and turned south. 'I went out and bought that paper first thing this morning. There was a cottage advertised that sounded so much the thing we wanted, I rang up about it straight away. The house agent said he'd arrange for us to see it this afternoon. So that's where we're going.'

Maggie leaned back in her seat. She didn't say anything. She felt as though she must keep her fingers crossed. Was it really going to come true?

Joe chattered, asking questions, as they gradually left houses behind and came out into open country. In just over half an hour they were near the border of Surrey and Sussex.

'I'll have to watch for a turning soon,' Mr West said. 'I looked it up on the map before we started. It's not far now.'

Presently he said, 'This looks like it,' and after peering at a signpost, swung the car on to a narrower road. They passed a farm and drove into a village. A little square of cottages and a church with a pointed spire.

Maggie cried in amazement, 'Joe, it's *that* one? The one we saw!'

'What one we saw where?' Joe asked. Then he recognised it too. 'That's right,' he said. 'The poster down at the station. Cheap day tickets for ramblers. It is the same village. Where's the cottage?'

'Straight through the village,' his grandmother told him. 'Just on the outskirts.'

'This it?' Mr West asked, drawing up.

It was. Joe scrambled out instantly, but after all the disappointments, Maggie hardly dared look. The owners were expecting them, and came down the path to meet them. Joe and Maggie had been told about them on the journey. The house agent had told their grandfather that they were anxious to sell the cottage and move out quickly, because they were going to live with a married son in Canada.

Maggie followed her grandmother through the gate, and then looked at the cottage. It was built of stone, the knobby, flinty stone of chalk country. It had a thatched roof that looked fairly new. It was very simple, like a child's drawing, with a door in the middle and a window on either side, downstairs, and three windows upstairs. A big purple clematis in full flower climbed the wall on one side of the door.

The little plot of grass in front of the house was bordered with beds brilliant with a confusion of flowers: stocks, pinks, pansies, lobelia and petunias, with taller tobacco flowers and scabious. It was right. It was exactly right. Maggie felt reluctant to look at it much, all the same, in case there was some snag.

Mr Ashby, the owner, showed them over the house while his

wife went into the kitchen, saying she would put the kettle on and make them all some tea. The inside, like the outside, was simple, with two living-rooms and a kitchen downstairs, three smallish bedrooms and a bathroom upstairs. It was clean and light and bright. When they had seen all over it, and looked at the back garden with its flower-beds and grass, fruit bushes and apple trees and vegetable plot, Mr Ashby said, 'Perhaps you'd like to talk it over by yourselves. Walk round again, if you like. I'll go and help get the tea.'

Maggie said, 'Can I go upstairs again and look out of the window?'

'Let's all go up,' her grandfather said. When they were standing by the window in the largest bedroom, looking out at the fields beyond the village, he asked, 'Well, will it do, Gran?'

'I don't see that we would find anything better,' she said. 'Fancy us moving at our time of life! And all because we were put up to it by these two.' She smiled into the excited faces of her grandchildren.

'But you're sure it's all right?' Maggie asked, suddenly anxious. 'You really want to move and come here?'

'Of course. It's a real adventure. It makes me feel like a girl again. How soon can we get everything fixed, Grandpa?'

'It shouldn't take long. I can call and see the house agent on the way home. If we start all the legal things moving today, there shouldn't be much delay. The building company will be quick enough, from what I've heard from the Washington Avenue people. With luck, we'll be moving in here about the middle of August.'

'August?' Maggie repeated. Just halfway through the holidays, she thought.

Her grandmother looked at her with mock severity. 'Well, if that's it, I hope you can spare a bit of your holidays to help us get settled in. We'll need two more pairs of hands.'

The cottage was exactly right

'You bet!' Joe shouted. 'Can we come for a week? Two weeks, if you'll let us?'

'All the rest of the holidays, if your mum doesn't mind.'

'Oh, Gran!' Maggie exclaimed, too happy to say more.

But Joe spoke for both of them when he remarked, 'That's better than a cheap day ticket for ramblers!'

The Land of Trees
and Heroes

by Joan Aiken

The children had been in bed with very bad attacks of flu, and although they had recovered and were feeling much better now, and had even been getting up for a few hours a day, they were still thin, pale, and cross. Mrs Armitage decided that they had better lose a bit more school and go to stay with Grandmother for a change of air. Mark and Harriet received the news listlessly. There seemed so many snags and prohibitions about going to Granny's.

'You'll have to wear sandals all the time.'

'Why? Can't Granny stand noise?' asked Harriet.

'It's not that. The floors are so slippery with polishing; I remember well the time your father broke his leg on the stairs. And you must amuse yourselves and not bother Granny; she hasn't much time for children.'

'Wouldn't it be better if we stayed at home?' Mark said.

'No, a change is just what you need. And we shall be busy here, with the election.' Mark's mother showed slight relief, indeed, at the thought that her children would be out of the way at this time; they had been known to upset local affairs.

Granny's house was huge, old, and dark; Mark and Harriet tiptoed about in it at first like two white mice in a cave. Not that Granny was unkind; in her vague way she seemed pleased to see them. But they began to understand what their mother had meant when she said that Granny hadn't much time for children. The old lady wasn't exactly busy, but most of the

169

time her attention was very much elsewhere.

'Put that bayonet away, Roger,' she would say absently. 'How many times do I have to tell you that it will rust if you don't give it a rub when you bring it into the tent. And hang up your balaclava and ask that Sepoy what he is doing.'

For Granny was very, very old, and had travelled with Grandfather (dead long ago) all over the world, and seen many a battle, from Inkermann to Mafeking. She was also very deaf and seemed to hear only a tenth part of what the children said to her as she sat knitting, placid and withdrawn, by the log fire that always burnt in the great hearth. They got most of their advice and information from Nursie, who was almost as old as Granny, but not at all deaf, and took an active interest in all their goings-on.

'Why is there a telephone in the orchard?' Harriet asked. 'Ah there, Miss Harriet, always asking questions like your father before you. Why should it be there but in case your Granny wanted to ring up the orchard, then?'

'But there's nobody to answer — only a lot of apple trees?'

'And if you're going to speak to an apple tree, better ring up than walk all that way at her age,' said Nursie, which only muddled Harriet more and didn't explain matters in the least. She thought it was very odd to see a telephone standing all by itself among the trees, on a pedestal on the grass with a dovecote roof over it to keep the rain off.

'And why does Granny keep all those musical things hanging in the trees if she can't hear them?'

'Aeolian harps, those are, Master Mark, and the others is wind-bells. And as for why she keeps them there — well, maybe the trees like to listen to them! Now run along, the pair of you, and leave bothering. Play anywhere in the garden, climb any of the trees, but don't break any branches. And don't go climbing the laurel tree or the Silver Lady will get you.'

'Oh, who is the Silver Lady?'

'The Silver Lady? Why, she owns the laurel tree, of course. Climb into her tree and she'll put you to sleep.

Sleep in the laurel but for an hour,
You'll sleep in the Silver Lady's power.

So mind you keep out of it — nasty dangerous thing.

The children wanted to hear more about the Silver Lady but Nursie pushed them out exclaiming that, Silver Lady or no Silver Lady, she'd got to get her silver polished by lunchtime. They wandered into the garden rather forlornly.

Many of the trees were hung with these strange Aeolian harps or with the silvery glass wind-bells, and it must have been a sheltered part of the country thereabouts, for only very occasionally did there come a twangling and a sighing from high among the branches. As he lay awake at night, coughing, Mark often hoped for a wandering gust of wind-music to breathe him off to sleep but, perhaps owing to the immense thickness of the solid old walls, it was seldom that a far-off note whispered against his ear.

At five o'clock every evening Granny took off her hearing-aid and settled down to watching TV; at the same time Nursie removed her thick glasses and dragged her favourite upright chair close beside the radio, turned on loud; from that minute the two old women were quite lost to the children, who would find their supper of bread-and-milk and beef tea set out on the kitchen table. The kitchen was one of the nicest rooms of the house: huge, but airy and warm with a great open range. Here they would eat, read, talk and play a leisurely game of ludo before taking themselves off to bed.

The nights were troublesome.

Their rooms were adjoining, and if Mark managed to get off to sleep for half an hour, Harriet was sure to have a fearful burst of coughing and wake him up. Then she would doze off until Mark waked her in his turn. It seemed as if their coughing shook the house from end to end, but Granny never

171

heard them at all, and it took ages before Nursie came muttering and tutting along in her red flannel dressing gown to give them hot drinks of lemon and barley. And sometimes, on account of not putting on her glasses in the night-time, she got muddled and rubbed their chests with the lemon-barley (very sticky) and gave them hot camphorated oil to drink. Still, it was nice to have her exclaiming round them like a cross, ancient ghost, and sometimes she sang them to sleep with old, old nursery rhymes:

'Intery, mintery, cuttery, corn,
Apple seed and apple thorn . . .'

in her wavering, quavering voice that seemed to search round all the corners of the room before finding its note.

'Now that's enough, you must go to sleep,' she would finally say severely, and at this point the children always pleaded (Harriet had come in and was sitting, wrapped in quilts, on Mark's bed):

'Oh, please, the Land of Trees and Heroes before you go please!'

And Nursie would sing:

'In the Land of Trees and Heroes
The great white owl is king
Who locked the door, who holds the key
Hidden beneath his wing.'

'Tell us some more about the land, Nursie?'

'That's all there is, and it's time you went to sleep.'

They never got more than one verse out of her, but there was something about the song that made them long to know more. Where was the land? And who were the heroes? And why was the key hidden? Nursie wouldn't say.

One cold afternoon they were rummaging in the summerhouse when they came across an old bow with a leather cover and a red velvet guard. There was a target too, but no arrows.

Mark dragged the target, moulting straw at the seams, out on to the lawn, and said, 'We can easily make some arrows. Never mind about feathers. Hazel's the best wood.'

'Nursie said not to break any branches,' Harriet reminded him doubtfully, but she rubbed her finger up and down the smooth springiness of the bow; it did seem a pity not to use it.

'Oh, she only meant big ones.'

They couldn't find any hazel, but there was an elder-bush by the summerhouse with a lot of straight young branches shooting out of the thick of it. Mark cut two or three of these with his penknife while Harriet, to be on the safe side, politely asked the elder tree if she minded their taking this liberty. There was no reply; she had hardly expected one.

'They're a bit light,' Mark said, 'but they'll do for a start.'

He whittled them clean and cut a bowstring notch while Harriet stood hugging her arms together.

'Now then!'

Stringing the bow he carefully fitted an arrow and fired, aiming high. The light, pithy arrow soared and began a beautiful curve towards the target, but just then a gentle wind sprang up and swerved it sideways so that it landed in the laurel tree.

'Oh, blow!' said Mark. 'That's the first wind there's been all day. Hark at the wind-bells. It would happen just then.'

He ran towards the tree.

'Wait!' shouted Harriet dashing after him. 'What are you doing?'

'Getting the arrow, of course!'

'But don't you remember — the Silver Lady!'

'Heavens, I'm not going to stay in the tree an hour! It won't take two ticks to nip up and get the arrow. I can see it from here.'

'Do be careful —' She had arrived at the tree just as he swung himself into the centre crotch, and stood anxiously looking up at him.

'I can almost reach it,' he called from somewhere in the middle of the tree. 'It's very thick, though. Goodness, there's a cat up here — it seems to be fast asleep! And a whole lot of birds, with their heads under their wings. How peculiar.'

'Oh, do hurry up!'

'And here's a satchel.' Mark's voice was muffled by the thick green leaves among which he was scuffling and flapping. 'Good lord, I say, there's a postman asleep up here. And something that looks like a butcher's basket full of chops. This is the oddest tree I've ever bee...' His voice trailed off on a tremendous yawn.

'Mark!' shouted Harriet, her voice sharp with anxiety.

No answer.

'Mark!' Twisting her head she peered up, looking into the dark cave of the tree. And then she saw Mark. He was fourteen or fifteen feet up, curled comfortably into a fork as if he were lying in a hammock, fast asleep, his head pillowed on his hand. In the fork above was a tabby cat, also asleep, and to the left she could dimly make out a butcher's boy in a striped blue apron, sleeping wedged in a nest of criss-crossing branches.

Harriet shouted till she was hoarse, and shook the tree till she coughed, but no reply came from any of the sleepers.

'Oh goodness,' she said to herself miserably, 'I *knew* something like this would happen. Now what had I better do?'

Asking Nursie seemed the first step and she went indoors, but five o'clock had struck, and Nursie was listening to a programme of Young Artists from the Midlands and was not to be disturbed. She waved Harriet away with a preoccupied hand.

'If I don't get Mark out of the tree before the hour's up,' thought Harriet, 'I don't know how we shall ever wake him. I wonder if I could drag him down.'

She decided this would be too risky; she couldn't lift Mark

The postman and the butcher's boy were asleep in the tree

to carry him down a ladder and if he fell from that height he would probably break a leg. Besides, there was the problem of the postman and the butcher's boy.

'I know,' she decided, 'I'll go for the doctor.'

Dr Groves lived a short way up the lane. Harriet ran to the shed for Nursie's bicycle; this was no time for loitering. She sped off down the front path and took the steps at a slither. Thank goodness it was not a surgery night.

Dr Groves was sitting by his fire, peacefully reading *The Lancet,* when Harriet arrived panting and gasping.

'Please will you help me,' she wheezed, trying not to cough. 'Mark's gone to sleep up the laurel tree.'

'Eh, dear me, has he now,' said Dr Groves. 'And you want me to help pull him down, is that it?'

'Yes, please. And there are two other people in the tree, and a cat. I expect they ought to come down, too.'

'Tuts, now.' The doctor sounded more disapproving than surprised. 'And what would they have been doing up there, I wonder?'

'Trying to rescue that cat, perhaps. One's the postman. Oh, please hurry.'

'I can't hurry, my lass, on account of my leg. Eh, well, now, the postman. We all wondered where he'd got to when he vanished last May.'

He pulled himself stiffly to his feet and Harriet remembered with dismay that he had an artificial leg.

'Should I get somebody else?' she said anxiously. 'Will it be too hard for you?'

'No, no, I'll manage very well. Just hand me that stick, will ye, lass.'

They made slow progress down the lane and Harriet did rings round the doctor in her anxiety.

'Ah, it's a great convenience to me, this leg,' he said imperturbably as he clanked along. 'Bitten off by a shark, it was, when I was a sea-doctor, and I fitted myself up with the best cast-iron peg I could have made. I can use it for poking the fire, or knocking over a charging tiger, and best of all, when some fussing female gets a pain in her little finger and thinks of sending for the doctor she thinks again and says to herself, 'With his leg it'll take him an hour and twenty minutes to get here, it's not worth it,' and that saves me a great, great deal of trouble, I can tell you, for I'm a lazy old man.'

'Oh yes, I'm sure it does,' said Harriet wheeling round him distractedly. 'Are you sure you wouldn't like to ride the bicycle?'

'No, thank you, my bairn. Riding a bicycle is beyond me. But we're managing very well, very well indeed.'

Dusk was falling as he stumped up Granny's steps, and Harriet, looking at her watch, saw with a sinking heart that it had taken them forty-five minutes to do the return journey; Mark must have been in the tree for nearly an hour.

'Ah yes,' said Dr Groves, pulling a flashlight from his pocket and shining it into the tree. 'Fast asleep the three of them. And Pussie baudrons too, after birds, nae doubt, the naughty grimalkin. That's an interesting thing, very interesting indeed, that the laurel tree should have such a soporific power. When I was a boy I was aye using laurel leaves for putting butterflies to sleep. In a jam jar.'

Without listening to his reflections Harriet dashed off and came back with Granny's aluminium fruit-picking ladder, which she planted firmly against the trunk.

Dr Groves had embarked on a learned chat with himself about the medical properties of various plants, so she started up the ladder, saying, 'If I pull them down, Dr Groves, do you think you can catch them?'

'I'll do my best, lass. Feet first, now. Don't let the poor slumberers fall on their heads, or you'd do better to let them bide.'

The butcher's boy was the nearest, and Harriet tugged him down cautiously, taking care herself not to step into the tree even for a moment. Dr Groves received the legs and flopped the boy on to the ground, where he continued to sleep. Harriet dropped the basket of chops (they flew in all directions) and moved the ladder round to Mark, who was harder to shift. Half lifting and half dragging she at last managed to get him clear of the branches and lower him down. He was laid among the chops while they tackled the postman, who was the most troublesome of all. In the end Harriet had to get the clothes-line and make a very unseamanlike hitch round his shoulders so that she could let him bumpingly down. She herself had to come down from time to time for a breath of fresh air; even perched on the ladder she found that she was becoming uncommonly sleepy.

'I can't reach the cat, and I'm not going to risk being caught by the Silver Lady for a lot of starlings,' she said, coming down. 'Now, what shall we do with them?'

'Eh, well, there's little can be done till I've reflected,' said the doctor, who seemed to have caught the general somnolence, and was yawning dreadfully. 'We'll get them indoors safe and snug and then I'll be off home. I'll come along in the morning for a confabulation with your granny. Meanwhile they'll take no harm.'

Using the wheelbarrow they carted the sleepers into the garden-room, and left them on deck chairs, covered with tartan rugs. The rising moon silvered the three inert bundles as Harriet and the doctor stepped out, closing the glass door behind them, and the doctor's peg-legged shadow stretched out, long and strange, across the misty lawn, as he stumped off.

Harriet went straight up to bed, feeling rather forlorn. The house was as quiet as a stringless harp and she missed Mark's coughing from next door. She fell asleep and drifted into some very strange dreams about flying cats, laurel trees full of sharks, and a Silver Lady with a wooden leg.

'Give me back my brother!' shouted Harriet, and became aware that she was coughing, and that she was awake.

'Eh, nonny, nonny, what's all this?' said Nursie, materialising beside the bed with her candle and red dressing gown. 'Here you are, then, my duck, here's a drink of blackcurrant for you.' Harriet obediently swallowed it down. It tasted very like permanganate.

'Nursie,' she said miserably, 'we've lost Mark. The Silver Lady's got him. He's asleep and won't wake.'

'Laws-a-me,' said Nursie sharply, 'he's been up the laurel tree, then? They're all the same—tell them not to do a thing and they run off and do it straight away. A good sleep'll do wonders for his cough, that's one comfort.'

'But how are we going to wake him? The postman's been asleep since May.'

'As to that,' Nursie answered, 'we'll have to think. The rhyme says,

Those by the silver slumber taken
Only the great white owl can waken.

We'll think about it in the morning, Miss Harriet dear. I reckon it would take more than an owl to waken Master Mark in the ordinary way, let alone when the Silver Lady's put her finger on his lips.'

She left Harriet awake and worrying in a patch of moonlight. Something must be done about Mark soon, she was sure, otherwise he might sink into so deep a sleep that he could *never* be awakened. And then all their plans for Christmas would be spoiled. Let alone Easter.

The great white owl, Nursie had said. There was an owl, too, in the rhyme about trees and heroes. Perhaps it was the same one? In any case the time to find an owl was now, while it was dark and the owls were abroad, not tomorrow morning, when they were all fast asleep, hidden away in thickets.

Harriet got up silently and put on her clothes. She had had
an idea. It seemed so wild and odd that she hardly liked to put
it to herself, but she slipped out of her room and downstairs to
the little telephone closet off the front hall. The house was
silent. Nursie and Granny had gone to bed. Only the faint
crackle of coal came from the kitchen stove settling for the
night.

Harriet sat looking at the telephone in its little pool of
moonlight. How did you ring up the orchard? In the end she
dialled O.

For a long time she could hear ringing but no one answered.
She almost gave up and put the receiver back. At last there
came a click and she could hear a far-off sighing, like wind in
branches.

'Is—is that the exchange?' she asked rather nervously.

'No,' a whisper answered her. 'Cox's Orrrr-range Pippin
speeee-king.'

She realised that she had got straight through to the orchard.

'To whoooooom did you wisssssssh to speeeeeeek?' the
telephone murmured leafily against her ear.

'May I please speak to the great white owl?' Harriet's heart
beat hard.

'Hold on, pleasssssss . . .' whispered Cox's Orange, and there
was another long pause, a long, long pause, while Harriet
heard, down the receiver, the trees in the orchard all turning
their branches this way and that against the night sky.

Presently there came another click.

'I—is that the great white owl?' Harriet asked.

'Who?'

'I asked to speak to the great white owl.'

'To who?'

'You mean, to whom,' Harriet was on the point of saying,
when she realised   that she *was* speaking to the great white owl.
She explained the trouble they were in, and that he was their

180

only hope. 'Oh, please, sir,' she ended despairingly, 'Won't you help us? I'm sure Dr Groves won't have much idea what to do.'

'You will need ammunition,' said the owl. 'To wit, a bow and some arrows.'

'I can manage that.' Harriet was much encouraged by his voice—a friendly, warm, furry sort of voice. 'What shall I do?'

'Bring them to the laurel tree. Do not delay. I shall be there.'

'Oh, *thank* you,' Harriet said gratefully.

'Who.'

'You—oh, I mean whoo,' she replied politely, put the receiver back, and ran to fetch the bow and the two remaining arrows. Then out, making snail-tracks in the moony dew, across the lawn to the laurel tree.

She had not been there a moment when the branches parted and a large white shape coasted silently down and landed as lightly as a dead leaf on her shoulder. She felt the smoothness of feathers against her cheek.

'Whooo,' the owl said gently in her ear. 'The arrows—of what wood are they?'

'Elder.'

'A moody personality. Was permission obtained? It would not do to be rude to her.'

'We—we asked,' Harriet said anxiously. 'But she didn't answer.'

'I will inquire anew. Go you, procure a bicycle and return hither—be swift. Adieu.'

Quick as she was, he was back at the tree first.

'Elder is graciously pleased to allow the use of those two. It is a propitious wood. Now! We must go fast. I will instruct you as to the route.'

He flew ahead and Harriet followed. Whizzing after him down the front path she realised that she was not going to have time to dismount for the steps, but discovered, without much surprise, halfway down them that she had become airborne and was pedalling briskly after the owl ten feet above the white surface of the road, which streamed away like nylon ribbon beneath.

'Where are we going?' she called.

'To the land,' his hoot came faintly back between wingbeats, 'to the land of trees and heroes...'

It was a wonderful ride. Harriet would not have minded going on all night, seeing the moon-silvered fields sliding under her feet and breathing the sharp cold scent of the trees when they swooped through the darkness of a wood. But presently she found they were toiling up a long, cloudy ascent; the owl went more slowly and she herself was glad of Nursie's threespeed. Great cliffs of cloud built up on either side, drifts of loose mist sometimes obscured the path, and at length they came to a door.

The owl flew up against it and clung rather like a woodpecker to the side of a tree, and in a moment or two the door opened and they passed through.

Harriet often wished afterwards that she had had more time to notice the beauties of that land. It was smooth and rolling: a country like a counterpane of grassy downs with small groves on the hilltops, set with statues that shone white here and there against the trees.

Strolling on the grass or lying in the shade, some near, some far, were the heroes. Many of them Harriet recognised at once. There was Hercules, doing his best with the assistance of two grass-snakes to copy the position of a statue of himself. But the snakes were not being very co-operative. There was Jason with one sandal. There was Prince Hal, galloping about on a fiery horse chasing Ivanhoe; Davy Crockett and Robin Hood having a shooting-match; Captain Nemo and Captain Ahab chatting in the shade. Harriet saw with wonder, not unmixed with envy, that the postman was with them, that the butcher's boy was playing bowls with Drake and Raleigh, and that Bellerophon was giving Mark a ride on Pegasus.

'How did they get here?' she asked in astonishment.

'They dream,' the owl answered her. She had propped her bicycle against an ilex tree and he was once more perched on her shoulder. 'But now you must not delay—the Silver Lady will soon be returning and you must shoot her!'

'I don't much want to shoot anybody,' Harriet said doubtfully.

'She will take no harm. And only thus will you have power over her. Watch, now—'

'String your bow,' said Robin Hood, who had strolled up and stood watching with friendly interest. 'Then you'll be ready. Like this—'

Several other heroes gathered round with encouragement and advice as Harriet pointed her bow at the sky. Bellerophon grounded Pegasus in case of accidents. 'Isn't this a grand place!' Mark shouted to Harriet.

'There she goes!' came a cry from the watchers, and Harriet saw something silvery and unbelievably swift streak across the sky towards the moon.

'Shoot!'

'Quick,' the owl murmured, 'before she hides. Or you will have twenty-four hours to wait.'

Harriet shot after the speeding figure.

'Oh!' came a long-drawn cry from the watchers. 'You've shot the moon!'

And so indeed she had. Down it came tumbling and drifting, like a great silver honesty-pod falling through leaves of air. All the shadows rushed upward.

Harriet was horrified. But Ivanhoe, galloping to where the moon lay blazing coldly, shouted, 'You've caught her!'

'Make haste!' called Jason.

Harriet ran to the moon. It had fallen on its edge and was standing upright, like a silver coin the size of a small table.

The arrow, thrust clean through, was still quivering. And on the far side of the moon the Silver Lady struggled angrily to be free. The arrow had caught the bracelet on her wrist and she was a prisoner, fastened by one hand to the shining disk. She was very beautiful but her rage was frightening and made the air all round her freezing cold; Harriet hesitated to approach.

'Do not fear,' said the owl in her ear, and he called to the lady, 'Mistress, the child has beaten you fairly.'

'Not without your help and counsel,' the Silver Lady replied, giving him a black look. 'Well, child, what is it you want? Quick! Selene is not to be humiliated for long.'

'I—I want you to set my brother free, please,' Harriet said hurriedly, 'and the postman and the butcher's boy.'

'Is that all? You might have asked for kingdoms.' The lady blew in the direction of Mark, who vanished like a pricked bubble. The postman and butcher's boy disappeared too. Then, twitching her bracelet free from the arrow, the lady gave Harriet an enchanting smile and shot upwards like a spark.

'You must put back the moon,' she called over her shoulder. 'Or you will be my next prisoner.'

Put back the moon! Harriet stared at it in horror. How was that to be done? But Perseus grinned at her reassuringly, tugged it out of the ground and, leaning backwards, slung it up with a mighty swing of his arm. Higher and higher it soared, and finally steadied, like a kite that feels the pull of the wind, and sailed among its accustomed stars.

'Homeward, now,' the owl warned Harriet. 'Dawn approaches.'

It was a race home, through the mighty door, down the slopes of paling cloud. The stars were thin as they covered the last furlong, and the bearings on Nursie's bicycle were red hot.

'Owl,' said Harriet when they stood again below the laurel tree, 'is the tree disenchanted now?'

'Oh no,' said the owl. 'The tree is Selene's, and will always

184

be hers. Just as the other trees in your grandmother's garden each belong to a different power. Did you not know? The elder, the quince, and the dark-berried yew...'

His voice was trailing away as if he were yawning, and he murmured 'Adieu,' and gave Harriet's ear a little peck just as the sun rose and he flitted silently off to a lilac thicket.

Harriet watched him go with regret. There were so many things she wanted to ask.

'There!' Nursie clucked in triumph at breakfast. 'Didn't I say a night's rest would break the spell?'

'No,' Harriet said, but she yawned as she said it, and the clatter of knives and forks drowned her voice. Mark and the postman and the butcher's boy were eating an enormous breakfast. In the middle, Dr Groves stumped in and heard their tale with interest and envy.

'Did ye now? Do they now?' he exclaimed at intervals, as Mark told Harriet how he had gone chariot-racing with Phoebus and Boadicea. 'Well, something has cured your cough at all events, whether the sleep or the change of air.'

It was true. Mark had not coughed once, though Harriet still had a fit of it from time to time.

'It's unfair!' she exclaimed. 'When I had all the trouble of fetching him!'

They had been arguing about this for some minutes when they noticed that the doctor and the postman had left the room. Glancing out of the window Harriet saw them cross the lawn to the laurel tree. The ladder was still propped against it and now, helped by the postman, the doctor hauled himself up with surprising agility. The postman followed.

'Hey!' Harriet shouted, leaning from the window, 'that's dangerous! It's still enchanted...'

But they were gone, and when the children ran out and stood under the tree they could hear only contented snores coming from the upper branches.

Pip and the Famous Author

by MARGARET BIGGS

Pip, who was never called Philippa save when in dire disgrace, sat with her long legs curled up under her, listening to the pops on the wireless, and nodding her head in time to the music.

Outside it was snowing for the twentieth day in succession, and even in Pip's bedroom, despite the electric fire, it felt chilly. It was a month after Christmas, when the winds were keen and the air frosty. But Pip never bothered about the weather. She was always cheerfully absorbed in her own affairs. She had a round freckled face, and long red-brown hair falling in loose curls to her shoulders. At school she had to tie it back, but at the weekends she let it go where it pleased. Her mother liked it long, so Pip had no objection, though she found it rather in the way sometimes.

The afternoon was darkening already, though it was only half past three. Lazily Pip stretched, and got up to switch on the lamp by her bed. In the pool of warm light her hair sparkled like bronze.

The music ended suddenly, and with the roar of applause the programme was over. Pip sighed, and switched the wireless off. In the sudden silence she could hear her mother apparently arguing with Valerie, her elder sister. Pip could not hear the words, but she gathered that her mother was rebuking Valerie, who was answering in peevish self-defence. Then light footsteps sounded up the stairs and Valerie, now near Pip's door, called: 'All right, all right, let's forget it! Then her bedroom door, across the landing from Pip's, slammed.

'Sounds like trouble,' thought Pip. 'I expect someone'll come and tell me about it any minute.' She was the only calm one in a turbulent family. The Graves frequently stormed, yelled and shrieked at each other, enjoying themselves in the process. Pip usually stayed on the sidelines during these encounters, rather bored by the whole business. It was such a waste of time, she felt.

A few minutes later there was a knock at the door, and Valerie's disgruntled voice said: 'Pip—are you there?'

'Yup,' answered Pip, shutting her book, *The Mill on the Floss*, with regret.

Valerie poked her yellow head round the door. She was tall and very pretty, but at the moment her face was dark and stormy. 'I want to talk to you,' she said, and bounced in, slamming the door after her with her sandal. Valerie was sixteen, four years older than Pip.

'Move up,' she said, flinging herself down beside Pip on the bed.

'What do you want? I've got my homework to do yet,' said Pip.

Valerie was not to be put off. 'Oh, you can do that any time,' she said brusquely. 'Did you hear the row I was having with Mother?'

'Well, I heard *something*,' admitted Pip. 'But I really ought...'

Valerie unceremoniously interrupted Pip. 'Do listen, for goodness' sake! I'm really fed up with this course I'm doing, and I've been telling Mother I want to give it up, and do something else. But she won't listen, she just keeps saying I ought to stick at it, and I'll be glad later. It's absurd, because I know *now* I shan't alter.'

Valerie was doing a one-year secretarial course at the local Grammar School, which Pip also attended. Valerie had been mad keen to do the course and get a secretarial job at the end of the year, but after a few weeks struggling with shorthand and learning touch typing she was regretting her decision. She had been moaning about it for days, and Pip knew a row about it had been brewing up.

'Well, you want to get a typing job, don't you? You kept saying so earlier on, she said unsympathetically.

'I didn't know how dull and dreary it all was then,' said Valerie, frowning. 'All these shorthand phrases to do over and over again, and working speeds up with Miss Matthews giving us eternal dictation—to say nothing of typing till my fingers feel they're wearing out!'

Pip chuckled. 'You always think you're overworked, even when you're not doing a thing!'

Valerie tried to look menacing, but dissolved into a reluctant giggle. 'A fat lot of sympathy I'm getting from you, you wretched child,' she said. But talking to Pip usually made her feel better, and there was no animosity in her tone. She clasped her hands behind her head, gazed out between the yellow curtains at the silently falling snow, and went on dreamily: 'I wouldn't mind if it was going to end up getting more interesting, but it isn't, I can see that. Miss Matthews keeps telling us shorthand-typing is the foundation to build on, but that's just rubbish.'

'I suppose she ought to know,' said Pip, her eyes wandering back to her book. 'And now, if you've quite finished...'

'I haven't,' Valerie told her. 'I've hardly *started*. Anyhow, Mother's told me I've got to keep it up until the end of this term and see what I feel then, so I'm stuck at the grindstone, but once the term ends Miss Matthews won't see me for dust.'

What would you rather do instead?' enquired Pip, without much interest.

'Anything—even be a char! It's the dullest job in the world,' said Valerie. 'Oh well...' She sat up, and gazed at herself in Pip's battered mirror. 'I look a bit of a mess. I've just got time for a bath before going down to the club. See you later—and mind you support me if Mother brings up the subject.' She gave Pip a wink, and departed. A few minutes later Pip heard the taps cascading, and her sister singing at the top of her voice as she undressed. Obviously she had regained her usual good humour.

Pip yawned and looked at her wrist-watch. Soon it would be tea-time—thank heaven, she felt ravenous, as usual. Pip was at the stage of growing like a magic beanstalk.

'I suppose it must be pretty dull,' she mused vaguely. 'But I daresay Val will change her mind again about twenty times before the end of term. She's funny.' Pip seldom changed hers, having once made it up, which Valerie called pig-headed.

Later, at tea, in the big warm kitchen of the rambling old house, Mrs Graves glanced round the table and felt glad the rest of her family were not, just at present, as unmanageable as Valerie. Roger, who was fourteen, was too occupied in working for his G.C.E. to have much time to spare for argument. Pip was always easy, thank goodness! And nine- -year-old Paul could always be side-tracked with a doughnut when he was preparing to make a fuss.

'I suppose Valerie poured out her woes to you?' she said to Pip as she watched her take a sixth piece of bread and butter, and begin her second boiled egg.

Pip, her mouth full, nodded.

'The trouble with Val is, she's bird-brained,' said Rodger weightily. 'She keeps hopping from one thing to another— there's the phone, Mother.' He stretched his long legs out in front of him.

'How about you going, you lazy lout?' said Pip, kicking him.

'Too exhausted from my studies,' said Roger sadly.

The phone continued to shrill imperiously. 'Pip dear, do you mind? You're nearest the door,' said Mrs Graves, mildly.

'Oh, all right—but I don't know why nobody ever thinks *I'm* exhausted,' said Pip, and went off carrying a slice of bread and butter to keep her strength up.

'Larchester 2828,' she said politely, leaning heavily against the hall table.

'May I speak to Valerie Graves, please? Miss Matthews here,' said a clipped, hurried voice.

'Oh, hullo, Miss Matthews,' said Pip, standing up straight. She went in some awe of the secretarial teacher. 'Pip speaking. I'm sorry, Valerie's gone out. Can I—?'

Miss Matthews interrupted unceremoniously. 'Gone out?— oh, how maddening! I told her I might want her help this evening!' She sounded really put out, and Pip tried to be tactful. 'She's helping at the church youth club, Miss Matthews— they're holding a beatle drive to help the church funds.'

'Oh, I see—I suppose she forgot what I said—she's certainly scatterbrained,' said Miss Matthews. 'Well, I shall just have to try to get hold of somebody else, that's all.'

Rather curious, Pip said: 'If it's urgent, I could go down to the church hall and get hold of Valerie. She'll be sorry she wasn't here, and I could give her a message.' She wanted, if possible, to protect Valerie from Miss Matthews's wrath. Valerie was often in trouble with her elders for forgetting things. No doubt after the row with her mother she had completely forgotten about whatever Miss Matthews had said to her.

'Could you, Pip?' Miss Matthews, rather to Pip's regret, took her up on this. 'I wish you would. I'll explain. My cousin, James Travers, has come up for the weekend—'

Pip had to interrupt. 'Not James Travers the writer?'

'Yes. You've heard of him, I presume?'

'Ooh yes. I think his books are out of this world!' said Pip enthusiastically.

'I gather that means you enjoy them,' said Miss Matthews, with a smile in her voice. 'I'm glad of that.'

'Fancy *him* being your cousin!' murmured Pip, wide-eyed.

'Yes—well, I can assure you he is. Now will you let me

explain, Pip? I promised my cousin I'd send him along one of the girls from my secretarial group to do some typing for him. It won't be anything complicated—one or two letters and possibly a bit of his current novel. His secretary's been ill this week, he tells me, and work has piled up on him. He's staying at the George, in the High Street—I haven't got room in my flat—and I promised him I'd send one of my girls to help him out. So now you see why I want to get hold of Valerie!'

'I thought she wasn't much good,' said Pip doubtfully.

'They're all at the same stage, and there's nothing to choose between them,' said Miss Matthews. She sounded as if she was smiling again. 'Valerie lives near, she's not the type to be overawed and awkward, and I thought, to tell you the truth, she'd enjoy it. She's been a bit depressed this week. I'd help my cousin myself, of course, but he won't hear of it. Says I'm on no account to put myself out for him! He's a delightful man to work for—no temperament. Now you've heard all about it, can I rely on you to get Valerie down to the hotel as soon as you can, or had I better try to get hold of some other girl? Not that I'm likely to succeed, on a Saturday evening!'

'Oh, I'll get Val. She'll be thrilled,' Pip assured her eagerly. Who wouldn't be thrilled to meet James Travers, who wrote those wonderful travel stories? 'You can rely on me, Miss Matthews. I'll dash along and get hold of her right away.'

'You're sure? Well, that's fine, a weight off my mind,' said Miss Matthews, sounding much relieved. 'Thank you, Pip. If by any chance you can't get her, will you ring me straight away? My number's in the book.'

'I will, but I'm sure it'll be O.K.,' said Pip.

'All right, then. Goodbye, Pip.'

'Goodbye, Miss Matthews.' Pip dashed down the receiver and tore back into the kitchen. Ten minutes later, having gulped down her tea, she was hurrying down the road to the church hall, just on the corner and only a hundred yards away. 'Lucky old Val,' she thought, as she sploshed through the snow. 'Wonder if she'd be able to get his autograph for me? It wouldn't hurt to ask. Fancy James Travers in *our* town! 'It seemed too astonishing to be true.

But at the church hall she came on a snag. Valerie was not there. The beatle drive had been cancelled (the vicar deciding the weather would keep anybody but the insanely determined at home) and the hall was locked and bolted, and obviously deserted. Doggedly Pip ploughed her way down the street to the vicarage for any information she could glean. Perhaps Val might be there. She knew the vicar often invited members of the youth club in to hear records and drink coffee. But no, although lights shone from the vicarage bow window, the vicar's housekeeper told her that the vicar had gone visiting at the hospital, and she didn't know anything about where Valerie Graves might be.

'I believe the vicar did say some of the young ones had gone to the cinema, now I come to think of it, but I've no idea which one,' she said vaguely, moved by Pip's earnest face and snow-encrusted hair. 'Is it urgent you get hold of your sister, then?'

'Well, in a way—but it can't be helped. Thank you,' said Pip politely.

'I should get home if I were you,' said the housekeeper. 'It's a wretched night. I told the vicar it wasn't fit for him to go out, but he only laughed! Well, goodnight.' She closed the door, and Pip went slowly down the steps, thinking hard. It was hopeless to try to find Valerie. There were three cinemas she might have gone to, all equally near, and she might even not be at any of them! The housekeeper might have got it wrong. No, she would simply have to ring Miss Matthews and apologise profusely and go home and forget all about it. But it did seem a shame to lose the chance of James Travers's autograph! And suddenly Pip's eyes gleamed and her chin jutted. 'I'll go myself,' she decided. 'I know jolly well I'd be as much use to him as Val ever would! It'll be great fun, and I bet Miss Matthews will think I'm full of initiative!' With a beaming smile on her face, delighted at the thought of meeting her hero, she set off for the George, where James Travers was staying. Full as always of boundless confidence, she had no apprehension of any difficulties. She could type a bit on her father's battered portable, and that was the main thing, wasn't it? Wouldn't Val be astonished and envious?

The George was a quiet hotel set back from the High Street behind a high arch. Pip tramped into the entrance hall, pausing by the swing door to kick the snow off her boots. She looked round curiously. She had passed the George hundreds of times, of course, but never been inside. At first sight she liked it. It looked comfortable, it felt warm, but it was not intimidating. Pip marched up to the girl at the desk, who was rubbing her hands over a radiator, and asked for Mr James Travers, please.

'If you tell him I'm from the Grammar School, and Miss Matthews sent me, he'll know what it's about,' she said reassuringly, as the girls stared uncertainly at her. 'He won't know my name, but you might as well say Miss Graves, if he asks.

'Well—if you just wait, I'll ring through to his room,' said the girl dubiously, and retreated into the shadowy little office behind the desk. Pip waited willingly by the crackling fire in the hall, staring round at the old maps framed on the walls.

'That's quite all right, Miss Graves,' said the receptionist, reappearing abruptly and looking relieved. 'Do you mind finding your own way to Mr Travers's room? It's only through the passage, on the ground floor. Number Five. You can't miss it.'

'Oh, I'll find it,' said Pip confidently. 'Thanks.' She gave her beaming smile and set off.

The room with 'V' painted on its door was only a few yards

away. Pip raised her chin, squared her shoulders, and knocked.

'Come in!' called a muffled voice.

Pip crossed her fingers in her coat pockets, and opened the door.

The tall, thin man sitting at the small table by the window got up and came across to her. He looked first relieved, then surprised. 'Er—has there been a mistake?' he enquired dubiously. 'Are you the girl my cousin promised to send along?'

'I like his face; he looks as if he's got a sense of humour,' thought Pip approvingly. 'I think I'll own up straight away, and see how he reacts.'

'I'm Pip Graves, Mr Travers, she said, looking guilelessly up at him. 'I'm at the Grammar School—'

James Travers went on staring at her. 'Surely you can't be taking the secretarial course?' he interrupted, puzzled. 'You aren't more than fourteen at the most!'

Immensely flattered by this, Pip hurried to explain. 'No, actually I'm not. Miss Matthews was going to send my sister, but I couldn't find her, and anyhow she's not much use, so I thought I'd come and help instead. I *can* type, honestly, and I've read all your books and I think they're heavenly!'

The last part of her speech seemed to amuse James Travers. 'I see,' he said, smilling. 'How nice to know. I'm delighted to meet one of my readers, but what I want just at the moment is someone to take a few letters and type out a few sheets of my manuscript. My secretary's away with flu, and I've got into a fearful muddle. It's good of you to think of helping me, Miss—Graves, is it?—but—'

'*Please* let me try,' said Pip earnestly. 'I'm quite as much use as Val would be! I can't do shorthand, of course, but I can write jolly quickly, and I've done typing for my father often. Do let me try, Mr Travers—I promise I won't waste your time!'

'Well, in that case I won't argue,' said James Travers, whose smile had broadened. 'I'm hopeless at typing myself, I can never find half the keys, so when Miss Matthews said she'd get one of her pupils to help I must admit I jumped at it. We'll try to do a bit for half an hour anyhow, shall we? Then I'll see you home. You're—well, forgive me mentioning it, but you *are* rather young to be out alone in the evening, aren't you?'

'I'm twelve,' said Pip. 'Getting on for thirteen, actually. So long as I'm back by half past eight, my mother won't worry. She's fairly sensible.'

'Well, in that case let's begin at once,' said James Travers, quite briskly.

Pip sat down at the table by the window, after Mr Travers had solemnly helped her take off her coat. She felt greatly responsible and grown-up. Mr Travers lugged out his portable typewriter, and set it before her. 'I'll dictate very slowly, and you can type it straight out, shall I?' he suggested.

'Just as you like, Mr Travers,' said Pip, trying to sound efficient.

She got on swimmingly. James Travers sat beside her, and dictated slowly enough for her to type without any difficulty. He began very slowly, but sped up when he realised, to his relief, that Pip could indeed type at a respectable speed. When Pip had typed two letters, one to his publishers and one to his literary agent, James Travers looked through them and signed them with a flourishy signature while Pip typed the envelopes. Then he asked rather dubiously if Pip really thought she could tackle a few pages of his latest manuscript. 'I'd be thrilled if you could, Pip. I've promised to get this chapter off to my printers by tomorrow at the latest, and I simply *can't* expect them to decipher my scrawl, I'm afraid!'

'I'll try. I'm sure I can, so don't worry,' said Pip reassuringly. She was quite at home with him by now, and had no doubts of her ability to cope.

So James Travers got out the manuscript, and showed her

Pip typed as James Travers dictated to her

how far his secretary had got with it before succumbing to flu. It was a story about diamond smuggling in Amsterdam, full of excitement and crooks and police coming to grips. Pip began at once, and though she found Mr Travers's writing rather difficult at first, and had to screw up her eyes and peer hard at some of his crossings-out, after a few paragraphs she found she could read it quite easily. Mr Travers sat watching her, smiling to himself at the multitude of expressions chasing across her face.

'What an astonishing child—I mean, *girl*, you are, Pip,' he remarked, over the tapping of the machine.

'It's a super story, Mr Travers,' said Pip blissfully. 'When will it be published?'

'In the spring, I hope. I'll send you a copy as a thank-offering, if you like,' said James Travers.

He was amused and touched by Pip's shining face. 'Oh, Mr Travers, will you really, honestly? Oh, how wonderful! All the family will be green with envy!'

'Why, you don't mean to say *all* your family read my books?' enquired the author.

'Oh yes. My father usually gets them out of the library, but we all read them in turn, even Paul, who's only nine and a half,' said Pip. 'And when they televised one of them in October, we all watched, and Mum let Paul stay up late, and we thought it was super! It was the one about the spy-ring, and I thought it was the best play I'd ever seen on TV.'

'Thank you very much, Pip.' James Travers sounded as if he really meant it. 'Now, how's that chapter going? I mustn't forget the time, or your family will be worrying.'

'I've only got one more page to do,' said Pip, returning to her task with alacrity.

Ten minutes later she had finished, and Mr Travers read quickly through. 'That's wonderful, Pip,' he said. 'You've only made one or two mistakes, and I can easily correct those.

And you've taken two carbon copies, as my secretary always does. Well done! I'm sure your elder sister couldn't have done better.'

'Well, of course, Val can do shorthand, and I can't,' said Pip, modestly.

'Well, we've managed without the shorthand, luckily,' said James Travers. 'Thank you again. I—' He paused, as there was a knock at the door. 'I wonder who that can be? I'm not expecting anybody.'

He went over to the door and opened it. Pip gulped uneasily as she saw who it was. 'Miss Matthews!' she murmured.

'I won't delay you, James, but I felt I must just call and see if Valerie Graves was helping you, or whether—' Miss Matthews here caught sight of Pip, and stopped short. 'Pip! For goodness' sake—'

Seeing the gathering cloud of wrath, Pip hastened to explain. 'It's all right, Miss Matthews. You see, I couldn't get hold of Valerie, so—'

'I told you to ring me if you couldn't find her, and I'd get somebody else!' Looking really put out, Miss Matthews turned to her cousin. 'James, I do apologise for this. I had no idea Pip would turn up here and bother you. I simply gave her a message for her elder sister, and she promised to deliver it. There's no excuse for her to come wasting your time—'

'Just a moment,' said her cousin hastily. 'Please don't be angry with Pip. She's been a great help, and we've just finished the work. She came along and offered her services, you see, and as I was in a desperate muddle I gave her the chance. I'm delighted with the result, and I'm sure in a few years, if she wanted to, she'd make somebody a very reliable secretary!'

Miss Matthews looked staggered and—unusual for her—wordless. 'Pip would?' she said after a long pause.

Pip glowed, and thought how exceptionally nice Mr Travers was. Miss Matthews when she lost her temper could be ferocious, as Pip knew to her cost.

'Yes, Pip,' said Mr Travers firmly. 'So you see I'm really grateful to her, and I'm just going to see her safely home.'

'Oh, don't bother, James, let me. I'm sure you don't want to—'

'No, don't worry, Beryl,' (Beryl! thought Pip appreciatively. She had often wondered what Miss Matthews's Christian name was.) 'I'd like to introduce myself to Pip's family—they're fans of mine, Pip tells me,' said Mr Travers, smiling at his cousin's face. 'The work's done now, so I can relax.'

'Well, if you're sure, James...' Miss Matthews gave up trying to take control. It was all most peculiar, and she couldn't quite understand how on earth Pip had managed to be of use, but thank goodness she had been!

So twenty minutes later Mrs Graves opened the door to find Pip, beaming triumphantly, and a complete stanger standing in her porch. 'Oh, Mother, this is James Travers, you know, the writer, and he wants to meet all the family!' Pip burst out in one breath.

Amid a torrent of explanations, with everybody talking and asking questions simultaneously, James Travers found himself swept into the Graves living-room and surrounded by the entire Graves family, all eyeing him with intense interest. Amid the hubbub Mr Graves, who was used to shouting his family down, saw the visitor's dazed expression and said loudly: 'Shut up, everyone!' In the brief pause that followed he smiled at Mr Travers and said his family was unruly in the extreme, he was afraid, but they all were thrilled to have a famous author in their home. Then he offered Mr Travers a much-needed cigarette, a comfortable chair, and asked courteously if Pip would mind explaining all over again.

Valerie in particular listened with her mouth open. 'Why didn't you come and find me?' she hissed into Pip's ear. 'It was *me* Miss Matthews wanted, not you, you little beast. You knew where I was—'

'That's not fair,' hissed back Pip indignantly, under cover of the boys begging for Mr Travers's autograph. 'I did try to find you. I went down to the church hall and even asked at the vicarage, but nobody knew where you were.'

'I was only at Jill's house, hearing her new record,' said Valerie. 'Oh well, I suppose if you tried, I can't blame you. I must say I'd completely forgotten Miss M. told me she might want me this evening. She didn't say anything about James Travers coming down here. You lucky little wretch, you always fall on your feet!' She sighed resignedly.

'Well, the way you were going on this afternoon about hating the secretarial course, and wanting to throw the whole thing up, I should have thought you'd be glad to have got out of anything like typing and shorthand,' said Pip, grinning.

'Well, if it's for someone like James Travers, it's a bit different, isn't it?' said Valerie.

'He thought I'd make a jolly good secretary when I'm a bit older,' said Pip smugly.

'He must be mad,' said Valerie.

'Thanks very much!' laughed Pip.

Valerie sat silent, listening to the conversation. Fancy Pip marching off to that hotel all by herself! It was just like her...

Mr Travers left reluctantly. He had made a hit with the whole family, who were loud in his praise when the door shut behind him. He shook hands warmly with Pip when he left, and murmured: 'I won't forget about the book for you—and thanks again!' Pip, her eyes shining, thanked him incoherently.

'You know,' said Valerie slowly, as she and Pip meandered up to bed a few minutes later, 'I think I'll give the secretarial course another try. I can see I *might* be able to land an interesting job when I've finished. After all, plenty of interesting people must need secretaries—writers, actors—maybe pop singers!'

'Exactly,' said Pip, yawning.

As she lay in bed she stretched luxuriously and thought: 'Perhaps one day I *will* be his secretary properly. How gorgeous!' She settled her cheek comfortably on the pillow, and went straight off to sleep.

The Biggest Catch

by Lois Lamplugh

The harbour smelled of tar and lobsters, and, in the early afternoon quiet, seemed almost deserted. Although it was only the beginning of September and there were still holiday visitors in the town, no speedboats or motor launches were taking trippers out. Perhaps everyone was on the pier, Marion thought, waiting to go aboard the next paddle steamer. She leaned on the wall and looked at the moored boats below. Here and there a man was working on a launch or cabin cruiser. A girl was just climbing into a broad-beamed old rowing boat.

Marion felt that something about the girl was familiar. As though conscious of being watched, she glanced up, and Marion recognised her as Janet Maddox, who went to the same school as she did. They had never been particularly friendly, and so she was surprised when Janet smiled and waved up to her with every appearance of delight.

'Hallo,' Marion said. 'Are you staying here too?'

'I *live* here,' Janet answered, appearing somewhat hurt that Marion did not know this. 'You don't, though, do you?'

'No. We're at a farm a few miles away. We came in here today because my brother wanted to go on one of the paddle steamers.'

'Why didn't you go too?'

'I didn't want to,' said Marion flatly. She hardly knew why she had been so stubborn about it—perhaps because nowadays she was apt to think that anything Jeremy did or wanted to do was much too childish for her. He was five years younger.

'Which steamer are they on? The Welsh one or the Four-hours-along-the-coast?'

'Four-hours-along-the-coast. The *Glen Usk*.'

'That won't be back for some while yet. I was just going to row along towards Great Hangman. Would you like to come too, to fill in time?'

Marion hesitated. She did not particularly want to go out in the rowing boat, but it would be something to do. The last three hours had dragged more than she had expected, although she had filled them as best she could by bathing and having lunch very slowly in a café filled with other holiday-makers.

She thanked Janet and climbed down into the boat by a slippery wooden ladder clamped to the sea wall. She was surprised to find Janet handling a boat at all: at school she was apt to be clumsy, and was widely known for her tendency to lose, break or drop things. However, she held *Maybelle* steady while Marion climbed in, and then cast off and poled them away from neighbouring boats with an oar.

Once they were floating freely she fitted the oars into the rowlocks and said, 'I'll row us out of the harbour, shall I? You can take over presently, if you'd like to.'

'I'm not much good at it,' Marion told her. 'I'll have a go if you get tired, but not otherwise.'

Janet nodded amiably. She seemed to enjoy rowing, though she caught a crab as they rounded the wall dividing the inner and outer harbours and came in sight of the short, wide pier that curved around the base of a big, conical, grass-grown rock called Lantern Hill.

Farther out at sea, a few small boats rose and dipped. The water was deep blue and fretted with little arcs and arrowheads of white. Only a light breeze was blowing, but all the previous night a westerly gale had roared in from the Atlantic —what Jeremy had once called an 'equinoxious gale', Marion remembered. She wondered if it was choppy on the *Glen Usk*. Her father and Jeremy would not care if it was, and her mother had probably taken travel pills. Janet rowed steadily, midway between the high, dark cliffs and the pier, looking over her shoulder now and again to check her course.

Marion leaned back in the stern and watched the herring gulls drift overhead, their wing feathers a brilliant white against the sky. She began to enjoy being in the boat.

Maybelle was some way seawards from the pier when Janet glanced over her shoulder. Then she stopped rowing and turned to look at something in the water ahead of the boat.

'That's odd. There isn't usually a buoy there,' she said. 'I wonder if the gale last night...'

She broke off and Marion leaned forward to see what she was staring at. It was more than half-submerged: a black rounded metal object with spikes projecting from it. It did not look like a buoy, she thought; there was something wrong about it.

And suddenly she knew what it was. She had seen pictures of these things when they had been washed up on beaches. At that moment Janet exclaimed, 'Marion, Marion, look at it! *It's a mine.*'

She said the last words in a whisper, as though the mine might hear her. The projecting horns that would detonate the mine if they struck anything seemed to leer at them with evil, knowing eyes.

'For goodness' sake, Janet, let's get back to the harbour,' Marion said. 'We'we got to tell someone. *Quickly.*'

But Janet said 'The tide's going out. That thing must have come just so far and turned back. It's floating away from us now, out to sea again.'

'But the *Glen Usk!*' Marion glanced at her watch. 'She's due in half an hour. Can we row on and warn her?'

'No, we can't risk it. She might not notice us. Her wash might swamp us.' Janet began to tug desperately at one oar, trying to turn *Maybelle*. In doing so, she lost her grip on the other oar. It slid out of the rowlock and was carried gently away. Janet made a grab at it, tipping the boat so that it nearly capsized.

Marion threw her weight the other way and kicked off her shoes. Under her dress she was wearing a bathing costume; she pulled the dress off and dived over the side.

Janet called, 'No, Marion, leave it. Listen...' but Marion took no notice. She was a fast, strong swimmer and she reached the oar in a few strokes and turned back, pushing it in front of her.

Janet leaned down and took the oar from the water but instead of offering to help Marion aboard again she asked, 'Could you swim to the pier?'

'Of course, but why?'

'I'll watch where the mine goes and follow it slowly. I'll shout to try to attract attention—and I can shout to warn anyone who comes near in a small boat. You can swim faster than I can row. Tell the harbour master—his office is up there on the sea wall.'

'All right.' There was no time for argument. Marion turned away at once and struck out towards the pier. She swam with fierce energy, thinking of the *Glen Usk* with her parents and Jeremy and a hundred or more other people aboard her sailing steadily minute by minute towards the treacherous waiting mine.

Face down in the water in a swimmer's smother of foam, lifting her head only enough to gulp air on alternate strokes, she began to picture other mines ahead of her or below her, though she knew it was absurd. The ugly evil look of the mine she had seen had turned the friendly harbour into a nightmare place.

Soon she knew she was swimming badly. In her eagerness to swim faster than ever before, she was pushing herself wildly through the water, tiring rapidly and getting breathless. She raised her head to look towards the pier. It was a little nearer,

'*Marion, look! It's a mine!*'

but not as much as she had hoped. Then she realised that the tide that was carrying the mine seawards was also pulling her back. How much time was left? Rescuing the oar must have wasted five minutes, and since then she had been swimming for—how long? Ten minutes? Fifteen? The *Glen Usk* must be almost due. There seemed no hope of warning her, unless Janet's shouts had attracted someone's attention.

Then she heard the putt-putt of a small engine. At first she thought the sound came from the harbour, but it quickly grew louder and she looked up to see a man in a dinghy driven by an outboard motor coming towards her from the point where the pier and the harbour wall met.

He slowed the dinghy to a stop beside her. 'Something wrong?' he asked. 'I saw you dive in and heard your friend shouting but I couldn't get the engine to start for a while. Can't hear what your friend's saying. What's up?'

'A mine,' she said. 'And the *Glen Usk* is due any minute.'

He looked quickly in the direction she pointed.

'Sure it's a mine?' he asked.

'Positive. Oh, do help me *quickly*. What time is it now?'

He looked at his watch and then reached down to help her clamber over the dinghy's side. 'We've got five minutes if she is punctual,' he said. He swung the boat in a sharp turn, opening the throttle.

'The name's Baker,' he told her.

'Mine is Marion Hunter.'

'Is it one of the old wartime mines, Marion, do you think?' he asked. 'I wonder where it's been. They turn up every now and again. The gale last night must have shifted it.'

'We must warn the *Glen Usk* somehow,' Marion said. She saw that they were heading towards a flight of stone steps on the outer side of the harbour wall below the harbour master's office.

'The harbour master can send out a speed boat, perhaps, or

fire a signal rocket or something of the sort,' Mr Baker said. 'Now when I bring the dinghy alongside the steps you jump out and off with you. I'll moor and follow. If there's nothing I can do to help I'll go out and fetch that friend of yours. That's no picnic, being where she is.'

Indeed it wasn't, Marion thought. Swimming for help had been easy; waiting out in *Maybelle* must have been an ordeal.

'Here we are,' Mr Baker said. 'Good luck.'

Marion jumped out on to the wet, slippery steps, stumbled, recovered and ran.

When she burst into the harbour master's office she saw a short broad-shouldered man scanning the sea with a small telescope.

He swung round as she gasped out her news and muttered 'So that's it.' In a moment someone had been sent running to open the main gates of the pier and shepherd everyone off; someone else was phoning the police.

The harbour master himself seized two objects from a cupboard and ran towards Lantern Hill. Marion followed him.

'Stay in my office,' he called over his shoulder, but she took no notice. She saw now what he had taken from the cupboard: a loud-hailer and a clumsy-looking pistol.

He and Marion climbed Lantern Hill by a steep zig-zag path, one behind the other. At the summit Marion shouted 'There she is!'

Fifty feet below was the sea, and the *Glen Usk* sailed majestically towards the pier head.

The harbour master fired the signal pistol across her bows, put the loud hailer to his mouth and shouted, 'Ahoy, *Glen Usk*. Reverse engines. There's sea mine near the harbour mouth.'

On the bridge the captain made a quick movement, a bell rang and the sea was instantly churned white as the great paddles stopped and were thrown into reverse.

The captain looked up and shouted, 'Thank you, harbour master. I'll stand out to sea until you signal that I can come in.'

And Marion, gazing down at the startled faces of the passengers, saw Jeremy staring up at her from the rails and her parents sitting on a deck seat nearby. The anxiety-stiffened muscles of her face relaxed and she was able to smile at them. They seemed too astonished to smile back, but they waved when she waved, and then the *Glen Usk* turned in a whirlpool of foaming white water and sailed at full speed in the direction of the Welsh coast.

The harbour master took his telescope from his pocket and began to search the sea beyond the harbour mouth. Marion saw that Mr Baker's dinghy, with *Maybelle* in tow, was just entering the inner harbour, and people were streaming away from the pier, shepherded by officials.

She heard the harbour master say in a sharp voice, 'It's heading for the Cheyne Rocks. The current's taking it . . .'

He broke off, snapped the telescope shut and pushed Marion towards the path. 'Run, girl,' he said. 'I don't think we're going to need those bomb disposal chaps for this one.'

Bewildered, Marion ran, and the harbour master clumped down the path behind her. At the now almost deserted pier gates they saw Janet and Mr Baker coming towards them.

Mr Baker said, 'You made it, then?'

And as he spoke there was a tremendous reverberating roar that echoed and re-echoed along the cliffs, and thousands of seagulls rose, mewing widly, and flew in over the town.

The harbour master smiled and said 'That's settled that,' but Marion clutched his arm in terror and said 'The *Glen Usk*?'

'Oh, she's all right, don't fret. She'll be well away by now.' He looked from Marion to Janet. 'When I saw your antics with your boat from the office window I wondered if I'd need to send out one of the fishermen to haul you in. I didn't guess you'd made the biggest catch of the lot.'

The Park

by Penelope Farmer

I yelled. But no one took any notice. Jim and Willy were hammering in the back kitchen. Ellen had the wireless on, loud as it could go. Margie was whining 'I want, I *want*' like a talking doll gone wrong, and the baby had found the rubbish bin and was wiping margarine papers in his hair, though silently. I could bear it no more, and so I yelled.

The only change was that the baby tore up the marge papers and began to grizzle for attention, so I yelled out again, bursting my voice. And this time the baby started to cry properly, and Mum came in and yelled at me for yelling at the kids.

She was a little woman, with neat hair like a dutch doll. She seemed to have wheels turning round in her all the time, one wheel setting off another, like clockwork, the work rolling in among the wheels and out again, neatly done, before you'd noticed it. Now, while scolding me, she was hanging up her coat, making Ellen turn the radio down, and comforting the baby, all at once.

I burst into tears and rushed out, slamming the door, rushing right to the end of our street. But there I stopped and leant against a wall, not caring who saw. There was nowhere I could go alone to weep where there was no noise; nowhere at all.

I'd never used to want to be alone like this. But lately the noise had seemed to rise and echo in my head unbearrably until I had to burst out, yelling, as I had done just now.

I did not understand why I felt this way. I should have been used to noise, with six kids in our tiny house. Four of us shared our bedroom, and Ellen and I shared a bed in that.

The one half bed was my own place I suppose; in the dead of night it was my one peaceful, private place. But I hardly dared move in case I woke Ellen, and the room all round me was filled with the snuffings and hummings of children asleep. It was a friendly, quiet sound. But I wanted a room of my own, with only my own sounds in it; I wanted it desperately.

It wasn't just home either. It was noisy everywhere. It was noisy in our street, which had been a little quiet back street once but had been made one way, the traffic rushing day and night, just as it rushed, roaring, now.

It was noisier still in the High Street beyond my wall, where the shops were. There the pavements also were jammed, with people, and you had to dodge crazily in and out among dogs and prams and shopping baskets and the people who'd stopped to talk.

It was noisy even at school; except when the headmaster came, but that was a frightened, not a peaceful quiet at all. Otherwise, in our classroom there was never quiet. I liked Mr Clarke, our class-teacher. He taught things you remembered afterwards. But he was too gentle to hold our roaring boys, who laughed at him, made jokes about him to his face. Sometimes they were very funny jokes, you couldn't help laughing, and sometimes even Mr Clarke laughed too. But behind the laugh his eyes looked hurt and sad at the cruelty of the jokes.

Poor Mr Clarke. But just now I was chiefly sorry for myself, wondering desperately where I could go, when I could go. For I had to help mind the kids out of school. Where, when, oh *where* could I go?

People passing looked curiously at me. After a while I stopped crying, and pushed myself upright, and went home again, to the kids and the noisy kitchen, though it was less noisy when Mum was there.

The next morning I went to school late. Mum had to go to the doctor, and there was no one else to look after Margie and

212

the baby. So she kept me back and gave me a note for Mr Clarke, explaining.

The shortest way to school lay along the river road, past the park. Usually in the mornings I was late and running too hard to look in over the park gates, and in the afternoons children screamed on the grass, as noisily as anywhere else. So I never went in there.

But this morning I was in no hurry at all. Playtime started in ten minutes time, I had no real need to get to school before it ended, at eleven o'clock. I looked over the park railings as I went by, and saw the empty paths and the river glittering beyond the plane trees.

I stopped for a moment and leant my elbows on the black railings. How quiet it was. My ears still echoed with the noise of home, but in a little while they calmed and I began to feel quiet too. I began to feel so peaceful.

I turned slowly back along the railings, trailing my hands from spike to iron spike. I came to the gate and pushed it open. Its hinges squeaked behind me; I was inside, shut in there, and quite alone.

For no one sat on the green-painted seats or walked on the path by the river. No one was there except me and I stood inside the gate and looked, quite dazed with it.

Of course it was hardly more than a strip of garden along the river, not a park at all. But they called it the River Park; the board by the gate had a notice saying, "The Park will open at—, and shut at—" with slots to put the times in.

It had a lawn and a path and several neat flower-beds, some round, some square, some longer and narrower ones. Like all official gardens the edges of the beds were sharp and neat, and the roses stood sternly in level rows. It seemed to me that if you counted, each bush would have the same number of roses on it.

But the river ran heavy and brown and glinting and no one could officialise that. And in the middle of the lawn stood the

great plane tree, its bark dappled over with patches of light
and dark like sunlight without sun. Its leaves and branches
spread shade unevenly, vaguely over the strict lines of the
paths and flower-beds. And no one could regularise that.

I went slowly to sit on the seat at the far side of the plane
tree, and looked at the river. A long low barge went by,
towing another. A ship with steaming funnels passed the other
way, hooting as it went. But in the park there was only me.

Why did I want quiet, I wondered. Having it, what should
I think about? I found I did not know. I just sat there happily,
under the plane tree, gazing at the river; until suddenly I heard
a clock strike eleven, and I leapt up with a jump and ran all
the way to school.

'Sir—' I panted, into the classroom and up to Mr Clarke's
desk, 'Sir—it was my mum kept me home. Sir . . .' But he was
trying to quieten the boys and hardly noticed me. When he did,
after a little while he nodded without hearing my story again.

'That's all right,' he said. 'Hurry up and sit down.' And it
wasn't till dinner time that I remembered, still lying in my
pocket, the note from Mum.

But he never asked for it. And Mum did not keep me back
from school again, so I had no chance to go in the empty park.
I stood a moment by the gate the following morning and
looked longingly. But I was already almost late for school, and
had to run on again, sighing a little.

The day after that, although it was already May, a harsh
wind came and driving rain. The full-leaved plane tree looked
bleak and unfriendly and the sparrows huddled, ragged with
wind.

At home everyone crowded noisily into the warm kitchen,
and at school the boys, unable to play cricket, spent their
noisiest energies baiting Mr Clarke. I felt miserable to see his
hurt and pleading face, but it was the noise I hated more than
anything, the jeers and cocky gigglings that beat on the walls.

Then exactly a fortnight after the day I went into the park, the sun came out again, and the pigeons lazed and blinked along the street. I set out early that morning. Reaching the park I looked round swiftly to see that no one I knew was in sight; then I lifted the latch on the black iron gates and slipped inside. I was alone in there, once more.

I had never meant to stay long; I meant to get to school on time. But as I sat on my same seat, under the plane tree, a ship came past all the way from Jamaica and set me to thinking, for we had some Jamaican kids in our school, who had told us about it. I thought of sugar cane, strong sun and calypso music, and how the lucky people on the ship would have seen it all. But before I realised it the time was gone and half past nine sounded from somewhere over the river.

Half past nine! That was the time for school assembly. If I went now I would be in terrible trouble for missing it without a proper excuse. For a moment I was too worried to enjoy the quiet.

Then all at once I knew what to do. If I was going to be late I might as well be properly late. I would stay till playtime and say that Mum had kept me again. Mr Clarke had said nothing last time, nor would he this time. I would have nearly an hour and a half to myself and no one need ever know.

I sat on my bench soaked in the sun. I still had nothing particular to think about. I didn't care, either. I watched the sparrows and the ships and the sun slipping among the five-cornered plane tree leaves. When an old man came I blushed and seized a book from my satchel, trying to look as if I was not playing truant. But he smiled at me and soon went off again.

It was wonderful: the best morning I'd ever spent in my life. I went to school, at playtime all hot and stretched and contented, with a grass stain on my skirt.

But explaining to Mr Clarke I could feel myself blushing, and I spoke more to his desk than to him. My heart jumped with relief when he sent me to my seat, and then jumped again, in terror, for he called me back.

'Don't worry this time,' he said, 'But next time ask your mother for a note.' And I turned away, scarlet-faced, relieved again.

Later I remembered Mum's note, still in my pocket from a fortnight ago. I took it out at dinner time and looked at it. She hadn't put the date, just the day, Wed., short for Wednesday. Today was Wenedsday again, so I could give the note to Mr Clarke now and say I'd forgotten before.

But then I thought he hadn't wanted a note today, only next time; so I could save it until next time, next Wednesday perhaps.

Next Wednesday: next time. I did not know how I'd decided to play truant again. I could not remember deciding, yet I must have, to be able to think "next time", casually, like that.

But I didn't use the note on the next Wednesday, though I went to the park again. Because by then I was thinking of the next time and the next. Again I could not remember deciding —I just knew I was going to go, again and again, for which I would need not just one note from Mum, but several. If I used up the real note now, I would have nothing to help me.

And so that Wednesday I copied the note. And when I gave Mr Clarke my careful copy he read it and nodded, unsuspecting. And I went, relieved, almost triumphant, to my desk.

And thus it went on. At first I did not play truant every week in case it surprised even unsuspecting Mr Clarke. But I grew more reckless as the term lengthened. I went once, twice a week and forged note after note in Mum's handwriting. I sent her to the doctor every week—or else to the dentist, and once, even to the chiropodist. I wondered sometimes how long it would be before I was found out.

That summer was the best I can remember. Almost every morning the river gleamed under the sun. In the park, wallflowers, tulips, delphiniums, and roses came and went. The sparrows and the pigeons reared families, and I watched them. The leaves of the plane tree darkened with summer to make a heavier shade.

I did not sit on the green seat any more, I sat on the lawn as if the garden belonged to me; and if other people passed I lay where I was, uncaring. Only when gardeners came did I move to sit primly on the seat, but they came rarely and then, though some looked curious to see me there in school time, not one ever asked what I was doing. I have always looked older than my age; perhaps they thought I had already left my school.

There were mornings, of course, without sun; windy mornings; still but cloudy mornings. The best morning I spent in the park it was raining. The rain began to fall quite gently when it was already too late for me to get school on time, so I stayed in shelter under the plane tree. It felt as safe and private there as if it was my own house.

No one came that morning. Almost no one went past on the other side of the railings and the traffic hushed by on the wet road. Inside the park there was no wind to move the tree, the earth smelt strong and good, and the rain hissed so softly against the leaves above my head that it was almost itself a silence. I stayed there till my usual time and went on to school with a gentleness inside me that the noisiest boys could not destroy.

There was sun the next time. I was unthinking of danger or rather of any more danger than there usually was in playing truant from school. But there happened at last what I had always feared; and which had surprised me really, not happening before. Someone who knew me came past. Her name was Carol Webb, and though she was in my class at school she did not live nearby at all. So what she did, passing the park at that time of morning, I never found out. The first I knew was her voice calling.

'Mary, Mar*ee*,' I jumped and twisted my body round to see her peering in at me over the points of the railings. She was a sharp, beady girl, whom I'd never much liked.

'Well, fancy seeing you,' she said. She moved along the railings, clicked the latch smartly, and came in.

'So this is where you come. Everyone was beginning to wonder. If we had any other teacher but Mr Clarke he'd have been wondering too.' She stopped her eager voice, and looked at me curiously. I still sat as if planted on the grass, too alarmed to move.

'You just *sit* here?' she said. 'Whatever for? We thought you must have a boy friend at least. But just sitting here? You must be daft.'

'Yes, I'm daft,' I said furiously. Then I remembered my weak position and changed my voice.

'I *like* coming. Please, Carol, don't tell them at school. I'd be in awful trouble.'

'Me tell the teachers?' said Carol. '*Me* tell the teachers anything? You must be daft. Course I wouldn't tell.'

I believed that. I did not like Carol Webb very much and I knew she despised Mr Clarke, laughing louder than anyone at him; so she would do nothing to help him, even to get me into trouble. But still might tell someone else, who might tell some other teacher. I couldn't see how she would bear keeping what she had found out to herself, if only to show everyone how daft I was. I would have to be very careful.

For about a week after that I went early to school each day. Passing the park I turned my head away, and in school I tried to keep my head turned from Carol Webb. But she kept catching my eye on purpose and grinning knowingly. I had to smile back, being more or less obliged to her, though I growled inside.

Of course, I could not keep out of the park forever; the next time I went it was very early and I meant to stay only a few

I sat on the lawn, as if the park belonged to me

minutes before school. But the minutes were twenty before I knew, so I had to stay as usual and forge another note for Mr Clarke.

This time as I came out, I bumped straight into my younger brother, Jim.

'And just what are *you* doing?' he asked.

'I just slipped in for a moment,' I lied. But my truthful face felt hot.

'No you didn't,' Jim said triumphantly. 'I had to stay at home for Mum and I've been watching you, see. I don't believe you've been to school at all. You'll catch it if Mum finds out.'

'All right then, *clever*, what are you going to do about it? Tell her?'

'Course not, keep your hair on. You'd better watch, that's all. It mightn't be me next time. But I won't tell.'

I believed him also, he was loyal despite his teasing and badgering. But still it might slip out accidentally, for at home he spent his time with Willy who never kept a secret longer than five minutes.

Yet, strangely, though there was danger all round my life, at home and school, it made me more reckless, not more careful. I didn't care any more. They were bound to find out sooner or later I thought, and I might as well enjoy myself while I could. One week I stayed out there mornings, and once not just till play, but right up till dinner time. Carol Webb winked and grinned continually, and so did her friends, so she must have told them. But I didn't care. I didn't even bother now to smile back.

And yet, though I went to the park so often I enjoyed it less. I was frightened in spite of my recklessness. Sitting under my plane tree I went over and over in my mind what might happen. I imagined how the discovery might be made, and what they might do to me. I knew that the school attendance

officer got after truants like me and I knew that they were
sent away to approved school. Whatever would Mum say if
that happened to me?

It wasn't peaceful any more, with such thoughts running
round my head like mice inside a wheel. In a way I didn't
want to go in any more, I almost hated it. And yet I couldn't
stop. I used to say to myself, I'll just stay for two minutes, and
go straight on to school, but twenty minutes would always
pass and it was always then too late. The tree and the river
were the same; so were the pigeons and the sparrows. It was
just me that had changed and become all jerky and restless
and unhappy.

Mr Clarke still never said anything, but he began to look
at me carefully, strangely.

And so, in a way, it was a relief when the trouble broke. It
was different from how I had imagined; neither Jim, nor Carol
Webb, nor even Carol's friends, had anything to do with it.

One day I came back from school to hear a strange voice in
the kitchen. I pushed the door open casually, wondering who
it might be, for though the voice sounded somehow familiar, it
was no home voice, and it spoke so softly that I recognised its
tone rather than the way any words were said. But its
familiarity did not warn me.

He sat in the armchair, his back to the door. I would have
slipped back and out again at once, but Mum had seen me and
it was too late.

'Yes, it was you we wanted to speak to,' she said in her
neatest, angriest voice. And then Mr Clarke had turned round,
a cup of tea in his hand, and was staring, as if he had never
seen me before. His face wasn't angry, and for a moment
I could not recognise the expression on it. And then I saw;
Mr Clarke looked puzzled. And as I started, my face growing
scarlet with fright and guilt, his turned red too, reflecting
mine.

Mum was cutting up vegetables for a stew. Onions, carrots and potatoes lay neatly heaped on the pale wooden table top. She watched me and felt her finger slowly up and down the blade of the knife as if she hardly knew what she did. Then she shook her head sharply and continued her chopping, the sharp knife blows falling drum-like behind her voice.

'Well,' she said, 'Well, Mr Clarke comes here, ever so nice, and wants to know why I've kept you from school so much this term. Bad for your work to be away so much he said. The headmaster was talking of sending the truancy man round he said . . .'

I was horrified. I had never imagined Mum in trouble, only me. Suppose they put her in prison, whatever should we do? I could not bear to look at her, nor at Mr Clarke stiff in the red armchair. I looked at the floor, at the patched brown rug.

Mum's voice swept on: not loudly, but with an energy of anger in it, as if all the clockwork wheels went round at top speed together.

'Kept her away he said, kept you away I said, except that one time I went to the doctor I never did any keeping; if anyone kept her it wasn't me. And then . . .' Her voice ran out. The chopping sound stopped and I looked up to see the knife blade pointing. My eyes followed to Mr Clarke's lap, where lay like leaves off a paper tree, a heap of crumpled paper pieces: the notes I had written in Mum's name.

Mr Clarke and I both spoke at once.

'She . . .' he started.

'Mum . . .' I began. But Mum's voice swept ours away.

'Truancy officer indeed; there's been no question of him in this house before, I'll have you know. And forging my name like that—the cheek of it. You'll end up in jail, my girl, you'll see. And then what will your dad say, a respectable man?'

I burst into tears at last. Mr Clarke turned to my noisy sobbing, and said 'Please . . . Oh please . . .'

'And well you may cry, too,' Mum swept on. 'What have you to say then? Where were you all those mornings?'

And then Mr Clarke drew his voice hard out and it was Mum's this time that got swept away. His voice was loud, but not angry at all. It was comforting and interested.

'Where did you go, Mary? What was the matter? Tell us now.'

Mum looked at Mr Clarke very sharply, and then at me. I stood with tears streaming on my face, not trying to stop them.

'And well you may cry,' she said. 'You just answer your teacher. Tell him what it's all about.' And suddenly she too had become more curious than angry. She was usually fair and now she was giving me my chance to explain. Both she and Mr Clarke were looking at me curiously, interestedly, waiting to hear.

I wanted to tell them everything; how I'd longed to be quiet, to be on my own in my own place. Even if Mum hadn't understood, and perhaps she would have, Mr Clarke might have done. They couldn't both misunderstand me. My mind groped after words to explain it all, but could not make them come. I stood, groping, saying, 'I—I—' till Mum lost patience and said sharply, 'Where's your tongue then, we haven't all day, Mr Clarke an' me.'

That drove out any pattern of words that I had made. I didn't mean to be sulky, but somehow I was; I said sulkily, 'I just went in the park, that's all, I don't know why. I just went in the park.' And I cried, harder than ever.

Mr Clarke looked hurt as well as puzzled. Mum grew angry again; sulks always made her angry.

'You went in the park,' she cried, 'In the *park*, that's all you did. Well fancy, wasting your time like that, all those mornings...' her voice died away again and she looked at me silently, pointing the dangerous knife. That turned me properly angry, properly sulky. What had she expected me to do

I thought furiously, write a book or something? Being angry, I would have said right out why I went, how I hated the noise and everything; the words seemed easy. But her voice swept on, not giving me the chance and afterwards my tears returned and it was too late.

On and on she scolded, wielding the knife in time; the vegetables falling out in neat rows like soldiers. On and on with Mr Clarke growing red and upset as me. Who would have thought such rage could come from my peaceful time in the park?

I had to promise never to play truant again; or Mum would take me to school every morning like a kid to the infant school. When she had done with me she turned on Mr Clarke. Though she was too respectful to attack a teacher directly you could see she blamed him for not finding me out before.

Seeing his unhappiness made me sorry all over again. He had promises to make too: that he would explain things to the headmaster, that the truancy officer would not come to see Mum. When they were made he went home again, without a second cup of tea.

We heard no more about it, so Mr Clarke kept his promises. And until I left school he was always especially nice to me, and he always asked very respectuflly after Mum.

Once or twice he asked again why I had played truant; but I couldn't, wouldn't tell him now. It was just too late. Soon it seemed as much a mystery to me as to him or Mum how I'd ever had the courage.

Passing the park every morning, I looked away to the warehouses on the other side of the street. I could still see out of my eye's corner the plane tree and the movement of birds, and yet, the worry over, it was almost a relief to have no more to do with them.

I decided that I did not want quiet or solitude any more; I did not need them or thought I didn't. After a while I could even pass the park without looking away.

Yet, deep in my mind, I never forgot those few park mornings. It all comes back when I least expect it: the sparrows, the waving plane tree, and the river, glittering savagely beneath the sun.

A Fair Deal

by ALAN C. JENKINS

Though the village of Belham was, as Clare's Uncle George was fond of remarking, as stuffed with odd characters as a Christmas pudding with sultanas, undoubtedly one of the most outstanding of them was Old Joe Floggit.

To Clare, Mr Floggit seemed like some dignified, mossy ancient monument, for the sight of him driving round in his flat-topped cart, with his pony, Bramble, in the shafts and his whippet, Swifty, trotting beneath the back-axle, was as natural a spectacle as the sun rising.

Nobody quite knew what Old Joe did. He called himself a dealer and that covered a wide variety of activities. Anything was fair game to Old Joe as long as he could squeeze a profit out of it and you were just as likely to see an old iron bedstead on his cart as a crate of chickens. Old Joe, the cart and Bramble and Swifty were inseparable. Certainly neither master nor pony nor dog would have survived without one another, while it seemed to Clare that even the ramshackle cart, with its creaking axle, would fall to pieces in sorrow if Old Joe abandoned it or Bramble was no longer harnessed to its shafts.

Old Joe was not only one of the most outstanding characters in Belham, he was also one of the most popular. The fact was he was simply a pleasant old chap, always ready to lend a helping hand or a cheery word where it was needed. He would bargain fiercely over the price of a load of scrap iron or a litter of pigs, but Old Joe would drive miles out of his way on behalf of anyone who needed help.

As for Clare, she was always delighted to go down to Belham for the holidays. Old Joe's breezy manner and sly but kindly jokes were a tonic in themselves. Even the glummest characters couldn't help smiling when Old Joe drove by with a wave of his hand and a cheeky quip.

'That man is one of nature's gentlemen,' declared Uncle George to Clare one day, as Old Joe trundled past, raising his whip in salute.

'I think he's a dear,' agreed Clare.

* * * *

But there came a time when even Old Joe Floggit's cheerful philosophy failed him. Clare found him one evening sitting on his cart, hat over his eyes, straw in mouth, knees tucked up to his chin, deep in gloomy meditation, while Bramble snuffled hopefully in the manger of the nearby stable and Swifty lay curled up by the door.

'Hello, Old Joe,' Clare said, frowning somewhat. 'You look very pensive. I hope nothing's wrong?'

'Ah, Miss Clare,' sighed Old Joe, pushing back his battered trilby, 'at this rate I shall be out of business as quick as water runs out of a leaky tub.'

'Why, what ever has happened?' Clare asked anxiously, jumping up on the cart. 'Are things as bad as they sound?'

She was worried, for she had never seen Mr Floggit in such a despairing mood. Old Joe's cheerful ways were so much taken for granted that to see him otherwise was like frost in July. Old Joe gloomily chewed his straw and squinted at the end of it.

'I've been given notice, Miss Clare,' he announced, in a hollow voice, while inside the stable Bramble suddenly neighed and Swifty shivered as if they understood what their master was saying.

'Given notice?' echoed Clare, tossing her plaits in surprise. 'But I don't understand. You're self-employed . . .'

'Ah,' agreed Old Joe, spitting out the straw with great

Old Joe Floggit was the most colourful character in the village

feeling; 'I am that, miss, and it costs me sixteen and tuppence a week for me stamp.'

'Well, then, how can you be given notice?' demanded Clare, clasping her hands round her knees.

'Why, miss, from this 'ere stable where me and Bramble and my little dawg lives,' declared Old Joe, jerking a thumb. 'His nibs has given me notice to quit. Wants the stable for himself, see? Going to pull it down and build a cottage for his blooming chauffeur.'

Now, as Clare knew, 'his nibs' was a certain Mr Carver Waye who lived in Belham Place. He also was, it could be said, a dealer, though instead of working in the pence and fivers, he transacted his business in terms of five or six figures. He hadn't long taken up residence in the village and the most people used to see of him was driving to the station at Swinkhampton, five miles away, where he caught the train to London every so often.

To the village of Belham he was still very much a 'foreigner' (Uncle George used to say it took at least ten years' residence before you could even apply for your naturalisation papers); and the villagers were suspicious of his breezy bonhomie, resentful of his obvious wealth and didn't think very much of his wife's poodles which, with their careful coiffure, looked a bit odd among the rag-tag and bobtail of the village dogs.

When Mr Carver Waye had moved into Belham Place, he had acquired a sitting tenant who occupied the stables and loft at the end of the grounds. This was none other than Old Joe Floggit, who was as much a part of the place as the cobwebs that festooned the stable. Clare thought it highly likely that the stable had actually been built round Old Joe, he seemed such a part of it. It was not only the stable where Bramble was housed, but Old Joe himself dwelt in the loft overhead.

'And now old Carver Waye has given you notice?' said

Clare, indignantly, as she sat on the cart listening to Old Joe's doleful news. 'The absolute beast! Why, he's positively oozing with lolly!'

(You can see that Clare was always very outspoken.)

'Ah,' sighed Old Joe, carefully selecting another straw as if he were choosing a cigar. ''Tisn't only a question of stabling my Bramble. 'Tisn't only a question of housing me. But 'tis my Haitch-Q, as you might say, Miss.'

He clambered wearily off the flat-topped cart.

'Yur,' he beckoned to Clare; 'come along o' me, miss, and I'll show 'ee something.'

Obediently Clare followed him through the dusky stable that smelt of oats and leather. Old Joe opened a door at the end of the building and, with a jerk of his head, signalled to Clare. In the adjoining shed an astonishing sight greeted her eyes. The place was piled roof-high with an incredible assortment of articles. Hip-baths rubbed shoulders with Victorian wash-stands, bales of hay jostled with ancient fire-screens, shapeless scraps of iron got under the feet of tottering wardrobes. A bag of coke communed with a mangle that was obviously suffering from that Monday-morning feeling. Festoons of cobwebs united everything like a complicated telegraph system.

One finger under her nose to stop herself sneezing, Clare gazed in fascinated wonder at this display of Old Joe's stock-in-trade.

'See what I mean, Miss Clare?' said Old Joe, gloomily, as they left the place. 'This 'ere is my 'Arrod's, as you might say. Maybe I could find somewhere to stable my Bramble. Maybe I could go and live with me sister over at Sedley...'

(He shuddered at the idea of having to do that; it would have been a really desperate measure.)

'But where in the world,' he continued dismally, 'would I put all that stuff? 'Tis from here I carries on my profession!'

'I quite see what you mean, Old Joe,' murmured Clare,

231

dusting herself carefully. Franky, she couldn't for the life of her imagine anyone buying all that junk, but Mr Floggit evidently found it worth while. To evict him from his business premises would be just the same as throwing him out of work.

'It'll be a rotten shame if old Carver Waye does make you leave,' Clare went on, as they resumed their perch on the cart outside. 'Have you tried talking to him, Old Joe?'

'Him and me don't talk the same language, Miss,' said Old Joe, tugging at his battered trilby. 'He talks through 'is nose and buttons up 'is mouth like a bad-tempered ferret. But he's made his meaning plain enough. He's had his lawyers send me an official letter setting it all out. They've told me I've got to quit these 'ere premises by next quarter-day.'

From the depth of his tattered coat he produced a severe looking typed letter and handed it to Clare, who looked equally severe as she glanced through its contents, which she found some difficulty in understanding: it was all couched in such terms as 'whereas' and 'heretofore'.

'No argy-bargy about that, eh?' Old Joe shook his head sadly, as he put the letter back in his pocket.

'I think it's a beastly shame, Old Joe,' protested Clare, her eyes filling with tears, for she realised how distressed Mr Floggit was. 'I tell you what, I'll get my uncle to talk to Carver Waye. Perhaps he can persuade him to let you stay.'

'I say, Uncle George,' Clare burst out at supper that evening, while she waited for Mrs Pilkington the housekeeper to bring in the soup, 'that horrid man Carver Waye has given Old Joe Floggit notice!'

'I know, my dear,' answered Uncle George, crumbling his bread.

'You know? How?'

'Well, he had to apply for planning permission to do what he wants, you see.'

232

'But, uncle, he can't just throw Old Joe on the street like that.'

'I'm afraid he can, Clare. You know Old Joe really has no right to be there anyway and the place has been condemned. I agree with you it's a shame, but what can be done?'

Uncle George shrugged with a resigned air and concentrated on the asparagus soup that Mrs Pilkington had now brought in.

'But Old Joe has nowhere to go,' protested Clare. 'If he has to leave his place he'll have to go out of business. The place is his Harrod's. Or his Maples, as you might say.'

'I know, I know, my dear girl,' Uncle George agreed, shaking his head regretfully. 'I feel very upset about the whole matter. Old Joe Floggit is part of Belham Village. He's a legend.'

'Couldn't you speak nicely to Carver Waye?' suggested Clare, putting down her soup spoon. 'Use your influence and all that sort of thing?'

'I could try, Clare,' said Uncle George, absently, wondering what Mrs Pilkington was going to produce after the soup. 'Though frankly I don't see much hope.'

'Well, we can't just stand idly by, while Old Joe is evicted,' said Clare, in that decided way of hers, and tossed back her hair. 'You'll simply have to do something, Uncle.'

Well, Uncle George did approach Mr Carver Waye on Old Joe's behalf, but to no avail. It was a perfectly friendly conversation, but Carver Waye wouldn't budge. He'd got the law on his side and Old Joe would have to quit.

'It's not as though it's a dwelling-house, Colonel,' Carver Waye explained to Uncle George. 'Then, of course, I would be obliged to find Mr Floggit alternative accommodation. As it is, I am perfectly within my right.'

'You'll be unpopular with the village,' Uncle George warned him.

'That will not influence me one iota, my dear Colonel,' replied Carver Waye. 'Have you seen Floggit's place? It's a standing disgrace. Breeding ground for vermin. I am surprised, Colonel, that as chairman of the parish council you have tolerated such a state of affairs...'

Very skilfully, Carver Waye had turned defence into attack and he smiled secretly as he observed Uncle George's discomfiture.

'He's happy there,' was all Uncle George could mumble. He knew Clare would be cross with him for being so feeble. He would rather face a whole swarm of dervishes than his niece when she was in a disapproving mood!

Anyway, it seemed as if Old Joe would really have to get out. Bravely the old man continued to shout out his cheery greetings as he went trundling past in the flat-topped cart, but it was easy to tell that beneath his happy-go-lucky exterior he was worried about the future. Even Swifty the whippet seemed to understand that something was wrong and tucked his tail further than ever between his legs.

"Twon't seem the zame when Old Joe zeases to zcrubble about Belham,' observed Bill Glanfield the smith, as he stood outside the smithy. 'Man and boy I've zeen 'un trundling round with thiccy cart these forty years.'

'Ar,' said Percy Maddacott the roadman, 'I hopes that there furriner, Mr Carver Waye, zuffers remorse o' nights for what he be doing to Old Joe. 'Tis a mortal shame to evict the poor old chap.'

'Hear! hear!' agreed Clare, who had just ridden round to the smithy to have her pony shod.

However, as Mr Carver Waye had said to Uncle George, not even unpopularity was going to sway him from his intention. The date of Old Joe's eviction loomed closer.

And then, as so often happens in the affairs of men, Fate took a hand in the matter of Old Joe Floggit's eviction.

Soon after breakfast one morning, Clare and her uncle were taking a walk along the lane that led past the church and eventually joined the road to Swinkhampton. It was one of those mellow September mornings, with red admirals and peacock butterflies flitting here and there, and the dahlias in the cottage gardens were burnishing the air with their many colours.

Suddenly with a purring roar this peaceful scene was shattered and Clare and Uncle George had to move smartly into the roadside verge as a snazzy, shiny, limousine came swishing past in a cloud of dust.

'Road-hog!' Clare said fiercely. 'That's Carver Waye, off to the station. Going up to town to carry out some smart deal, I suppose.'

'Yes, a very important one, I believe,' said Uncle George, as they walked on again. 'I met him last night at the Admiral's party and he mentioned it was the biggest contract he ever had. Important day for him, I gather.'

'It's funny how wealthy people can sometimes be so mean,' said Clare, scowling in the direction the car had gone.

Half a mile further along the deep-hedged lane, which was a mass of old-man's-beard and spindle berries, they turned a corner and came in sight of a stationary car. A purple-uniformed chauffer was bending earnestly over the engine, while a figure in homburg hat and pin-stripe suit hovered anxiously alongside.

'It's Carver Waye!' exclaimed Clare. 'Gosh, fancy that super car breaking down!'

'He'll lose his train if he's not careful,' observed Uncle George, glancing at his watch. Bound to be getting the 8.54, only through train of the day.'

As they approached the stranded car it was obvious that Mr Carver Waye was in a highly irritable mood. They could hear him upbraiding the unfortunate chauffer, who had by now divested himself of his smart jacket as he strove to discover the trouble.

235

'Can't you do anything, Blenkinsop?' he fumed. 'For goodness' sake get a move on, man. There's only ten minutes to go.'

'And nearly two miles to the station,' remarked Clare sweetly, as she and Uncle George arrived on the scene.

'Most unfortunate,' murmured Uncle George. 'I wish we could help.'

'This may cost me a fortune,' cried Carver Waye in a frantic tone, taking out his watch. 'If I don't get this deal signed-up today, there's a German firm on their way over to outbid me...'

'You might make it if you took the short cut over the fields,' suggested Clare, looking her most innocent. 'But you'd have to run. And unless you know the away it's apt to be a bit tricky, especially if Mr Ampleforth's bull is out.'

Carver Waye opened his mouth savagely as if to make some devastating remark but, unable to think of anything strong enough, closed it again like a snapping turtle.

'I shall be ruined,' he said. 'Five figures. Ruined. Just through missing a train.'

At that moment the familiar sound of a creaking axle and clip-clopping hooves could be heard approaching at a leisurely pace along the lane. Casually Clare and the others glanced round. Needless to say it was Old Joe Floggit.

'Morning, all!' Old Joe called out deferentially as the cart and Bramble came trundling past, with Swifty the whippet trotting tirelessly on beneath the rear axle.

Mr Carver Waye was clearly embarrassed and looked the other way. Uncle George and Clare returned Old Joe's greeting cheerily.

Suddenly Uncle George uttered a cry and raised his hand.

'Old Joe!' he shouted. 'Stop! Just a moment!'

In some surprise Old Joe reined in Bramble alongside the stranded car.

'What ever are you doing, Uncle George?' Clare demanded.

'We can't stand by and let Mr Waye lose his train and his contract,' said Uncle George. 'Old Joe! Can you get to the station to catch the 8.54?'

Ponderously Old Joe consulted a massive silver watch that adorned his tattered waistcoat.

'Five minutes and nearly two miles to go,' he mused. 'We can try, Colonel, sir. Wouldn't like to see anyone in trouble if I can lend a hand.'

'Up you get, Waye!' ordered Uncle George, turning round. 'It's your only chance...'

'But... I can't ride on this... this contraption!' protested Carver Waye, glancing at his impeccable clothes.

'It's either that or lose the train and your contract!' retorted Uncle George, hustling him towards the cart.

While Old Joe lent a helping hand. Uncle George and Clare half lifted, half hoisted Mr Carver Waye, elegant homburg and dispatch case and all, on to the flat-topped cart.

'Swifty will have to get up, too!' cried Old Joe, brandishing his whip. 'We'm got to move main fast!'

So Swifty the whippet was lifted up, too, and while Mr Carver Waye clutched his homburg with one hand, he put his other one round Swifty to make sure he didn't fall off.

'Giddup!' Yelled Old Joe, and, with a crack of his whip, he set Bramble at a gallop down the lane faster than the old horse had travelled in her life.

'Well,' said Clare furiously, as she and Uncle George and Blenkinsop stood watching the cart disappear in a cloud of dust that would have done justice to a troop of cavalry, 'if I'd been Old Joe I'd've let Mr Carver Waye stew in his own juice and miss his train. I can't think what you were thinking of, Uncle.'

'Ah, Old Joe is one of nature's gentlemen,' Uncle George pointed out. 'He's always ready to lend a helping hand. Pity other people don't live up to that principle.'

Well, eye-witnesses still recall Old Joe's record drive to Swinkhampton station. They still recall the sight of Mr Floggit standing up like a roman charioteer, urging the valiant Bramble to greater efforts. They still recall the even more extraordinary sight of the elegant Mr Carver Waye, usually to be seen lolling in the equally elegant limousine holding on like grim death to that bone-shaking cart, a look of agonised anxiety on his face.

But they did it. They caught the train. While the Swinkhampton Station porters rushed out to see what was going on, the cart drove up like a headlong buggy straight out of some Wells Fargo epic, just as the guard was beginning to slam the doors of the London train. Tripping over the feet of the occupants of the nearest compartment, Mr Carver Waye hurled himself on board and with his remaining strength waved gratefully to Old Joe.

'What, you turning taxi-driver, Old Joe?' the ticket-collector enquired, after the train had puffed sedately out of the station.

'No, just giving a lift to a fellow-dealer,' explained Old Joe as, followed by Swifty, he made his way out to the station yard again. 'Not that he's in quite the same line of business,' he added modestly.

So, thanks to Old Joe, not to mention Bramble, Mr Carver Waye caught his train after all and landed that important contract which meant so much to him. Nor was he ungrateful, for, as Uncle George had said, he was a decent enough chap at heart. It's true, Old Joe had to move out of the stables right enough, but that was a good thing, for the place was full of dry rot and rats. But Carver Waye showed his gratitude all right by building new premises for Old Joe further down the village on some land he owned. A neat little bungalow for Mr Floggit, handsome stables for Bramble, and a capacious storehouse for all Old Joe's stock-in-trade.

So, to everyone's satisfaction, Old Joe still goes trundling around the lanes in his flat-topped cart, with Bramble in the shafts and Swifty trotting demurely along under the rear axle (which still creaks as much as ever). And Mr Carver Waye has even been invited to join the Belham cricket club, proposed by Uncle George, seconded by Clare, who always acted as scorer during the summer holidays.

The Breadth of a Whisker

by JANET McNEILL

This was the time that the alchemist loved best. There was no sound anywhere in the house, and the dark quiet rooms lay round him like a spell. Sometimes the goldfinch in its wicker cage at the window stirred and slept again. He heard the little flame licking the bottom of the crucible. The liquid in it seethed and steamed, and released a large single bubble that swelled on its surface and reflected the solitary lamp by which he worked before it burst, with a soft plopping noise, and another bubble rose to take its place.

During the daytime the alchemist was busy with salves and potions and draughts and unguents, for children with bruised knees and young girls with broken hearts and noblemen with black melancholy and old people with the rheumatics; but the night — the night was all his own.

Not quite his own; it was so still that he heard the small brown mouse as he scuttered from his mouse-hole in the wainscot and came across the floor like a shadow, and sat down at his feet.

'You're late,' he said, without turning to look round. He was adding single drops of rose-red liquid from a phial into the crucible. As they fell, one by one, they filled the air with perfume, like a hedge of summer honeysuckle.

'Maybe I am late,' the mouse said, panting from his exertion, 'but if there were more crumbs from your supper table in the evening I wouldn't have to look so far afield to feed my family.'

The alchemist sighed. 'I daresay,' he agreed, 'but some

day — some day — there will be plenty of crumbs,' and he bent over the liquid again.

The mouse's eyes shone and he pricked up his whiskers. 'Tonight? Do you think it will be tonight?'

'It could be any night,' the alchemist told him, watching how one bubble more huge than the others had risen, sleek as steel, and with every colour of the rainbow streaking its arching sides. The mouse watched it too, and neither of them spoke until it burst. Then the little animal shook his furry face dry from the explosion.

'That's what I tell my wife when she grumbles,' he said. '*Any* night, I say. And I must be there on the night when it happens.'

'I know,' said the alchemist. He told his wife the same thing. She was asleep uptairs with her golden hair spread out on the pillow and the gold wedding-ring round her finger.

The sand in the hour-glass had almost run out. As the last of the grains hurried through — it was so quiet that the alchemist fancied he heard them rubbing and grinding together in their haste — he leaned forward and with a finger and thumb outstretched he dropped into the crucible a pinch of small crystals as bright as purple violets. They fell with a hiss and a stinging green steam rose from the liquid and filled the room.

'I like that one,' the mouse said when he had stopped coughing, 'I shall tell the children about it in the morning. Has anything happened?'

The alchemist wiped his streaming eyes with the long pointed sleeve of his jacket. The liquid in the crucible was now the colour of a jay's wing feathers and ran in a small whirling tide restlessly round the vessel's lip.

'No,' he said, unable to hide the disappointment from his voice, 'nothing'.

'But what a beautiful colour it is, even if it isn't the one you had hoped it would be!'

The alchemist turned over the pages of his great tattered book. He lifted a quill pen and wrote in it, adorning each letter with careful flourishes. The pen squeaked and the goldfinch turned round on its perch.

The alchemist lifted a handful of flowers with spotted out-thrust tongues. 'You're a good friend,' he said to the mouse, 'and if there's ever anything I can do for you —'

'There is just one thing,' the mouse told him and his black nose-tip was lively with nervous excitement.

'Well, what is it?'

'On the night when it happens — and I shall be here, mind you, to see it happen — may I — would it be too much to ask that I — could you allow me to — just dip one whisker into it — oh, not very deep — so that I may show it to my wife and family when I go down into my mouse-hole in the morning?'

The little animal stopped, panting. The alchemist was plucking the spotted tongues out of the flowers. When he had done this he put them into his mortar and ground them with a pestle.

'Very well,' he said, 'it's a promise. You're very sure, aren't you, that it will happen? After all these nights you are still sure?'

'Oh yes, said the mouse, 'aren't you?'

The alchemist didn't answer. From the bruised tongues of the flowers he had extracted a drop of liquid that he gathered in a bowl of a spoon. Although the tongues were purple the liquid was white and milky, like a pearl. The alchemist held the spoon over the crucible and tilted it, and the pearl fell in and was swallowed up.

As it fell they heard the sound of a deep note, like the single stroke of a bell. The whole room became dark, even the lamp went out, and the little flame below the crucible grew pale and lay flat.

The mouse cried out in terror and he ran and hid in the alchemist's sleeve, and they waited.

Something in the crucible was shining. Faintly at first, but always increasing until it grew and grew and filled the room to its furthest corner with brilliant yellow light. Then it flashed and darkened, and there was no light at all except from some small particle that lay in the bottom of the crucible, a mere trace, a grain, a drop, something bright, something — golden!

With shaking hands the alchemist lit the lamp and bent to look. The mouse crept from his sleeve. Yes, it was there, a bright bead, lying at the bottom of the crucible.

'Gold!' said the alchemist. 'Gold, gold, gold!'

They stared at it together.

The mouse was the first to find his tongue. He ran round and round on the stone floor, jabbering with excitement. 'You've done it! — I knew you'd do it! — I always told my wife you would! — you're famous! — no one has done it before! — no more stale breadcrumbs now! — no more rinds of mouldy cheese! fresh moist yellow cake rumbs! — mountains of them! — and a rasher of smoky bacon for the asking! — and you famous! — the whole house full of gold! — nothing all day to do! — and a golden ring on every finger of your wife's two hands!—and every feather of the goldfinch gold!— and his cage gold! — and nothing to do at night but sleep! — on a bed of gold! — go on now and wake your wife — tell her — what are you waiting for?'

The alchemist rose and went up the stairs. The goldfinch opened a sleepy eye at him as he passed the cage and thrust its head deeper into the shadow of its gold-barred wing. In the room aloft his wife was sleeping deeply. How thin the little ring of gold was that lay on her finger! He lifted a braid of her hair, wondering if it was as bright as the gold in the crucible. And then, without waking her, he came downstairs again to his workroom.

The mouse was still where he had left him, staring at the bead of gold with round dark eyes that reflected it, like the golden heads of twin pins.

'Did you not tell her?' he said over his shoulder, 'What are you waiting for?'

'What are you waiting for yourself?' asked the alchemist. 'There's nothing more to keep you here.'

That fact grew slowly in the little beast's mind. Excitement and pleasure ebbed. His whiskers drooped. Then the alchemist remembered. He lifted the crucible off the flame and held it out. 'There isn't very much of it,' he said, 'best go ahead before it cools.'

The mouse trembled from nose-tip to tail-tip. 'Do you mean it?' he asked.

'Wasn't it a promise?'

The mouse jumped on to the alchemist's arm. On small excited feet he went up the alchemist's wrist, out along his palm, down his long thumb, and there he stopped at the rim of the crucible and gently, so very gently, he tilted his head and dipped one whisker down.

When he lifted it again, the whisker was gilded, as bright and fresh as a springing sunbeam. But the crucible — the crucible was empty, drained, dry as a dried-out well, as a frosty stone, clean as a plate that a dog had fed from.

The mouse looked up. 'It has taken it all,' he said.

The alchemist nodded and smiled. 'Why, so it has!'

'It was the juice from the tongues of those flowers that did it.' the mouse cried, 'those curious spotted flowers — what was their name?'

The alchemist rubbed his chin. 'For the moment,' he said, 'I hardly remember. But I'll remember some day, I expect. And that may not be the only way. There may be other, better ways. Anyhow, I've been thinking — there's enough gold in

The mouse dipped one whisker in the crucible

this house for the time being.'

The mouse nodded slowly, because he understood.

'Go home now, said the alchemist, 'it will soon be morning.'

'And — shall I come back tonight?'

'If you're interested in joining me.'

So the mouse went off to his mouse-hole, with a proud tilt to his golden whisker.

Next day the miller called in at the alchemist's house for a potion. He had an angry thumb, swollen as big as a bun, poisoned from a fish-hook that had lodged in it, for whenever the sails of his mill were idle, he was out along the river with his rod.

'And I suppose you're still at the old game yourself,' he said to the alchemist.

The alchemist said he was.

'And where's your gold, eh? I've more to show from my fishing, when all's said and done. Well, nobody can say you ever put yourself out of a job. Tell me this, though, did you ever come near to it at all?'

'I did,' said the alchemist.

'Well, well. How near?'

The alchemist smiled. 'As near,' he said, 'as the breadth of a mouse's whisker.'

'Ah,' said the miller, and he nodded — nodded with sympathetic appreciation, because he was a fisherman himself.

Lake Island

by KATHLEEN MACKENZIE

The lake stretched before them like a huge looking glass, bottle green round the edges where it reflected the thick woods. There was hardly a ripple on its surface; only an occasional ring where a dancing fly touched it. Three quarters of the way down the lake, standing above its exact reflection, was the island.

Paul let out a great sigh as he looked at it. It was not, of course, a desert island, but it was uninhabited and it was, in fact, the first island he would ever have been on. All his life he had been mad about islands. He looked at his twin sister, Penny, and knew that, though she did not feel the magic of it he did, she too was longing to be on it and exploring it.

'Come on, Peter, let's do it. No one will mind.'

Peter, who was fourteen, looked at the twins and then at the boathouse, from the open, lake end of which projected the bow of a small rowing boat.

'I don't suppose they will,' he agreed. 'But I wonder if we ought to have asked.'

'There's no one to ask — as Sir Henry isn't here. Come on. We want a decent time there. No one said we couldn't, did they?'

Mr Bennett, Peter's, Penny's and Paul's father, had only three days ago come to farm Sir Henry's Home Farm, and it was only yesterday that they had discovered the lake. Terraces with flowerbeds and lawns sloped down from the big house Sir Henry lived in to a wild bit of garden, with woods and winding paths and open glades, and beyond that lay the lake. Sir Henry was away and no one had seen them when they entered the wild garden from one of the farm fields. Though they had not asked permission there did not seem any good reason why Peter should not take the boat and row the twins out to the island; they would not be doing any harm.

Peter moved round to the back of the boathouse where there was a door and lifted the somewhat rotten bit of wood that made the latch. Penny accompanied him, but Paul was still standing gazing at the island, completely lost in looking at it.

'You'd better not come barging in here, too,' said Peter. Wait till I get the boat out.'

'Hurry up then,' said Penny, hopping with impatience.

Peter climbed cautiously into the boat — he wanted to make sure the bottom planks were not rotten — and finding that they seemed safe he stood up in the boat and pushed it out by the low roof of the boathouse. Outside he put the oars in the rowlocks and paddled round to the low bank on which his brother and sister were standing. Penny, always light and agile, leapt in and settled herself in the bows.

'Wake up, Paul!' said Peter. 'Don't stand gawping like that, Hurry up!'

Paul withdrew his eyes from the island, sighed with pleasure and did as he was told. He would have left the knapsack containing their tea behind him if Penny had not reminded him it was still on the bank.

'Shall I steer?' he said, and sitting in the stern took the tiller ropes in hands that were trembling with excitement. He knew that it was no good hoping that even Penny would understand what he felt, because, close as they were, she never did feel things in quite the same way. The twins were not a bit alike in looks or temperament. Penny had curly red hair, green eyes and was practical, impatient and quick; Paul had brown hair, brown eyes and was slow and always in a dream. But they were very, very fond of each other. Peter was not like either of them; he was dark, big and strong for his age, good at games and going to be a farmer like his father.

Peter settled down to row strongly. The slight clunk of the rowlocks and the plop of the oars echoed back over the water from the wooded banks. Otherwise there was hardly a sound. Neither Penny nor Paul took their eyes from the island. As they came nearer they saw that it had one bigger bay and several other little creeks and a long promontory of rocks at one side. There were mountain ash trees, covered with berries, alders, birches and one tall scotch pine. The little bay had two sentinel rocks at each side of the entrance, one of them with a mountain ash hanging over it, and between the rocks they could see the white sand of a little beach.

'I suppose we had better go into that little bay,' said Penny. 'Doesn't it look absolutely wizard?'

'Is it deep enough? We don't want to hit a rock, or ground the boat or anything,' said Peter, glancing back over his shoulder. 'Can you steer me in, Paul?'

Paul nodded, he was far too excited to speak, and Penny said, 'I can see the bottom and it's quite a long way down. The water's frightfully clear.'

Paul steered straight for the centre of the two sentinel rocks. As they got near to them Peter, glancing over his shoulder again, gave a strong pull on the oars and then drew them into the boat and let it glide into the little bay just long enough to hold it till it grounded with a gentle crunch on the sandy beach.

'Here we are,' he said. For a moment no one answered him; both the twins were gazing at the island, Penny taking everything in. Paul almost believing that they were the first people ever to set foot on it — that it was a solitary, unexplored place and that he and Penny would be the first people ever to know what it was like.

Penny, of course, was the first out of the boat.

'Isn't it super?' she said. 'Are you sure you won't stay, Peter?'

Peter looked round. He felt rather torn. In some ways he would very much like to, but on the other hand he had told his father that he would be at home that afternoon to help unload the new horse they were buying and load the one they were selling. Mr Bennett, much to his annoyance, had to go to the nearest town to see the solicitor about something and had had to leave his wife and elder son to cope with this. Peter, who was mad about horses, of course wanted to be there when the new one arrived, but he also wanted to explore the island. He looked at his watch. He would have to go. It was nearly half past two and it would be getting on for three by the time he got back, and the lorry with the new horse might come by three.

'I can't stay,' he said. 'I told Father I'd be there. I'll have a look round when I come back to fetch you.'

'What time will you come?'

'I don't know exactly. It depends on what time the lorry arrives. It won't come after five, I should think, so I ought to be here by about six at the latest. You'll be all right, though.'

'Of course we shall. It will be heavenly. And we've got a decent tea. Sling it out, Paul, and get out, do. Don't sit mooning there all day.'

Roused by her words Paul did as he was asked, handed out the heavy knapsack and climbed out himself. But once he was on the beach he took no notice of the others and simply stood, looking around him, not even hearing Peter's demand that they should push the nose of the boat off. Penny, too used to Paul's dreaming even to feel annoyed, gave the bow a shove, and Peter punted it with one of the oars out of the little bay backwards, then he turned it and set off rowing steadily back to the boathouse.

As soon as the boat was out of the bay Penny turned to

It seemed as if they were the first people to set foot on the island

clamber up the bank behind her, but Paul stopped her.

'Don't go yet,' he said. 'It will make it more like really being on a desert island if we wait till he's gone.'

Impatient as she usually was, Penny nodded, and they stood quite still till Peter had disappeared with the boat into the boathouse, and even then they did not move away till they had seen him wave and then disappear into the trees that bordered the lake.

'Now!' said Paul, and turning led the way, scrambling up the steep bank from the little beach.

* * * *

Mrs Bennett, in the kitchen, was making a Victoria sponge when Peter got back. 'There you are,' she said. 'Where have you been? Father didn't have time to get Tom-Noddy out of the field before he went. You'd better get him at once. The box may be here at any minute.'

'Okay,' said Peter, and without answering his mother's question as to where he had been, he went across the yard, picked up a halter from the harness room and ran down to the paddock where Tom-Noddy, the rather heavy, thick-set hunter his father was selling, was standing under the shade of a tree. It was very hot and the flies were buzzing round him.

He was, as usual, tiresome to catch and Peter had a most exhausting twenty minutes. Tom-Noddy would wait till the person catching him got right up to him and then would suddenly swerve and trot off a few paces, and repeat the performace all over again. And again. At last, however, Peter managed to make a grab just as he was swerving and this time hang on to his mane, and once he was caught he was no further bother. Feeling very hot Peter walked with Tom--Noddy into the yard. He only just had time to put the horse into the stable before the horse box turned into the yard.

There was only one man with the box and he was in rather a bad temper. He had just narrowly missed having an accident, and had had to brake so suddenly that he was afraid he might have hurt the mare, Stella, inside the box. He had heard her slither dangerously in the sudden halt. He and Peter opened and let down the back with some anxiety. (The whole back of the box let down to the ground, making a sloping ramp for unloading.) Stella had not been hurt physically as far as they could see, but she seemed upset in her nerves, because she was extremely difficult to unload, dancing and tittupping about in the box and refusing to come out. Twice they got her as far as the ramp and each time she turned back, with a hollow thudding of hoofs, and when they did finaly get her down she galloped round and round the yard before they could catch her. And even when they got her into the stable they could hear her pawing the ground and chucking her head about, making the halter rings rattle and clink.

'Goodness!' said Mrs Bennett, hot and dishevelled. 'This would happen when your father's away. Well anyhow, Tom-Noddy's quiet enough. He won't be any bother to load.'

Peter agreed and went to get him. But whether the mare's wild behaviour had upset the horse, or whether it was the heat, or whether the driver of the box was to blame by giving a shout just as Peter was getting him to the ramp, no one knew. All that they did know was that the usually quiet Tom-Noddy flung up his head, dragged the halter out of Peters' hand, dashed up the ramp and into the box where the hollow sound of his hoofs seemed to terrify him more, for he swung round and came hurtling out again. Peter tried to stop him, the horse slithered to a halt, skidded round, gave a wild leap sideways and as he jumped caught Peter's head a blow with his hoof. Peter dropped as if he had been shot; the horse, his shoes striking sparks out of the yard cobbles, galloped to the corner and then stood with heaving sides.

Mrs Bennett gave a gasp and ran towards Peter, who was laying in a crumpled sort of heap on the ground, very still, with a little blood trickling down the side of his head.

Mrs Bennett could never afterwards remember how things happened next. She knew the driver of the box was most helpful. It was he who telephoned for the ambulance and the doctor, and it was he who made Mrs Bennett a cup of tea, which he insisted she should drink before she went with the ambulance to the hospital. She did remember to leave a note on the kitchen table for the twins (whom she thought were picnicking in one of the fields of the farm) telling them to go to the neighbours down the road for their supper, and to stay there till she got back, even if it meant remaining there for a long time.

It was just after four o'clock when the ambulance drove out of the yard, with Peter, still silent and white in it, and Mrs Bennett sitting beside him.

* * * *

Penny and Paul found the island even more satisfying and wonderful than they thought they would. When they scrambled up the bank they found themselves in an open, grassy space, at one side of which was a tiny wood, and on the other the ground sloped up to a hill, covered with bilberries and shoulder high bracken just turning bronze, and then bare patches with heather and rock. On the far side of the hill there was a narrow winding creek which opened out into a little pond, very deep and clear. Some of the sand at the bottom of this pond glinted in the sun like gold and they spent a long time trying to fish out the golden bits. It was Paul who first decided that it was not gold but just bits of quartz in the sand, and though for a long time Penny would not believe him, in the end she had to.

'Oh well,' she said at last, 'it's a pity, but it can't be helped. And perhaps if it was gold it wouldn't belong to us but to Sir

Henry, so we shouldn't make our fortunes. Anyway, one could't really expect to have buried treasure and a desert island, I suppose. I'm boiling. Let's bathe.'

Paul agreed and they went first to the little bay and bathed there, and then to the long promontory of rocks and practised diving, at least Penny did; Paul very soon went back and climbed to the top of the little hill and, looking round, hugged himself as he realised that he and Penny were really on an island and that there was no one else on it but they two. It did not even look as if anyone ever had come there, and he hugged himself afresh as he thought how he and Penny could make it their secret place and come there whenever they wanted to. He would just have to learn how to row a boat, but he was sure that would not be difficult.

Penny was hungry after the bathe and came to find him so that they could have the picnic. Paul rather wanted to light a fire, but Penny was against it.

'Fires are fun,' she agreed, 'but it's so boiling hot we don't need it a bit. And we don't want to make tea. Mummy gave us a whole bottle of orange squash. Besides, we don't want anyone to see the smoke and come to see who's here.'

'Gosh no! But do you think anyone would? There's no one to come, is there?'

'We don't know when Sir Henry's coming back. And anyway I suppose some busybody might.'

'It doesn't look as if anyone ever does come here,' said Paul.

'No, it doesn't,' his sister agreed. 'I suppose Sir Henry isn't the kind of man who ever comes to a place like this. Lots of grown-ups wouldn't, you know. I can't imagine why not, but they wouldn't. Though he has got a boat of course. I don't know what he'd have a boat for if he didn't want to come here, do you?'

Paul looked round. The sun was just beginning to come

slanting through the trees. It was extraordinarily peaceful and still. The scarlet-orange berries of the mountain ashes glowed as the sun caught them.

'You'd think, if it was your island, you'd never want to be anywhere else,' he said. 'But I don't think he can want to. That boat didn't look a bit used, and there are no footpaths.'

Although Penny liked being on the island nearly as much as Paul did, it was she who first began to wonder what was keeping Peter. The slanting shadows of the trees grew longer and longer, and quite suddenly she began to feel it was getting late. She looked across the lake to the boathouse again. There was still no sign of Peter.

'Paul,' she said, 'what time do you think it is? Shouldn't you have thought Peter would have come by now?' She picked a large, blue bilberry as she spoke and ate it, disappointed to find it was rather sour.

'I don't know. I don't know how late it is. How long do you think we've been here?'

'I don't know. But last night when we walked back across the field with Father the trees had shadows just like this, and that was after six.'

'Well, I suppose Peter's doing something. He'll be along I should think. I wish he wouldn't; I'd like to stay here much longer.'

But when another twenty minutes had gone and Peter had not appeared, even Paul agreed that it was perhaps a little odd. It wasn't like Peter to forget. They always had their supper about seven and as one of their jobs in the evening was collecting the eggs from the few hens they kept it was strange their mother had not reminded him to go and fetch them.

'Mummy didn't know that Peter was going to row us here,' said Penny. 'She knew we were going for a picnic, but I didn't say anything about where. I hope he comes soon. She'll be a bit mad if we're terribly late.'

258

'Would you hate to have to spend the night here?' asked Paul, also eating a bilberry — a riper one this time.

Penny looked round. There was nothing in the least alarming about the place now, and it was still beautifully warm, but perhaps when it got dark... She tried to imagine what it would be like in the dark.

'I shouldn't terribly want to,' she said frankly. 'Of course, with two of us I suppose it wouldn't be so bad, but we never have been out in the dark all night, and I should think it might be rather beastly.'

Paul was trying to picture it, too. 'It would make being on a desert island awfully real,' he said.

'Too jolly real if you ask me. And beastly cold.'

'In books people sleep in the heather and that seems to keep them quite warm. There are big enough clumps of heather for that.'

Penny looked unimpressed. 'What people in books do and what ordinary people do seems to me to be quite different,' she said. 'Just don't believe heather is a bit warm to sleep in. And horribly scratchy. But I do wish Peter would hurry up. I can't think why he is so long.'

Somehow neither of them seemed able to find anything to do on the island now but sit watching the boathouse, and gradually they both became aware that it was getting harder and harder to see it clearly; it was certainly getting much darker.

'What *do* you think has happened?' asked Penny. 'Do you think Pete's broken his leg, or what? Surely he'd come before it gets dark.'

'And if he had broken his leg he'd tell Mummy and she'd come.'

'Does she know the way? I don't believe she does. Perhaps she's got lost looking for us. Do you think it would be a good idea if we shouted?'

259

Paul nodded. 'It couldn't do any harm, and if she was not sure of the way she might hear us.'

'Right! One ... two ... three ...'

Their combined yell died away across the water. Some mallards started fluttering under one of the far banks and a pigeon, disturbed, clattered in the branches of a tree in the woods, but when these noises too died away it only made the silence deeper and more lonely. They shouted several times more, but there was no welcoming shout back, only the dying echoes of their own voices. Shouting and getting no answer seemed suddenly to make them feel very far from everyone and very much alone.

'Paul,' said Penny, and because her voice shook a little he knew that she was beginning to feel scared. 'What are we going to do?'

'We can't do anything till Peter comes. It's too far to swim.'

'But suppose he doesn't come?'

'Someone must.'

'But suppose they don't. Suppose something awful's happened and they don't?'

'Then we shall have to stay here till ... till the morning.'

He felt Penny's panic at this thought, though all she said was, 'I shall be awfully scared, won't you?'

'I shall a bit. But I suppose there's nothing really to hurt us.'

'No crocodiles or snakes or lions you mean, like a real desert island?' There was a pause, while Penny thought this over, and when she spoke again her voice was less panicky. 'There isn't really. It's just the dark ... and not knowing what's happened ... We shall be beastly cold. Do you think we ought to make some sort of a camp before it gets too dark to see?'

With the thought of making a camp Penny's voice became even more normal. She always felt cheered when there was

something to do. Paul agreed, partly because he, too, felt
doing something would make waiting better, and partly
because he had enormous faith in his twin. Somehow, no
doubt, Penny would make things much more bearable.

There was not, in fact, much to do. They both had jerseys
with them, but there was nothing else of which to make
a covering if the night got very cold. Paul could not in the
least remember if it did get cold at night; he was always
warm enough in bed at home, but what it would be like on the
island he could not imagine. Penny broke off some bracken
to make something to lie on, and they discussed making a
fire — both felt this would be an excellent thing to do because
not only would it warm them, but someone might see it.
When, however, they discovered they had no matches this
idea had to be abandoned. Unfortunately they had eaten
all the tea, so there was really nothing left to do but wait.
The both sat where they could look out towards the boathouse, thought it was now growing too dark to see it, and
after putting on their jerseys huddled together, both trying to
pretend they were not hating this adventure as much as
they were.

* * * *

Peter was aware of someone whirling round and round and
he very much wished they would stop. Then he gradually
realised the person going round was himself. Cautiously he
opened his eyes. The light seemed so bright (it was really
a shaded lamp) that he shut them at once and then someone,
whom he was surprised to realise was himself, groaned. The
whirling feeling stopped, but he still seemed to be a very long
distance away from himself. If only he could bring himself
nearer he might be able to remember the thing that he must
remember ... it was awfully important he knew, but what it
was he could not think.

He heard voices which seemed terribly loud, though they were in fact whispers, and suddenly he remembered, and making a tremendous effort said, 'Penny!'

He felt rather than saw someone — a huge someone it seemed — in white bend over him and a voice said. 'Are you feeling better? Just lie quite still.'

The crackling of the nurse's starched apron seemed to Peter like the noise of crashing thunder and her voice, though she was speaking very low, like a trumpet.

'Penny!' he said again, in what he thought was a bellow. But like his first remark it was merely a mutter, which the nurse did not hear.

'You just lie quiet,' she said, 'and you'll feel much better.'

'Penny!' said Paul again, desperately, making a huge effort to speak distinctly. The nurse, however, simply took his wrist, felt his pulse, put his wrist down on the bed again and disappeared. Peter began to feel frantic. He kept on floating away and trying to drag himself back to tell people that Paul and Penny were on the island, that someone must go for them, but no one seemed to take any notice until, suddenly, a dark figure bent over him and a voice said intelligently, 'Penny? What do you want to tell me about a penny?'

'Paul, Penny... on the island... I was going... to fetch them...'

It was such an effort to speak that Peter's voice trailed away, but the Matron had heard him.

'Do you mean that someone called Penny is on an island and you were going to fetch her from there?' she asked distinctly.

Peter would have nodded only his head felt too heavy and painful to move. 'Island... lake...' he whispered.

'Very well,' said the Matron. 'Don't worry any more about it. We'll fetch them. You just go to sleep. I understand, don't worry.'

Peter started to drift off again, but this time he did not mind. Someone understood and would fetch the twins.

* * * *

Penny and Paul had stopped suggesting to each other the things that might be keeping Peter from coming for them; they were just sitting very close together, trying not to let themselves get terrified at all the unexplained rustles and noises on the island, and the strange 'plops' that sounded from the lake, and also trying not to think of the long dark night that stretched before them. Paul was attempting to comfort himself with the thought that this was more like being cast away on a real desert island than anything he had ever expected would happen to him, but Penny was just thinking of what her mother and father would be feeling, and wondering what it was that had prevented anyone coming for them.

The stars were brilliant overhead and were reflected in the water, and Paul was sure that the faint glow in the sky was the moon getting up. It must have been nearly nine o'clock and Penny had fallen into a sort of daze of misery when suddenly Paul seized her arm and said, in a whisper, 'Oars!'

As she became fully awake she heard, quite distinctly, the noise of oars dipping gently into the water, but though the moon had now appeared just above the trees and was shining over the lake, there was no sign of a boat coming from the boathouse. The noise of the oars was getting louder and there could be no doubt that a boat was approaching the island.

Penny did not really know why the idea of a boat coming from another part of the lake was so alarming, but it was.

'Who can it be?' she whispered, and felt her heart thumping uncomfortably much nearer her throat than she thought was the proper place for a heart.

'I don't know. It can't be Peter. I can see the bow of the boat still in the boathouse.'

263

'Oh gosh! Do you think it's coming here? What do they want?'

'It might be poachers.'

Penny really knew nothing about poachers, but something in the word and the way Paul said it made her feel absolutely terrified. She clutched Paul, her heart pounding wildly as away to the right, through the trees they heard the water chuckling softly under a boat, then a few rustles and then, quite loud, the snap of a twig as someone stood on it. A dark shape loomed through the trees. Penny lost her head completely and let out a yell of fright.

A narrow beam of a torch shone on them and a voice — a very nice voice — exclaimed 'Good heavens! Who on earth are you?'

Paul stood up. 'We're marooned,' he said.

Penny scrambled to her feet, too. 'Oh, please, do take us home,' she said. 'Please do.'

And this, of course, is what the man did. He was interested to hear why they were there, and sorry for them. He was a birdwatcher and had intended to spend the night on the island, hoping to see some ducks flighting in the morning, but he took them home first. He not only rowed them back across the lake, but walked all the way home with them to the farm too, for which both Penny and Paul were very thankful — they had had enough of being out on their own in the dark.

Back on the farm, of course, panic had been reigning. When Mrs Bennett came back from the hospital, naturally terribly worried about Peter even though the Sister had told her she was sure he would be perfectly all right in a day or two, and had found Penny and Paul not at the neighbours and not at home, she did feel quite frantic. She had no idea, nor had Mr Bennett when he got home, where they could be. She had been all round the farm, shouting for them before her husband returned and was quite mystified.

It was a good thing the twins got back when they did because Mr Bennett was just about to get the police and all the neighbours he could to go out and search for them. Paul was thankful they had arrived in time to stop this; he would have hated people to have had all that trouble about him when it was not needed.

Once back safely it was rather marvellous to have been marooned, though Paul wished he had made more use of his time on the island. He certainly meant to go back there. When Penny told the children in school about it they were rather scornful and all maintained they would not have been in the least frightened at staying the whole night.

'You can say that now,' said Penny firmly, 'but you just try it, that's all. You just stay on an island in the pitch dark, not knowing why people haven't come to fetch you and see what you feel about it. I bet some of you would be bawling with fright.'

'Was Paul scared, too?'

'Yes, I was. I daresay it was silly, but I was. It isn't as much fun being a Robinson Crusoe as you'd think.'

'I suppose it's put you off islands, then?'

Paul shook his head.

'Nothing will put me off islands. Ever. They're all right. It's just that I must learn to be braver, that's all.'

Grandpa's Gold Watch

by KATHLEEN O'FARRELL

Susan Campion hated Grandpa's watch.

It was golden and shiny and had a message inscribed on the back, and it hung by its chain on a nail beside Gran's bed. It had hung there for three years, ever since Grandpa had died, and Gran had come to live with Mum and Dad and Susan and the boys.

Susan didn't like Gran very much either, although she did her best to hide it, especially from Mum. It upset Mum so dreadfully when Susan and Gran had words. Mum was such a kind, gentle person, the sort who would do anything to avoid a quarrel, and Dad was peace-loving too, while the boys, Tony and Martin, were always too full of their own interests to wage war on Gran. It was only Susan, nearly ten years old, and red-haired, with freckles all over her nose, who ever dared to stand up to Gran.

The Campions lived in the New Town of Foxbridge, about thirty miles from London, and had a pleasant, though rather shabby, little home, and a garden that boasted the best show of dahlias in Sycamore Crescent. Dad had green fingers, and was wonderful with flowers. He worked — when he *was* in work — at one or other of the local factories.

It was because of Dad that Susan hated Grandpa's watch.

It was so unfair, she thought, the way Gran always had to bring it up when Dad was down on his luck. Dad wasn't strong, he was quiet and shy and people didn't always understand him, and somehow he could never keep a job. Sometimes it was because he stayed away too much, and sometimes it was because the foreman didn't like him, but at other times it

267

was simply that he wasn't quite quick enough or good enough at the work he was given to do. But, whatever the cause, whenever Dad came home, sad and bewildered and crushed-looking, to explain that 'they said they wouldn't be needing me any more,' Gran had to lead off to Susan in the same tiresome fashion.

'I just can't understand your Dad, Sue. He never holds a job more than a few months. When I think of your Grandpa, and how he worked for the same firm for fifty years, *and* had a gold watch to prove it, then I wonder what the people of today are coming to. I often lie in bed and look at that watch, winking at me like a big gold eye, and I tell myself how lucky I was to have had such a husband. Which is more than your poor Mum can say.'

'Dad's all right,' Susan would answer fiercely. 'He's just unlucky, that's all.'

'Maybe,' Gran would mutter dubiously. 'But he'll never get a gold watch for long service. Why it was the proudest day of your Grandpa's life when they presented him with his watch! He wore his best suit to work, and a new shirt *and* a new tie — I'd never seen him look so smart, not since our wedding-day — and the Managing Director shook hands with him. And when he came home ... I'll never forget his face. Oh, but he did treasure that watch, just as I do now! But there, he was a real worker, your Grandpa was, a real honest-to-goodness worker. Not like *some* folks I could mention ...'

And Susan, hot with fury on Dad's behalf, would wish Grandpa's watch at the bottom of the sea. Or underneath a steam-roller ... or under a bus or a train ... anywhere, so that it wouldn't be upstairs in Gran's bedroom, mocking poor Dad in his failure and misery.

The funny thing was she had loved Gran and Grandpa very much in the past, when she and the boys had been taken up to London to visit them in their flat near Victoria Station.

268

Susan hated Grandpa's watch

It had been all hugs and kisses and chocolate bars, with cream cakes for tea, and she had thought Gran the jolliest, kindest old soul alive. It was only sice Gran had come to live with them that things had been different.

'*Why* does Gran have to live with us?' she asked Mum one day, when the old lady had lectured Susan on not helping enough with the housework. 'Oh, Sue,' Mum had said, looking hurt. 'You mustn't take everything your Gran says to heart. She's the kindest and the bravest soul that ever lived, and it's only right that we should have her here. She brought up twelve children, Sue, and was the best mother you could wish for, so how could I have let her stay alone in London, now that she's old and poor and needs someone to keep an eye on her?'

Mum was the youngest of Gran's twelve children, the rest of whom were scattered far and wide, and perhaps that was why Gran seemed so ancient. She was far older than Linda Todd's Granny — why, Linda's Granny wore high-heeled shoes and lipstick and still went to dances — and not a bit like Janie Robinson's, a timid little lady who called everyone 'dear' and couldn't be bossy if she tried.

No, Susan's Gran was different. Very old, very large, very fat, and very interfering. She had shrewd dark eyes that looked right inside you, and grey hair braided all round her head. You could never hope to tell her a fib and get away with it... 'A real old character,' the milkman called her, when what he really meant was 'a real old Tartar'.

And yet, for all her sharp words, Gran really was kind and generous — Susan had to agree with Mum there. Even when she interfered or scolded she meant well. If only she had let Dad alone... Yet Dad, sensitive though he was in some respects, rarely took offence at Gran.

'I know she does rather harp on things,' he admitted to Susan one evening, when she was sitting on his knee before the fire. 'But old folks are like that. You just have to make allowances.'

'It's when she keeps on about that beastly watch that I get cross,' said Susan. 'Sometimes I feel like throwing it on the ground and jumping on it.'

'Don't you ever *dare* to say such a thing again,' cried Mum, who had just come in. 'You'd break your Gran's heart if you harmed her beloved watch. It's the only thing your Grandpa had to leave her. Her one and only treasure. Besides, he earned that watch a hundred times over at least. He started work at Benson's Biscuit factory when he was a little lad of fourteen, and carried on there until he was a little old man, bent nearly double from lugging heavy boxes and tins to and fro. Loading up the vans, that was his job.'

'And a decent, regular job it was, too,' came Gran's booming voice. (They had thought her safe upstairs.) 'I've come down to look for my knitting — it's tucked behind one of the cushions so somebody must be sitting on it. Yes, he was a great one for work, your Grandpa. Not a single day did he have off in fifty years — not even a day off sick.'

'Oh, Gran,' muttered Mum reproachfully, 'he *must* have had a day off sometimes.'

'Well, maybe he did,' Gran conceded grudgingly. 'But if so I don't remember it. Ah, here's my knitting!' She picked up the pretty green jumper she was making for Susan, then slowly heavily, made her way back upstairs.

It was springtime then, and for several weeks Gran had no reason to nag at Dad, or even mention Grandpa's watch. As though by magic the atmosphere in the little house seemed happier, more light-hearted. Dad was settled in a job he liked at long, long last, and Mum was so pleased about it that she became young again and fun to be with.

'We'll soon have to start thinking about your birthday,' she said to Susan one day, as she arranged daffodils in the front room window. Although the furniture was old and the wallpaper faded, there were always flowers from the garden to brighten up the rooms, and pictures that Dad had painted himself — he was really quite good at painting seeing that he'd never been properly taught. 'Shall we have a party?' went on Mum.

'Oh, *please*, Mum. Last year's was such fun. We'll ask Linda and Janie and Sarah and Jennifer — they all asked me to theirs. And there are two or three nice girls at school I'd like to ask as well.'

'Then I'll start putting things by,' promised Mum. 'A tin of fruit this week, two or three jellies next week, and by the time your birthay comes we'll have no end of a collection. By the way, Sue, is there anything special you'd like for your present?'

'Yes,' answered Susan quietly. 'You know there is.'

She didn't say any more, she just looked at Mum beseechingly, and Mum looked back in sympathetic understanding.

'So you're still hankering for a bicycle,' said Mum softly.

'Oh, Mum,' and Susan clasped her hands together, her eyes shone. 'If you only knew how much I long for one! And you've always said you and Dad would think about it when I was ten. Oh, Mum, it would be so wonderful. I know how to ride one — I've learnt on Jennifer's. All my friends have got bikes, and they go to such lovely places. Last Saturday Linda and Janie went primrosing and got simply *thousands*. And they saw a real windmill, and daffodils growing wild in a wood, and little lambs with black faces.'

'Steady on,' Mum told her. 'You mustn't get so excited before I've even talked it over with Dad.'

'Oh, but he'll say yes — I know he will.' Susan could count on Dad, they were old allies. 'And I'll be able to go fishing with Tony and Martin, and I'll go to the shops for you on it, and change Gran's library books ... Oh, I can't wait till June!'

'But I haven't actually promised,' Mum reminded her. 'I've only said I'll ask Dad.'

The next day she told Susan that Dad quite agreed. If he kept his job and everything else went well, Susan would have a beautiful, brand-new bicycle for her tenth birthday.

For a full moment Susan was stunned with the sheer joy of it. She stared at Mum, as though in disbelief. Then, with a shriek of pure bliss, she rushed round the house, telling the boys, telling Gran.

Martin and Tony were delighted. They, being older, (Martin was thirteen, Tony twelve), had been able to earn the money to buy their own cycles, Martin with his paper-round, Tony by helping the mobile greengrocer on Saturdays. They had often thought it a shame that Susan had to be left behind when they set off on country picnics of fishing trips. Soon, very soon, she'd be able to go with them.

To Susan's surprise, Gran was just as pleased at the news as the boys were. She said nothing about extravagance, or about the children of today being spoilt.

'A very good idea,' applauded Gran warmly. 'Living in a New Town like this, with all that pretty countryside on your doorstep, so to speak, it's a shame not to get out and about to see it. A Londoner born and bred I may be, and proud of it, too, but I've always had a soft spot for the country.' Her rugged old face softened. 'Your Grandpa and I always said we'd have a holiday in the country when our ship came in, but somehow we never managed it. Come to think of it, we never had a holiday of any sort, not once in our whole lives! Not that we were any the worse for it,' she added, with a touch of defiance.

For several weeks Susan lived in a little world of bicycles. She dreamed of them by night and by day: gorgeous new, shiny bicycles, blue and silver, red and silver, pink and black, or just plain black and white, but all complete with saddle-bags and

pumps and gleaming bells. When she went to the Shopping
Centre she haunted the cycle shops, standing with her little
freckled nose pressed against the window, her hungry eyes
taking in every tiny detail of the elegant models on display.

Which kind would she have? Would Mum and Dad let her
choose, or would they want to surprise her? When she asked
Mum she only received the tantalising answer: 'Wait and
see.'

For Mum, meanwhile, was full of plans for the party. It was
to be a wonderful party, as good as any of those given by
Susan's friends, and each week the collection in Mum's store-
cupboards became more mouth-watering. Strawberry jam,
and turkey paste, and packets of chocolate ciscuits, and big
tins of fruit-salad, jellies and sweets and bottles of squash —
the more the hoard grew the more enthusiastic Mum became.
Perhaps it was because, in Mum's eyes, this was more than
just a brithday party. It was a celebration in honour of Dad,
too, because, after all this time, he at last seemed settled and
secure in his job.

As the birthday grew nearer and nearer, Susan grew more
and more impatient.

'Oh, Gran,' she cried one Saturday, as she got ready to go
to the Library, 'it seems as if my birthday is never going to
come. I'm longing so much for my bicycle that it almost
hurts . . .'

'It won't be long now,' Gran consoled her. 'The trouble with
you youngsters of today is you haven't any patience. Now,
be sure and find me a couple of nice books, won't you? With
big print if you can.' She thrust into Susan's hands the books
that had to go back. 'You won't have to walk in many more
times, will you, Sue? You'll soon be skimming along like
a swallow when you've got your smart new bike.'

Susan took the books and set off happily, despite her longing
and impatience. Gran liked love stories, the old-fashioned sort

of love, with beautiful girls being carried off by sheikhs, and gypsy violins in the moonlight, and dukes in disguise — all that sort of thing. Her heroes were all wildly unlike Grandpa — dear, rather pathetic old Grandpa, with his cloth cap and bent back and droopy whiskers. Not one of them would ever have been presented with a gold watch for hard work.

It was a pleasant walk to the library, under chestnut trees shining with pink and white candles, past little gardens drenched with the scent of early summer, and the playing fields where dogs romped and children shouted on the swings. Susan exchanged her books, finding and new gardening guide that Dad had specially wanted, and a highly suitable one for Gran called 'His Desert Rose,' and then went to gaze at her favourite cycle-shop before starting off home.

'It still doesn't seem true,' she thought, gazing at the glittering new machines. 'Will I really and truly have a bike like one of those?'

On the way home the sharp clamour of bicycle bells broke into her dreams, and there were her three friends, Linda Todd and Janie Robinson and Jennifer, whom she liked best of all, dismounted, and walked home by Susan's side. She lived quite close to Sycamore Crescent, in a little road called Willow Close, and was a very pretty girl, a year older than Susan, with grey eyes and a long gold pony-tail.

'I've been to see my Aunt Betsy,' said Jennifer, 'and guess what she said? When you've got your bike, you and I can go and spend a whole day with her sometimes — that's if your Mum will let you. It's a lovely ride there, quiet lanes nearly all the way, so I expect she will.'

Jennifer's Aunt Betsy and Uncle Jack had a little farm at Forest Ridge, ten miles outside Foxbridge, and Susan had heard so much about it, about the big farmhouse kitchen, the orchard, the well in the lovely old garden, not to mention the various animals, that it had become a sort of fairyland to her.

275

The thought of spending a whole day there, and eating Aunt Betsy's much-taled-of cakes and pies — she won prizes every year at the Flower and Produce Show — made Susan catch her breath.

'Oh, Jennifer, of course Mum will let me!' she cried, eyes shining in her freckled face. And then, more quietly: 'Do you know, Jennifer, I'm longing for this bike so much that it quite frightens me. Sometimes I wake up at night and think "suppose something happens and I can't have it after all?" If it did, I honestly think I'd die of sheer disappointment.'

'But what could happen?' asked Jennifer, a little puzzled.

'I don't know,' Susan admitted. 'It's just a funny feeling I get sometimes. A feeling that it's too wonderful to be true . . .'

And, although she continued to dream of bicycles by night and by day, the feeling persisted. It was silly, of course. Mum and Dad had promised, and she had never know them to break a promise. Besides, Dad was working so hard, and Mum was so happy, that there was a new warm feeling of security in the home. There were more little treats, more ice-creams, and fancy cakes began to appear on the tea-table. Mum and Dad even began to talk about buying a television set. One way and another it looked like being the happiest birthday ever.

It was the following Friday when all Susan's forebodings came to be realised.

She came home from school to find Mum and Dad in the kitchen, and Mum looked as if she had been crying. She had just poured a cup of tea for Dad, and her hand was on his shoulder as though she were trying to comfort him. The boys were nowhere to be seen, so Susan fled upstairs to Gran.

'What's the matter, Gran?' she burst out anxiously. 'Something's happened, hasn't it? Mum looks awful.'

Gran looked older than usual, more tired and very sad. She put a gnarled old hand on Susan's hair.

'It's the usual,' she said wearily. 'Your Dad's lost his job again. Oh, it's not his fault this time,' she added quickly, as Susan stared at her aghast. 'The firm he worked for have just lost a big contract, and they had to lay off a number of men — all those who started work there this last year or so. It's just bad luck, Sue. It's nobody's fault.'

Dismay spread through the little house, the happy, serene atmosphere vanished. Dad looked crushed and forlorn again, and Mum cut down on fancy cakes and said no more about buying a television set. As for Susan, she waited, with a sick feeling of dread, for Mum to say something about the forth-coming birthday.

And when Mum did, her worst fear turned into certainty.

'I'm so sorry, Sue,' Mum murmured, trying to break things gently, 'but you know how things are at the moment. Money is so short — I'd take a job myself, only Gran has been feeling poorly lately, and I wouldn't like to leave her. You wouldn't be able to have a party if I hadn't put all those little luxuries by. As it is, you'll have your party, Sue — a lovely party, too — but I'm afraid, terrible afraid, you won't be able to have your bike.'

Susan's face turned pale under the freckles. She felt sick with disappointment.

'Perhaps,' went on Mum, soothingly, 'we might manage one at Christmas, if things look up in the meantime. Or we might come across a second-hand one going cheap...'

'No!' cried Susan. 'No, I don't want an old one. It wouldn't be the same...' Her voice trailed off, and big tears rolled down her cheeks. 'It's all right, Mum, it really is. But I just don't want an old one.' And she crept away, to sob out her disappointment in the quietness of her bedroom.

The boys were very sympathetic when they heard and did their best to cheer her up with sweets and ice-lollies out of their pocket-money. 'Poor old Sue,' they said kindly. 'It's rotten luck, but you'll have one by and by. It just means waiting a bit longer.'

Sue was very quiet after that. It wasn't that she blamed Mum and Dad for her disappointment, because she knew it was just bad luck. But she wanted to forget all about bicycles. She never mentioned them now, and was careful not to go near the shops that sold them. She even found herself avaiding her friends, an case they should ask her what type she'd be having for her birthday.

And then Jennifer called round one day, and was so warm and friendly and easy to explain things to, that Susan told her, quite candidly: 'I'm not having a bike for my birthday after all, Jennifer. You see, Dad's out of work at the moment, so I've got to wait. If you like, you can tell the others, so they won't keep rubbing it in.'

Jennifer nodded. 'I will,' she said. Then she gave Susan's arm a little squeeze. 'Cheer up,' she whispered. 'Don't forget you can borrow my bike whenever you like. You want to keep in practice.'

In the meantime Dad kept applying for jobs without any success. It seemed as if it were one of the quiet spells, when the local factories just weren't taking on any new men, and Dad grew more and more disheartened. Something inside Susan ached to see him, as he strode to and fro in the little house, hand thrust into his pockets, a look of utter defeat on his plain though kindly face.

'It's no good,' he sighed ruefully, when he came in one morning, dressed in his best suit, and the tie Susan had given him for Christmas — ('I'll wear that for luck,' he'd said, before setting out for an interview he had high hopes of) — 'Nobody wants me. It seems hopeless.'

Gran, who was sitting knitting in the most comfortable chair, fixed her dark eyes on him.

'If you ask me,' she told him firmly, 'you aren't cut out for factory work anyway. Why don't you try for something quite

278

different? I see in the local paper that the Parks and Gardens Department of the Council are needing men.'

'Parks and Gardens?' Dad's face lit up.

'Yes,' nodded Gran. 'I'd say it was just your cup of tea, seeing what green fingers you've got. Better for your health, too, being out in the air. Why don't you try your luck? Of course, the money might be less than in a factory...'

'Never mind that,' put in Mum quietly. 'We'd manage.' And Dad was so keen on the idea that he applied for the job that very day.

Soon after that Susan's birthday arrived. Her tenth, and much longed-for birthday!

Had it not been for the disappointment about the bicycle, which still hung over her like a cloud, it would have been the happiest birthday ever. To start with, Dad heard that he had secured the job. The postman brought the letter, along with Susan's cards and parcels, and it said that he could start the following week. The hours were rather long, and the pay was certainly les than in the factory, but Dad was really excited. Although he would be doing the humbler jobs to start with, such as weeding and grass-cutting, he wouldn't be far from his beloved flowers.

'This is a new start,' he declared. 'I'll never go back to factory work now.' He looked a different person, somehow, stronger, more sure of himself, and Susan knew that, this time, Dad would really settle.

He might — it was a big might, of course — but he might even get a gold watch one day!

She was pleased with her presents. Mum gave her a pencil-box, while Dad had painted a little picture to hang over her bed — a bunch of daisies and buttercups and clover thrust into an old blue jug, as though by a child's hand. Tony gave her a box of hankies with her initial on, and Martin gave her a little bottle of scent, but she was rather surprised that there was nothing from Gran.

But then Gran herself hadn't appeared...

'She's going to stay in bed today,' Mum told them. 'She's been a bit up and down lately, as though she's feeling her age, poor old soul. I expect that's why she forgot to buy you a present, Sue. She doesn't usually forget.'

'It doesn't matter,' Sue assured her. Deep down she felt a little relieved that Gran was staying in bed. Gran meant well, and was very jolly at parties, but she had a way of taking charge of things, of bossing everyone about and running the show completely. This year, thought Susan, she would be able to do just what she wanted to — it would be *her* party, not Gran's. But she was careful not to let Mum know what she was thinking.

The party started at four o'clock, and Jennifer, Sarah and Linda arrived within a few minutes of each other, followed by some of Susan's school friends. Janie was going to be late as she had to mind the baby until her mother came back from the hairdressers so Susan tried, amid the tumult of happy voices, to listen for the doorbell.

And when at last it *did* ring, she ran to the front door in some relief. Perhaps Janie would help to brighten things up, Janie with her laughter that bubbled up over nothing at all. Because they need someone like Janie... The party wasn't as good as usual, it was rather flat as though something were missing.

But when Susan opened the door it wasn't Janie who stood there. It was a young man, a delivery man, and he was holding a bicycle.

She gave a little gasp. It was, she decided, the dreamiest bicycle she had ever seen, all shining chrome and ruby-red enamel, with gleaming white mudguards. There was a saddle-bag, a white pump, and a bell that sparkled in the sunshine. There was even a small neat basket on the front, just big enough to hold school books or a little shopping. Breathless with delight, she just stared and stared. And then her pleasure ebbed away. It was a mistake. It *must* be a mistake. Mum had ordered it, then had forgotten to cancel it.

'Are you sure it isn't a mistake?' she asked the vanman. She knew him slightly; he was an elder brother of a friend of Martin's.

'Mistake?' The young fellow raised his eyebrows. 'Course it's not a mistake! The old lady — your Gran — came in and bought it the other day. Took about half a day choosing it — making sure it was the right size, the best sort, and so on. Wanted all the trimmings, too. She made us promise to deliver it this morning, only our van broke down...'

Gran? But how on earth could Gran, who only had her pension, who sometimes couldn't afford to collect her shoes from the mender's, go out and buy an expensive bicycle?

Susan propped it up in the hall, then rushed upstairs, her guests forgotten, to seek an answer to this puzzle.

Gran was sitting up in bed, the shawl around her shoulders making her look like a vast purple mountain. She was eagerly reading the last chapter of 'His Desert Rose'.

'Oh, Gran,' murmured Susan, 'Oh, Gran, I don't know what to say.' She was nearly crying with sheer happiness. 'It's the most wonderful surprise I've ever had. The best bike I've ever seen! Thank you, Gran. Thank you...'

She broke off, gazing at the nail beside the bed where Grandpa's gold watch had hung. It wasn't there now. Instead there hung a little framed photo of Grandpa.

'Gran!' Susan looked at her suspiciously. 'What's happened to Grandpa's watch?'

'Oh, that?' Gran pretended to be casual. 'To tell you the truth, Sue, you won't be seeing it any more. I thought I'd hang his picture there instead. What do *I* want to be watching the time for? Now, tell me how the party is going.'

281

Susan stood there, mystified. But the gold watch was Gran's greatest treasure, her proudest possession! Surely she would never, never part with it? It took her a few minutes to realise the truth. Then:

'You've *sold* Grandpa's watch, haven't you, Gran? *To buy my bicycle!*'

Susan was aghast — even as she uttered the words she could scarcely believe them 'Oh, Gran, how *could* you?'

'Now, don't make a fuss, Sue.' Gran didn't like scenes. 'It's just what your Grandpa would have wished me to do. "Annie," he used to say to me, "if there's one thing I can't bear it's to see a child disappointed." So you see, the bike is from him as well as from me. He really loved children, your Grandpa did, as your Mum knows only too well — the things he went without for their sakes! The best husband and father in the whole world he was. And such a worker, too! Why, they said Benson's wasn't the same place after he left...'

'Gran,' Susan broke in, 'you were asking about the party.'

'Oh, yes, so I was!' Gran came back to the present day. 'How's it going, Sue?'

'It isn't,' Susan told her in a flat voice. 'It's funny, but it doesn't seem to be as good as usual. Something's missing...'

'What do you mean, Sue?' The dark eyes were full of lively curiosity. 'What's wrong with the party?'

'Oh, Gran, I think it's because *you're* not there. It's not the same without you. The girls were asking where you were. They say you always make them laugh so much — you're such good fun! You've always been there before... I — suppose you don't feel a bit better now, do you? Because, if you do...'

Gran sat bolt upright in bed. She couldn't hide her eagerness.

'You mean — you want me to come down and jolly things up a bit?' She tossed her book aside. 'Of course I will! Nobody knows more about parties than I do. Why, the parties we had

282

when we lived in London! But it only goes to show — you youngsters can't *really* get along without us old ones. You may think you can, but you can't.' She chuckled with satisfaction. 'And now I must get up and dressed, and you must get back to your guests. Trot along now, there's a good girl. I think I can hear footsteps on the path.'

'That will be Janie,' said Sue.

Obediently, she ran downstairs. But before she opened the front door she stood for a moment in the little hall to take another long, loving look at the gleaming bicycle.

'Thank you, Grandpa,' she whispered. And hoped that he could hear.

The Lime Tree Den

by Anne Barrett

Cathy took hold of a leaf from the tree beside her and pinched it hard. Was she really here? But as she smelt its green protest and felt the thin ridge of veins between her thumb and forefinger she relaxed, reassured. It wasn't a dream. As she stroked the leaf's papery surface in apology she saw that one edge was clipped with a round caterpillar hole, like a London tube ticket.

Tube tickets! No more of those for six weeks, for six long, lovely weeks! She held the leaf against her cheek for a moment and then let it go, so that the twig sprang back into place. It was a perfectly ordinary leaf like a milion others but to her it seemed a most special and enchanted one. Because it was growing in Ireland, where magic lurked behind everthing, out of the very earth of Kileen; fluttering from a branch that hung over their own lime tree den. She was really and truly here. No measles, no street accident, nothing at all had happened to stop it; the summer holidays had come and she was back again.

The hundreds of leafy twigs which made the roof of their den were interlaced over their heads and Cathy watched the sun trickle down through them like golden syrup, making a strange sort of underwater light which dappled the others' faces with green. A green Tim, a green Sheena and a small, excited green Rory. Cathy, who was an only child, living with her mother in London, looked at her cousins happily, so thankful to be back with them again. But then, as she went on looking, her brown eyes grew puzzled and she gave a small frown. What was the matter? This year, for some reason she couldn't understand, things didn't seem to be quite the same.

Cathy pushed back her hair and tried at the same time to push the thought away. She was just being, silly, of course she was. Nothing ever did seem quite real on the first day, after all that travelling; it was as though bits of you got left behind in London and bits on the train. Like luggage, they followed after and wouldn't get collected together until she'd been there a while, till she'd unpacked and had slept her first blissful night at Kileen.

At the beginning of each summer holiday, during the long journey to her uncle's house in Ireland, Cathy's excitement always mounted to fever pitch. The first few days out of school, in the flat, were strange anyway and seemed stranger still because London was so pressed-down hot and thundery at that time, making one feel that something ominous was bound to happen. Year after year Cathy was sure that she would get knocked down by a car, or develop some disease, in those few days before they sailed.

But somehow, hour by hour, they passed, and there was always plenty to do. School clothes to be flung joyfully into the washing bin and polite clothes to be put away. The old threadbare jeans, the shorts, the cotton skirts which were all that Kileen ever needed mounting in piles on all the chairs, waiting to be packed. Then, miraculously free of mumps or broken legs, the last evening would come; the front door would be closing behind them, the taxi, the train. Getting out at the other end in warm summer night time, climbing the gangway to the boat, with glimpses of dark, oily water down below. Then morning and the magic grey wisp of land ahead that was actually Ireland.

'. . . if I get whooping cough now, at least I'll have it at Kileen, in my room where I can see the mountain, where the sun comes through the window in leaf patterns, where. . .'

But she hadn't got measles, mumps, chicken pox, whooping cough or suffered any other disaster; hale and hearty, though

286

rumpled and dusty after the long train journey across Ireland, she was here, with the others, in the lime tree den. The moment she and her mother got out of the car and Aunt Eila had come out to greet them, the moment she had returned her aunt's kiss and had a pat on the head from Uncle Martin, Cathy's connection with grown-ups was over. Like leaves blown in the wind or Indian scouts melting into the forest, she and Tim, Sheena and Rory, with Dingo dashing behind, would be across the drive and away under the trees, running for the lime den, to crouch there and look at each other, to compare notes for the long ten months that Cathy had been away. At least, that was always what it had been like before. Was it Cathy's imagination that this time the others had hung round the grown-ups longer, seemed not quite so keen to move away?

As the bees buzzed sleepily in the thick mat of leaves overhead and the honey sweet smell of lime blossom came sifting down the shafts of sunlight, Cathy looked at her cousins to see if they had changed. Tim had, she saw with a shock; he had gone to a new school last year and now he looked almost frighteningly older. Even his freckles seemed to have stretched, like the rest of him, as she looked at them in the chequered shade. Sheena, dear vague, good-tempered Sheena, looked just the same, thank goodness, as she always would, in last year's jeans, with the same old tear in them, grown a little bit shorter and tighter.

And Rory— Cathy looked at him and laughed. Well, she certainly wouldn't be able to pick him up and hug him any more; he was a small boy now and no longer a baby. He sat there, looking up at her as eagerly as Dingo, who was panting and grinning and looking up at Rory.

Cathy patted the dog's head and looked up at the thick wall of leaves. The curtain of twigs, so closely interwoven that it was like being inside some very clever bird's nest, made them a wonderful hiding place which was almost completely weatherproof. It was cool there in the hot weather, when the fly-tormented cows sometimes got there first, and feathery warm and dry when the rain pittered down on the far-away outside leaves. The den was their playroom, council chamber, reading room and everything else, for the only people ever likely to disturb them were the errant cows and the odd farm hands who came after them.

The children rushed down there after breakfast to discuss their plans for the day and returned with their books after lunch when they were too lazy to do anything strenuous; it was only after sunset, when strange fair beings were still said to haunt the ancient barrows and twisted trees of Kileen, that the den lost its friendly character and they gave it a wide berth.

'The trees grow on the edge of the Mound, you see,' Sheena had once explained to Cathy earnestly, 'which is a rath, a fairy place, and their roots must go right down deep inside...' and Tim, half believing the old legends and half teasing, used to tell her about old Doolan, who was said to have vanished for a hundred years when he went after a cow and Maggie O'Leary who was greedy for fairy gold and came back one evening all queer and twisted and clutching a handful of withered leaves. And about the handsome young man, of course, who was the most dangerous of all because you wouldn't ever recognise him, the one that you must never smile at or talk, to, however much he beguiled.

'Any new stories?' laughed Cathy now, for in the broad, sensible daylight she loved hearing these unlikely tales which made you shiver in spite of yourself. They were all part of the enchantment of being back at Kileen again, among the cool grasses and the wildness of a country where people could really believe in such things; away from hot, matter-of-fact London. Thinking of the dusty park grass and then of the meadows of Kileen, Cathy kicked off her shoes and wiggled her squashed, towny toes, but Tim and Sheena still didn't say anything. Oh well, perhaps fairy stories were rather childish, she supposed, and Tim had probably grown out of them at his new school, but still... Determined to break the silence, Cathy plunged in again.

'How are the oats this year, and how's the new barley in the far field?' she asked, thinking to get things back on a more sensible basis.

The peak of each summer holiday at Kileen was the harvest when the children and every one else about the place helped to get in the corn before the weather broke. Then time went for nothing as they used up every possible minute of the day, snatching their meals from the great hampers which Aunt Eila sent down to the fields and dropping exhausted into bed by the light of the great apricot-coloured harvest moon. They rode on the carts, raked up the corn and helped stook the sheaves and at the end of it all, sunburnt, scratched and gloriously aching from all the new muscles they had used, they romped, danced and laughed their way through the Harvest Home party.

'How's Morrisey,' asked Cathy, before Tim had time to answer, remembering all her old friends, 'and Conlan and Murphy and — how's old Mrs Keane? Can we go down and see her tomorrow? She was a special favourite and this was part of the summer holiday ritual.

Rory's eyes lit up.

'The oats?' Tim said vaguely, and Cathy realised that his voice had changed, too, 'Oh, they're all right, I suppose; I really don't know,' and to her dismay she saw that he didn't care either. She stared at him across the green shade. Tim not care about the harvest any more? The bottom seemed to fall out of her summer world. Tim was the leader and they tagged along behind him, if he dropped something in scorn then they had to let it go, too. But that held only for little, unimportant things. Surely he couldn't lose interest in the harvest, the wonderful golden harvest? It was the life, heart and soul of Kileen.

Sheena, ill at ease, but anxious to smooth things over, looked from Tim to Cathy.

'Tomorrow,' she said hesitantly, answering the last half of Cathy's question, 'well, I don't think we can go down to old Mrs Keane's tomorrow, Cathy; Fiona's coming over. Fiona Browne, you know. She's going to show us how to take Scruffy on a lunging rein.'

As Cathy looked from one to other of her cousins her heart sank. Indeed she did know Fiona, she knew her all too well and now she realised what had happened. She didn't say anything, her dismay was too great, but the thought took the warmth out of the sun as they went home across the fields and blurred the long-awaited mountain view from her window when she went up later to bed.

She stood there, fidgeting with the blind cord, and looked out. Night after night, as she had looked out at the roofs of London, she had longed for this moment but now, as she stared miserably at the dark outline of the hills against the sky, she almost wished she were back again. Nothing had gone right since she had arrived; nothing, she thought angrily, and now she knew why. It was Fiona's fault. She thought back to last year.

Up till then she and her cousins had been all in all to each other; they never wanted anybody else. When Aunt Eila used to tell them that the Brownes were back from abroad and that they must be nice to Fiona, they all used to groan. The Brownes were rich and lived very grandly and Fiona, fat, bumptious and unattractive, evidently thought nothing of Uncle Martin's small unmechanised farm of his scruffy children. They did their best, but it was always a great relief when Colonel or Mrs Browne collected their correctly dressed little darling

290

and took her home to Carrig again.

That was how it had been until last year, but then things had suddenly changed. When Fiona, who had been abroad with her parents for two years, came back again, Cathy, Tim and Sheena had the shock of their lives. Like the fairy story, it was as though the fat Fiona had burst and someone thin had come out of her. Her arms and legs had grown long and her podgy face pointed and lively while her lank hair now shone like a well-groomed horse. The change in her manner was more startling still. The sulks and bossiness of the old days were gone and she seemed interested in everything, while she had endless stories to tell them of all the strange places she had visited abroad. Sheena and Cathy, still suspicious of Fiona, and only wanting life to stay comfortably as it always had been, hung back, but they could see that Tim was fascinated by all the new ideas that she brought, by the Brownes' modern car and new farm machinery, and that he was beginning to move away from them again.

Sheena, of course — loyal sister that she always was — soon followed, and at the end of last summer it had only been Cathy who refused to be won over and was left behind. How she had hoped, when she got back to England again, that the others might have got sick of Fiona! Or that she might have gone abroad again, at least! But they hadn't and she was still here, at Carrig, and to Cathy's despondent spirits it seemed that she had won. But she was far too sleepy to go on standing here and brooding about it. She got into bed, touched the pillow and brushed a moth away. Then she was asleep and past caring about Fiona or anything else.

When she woke the next morning the weather was glorious and out in the fields, on their way to Scruffy's paddock after breakfast, all seemed to be well again. As they fooled about in the long grass and ragged each other, with Rory and Dingo ambling between them, Cathy, now dressed exactly the same

291

as Sheena, revelled in the freedom of her shabby, three-year-old jeans.

'Look!' She vaulted a gate in style, to show Tim what she had learnt in the gym that year, but as she came down amongst the thick grass and sorrel on the other side she realised that he hadn't even bothered to look. He was hurrying on ahead.

'She's here already — get a move on, you two!' and Cathy, furious, obeying him out of long habit, found herself hurrying towards where Tim was standing beside Fiona. Queenlike, the tiresome girl was sitting on top of the fence rail and was swinging the legs that were now so long and thin.

'Hallo Sheena — oh, hallo Cathy,' Fiona's voice was as cool as her glance and as this flickered across her Cathy felt instantly as scruffy as the pony and as rough and cross as an old file. Because, instead of the old jeans which she and Sheena were wearing, Fiona had on brand new cord jeans, which were flared at her ankles. They made her look very dashing and efficient, and in the clothes which had pleased her so much a few minutes ago, conscious of every potato and every chocolate that she had ever eaten, Cathy now felt exactly like a sack of flour.

It wasn't fair! she thought childishly, it wasn't fair to be Fiona's shape and then to be able to buy clothes that made you look even better! It wasn't fair for Fiona to come and spoil her holiday when all she wanted was just to bask in the old, effortless relationship with Tim and Sheena again! As Fiona laughed and made easy jokes with them, as she showed them how to manage Scruffy, calling out to him in that cool, tiresome little voice of hers, Cathy grew more and more cross and sulky.

The more she tried to get back on good terms with the others, the more, in desperation, she tried to impress them, the more it went wrong. As they flicked on the end of the rein and tried to rouse the reluctant Scruffy they shouted out all their new plans to each other and instead of being listened to

Cathy found that it was she who had to hear about all the things which they had been doing together and she had missed.

The boat in the loch... the new canoes in the stream... Trying to re-establish herself, Cathy blundered worse and worse and started to boast about the things she had done in London. But of course it would happen that Fiona often went there too and in a much richer way than Cathy could; she has seen ballets and theatres and tournaments which Cathy could never dream of. Fuming, as Tim and the others listened briefly to her angry pronouncements, and then started talking to each other again, Cathy at last turned her back on them and held out a hand to Rory.

'Come on, let's go down to Mrs Keane's,' she said, and, though Rory was delighted, Cathy was sulkily aware that her jeans had bagged into a seat like an elephant's as she stumped away down the road to the bog.

The white tufts of bog-cotton waved like little flags in the breeze, and Cathy could feel it rumpling through her hair. Her bare toes wriggled easily in her sandals and Rory's dry hand clutched happily at hers; Dingo bounded along beside them, but, although the day was lovely, Cathy's heart didn't match. She could still hear the others laughing behind her and realised from their easy familiarity that the three of them met most days now. Before she left she had heard about the birthday party and dance that Fiona's parents were giving for her soon and was horrified to realise that even Tim was pleased at the thought and wanted to go.

Tim! At a dance! Last year he would have howled with mirth at the very idea. They obviously expected her too, but how could she possibly go? Even if she had wanted to she hadn't brought anything but old cottons and jeans over with her.

Everything was spoilt! Instead of the long evenings out in

the fields, instead of paddling down the clear brown water of the little stream or climbing the mountain to see the sun set and the far-off sea; instead of pleasurably frightening themselves with all the old stories as they saw the shadows lengthen across the den, the others would now dress themselves up and go trekking over to Carrig, spend the evening indoors shuffling about to Fiona's records, things which Cathy could have done in London, if she has wanted to, anyway. Her thoughts swung round. Oh why hadn't she! If there had to be new things why couldn't she have been the one to teach them, instead of that horrible, smug Fiona! Cathy tugged at Rory's hand and hurried on.

Even at dear Mrs Keane's cottage, down at the edge of the turf bog, things seemed to have saddened and changed. The low walls were as white as ever behind the bright bushes of fuchsia and the scent of turf smoke and baking bread were still the same. Mrs Keane was as smiling as ever, too, when she came out to greet them, but there was a tightness behind her faded blue eyes and a new sort of tiredness in her walk.

'Ah, Miss Cathy! 'Tis pleased I am to see you!' She held Cathy's hands for a minute as she gazed up into her face. 'And you growing up too, like the others, I see!' and though Cathy hotly tried to deny that any such thing was happening to her, Mrs Keane smillingly shook her head. As Rory went off to see the donkey, Cathy looked round the little garden patch. It was usually as neat and tidy as Mrs Keane herself, but now it was straggling and wild.

'How's Jim, Mrs Keane?' she asked, for Jim was widowed Mrs Keane's only son. He did casual work round the local farms and he came back every now and then to work on his mother's little plot for her. Would he be coming soon, Cathy asked, but the old woman looked sad and shook her head.

'Ach, and it's right you are to be asking, Miss Cathy, for sure he'd always come back now. When the haying has over and before the harvest was ready he'd always find time to come back and tidy things up for me here. It was like the swallows, he'd say, how they'd always find their way back, each year, from wherever they were. But he had a fight, so they're been telling me, and no one has seen him since...' The old woman looked away. 'He'll be frightened, you see, for they told him once that they'd have to charge him the next time and perhaps shut him up for a while. Jim could never stand that.'

Troubled, Cathy looked at Mrs Keane. She remembered when Jim had been working at Kileen, his slow ways and his red thatch of hair, his big gentle hands and round eyes.

'But ... surely Jim would't hurt anyone ...' she began.

'Not a fly even,' his mother said vehemently, 'Unless he thought they were going to hurt someone else first. But he takes these ideas ...' She shook her head again. 'It's animals, you see; he doesn't like to see anyone treating them wrong. And there was this man with the donkey, so they tell me, and Jim took the idea he was hitting it too hard. Ach, what's the use, 'tis done now. But if only I'd been by, Miss Cathy, if only I could have said to him "Wisha now, wisha, Jim," the way that I used when he was a boy ...' She looked at her neglected garden sadly and then bustled off to get some of her soda bread. She called to Rory and when he came clattering back Cathy and he watched the creamy butter melt into the fragrant dough and had to cram it into their mouths as they realised how late it was and that they must start back for Kileen.

Fiona hadn't stayed to lunch, thank goodness, and it seemed as though the others felt a little guilty towards Cathy and wanted to make amends. When they asked her what she'd like to do afterwards, before it was time to bathe, she said the tree den. However frightening it might be at night she felt that by day it was a magic place; everything would come right there and it would be like the old days again.

Taking their books and sweets with them, they set out.

It *is* magic, thought Cathy as they lay there happily, with the sun trickling down warmly on to their bare legs. This is really our own place, we're safe from Fiona here, and she looked round at the others. Sheena, bothered about the dance, had brought down a magazine with pictures of dresses in it, but she soon got bored and put it down. Tim seemed to have forgotten all about it and was absorbed in his favourite task of whittling wood. With his special penknife, one that his godfather had given him two birthdays ago, he was carving something out of a root. Was it a seahorse? Might he even give it to her as he had done the little cat she always kept on her London window sill? As Cathy lay propped on her elbow among the warm leaves, watching him idly, everything seemed well again.

Even Mrs Keane's troubles, as she asked Sheena about Jim seemed far away. In that warmly golden afternoon it sounded like one of the fairy tales, a story heard long ago.

'Poor old Jim! Yes, he's been missing for weeks,' said Sheena. 'They're frightened he may have fallen in the bog, or wandered right away. The stupid thing is that the man wouldn't have charged him anyway; everyone knows Jim. And all for an obstinate donkey . . . !'

'A donkey — that's what it is,' said Tim, who had only been half listening, holding up his root; and thinking of donkeys, Cathy told them how she had seen *Midsummer Night's Dream* in Regent's Park. Their talk drifted here and there, as lazily as the sunlight.

'Coo-ee! Where are you?' The shout came ringing across the field.

Oh not here! Surely they wouldn't let Fiona come here, into the den? But Tim had put his carving down and was standing up.

'Here!' he called out in answer, cupping his hands round his mouth. 'Under the lime trees!' and guided by their voices, Fiona came.

Shrinking back into one corner, and into awkwardness again, Cathy watched her. One of those thin legs came first and then there were her long hands parting the dense leaves about it; a second later her mocking face was looking down.

'Good heavens!' she said laughingly, 'What's going on? Secret confabs, midnight picnics in the dorm? What a funny little hole!'

Cathy scowled and Sheena looked uncomfortable but Rory was the only one to speak.

'It's not a funny hole!' he cried out furiously, 'It's our Tree Den! And you look out what you say, Fiona Browne, or the Little People will get you. It's one of their places, it's a fairy mound. They let us come here but they don't want you here any more than we do!'

'Shut up, Rory,' said Tim, but Fiona laughed. She stepped down and sat on a twisted branch, looking round at them all in the green light.

'Goodness,' she said, 'You don't believe all that old rubbish do you? I suppose you think you'll get Rip van Winkled and sink into the earth for a hundred years! Well, in that case you'd better come on before they get you, because all the new records have just arrived and I'm dying to try them out. Are you coming, Tim and Sheena? Coming, Cathy?' she added, but Cathy shook her head.

She knew at once that she should have gone with them, hidden her feelings and pretended that she wanted to hear the records, too. But she couldn't, and she found herself left behind with Rory again, turned back into a sort of baby. This and the knowledge that she was really behaving rather stupidly made her even crosser through the rest of the afternoon.

'Aren't we going to play cards?' she asked after supper, remembering the old hilarious sessions of racing demon in all

297

the past years, 'Oh no, Tim!' as she saw him starting to get up, 'You're not going over there again!'

'Why not? The new records are terrific and there's only a week before the dance to practise in. Father's giving us a lift down in the car. I can't think why you don't come too,' Tim said casually, going through his pockets as he looked for something.

How she wished she could! Cathy was beginning to feel that she had been a very great fool, but somehow it was too late to change. 'Go to Carrig? I didn't come to Ireland to stay indoors and see nothing but Fiona,' she said scornfully. 'That stuck-up, affected...'

'I don't think she is,' said Tim mildly, but all the more infuriatingly, 'You ought to give her a chance. She's jolly amusing and she's got lots of guts, you know—you should see her on that pony her father's given her,' but his main thoughts were on what was missing from his pockets and as he went through them again Cathy's heart sank to the ground. Oh why had she made such a jealous idiot of herself! All her life Tim had been like a brother to her and now she felt that she had lost him for good.

'I've lost my knife,' said Tim despondently, his search fruitless. 'I must have left it in the den.'

'Oh dear,' said Sheena in dismay. The knife was Tim's most precious possession and now it would have to be left out all night and get rusted, for whatever Fiona said Sheena had no thought that anyone could possibly go to the den after dusk. 'Tim! You can't to out there now to look for it! The sun's gone down!' She tried to pull her brother back as he started towards the door, but just at that moment they heard the car hoot at the door.

'Oh, bother,' Tim said, 'There's father and he won't wait. Well, it'll just have to get spoilt now; it'll never be the same.'

As they rushed off, without even time to say goodbye to

her, Cathy was left alone in the hall. Oh why had she been so stupid, why hadn't she swallowed her pride and gone with them! She blinked away an angry tear as she looked out through the door. And then, as she watched the car's tail lights dwindling away, the terrifying thought came.

She had to do it; she must. It was the only way she could get back again, show Tim and Sheena that she was as good as Fiona. If she went out and got Tim's penknife now it needn't be rusted after all. But to the den...

Trying to give herself courage, Cathy saw herself handing it casually back to Tim at breakfast, but then all the other pictures came into her mind, too. Of the dark trees and the eerie light and long shadows; of old Maggie O'Leary and... But she had to go. A she heard Rory running his bath water upstairs and Annie rattling away with the supper things in the kitchen, Cathy grabbed hold of a torch from the hall table and stepped out into the dusk, towards the tree den.

The tall trees in the drive that rustled so peacefully by day seemed like sinister enemies now, towering over her head and stretching out wavering fingers to catch her. As Cathy hurried away from beneath them and climbed the fence into the field she still seemed to feel them behind her, playing a dreadful sort of grandmother's steps. Could she really hear them rustling or was it only the beating of her heart?

Out in the field there was just enough light left to tell grey from black and as Cathy's feet dropped down into the cold and dewy grass she could see the dark block of the den trees ahead of her, neither moving nor rustling, but solid and fearful and dense. To think that they could sit there in the daylight! Every story that Tim and Sheena had ever told her, everything that Annie had ever said, magnified a hundred times by her own imagination, was whirling, through her mind.

Old Doolan... the terrible fair host, buzzing like angry bees... But all the time, as well as the stories, there was something else whispering in Cathy's head which drove her on.

'Fiona ... she's got plenty of guts, you know ...' Well, she was going to have them too. Even if she was found clutching Tim's knife in her withered hand, even if ...

As she stood in the middle of the field, trying to stiffen up her courage, something leafy touched Cathy on the back of the legs and she gave a little scream.

A warm tongue licked her and she was brushed by a feathery tail.

'Dingo!' Cathy bent to hug him in her relief and then started out again. But even with Dingo beside her it took all her resolution to part the leaves at the edge of the Mound and climb down into the den.

She couldn't go forward, she couldn't! But somehow she knew that she had to go on. She remembered where the knife was, where Tim had put it down when Fiona called. Fiona! The thought of them laughing together at Carrig gave Cathy the last bit of strength she needed; with Dingo panting beside her she dropped down into the leafy darkness.

She couldn't see anything at all, she must put on the torch. As Cathy held tightly on to Dingo for reassurance she fumbled with one hand for the switch. And then the terrible thing happened. Dingo gave a low growl and she felt him stiffen as his hackles rose and he stared at something across the den. Frozen with terror she heard a rustling there, a rustling stronger than the leaves, or even a small animal could make. Her heart seemed to stop. It was all true, the dreadful thing had happened; there was Something in the den. Oh Dingo! she tried to will the dog at her side, don't bark, don't bring it after us! and with her one free hand she held tight to his nose.

But her other hand was shaking so much that quite without meaning to she switched on the torch. The feeble beam wavered wildly, swinging first up to the still leaves above her and then down to the thick layer of dead ones on the ground. She

Frozen with terror, she heard a rustling

saw the blade of Tim's dropped knife glinting, and as she bent swiftly forward to pick it up she saw something else—a pair of feet. It had happened, the worst thing of all had happened; it was the dreadful, beguiling young man.

From far away words echoed in the back of Cathy's terrified mind: 'You mustn't speak to him . . . you mustn't even say . . .' But as Dingo strained and choked beside her and she looked slowly up, at the angry blue eyes and the thatch of red hair, at the large hands that were lifting towards her, Cathy did say something after all.

'I'm not hurting him, really I'm not! Look!' and she let the dog go. 'Wisha now, oh wisha . . .' she heard herself whisper, and as the torch fell out of her shaking fingers and Dingo sprang forward, wagging his tail, Cathy tripped over a tree root and fell against the comforting human solidity of Jim Keane.

* * * *

Instead of the mountain there was a purple line of bog through the window and a trail of fuchsia was nodding against a sky of pure blue. It must be morning, thought Cathy, puzzled, but as she rubbed her eyes she saw that she was still dressed and lying under a blanket on the sofa in Mrs Keane's best room. The door was ajar and from the kitchen next door she heard three voices, Mrs Keane's, which even from here sounded quite different now, a man's deep one, and Tim's.

Trying to smooth her hair down into some sort of order and straighten out her crumpled clothes, Cathy got up and went through.

'Ach, Miss Cathy, have ye slept well now?' Mrs Keane was beaming. 'Are ye hungry? The table's all set. Jim, ye great gaby, go and bring in some eggs.' Smilin at her son as though he were the same age as Tim, Mrs Keane pushed the red-haired giant through the door. 'I sent to let them know that

Jim'd brought you here last night, Miss Cathy, and they sent over Master Tim.' From where he was whittling away at a piece of kindling wood by the window, Tim held up his penknife and grinned.

'First thing I saw. It's quite O.K.' he said briefly. 'Thanks,' and the sunshine that was flooding in through the doorway seemed to Cathy doubly bright, the smell of the new bread and steaming chocolate specially good. When they had eaten Jim's brown eggs for breakfast and said goodbye she and Tim set out for Kileen.

'Gosh, you didn't half give us a fright,' said Tim, 'till Mrs K. sent over to say you were there. We began to think the old stories were right after all. And fancy you finding Jim in the den! He must have been hiding there. D'you know what Dr King said?'

Cathy shook her head.

'That Jim might be all right now; that he mightn't get these violent fits any more after the shock of finding it was only you.' Tim turned round for a moment and looked at her.

'Just imagine you having the nerve to go down into the den after sunset!' he said, and Cathy's cup was full. It had been horrible, but it had worked; now she knew that she had moved on with them all, that she was back in the stream. But she didn't want to talk about it any more.

'I suppose Jim remembered it was the time when he always came back,' she said ' "like the swallows" Mrs Keane said, and he really did come home. How was last night?' she went on, and Tim shrugged.

'Oh it was all right, I suppose, but I don't now that I enjoy dancing all that much.'

Cathy looked at him in surprise.

'I thought . . .' she began.

'Well, you've got to try things,' Tim said, 'Haven't you? To find out whether you like them or not; you can't stand still when you get to the edge of something . . .'

Cathy remembered another edge. She wondered what would have happened if she'd never gone over it, if she had never found Jim Keane.

'I know,' she said happily, suddenly seeing a life full of new excitements ahead of her, feeling able to cope with boats dancing, Fiona, with anything at all, 'You've got to go on.'

Au Pair

by Elisabeth Kyle

The little room the Favarts had given Susan was much simpler and barer than the one she had at home. The plain polished floor-boards still looked queer to her, and so did the old-fashioned china basin and ewer taking up most of the room on top of the chest of drawers. The wardrobe was huge and beautifully carved, but it creaked madly each time you opened it. Even the table, on which she was scribbling her first letter home, had a marble top.

This was France, and a very small provincial town too. Susan was staying with the Favarts 'au pair'. 'They couldn't be kinder,' she wrote, 'though it's a bore having to talk French to Madame Favart because she doesn't understand anything else. This morning she took me to the market to buy mushrooms for supper. (The French for mushroom is *champignon*.) Genevieve's all right but she's seventeen; two years older than me, and she's sometimes rather silly. Still, I do think I'm old enough to wear lipstick now. For parties anyway —'

There was that church bell again! It came floating in at the open window, interrupting her thoughts. French people went to church at the oddest hours. This would be for the evening Service, the one they called Benediction. Susan left her letter and went over to the window to look out. The narrow house of the Favarts stood halfway down an equally narrow street. By leaning over the sill you could just catch a glimpse of the big open *Grand Place* at the end of the street, and the *agent de police* on traffic duty whirling his white baton about.

Susan leaned over it. Below her, a few doors opened up, and down the street women hurried out, clutching their rosaries, making for the invisible church. It was a warm evening. Right opposite stood the town museum, where Monsieur Favart was Curator. Genevieve worked there as his secretary during the day. In the evenings she practised her English with Susan, because you had to know English if you wanted a really good job as a secretary.

The bell had suddenly stopped. For a moment the street was empty. Then Susan saw Monsieur Favart emerge from between the glass doors of the museum. He passed under the hooded canopy, down the two steps to street level and between the big wrought-iron gates that would be closed for the night very soon. He walked briskly up the street towards the busy *Grand Place* at the end of it and soon passed out of sight.

Susan remembered now, he had said half-jokingly at lunch that Genevieve must look after the museum's treasures till lock-up time, as he had an important meeting to attend. For a moment or two she remained staring at the grim, motionless figure standing to the left of the glass doors, just under its protecting canopy. It was only a suit of Japanese armour, placed within sight of passers-by to lure them into the museum and improve their minds. But the way it was propped up made it seem oddly real. And though, from this distance, she couldn't really see the hideous yellow mask showing under the visor, she always felt it was looking her way...

Suddenly Genevieve apeared on the steps beside the dummy. She was staring anxiously across the street towards Susan's window. Susan waved to her. Genevieve waved frantically back, calling '*Su-san! Venez ici immédiatement! Vite! Vite!*'

'Coming!'

She left the window and ran downstairs and across the street. Genevieve grabbed her, drawing her inside the museum. Genevieve was exceedingly pretty and dressed very smartly in cool blue linen. Usually she made Susan feel awkward and freckled, but not now. In an emergency, Susan would always score.

'What's the matter?' she asked.

'You know my white summer handbag? I had it lying on my desk. It's been stolen!'

'Stolen!' Susan glanced round the little gallery. It seemed to be empty now. 'You'll have to tell the police. Was there much money in it?'

Genevieve made a French gesture with her hands. 'Only a few francs. The money doesn't matter. But the museum keys were in it so I can't even lock up. And Papa will never trust me with them again!'

'You can close the outside gates behind us.' Susan pointed out. 'They lock themselves automatically, don't they?'

'So I can! Papa has the key to them all right. He always carries it in his pocket —' Genevieve paused, thinking. 'It must have been those two boys.'

'What boys?'

She explained. They had come in together — 'au pair' —she essayed the weak joke but Susan just gazed at her sternly and told her to get on with it. One of them had interrupted her typing in the little office, to ask for assistance. His friend had wanted to examine the case of Brazilian butterflies, but the blind protecting their colours from fading had stuck on its roller and he couldn't get it up. Would Mademoiselle have the graciousness to show them how it worked?

So she had left her desk, with the bag, she was sure, lying on it, and had gone into the gallery beyond. The other boy was fiddling with the blind. He was of a handsomeness quite incredible. Not like the first, who was plain. She hadn't noticed whether the plain one had followed them or not Anyhow, there didn't seem to be anything the matter with the blind. It snapped up at once when she pulled the cord. She had remained for a minute or two, talking about butterflies and one thing and another.

'That must have been when the plain one went back to the office and took my bag. They left a minute or two after, and he could easily have hidden it under his coat. He was of an ugliness to do anything.'

'The handsome one must have been in it too. You don't really think people are thieves because they are ugly?' Susan felt half-amused, half-cross with Genevieve for her silliness.

Genevieve sighed. 'I suppose I must tell the police.'

'Let's have one more look first.'

They searched through all the papers on top of the desk, and then throughout the museum itself. It was rather a humble little museum with everything ranged together for want of room; all the fossils, the African pottery, the butterflies and the collection of snuff-boxes, including a gold one set with diamonds that had belonged to King Louis the Sixteenth and was the museum's special pride.

Genevieve, following listlessly in Susan's wake, called out 'Now that they have the keys, those boys will come back to steal the gold snuff-box. The ugly one will anyhow. It's the only thing of real value —'

Susan's voice called back from the other end of the room. 'Nonsense, your bag's here!'

Genevieve ran to where she stood pointing. There it lay, half hidden under the butterfly case. She snatched it up from the floor, her fingers feeling inside it. Then she gave a long sigh of relief and closed the bag again.

'*Grâce à Dieu!* And everything's in it, too. Even the keys!'

'You must have picked it up out of habit and taken it with you,' Susan suggested, adding, 'You know you always cling to it anyway. Then you would lay it on the glass lid of the case while you were talking to that boy, and it just slid off.'

'Perhaps.' But Genevieve still looked puzzled as well as thankful.

It was closing time now. She carefully locked the inner glass doors and then slammed the outside gates after them both. Crossing the street again, she murmured 'You won't tell anyone, will you? I don't want Papa to think...'

Monsieur Favart hadn't come home yet from his meeting. They had supper without him. A huge omelette oozing with mushrooms, which Susan found quite delicious. She copied the sensible French custom of chasing the last bits round one's plate with a piece of bread. Then she and Genevieve washed up the dishes together.

After that, she went back to her room to finish her letter to her mother and take it out to post. She licked down the flap, stamped it, and crossed by the window to get her coat out of the vast cupboard with the creak. She glanced out. Dusk was beginning to fill the street. All its doors were closed now. Everyone would be inside having supper. Even the big museum gates were growing indistinct, while behind them, the figure of the Japanese Warrior...

Surely the figure had moved!

Her fingers froze and the letter fell to the floor. It slid in the draught over the polished boards, and she had to scramble under the table to get it again. She straightened up and then, half fearfully, stepped to the window once more. But the street seemed to have grown darker already. Of course it had just been a trick of the failing light. Because now the space under the glass dome was so shadowy, you couldn't really see any figure at all...

'Susan Blake, you've a nerve to call Genevieve silly!' She told herself and she ran downstairs and opened the front door. Genevieve appeared behind her.

'You are going to the *poste*? I will come with you. I want to buy some chocolate at the *confiserie* on the corner.'

They crossed the street again because the post box was on that side. Far down, at the end of it, the lights of the *Grand*

Place were winking and blazing already. The distant sound of its traffic came to them as they walked towards it, but the street itself was still dark and quiet. Susan's heart thudded a little as they passed the outer gates of the Museum. She tried not to turn her head and glance through them, but she did. It was *very* dark under the glass hood at the top of the steps. The space seemed filled with emptiness now.

In fact, it *was* empty. The Japanese Warrior had gone.

She stared unbelievingly, her heart thudding louder than ever. Louder even, than Genevieve's voice saying in her ear, '*Regardez!* Is that not a light inside?'

The fireflly light flickered aross one of the museum windows facing the street, then was gone. 'Somobody's moving through the gallery with a torch!' Susan whispered back.

'What shall we —'

Now for the first time the silent street seemed to hold somebody else besides themselves. Footsteps sounded, approaching briskly. It was Monsieur Favart. 'Genevieve! Susan!' He exclaimed. 'Is anything the matter!'

'There's someone inside the museum, Papa. Do you see the light?'

He took a step back to survey the whole frontage of the building. Again that pale flicker of light catching the glass for an instant.

'But how did the fellow get in? The iron gates are locked and I have the key in my pocket.' His voice sharpened suddenly. 'You have the other keys safe? You didn't lose them?'

Genevieve answered hesitantly. 'Yes, yes, I have them now. I lost them for a few minutes and thought my whole bag had been taken. But it hadn't.'

'Give them to me.'

She pulled them out of her hadbag. His fingers first grasped, then seemed to pass over the keys exploringly. 'What is this I feel?' A cigarette lighter flared for a second to let him examine the pellet dislodged from one of the keys.

'Wax! Somebody took them out of your bag and made a wax impression, then put them back. They must have got new keys cut from the impression and come back with them after dark.'

He took the other key from his pocket and inserted it softly into the lock of the outer gate. Genevieve clutched his arm. 'Don't go in. He may have a gun!'

Monsieur Favart paused, then withdrew the key. 'It is true. One must be prudent. I will go back to the *Grand Place* and fetch the policeman.'

His footsteps receded again. The two girls waited, shivering, their eyes on the door. But nobody came out yet. Once Genevieve suggested going back to the house. But though Susan's teeth were chattering she said stoutly 'No fear! It's too dark for him to see us if he does come out. And we can tell them which way he went.'

It seemed a long while, but could only have been a minute or two, before Monsieur Favart returned with the policeman from point duty. Susan was glad to see the man still had his baton strapped to his wrist.

'Perhaps the young ladies had better retire,' he suggested.

Susan muttered 'No fear' and followed them through the iron gate which Monsieur Favart had opened with his key as noiselessly as possible. Genevieve hesitated, then came too, clutching Susan's arm. Unnoticed, they peered past the two men who now stood between the glass doors left open, with the keys still dangling from the lock.

The gallery was quite dark, except for a stream of light from a torch now stationary on top of one of the show cases. There came the sharp tinkle of broken glass. A grotesque, helmeted figure suddenly outlined itself against the light, groping inside the shattered case. A taloned gauntlet withdrew itself, talons curved round something that glittered . . .

The Japanese warrior turned its grinning mask towards them

'*Halte!*'

The policeman sprang forward. The Japanese Warrior turned its grinning mask towards him, moving cumbrously to attack. But the floor was slippery and he crashed, with the other man on top of him, while Monsieur Favart groped his way to the light switch and turned them all on.

They blazed up suddenly, illuminating the figure lying sprawled on the floor like a creature out of a nightmare. Monsieur Favart gazed down on his precious suit of armour which, being mostly of wickerwork, was now bashed and spoiled.

'*Le malin!* He must have hidden behind the armour so as to find himself safely behind the iron gates. The other would meanwhile have the keys to the glass door cut from the wax impression, and then push them through the ironwork so that they could be retrieved and used by his friend.'

'Indubitably, monsieur.' The policeman picked up the gold snuff-box and handed it back to the curator with a bow. 'This, I think, was what they were after.'

Genevieve had plumped on the floor and taken the Warrior's head on her knees. 'He's not moving. You may have killed him!'

'*Au contraire, Mademoiselle.* He is merely stunned by the fall. A little moment and he will be sufficiently recovered to walk as far as the police station!' the policeman said dryly.

And indeed, the young man inside the armour seemed to be coming round. He stirred slightly. Genevieve snatched her handkerchief out of her bag, drenched it with perfume and tenderly removed the hideous mask, murmuring '*Ah, le pauvre!*'

Then, catching sight of his face at last, she dropped the handkerchief, letting his head fall back on the floor as she turned to Susan exclaiming disgustedly, '*Tiens!* It *is* the ugly one. What did I tell you?'

The Cat and the Quince Tree

by JOAN AIKEN

Harriet was sitting alone upstairs in the dormer window over the porch. There was an old basket chair and a shelf full of entrancing books — *Jackanapes. The Silver Skates, At the Back of the North Wind,* and many others with thick glossy old bindings and gold lettering. The afternoon sun shone in and made a pinkish patch on the floor. Harriet felt drowsy and comfortable. Her throat and cough were still troublesome and kept her awake at night, so that she tended to be yawnish after lunch, and Granny, with whom she was staying, had said that she must rest every day for an hour from two to three. She was resting now, while Mark practised archery in the garden. Granny had gone off to call on a friend and Nursie was at her weekly W. I. meeting, so Harriet was alone. It was nice, she thought, to hear the aged house stretching itself and creaking a little round her; the only thing she did wish was that Granny kept a cat, a comfortable tabby or marmalade to stretch beside her in the parch of sunshine and let out a friendly purr now and then.

Cars passed occasionally in the lane, but they never stopped. Most of Granny's friends were very, very old now, and exchanged letters with her in crabbed trembling handwriting, but they seldom came calling. Now, however, to Harriet's surprise, a large glittering car did draw up by the gate and a lady jumped out of it and came purposefully up the steps.

Oh bother, Harriet thought, now the bell will ring and I shall have to answer it.

She waited. The bell rang.

Uncoiling herself from the squeaking chair (which had left

basket-marks all over her legs) she went down the stairs, stepping over the patch of sunshine where a cat should have been lying.

The lady was standing outside the glass-paned front door looking sharply about. She had on a most interesting hat, Harriet noticed, flowerpot-shaped and made of some reddish material. Out from under its brim curled green-and-white tendrils of Wandering Jew which then turned round and climbed up the sides of the hat. The lady's pale smiling eyes peered from under it in rather an odd way.

'Well, little girl,' the lady said, and Harriet took an instant dislike to her, 'is your mummy in?'

'She doesn't live here,' Harriet said politely. 'This is my grandmother's house.'

'I *see*,' the lady said. 'Well, may I see her then?' She spoke with a hint of impatience.

'I'm afraid everyone is out.'

'*Oh*, dear,' said the lady smiling crossly. 'Then I shall have to explain, shan't I? You see I am Miss Eaves, Wildrose Eaves, and I have been looking everywhere, but *everywhere,* for a quince tree. Well! I was driving along this lane and I looked up, and I said to myself, There's my quince tree! So I came straight up here to ask if I could buy it.'

'Do you mean,' said Harriet doubtfully, 'buy *Granny's* quince tree? Or do you want to buy some quinces? Because I don't think they'll be ripe for another week, but we could let you have some when we pick them.'

'No, dear,' said Miss Eaves patiently, 'I want to buy the *tree.*'

'I'm sure Granny would never think of selling the whole tree,' Harriet said decidedly. 'For one thing, wouldn't it die? And she's very fond of it — it's almost as old as she is.'

'I can see that you don't quite understand, dear. I am Wildrose Eaves, *the* Wildrose Eaves.'

316

Harriet looked blank, so the lady explained that she wrote a very famous gardening article which appeared every week in a Sunday paper. 'And people all over the world, you see, know every inch and corner of my mossy old garden just from reading about it in the *Sunday Tidings*.'

'How nice,' Harriet said.

'Well, it *would* have been nice, dear, if there *were* such a garden, but the fact is the whole thing was made up. But now I've had a very temping offer from an American magazine who want to come and take pictures of it, so you see I'm quickly putting the whole thing together, my charming old cottage, Shadie Thatch, and the yew hedges and pansy beds, but the one thing I couldn't get hold of was a quince tree and that's very important because I've mentioned it more than once.'

'Couldn't you say it had died?'

'Oh, no, dear! Nothing in the garden at Shadie Thatch ever dies!'

'Well,' said Harriet, 'I'm afraid it's not at all likely that Granny will want to sell the tree, but I'll tell her about it. Perhaps she could phone you?'

'I'll pay five hundred pounds for the tree — with all its quinces on, of course. That's most important.' And the lady ran down the steps again to her shiny car.

'I never heard such impertinence,' said Granny, when she came home and Harriet had made her put on her hearing-aid and pay attention to the matter. 'Sell the quince tree! What next!' And she stamped off to the telephone to give Miss Eaves a piece of her mind.

Harriet heard her shouting, 'I wouldn't take five hundred pounds, nor yet five thousand. And that's my last word!'

'Why,' she went on, coming back and picking up her knitting, 'your grandfather planted that tree the year we were married. I've made quince jam from it for the last fifty years. The idea! But it's all the same nowadays — people think they

317

can have everything without working for it.'

And then it was time to watch television and, shortly after that, time for Harriet and Mark to go to bed.

The children generally woke early, and if it was fine they got up, took biscuits from the pantry, and went for a walk.

'We could go to Cloud Bottom,' Mark was saying as they crossed the garden. 'We haven't — good heavens, look!'

They both stared in astonishment and horror. For where, yesterday, the quince tree had grown, beautiful with its rusty leaves and golden fruit, this morning there was nothing but a huge trampled earthy hole.

'Tyre marks,' said Mark. 'And big ones. Someone's been here with a truck.'

'The beasts!' exclaimed Harriet. 'It's that woman! Now what shall we do?'

'I wonder how long they've been gone?'

'Granny'll be most dreadfully upset when she finds out.'

'It's early still,' Mark said looking at his watch, 'and they can't have dug it up in the dark. They probably haven't gone far. Let's follow the tracks.'

They went into the lane. It was easy to see, from tyre tracks and broken hedges, which way the truck had gone. The children went on like bloodhounds. They hadn't much idea what they would do when they caught up with the thieves, but they did feel very strongly that the tree must be put back before Granny discovered its loss.

'Remember the time when someone came and stole the holly from the two round bushes. That made her ill. Goodness knows what this would do to her.'

'I say, look over there!' interrupted Harriet. The lane curved round a couple of meadows here, and across the three intervening hedges they could see what looked like the top of a big removal van, stopped by a little wood.

'I bet it's them,' Mark said. 'We must make a plan.'

They cut across the fields, skirted the copse, and came out in the lane farther along. Here there were no tyre-tracks. 'It's them all right,' pronounced Mark. 'You'd better start limping.'

Harriet picked out a good sharp flint from the mud of the lane, and stuck it in her shoe. She never did things by halves.

As they neared the van they saw two men beside it who had evidently just finished changing a flat tyre.

Harriet hobbled pathetically, clutching Mark's elbow.

'Hello, up early aren't you?' said one of the men. 'What's up? Little girl hurt her foot?'

'I think I've sprained it,' moaned Harriet.

'Could you possibly give us a lift?' said Mark.

'Where do you live?'

'Lower Little Finching,' answered Mark, inventing quickly.

'Never heard of it. We're going to Gorsham.'

'Oh, that would be fine.'

'Okay, hop in.'

The van was of the enormously high furniture-removal type. Mark noticed that a couple of rusty leaves were jammed at the bottom of the roll-down steel back.

'Lift the kids up, Alf,' said the driver, and he added, 'First filling-station we see, I must stop for some juice. All that winching nearly cleaned us out.'

The other man scowled at him in a silencing way. So they've got a winch in there, thought Mark, run by a belt-drive off the engine. He had been wondering how they got the tree out of the ground.

The van edged its cautious way along the narrow track, which was called Back Lane because it swung in a semicircle behind the village and joined the main road again beyond. Just past this road junction was Smalldown Garage, and Ken Clement, who owned it, was a friend of the children's; it was Ken who came and mowed Granny's wide lawns with her temperamental, crazy old motor mower.

The driver pulled in as soon as he saw Ken's sign.

'How about a bit of breakfast?' suggested Alf, noticing the Snacks sign.

'Okay. You want a bite, kids?'

'No, thank you,' said Mark, who was afraid that Ken would greet them and give the show away. 'We've had ours.' He wished it were true.

'Well, we shan't be long. You can stay in the cab.'

Both men jumped out, and the driver asked Ken to fill up his tank. Then they went in at the café door, which was round at the side.

'Now,' said Mark to Harriet. 'you go in and make sure their attention is distracted. Play tunes on the jukebox or something. Don't forget to limp. Get a packet of mints.'

Harriet hobbled off. Her foot was really sore by now, she didn't have to pretend. In the café a fat girl whom she didn't know was serving the men plates of bacon and eggs. Harriet bought mints and then limped over and put sixpence in the jukebox which jerked and rumbled once or twice and began to play a gloomy song:

'I get along without you very well
Of course I do ...'

Oh, blimey!' said Alf. 'I can never hear this song without crying.'

'Why!' asked the other man.

'It reminds me so of the missus!'

'Well, she's waiting at home for you, ain't she?'

'Yes, that's just what I mean!' Sure enough his face was all creased up sideways like a cracker that is being pulled, and as the song went on its sad and gloomy way he fairly burst out boohooing.

'Here, shall I turn the perishing thing off?'

'Oh no, Fred, don't do that. It's lovely—makes me feel ever so sad. Put in another sixpence and let's have it again. You don't often hear it nowadays.'

'No accounting for tastes,' Fred said, but he kindly put in another sixpence and started the tune again while Alf sat happily crying into his huge mug of tea.

Harriet went out quietly.

'It's all right,' she said to Mark. 'They're good for another twenty minutes.'

'That should do us; come on quick. Ken's waiting. He's filled up the tank and we had a look inside—lucky thing that twig stuck out, it stopped the lock on the back from engaging properly. It's our tree all right.'

They ran round the corner. Ken was in the cab already, and his son Laurie was in the back. Harriet and Mark piled in with him and he pulled down the steel door. Before he did so Harriet had noticed Ken's other son, Tom, starting a tractor with a shattering roar that drowned the sound of their own departure.

It seemed queer to be riding along in a van with a quince tree.

A few of the quinces had fallen off, but not so many as might have been expected.

'It's a very well-sprung van,' Mark said.

'Proper shame, to take your granny's quince tree like that,' Laurie said. 'Why not put them on a charge?'

'We don't want a lot of fuss. And I expect they were only hired to do the job. The main thing it to get it back before Granny notices.'

'It's going to be a rare old fetch-me-round getting her out and back in the ground. Good thing there's this here crane,' Laurie said.

They could feel the bumpy slower progress as Ken edged

the van up the lane, and the occasional swish of a branch against the roof. Then they stopped.

'Coo,' said Laurie as he opened the back, letting in daylight, 'I never noticed there was a cat in the van.'

They all saw the cat for the first time. She was sitting in the tree looking at them somewhat balefully—a big tortoiseshell with pale green eyes. Harriet was rather upset to notice that the red flowerpot hat which had attracted her attention on Miss Eaves's head was lying at the foot of the tree.

'Do you think it's Miss Eaves in disguise? she said apprehensively.

'If she's a witch, why go to the trouble of hiring a van to steal the tree?'

'She couldn't take it across running water.'

'That's true,' Mark said. 'Well, we'd better put her somewhere out of mischief's way.'

Harriet picked up the cat, who was very heavy. Then she blushed, thinking how undignified this treatment seemed for the ladylike Miss Eaves. If it *was* Miss Eaves. 'Still, it was pretty low to steal Granny's tree,' she said to the cat.

There were lots of unfurnished rooms at the back of Granny's house, apple rooms, onion rooms, tomato rooms, herb rooms, and chutney rooms. Harried popped the cat into an apple room with a saucer of water, shut the door and window carefully, and raced back to the garden.

The men had backed the van right up against the edge of the big hole, pulled down a sloping ramp, and were now swinging out the crane. Its padded clench was still holding on to the quince tree's trunk. When Ken got back into the cab and started the engine the crane cable tightened and began to throb.

'You kids get in the back there and push,' Ken shouted. 'Laurie, get a rope round the tree and control where it's going.'

Ken himself manoeuvred the crane. Little by little the tree slid along the van's metal floor, and moved down the ramp. Its roots, which had been pressed upward against the walls, sprang out straight.

Laurie gave the rope a tug to swing the tree round. 'Now we're going to have fun, getting her back in the hole,' he said, wiping his face with an earthy hand.

It wasn't so bad as he had feared, though: the hole was enormous, far larger than the roots, and all they needed to do was lower the tree, and tump it up and down to make sure the roots were comfortable. Then they piled the earth back on top and trampled it down.

'The ground looks terrible,' said Harriet. 'As if wild pigs had been here.'

'Turf, that's what we want,' said Laurie.

'Down by the cricket pavilion, ready for the new pitch,' Ken said. 'Hustle off, boy. The club won't grudge old Mrs Armitage a few.'

They swung the crane inboard again, hauled down the back of the van (Mark jammed in a twig, just as it had been before) and all piled into the cab. Ken turned with cautious speed and bustled the van back to the garage.

Tom was still exercising his tractor in the drive. He gave them a reassuring wave. 'Haven't come out yet,' he mouthed.

Sure enough, when Harriet strolled to the café window and peeped in the van men were still drinking tea, and Alf was crying while he listened to a tune that went:

> '*I never mention your name,*
> *Oh no!*'

They seemed set for hours to come. Harriet often wondered how much later it was when they discovered their tree had gone.

'*Do you think it's Miss Eaves in disguise?*'

THE CAT AND THE QUINCE TREE

Tom and Laurie fetched a load of turf in the tractor's trailer and, working like beavers, they all laid the turves round the foot of the tree, working outwards.

'Lucky it was lawn underneath and not summat like rose garden,' Laurie said. 'That wouldn't have been so easy to fake. Now, a bit of a roll, and she'll be as good as new, specially if we get a nice drop of rain.'

'We ought to pick the quinces as quickly as possible,' Harriet said, 'in case Miss Eave has another try, once they're off, the tree isn't any use to her.'

'I noticed the telephone linesmen as we came through the village,' Mark said. 'I'll run down now, and ask them to help.'

The linesmen always helped Granny pick her fruit, and when Mark told them the story they said they would be along right away. Laurie and Tom supposed they had better get back to work, and drove off amid many thanks from Mark and Harriet.

'It's just breakfast time,' Mark said, looking at his watch as the linesmen brought up their self-supporting ladder.

Granny was delighted to hear that the men had begun on the quinces; she said that ever since Miss Eaves had called she had been thinking about quince pickle, and as soon as breakfast was over she brought out a cookery book and a cauldron, told Nursie to make the men plenty of strong tea with golden syrup in it, and instructed the children to bring in the quinces as they were picked. Soon the house was full of aromatic smells, and Mark and Harriet were kept busy peeling, shopping, and running to and fro, while Nursie doddered around ordering everybody about and making the men huge jam tarts.

'D'you think the tree will be all right?' Harriet said to Mark as they watched the last of the quinces come down. A nice gentle rain was beginning to fall.

'Oh, I should think so,' he said. 'There, now we can let out

Miss Eaves.' Harriet ran in with the last basketful.

'Put them in the quince room, child,' said Granny, stirring away at her pungent brew. 'And then come back and have a good sniff at this steam; it will cure your cough. By the way—'

'Oh!' exclaimed Harried, stopping on the kitchen hearth. 'How did *she* get here?'

'I was going to ask you that?' Granny said mildly. 'I found her shut in the apple room. She's not a village cat.'

Miss Eaves was sitting comfortably on the hearth, washing her face. If it was Miss Eaves.

'I need a cat,' Granny went on. 'Ever since old Opussum died the mice have been getting at the codlins. I've buttered her paws and I shall keep her, if no one turns up to claim her.'

Harriet was taken aback. Miss Eaves looked uncommonly placid and pleased with herself. An empty sardine-saucer stood beside her.

After sniffing the steam (which did indeed cure her cough) Harriet ran off to consult with Mark.

'If she's had her paws buttered,' he said gloomily, 'she'll probably never want to leave, unless we can get her away across running water.'

The opportunity for this did not come immediately. Meanwhile, to the children's relief, the quince tree showed no signs of ill-effects.

A week later Nursie was out at her W. I. while Granny was making very beautiful and potent quince honey when Harriet saw the Brushitoff Brush van stop at the gate.

'Do you want any brushes today, Granny?' she shouted through the steam.

'No, child. Last week we had an onion brush, the week before a tomato brush, and the week before that a tin on apple polish. Not today, thank you, tell him.'

On the way to the front door Harriet found Mark and hissed her plan to him, while borrowing all the money he had, which was not very much.

'Have you anything less than twenty pence?' she asked the man. He undid his case and spread out a most multifarious display of brushes, straight, curved, circular, pliable, stiff, nylon, soft, bristly, and all colours of the rainbow. After much thought Harriet bought a tiny button-brush. The man collected his stock together again and drove off, unaware that he had an extra passenger in the back of his van.

The children hoped they had heard the last of Miss Eaves, but next morning Granny sat at breakfast looking very puzzled over a letter on pink writing paper at the top of which the heading Wildrose Eaves nestled among a cluster of flowers.

'Most extraordinary,' said Granny suspiciously. 'Here's some woman writing to thank me for her delightful visit. She's never been near the place. Must be mad. Says how much she's looking forward to another visit.'

And indeed it soon became apparent that Miss Eaves found catching mice among Granny's stored fruit much more to her taste than writing untruthful gardening articles for the *Sunday Tidings*. Three days later she was back again, purring beside the kitchen stove, and the children finally gave up trying to persuade her to leave. But Harriet never really got used to waking up and finding a lady journalist who was also a witch purring on the end of her bed.

'Dear me,' Granny said one day, a month after the children had ended their visit and gone home, 'there must have been a gale in the night. That big quince tree was blown completely round. The crooked bough used to be on the south side. And I never heard a thing. Just fancy that, puss.'

But Miss Eaves, purring round her ankles, said nothing, and Granny strolled on to look at the medlar tree murmuring, 'I'm getting very old; very, very old, puss; very, very old.'

Jane Rings a Bell

by E. W. HILDICK

'Why don't you do something good for a change? Why must you always do things like *that*? Aren't you ever ashamed of yourself?'

Jane Rebecca McNulty was in trouble again. She bowed her head as her mother went on and on and on. She bowed her head so low that her fair pigtals dangled in front of her, slowly swaying. She was sitting on a kitchen stool, sipping bicarbonate of soda and wishing her mother would sit down or stop nagging or do both. Always when her mother told her off—which was about seven thousand times a day—she did it like this. Always it was out of the side of her mouth, over her shoulder, while she flitted about doing other jobs, dusting or washing up or cleaning out cupboards, as now.

It was upsetting enough at most times, but this morning it was terrible. Jane felt that if her mother went on one minute longer the dizziness would come over her again.

'Oh dear!' she softly groaned.

'Oh dear, indeed!' her mother echoed. 'Don't come to me for sympathy. Cigarettes, at twelve-years-old! A girl! And *eating* them, if you please!'

'Oh mother!' groaned Jane.

'Cigarettes of all things!'

'It was only *one*,' said Jane.

'Yes, but *eating* it—actually spreading it with syrup and *eating* it! I don't know where you get these ideas from.'

Jane could have told her. Just as she'd told her younger sister, Sally, twenty minutes earlier, up in the bedroom.

'Cowboys,' she had said, squeezing the cigarette tobacco

into a soft plug. 'Haven't you ever seen them on the telly—chewing it and spitting out? Looks absolutely delicious. Sure you won't try some?'

Sally had backed away.

'Bet *you* don't!' she had said.

'Bet you I do!' said Jane, taking from the pocked of her trews a small flat sticking-plaster tin she had filled with syrup.

'What's that for?'

'To roll it in. Before I chew it. Actually real chewing-tobacco's got molasses in it. That's a kind of rough treacle. This should be better. Sure you won't try some now?'

Sally had simply shaken her head, wide-eyed. Then, as Jane lifted the sticky brown ball to her lips, the younger girl's nose had wrinkled.

'Ooh—it looks *awful!*'

'Nargh!' said Jane, popping it into her mouth and hitching an imaginary gun-belt. ''S 'lishous!'

For about three seconds it had been delicious, too—soft and juicy and sweet. Then it had happened. Her mouth and throat had seemed to catch fire and the fire to spread at once—to her ears, her nose, her eyeballs. Flashes of it flew to every part of her body. It was like being struck by lightning. It scorched and it staggered. Never in her life had Jane tasted anything so bitterly vile. She felt tears gush from her eyes. And she would have spat the whole lot out on the bedroom carpet there and then if the tears hadn't cleared a little and allowed her to see Sally's face.

Smirking . . .

Though she was only six, Sally had a very mature smirk. Many a woman of forty would have been glad to have a smirk like Sally's. It made other people feel so small, so inferior, so stupid. It made Jane feel all those things and mad into the bargain. She was dashed if she was going to let Sally see she'd made a mistake.

So, with a mighty effort, Jane had put a brave smiling face on it. She had even managed to roll the horrible wad round her mouth a few times and make hearty champing noises. But the human stomach can stand only so much. Even Jane Rebecca McNulty's—which had been known to tackle eighteen chocolate éclairs in one afternoon and, on other occasions, such things as garden snails fried in butter, home-made bird-nest soup, secret messages and vast quantities of bubble-gum . . .

That was why her mother was scolding her. That was why Jane was feeling so sorry for herself, sipping bicarbonate of soda in the kitchen and wishing her mother would keep still and shut up.

She put down the empty glass and started to get off the stool.

'And stay where you are when I'm speaking to you! You're not fit to go out yet, anyway. Just look at your face. White as a sheet.'

Jane raised herself a little and looked at her face in the kitchen mirror. True enough, it was white. Very white. It was—well—even rather nice like that. Smooth. Like ice-cream. With the freckles like a sprinkling of broken biscuit and the eyes like dark blue grapes. She stuck out the tip of her tongue to try the effect of a strawberry or cherry.

'Jane McNulty—are you making faces behind my back?'

Not for the first time, Jane wondered if there were eyes in that thin narrow back of her mother's. Somewhere just above the top of the dress—a pair of small steely ones, as sharp as pins, one on either side of the zip.

'No, Mother.'

'And stop calling me Mother, you make me feel fifty!'

'Yes, Ma,' said Jane—but under her breath, knowing full well that that was worse than ever. Aloud, she said. 'Yes, Mum.'

'Heaven knows what you'd get up to if you were a boy!'
continued Mrs McNulty, giving some jars at the top of the
cupboard an irritable rattling.

Jane silently supplied part of the answer by rubbing her
face with the tip of her left pigtail, as if with a shaving-brush.
For that was the only thing she envied boys for—shaving—
and one of these days she'd have a real go. With a proper
brush. And soap. And her father's razor. She could always
try it out on her eyebrows...

'Mischief—nothing but mischief,' her mother was saying.
'You're thinking of it now, I can tell. I don't know where it'll
all, end, honestly I don't!'

Again Jane supplied the answer—or *an* answer. Wrapping
the right pigtail round her throat, she lifted the left high in the
air. Then she stuck out her tongue and rolled her eyes
upwards, looking for all the world as if she'd come to an
unpleasant end on the gallows. For something she hadn't
done, of course... Then she bent forward and, letting the
pigtails dangle, pulled each one in turn, like a funeral bell.
She could have cried, she felt so sad. Fancy being hanged for
something you hadn't done! It wasn't right...

'And what,' said her mother, 'are you up to now?'

Mrs McNulty had turned round. Her eyes—the real ones,
just above the sharp nose—weren't much bigger than pin-
points themselves as she scrutinised her daughter now.

Jane went on pulling.

'It's to make my hair grow,' she said. 'Something I read
about... somewhere...'

'Well, stop it this minute! You'll give yourself a headache!
Making your hair grow indeed! Why can't you do something
useful for a change?

'Why can't you do something *good*?... But I suppose that's
impossible.'

Now certain words have very powerful effects on certain

people. With some it's jelly-babies. You've only to say jelly-babies and they start giggling and can't stop. With others it's jukebox. Nothing else. Simply say jukebox and watch them get angry, furious, red in the face.

With Jane it was the word *impossible*. She didn't giggle. She simply couldn't stand the thought of anything being impossible. It offended her.

'What's impossible?' she said.

'You,' replied her mother, still with her back turned. 'You, ever doing anything good. Unless it's by accident.'

'Really!' said Jane, trying to sniff coldly, the way some of her favourite heroines were always doing in magazines.

'Yes—really,' said her mother.

'We'll see about *that*, then!' said Jane, getting off the stool.

Then she marched out, flinging back over her shoulders first one pigtail, than the other. She did it in the manner of a princess tossing back her cape—a really haughty princess —a Crown princess—and when Jane Rebecca McNulty did that she meant business.

* * * *

She hadn't been out of the house more than a couple of minutes before she saw her first subject for a good deed.

He was standing at the edge of the main road, near the shops, gaping at the traffic, looking bewildered. He was standing the way frail old men do stand sometimes, slightly leaning back, with his hands dangling helplessly behind him and his head thrust forward.

Jane went straight up to him. She plucked at the sleeve of one of the dangling arms and the old man gave a hoarse little cry.

Poor old man, thought Jane. He's absolutely terrified.

'I'll see you across, sir,' she said, taking tighter hold of the sleeve. 'Don't worry!'

'Eh?' croaked the old man, looking down at her with a mixture of terror and suspicion in his eyes.

But Jane didn't bother to repeat her kind words. She was too busy watching the road. She felt responsible for the old man and she meant to do the job properly. A bread van went past. Then a petrol tanker. That left a bus in the distance and a car coming from the opposite direction. The bus stopped. The car turned left. The road was clear.

'Now!' said Jane.

She was feeling very pleased with herself. Apart from the fact that she was doing a real full-sized good deed, this looked like solving an extremely important problem. For at least three days she hadn't been sure of what sort of job to do when she left school. Now, at last, she saw what she'd been cut out for. A policewoman, of course.

'Now!' she repeated, and very firmly drew the old man into the road.

'I—but—I—I...'

There was no doubt about it: the old man *was* terrified. He was trembling so much that he could hardly stammer out his words of gratitude. But they were now in the middle of the road and the bus had started up again; 973 W.P.C. Jane Rebecca McNulty, still holding the old man by the sleeve, placed the flat of her other hand firmly in the middle of the bony back.

'You can tell me, after, sir,' she said. 'But let's not hang about just here. We don't want them scraping us off the bottom of this bus, do we?'

So they continued—Jane steering, the old man choking down his words.

It was not until they reached the other side that she released his arm. Then she looked up, smiling. She wanted to tell him that it was quite all right, no trouble at all, but she thought she'd better wait until he'd actually managed to stumble out his thanks. He was looking calmer already. He had closed his eyes and that seemed to steady him. He cleared his throat. He began.

'Girl,' he said (and that in itself was a strange beginning), 'I've a good mind to report yer!'

Jane blinked. She couldn't quite see what he was driving at. Report her to whom? The Road Safety Committee? Her school, for being so kind, for setting such a fine example? But why say it in such a queer tone of voice? The old man rubbed his arm and continued:

'I've a good mind to report yer to the police! Shovin' an old man about like that, what's just watching the cars go by peaceful! I have! I've a good mind to do that—an' —an' if yer don't clear off...' He paused, his head nodding angrily. 'If yer don't clear off, outa me sight, I *will* report yer!'

Jane wondered whether to apologise and offer to escort him back to the other side. But he was looking so furious that she thought better of it. So, mentally handing in her policewoman's uniform, whistle, nylons and handcuffs, she gave her pigtails a couple of regal flings and stalked away.

* * * *

Her next two good deeds came in quick succession. Deciding to play for safety and get out of the ungrateful old man's sight, she turned down the first side street she came to, and there, with its back to a wall, bristling and spitting, she found Subject Number Two: a beautiful tortoise- shell cat.

Jane stopped. The reason for the bristling and spitting was a huge boxer dog. It was about a yard away from the cat and its head was down and its haunches were up. True, it wasn't moving any nearer for the moment, but its jaws were slavering and it was growling murderously. When it pounced, the poor cat wouldn't stand a chance.

Jane stepped forward. She faced the dog. She spoke to it.

'Rag, agrag, agar!' she said, and she frowned, just to show she meant every word of it.

She was speaking Dog Language, of course. And 'Rag, agrag, agar!' according to Jane—who'd once spent the best part of a week experimenting with the dog next door—meant, 'Go away, friend, or I'll chew you up into tiny little portions!' Naturally, just like humans, not all dogs seemed to understand their own language, and Jane had had many disappointments. In fact, she had sometimes suspected the dog next door to be a badly educated slob who had taught her the wrong pronunciation.

This time, however, it worked. The boxer gave a little growl and retreated. The cat relaxed. It arched its back and brushed against Jane's leg. Cats knew their manners anyway, she thought. But since the dog hadn't retreated very far—only a few yards—she decided personally to conduct the cat to a safer place.

She picked it up. The cat purred. She cuddled it as she carried it. It began to sing. At the end of the avenue, after making sure the dog was nowhere near, she placed the cat on a low garden wall. It stretched its back. Its singing changed back to a purr. Then all at once it stiffened again, stopped purring, and made a peculiar chattering noise. Jane was just thinking she'd start making a study of Cat Language, too, when it jumped off the wall, over into the garden and straight on to a bird.

'You *pig*!' yelled Jane, in language that was neither catlike nor ladylike—and she jumped straight over after it.

The cat was startled. It was so startled by this sudden change of manner in an old and trusted friend that it let the bird go. The bird flew twittering into some bushes. The cat turned its back in disgust and started licking itself, but Jane didn't mind that. She'd been getting rather annoyed at the way her good deeds were turning bad and now she felt better.

Then, out of the bushes into which the bird had flown twittering, a man flew stuttering.

'You—You—you ...' he stuttered, red in the face pointing at Jane's feet with a weeding-fork.

Jane looked down, and saw for the first time that she was standing on what had been a beautifully raked-over, newly sown lawn, and said 'Oh dear!' —and jumped back over the wall and out of that garden even quicker than she'd jumped into it.

* * * *

She had almost given up the attempt to do a really long-lasting nylon-pleated good deed, when she found the privet hedge sobbing.

At least it seemed like the privet hedge. She was walking past it on her way home when she heard the sound, and all she could see at first was the dense hedge with some of the leaves shaking in time with the sobbing.

But since the hedge was at the bottom of a garden, and the garden belonged to a bungalow where a friend of hers lived, and the sobbing had a familiar ring, and trees don't sob anyway, she guessed who it really was.

She bent to the hedge, pigtails swinging.

'Ruth!' she said, softly.

The hedge shook more vigorously. The sobs came louder.

Then a small damp voice said: 'Go away! Who is it?'

'Me. Jane. Jane McNulty. What's wrong?'

'Oh!' came the voice.

The sobbing began again.

'What's the matter, Ruth?'

The sobbing dwindled into a kind of regular sniffing.

'Do—d'you really want to know?'

'Yes. Course I do! I might be able to help.'

There was a sudden rustling. The privet twigs bobbed and bent and finally parted. A face appeared.

It had a fringe of dark hair over a bumpy forehead and a pair of glasses with a red patch over the left lens. The single visible brown eye looked bigger than ever, with its slowly spilling tears. The hidden eye wasn't exactly enjoying life either, judging from the trickle under the red patch.

'What's the matter, Ruth?' Jane repeated, gently.

Ruth was only nine and normally Jane wouldn't have had much to do with such a stripling. But Ruth had a lovely singing voice. You could tell that, even when she was crying. It was rich and sweet and this was what had attracted Jane, at a time when her one ambition was to be half of a Singing Sisters act. It hadn't worked out too well, because to be any good *both* halves of such an act need to have rich sweet voices. All the same, the two had been good friends ever since.

'It's—it's Golly,' snivelled Ruth.

Jane frowned. Rapidly she went through all the neighbourhood's most loathsome boys—the sort likely to have caused these tears. She went from Sneaky Simon, the boy next door, to the Sunday paper boy, a monster with great wide ears, a sneering manner but rather nice eyes. None of them was called Golly.

'Golly? Who's he?' she said.

Ruth broke into a long wail, at the end of which she said: 'He's—he's my golliwog and I love him and he's gone for good, for ev … for ev … for ever!'

Then the wail began again. Tears splashed into the soil under the privets.

Jane tugged thoughtfully at one of the pigtails. She looked hard at Ruth.

'I didn't know you had a golliwog,' she said. 'Aren't you a bit too old for that sort of thing?'

'I—I *haven't* got a—got one … Not now!' sobbed Ruth. 'And I thought I *was* too old. That's just it!'

And she went on to explain what had happened.

It was the old story. She had this golliwog, which she hadn't touched for years, well, months, and it was somewhere in the back of a cupboard, and when the men came round for old woollens that morning her mother had asked her if it wasn't time she got rid of this thing together with some old baby clothes, and Ruth had been sensible and said, 'Yes, go on then!' and for about two minutes had felt quite grown-up, and might have gone on feeling grown-up too, if she hadn't looked out of the window and seen these horrible men carrying him off at the top of the sack, with his poor old head hanging over the side, and looking back, and his poor old face, it looked so sad, and—and—and . . .

Jane began to see. She nodded wisely. She'd had exactly the same trouble when *she* was nine, only instead of a golliwog it had been Teddy, and instead of the old woollen men it had been the bonfire. She brushed her cheeks lightly with the tip of her right pigtail.

Then she brightened.

'Did you say this morning it happened?'

'Ye-yes . . .' sobbed Ruth.

'And I suppose they gave you something in exchange?'

'Huh!' growled Ruth. Her face became quite fierce. The tears stopped rolling and Jane could have sworn that for a moment the red patch on the younger girl's glasses glowed, as if something were burning behind it. Then the head disappeared and there was a muttering and rattling. 'Yes!' Came Ruth's voice. 'They *did* leave something . . . This! . . . Junk! Muck! Rubbish!'

With each word a fresh object was flung over the hedge. A large gaudy painting-book hit Jane on the head. A plastic brooch bounced on the pavement just behind her. A black flapping thing flew over and a shower of coloured lozenges spilled from it as it landed with a tinny crash—a cheap box of paints.

339

'There!' said Ruth, poking her head through again. 'That's what I got. For—for poor Golly . . . and—oh dear!—I'd forgot. He's missing his injections. He needs his injections every six hours or he'll die!'

From a girl who'd not played with the thing for ages, this sounded a bit odd. But Jane knew how it was.

She started picking the objects up.

'Don't bother!' cried Ruth. 'I don't want to *see* them again.'

Jane shook her head.

'We need them' she said.

'*We? Need* them?'

Jane nodded.

'Yes. To return to the men. We're getting that Golly back. Right now!'

The woollen men's warehouse was not far from where the girls lived and, since it had turned tweve, Jane guessed the men might have got back for lunch.

She was right. As she and Ruth approached the small shabby building, she saw the lorry in the yard at the side. A man in a shirt with broad horizontal stripes was unloading the sacks of old clothes and a big man with ginger hair was telling him whereabouts to put them.

'That's the boss,' said Jane. 'The ginger one.'

'Yes, I know,' said Ruth. 'And he—he looks nastier than ever. Do you think we *should* ask him now?'

The man certainly didn't look the sort to argue with. He was scowling at the other man and telling him to look sharp before the fish-and-chips went cold.

'Maybe after he's had his dinner,' mumbled Ruth. 'Maybe that would be better . . .'

Jane glared at her.

'Are you turning chicken?' she said.

'No, but—'

'What about poor Golly? Suppose they put him in the

340

machine straight away?'

'What machine?'

'The machine that tears the old woollens to pieces! Come on!' said Jane, having alarmed herself almost as much as Ruth.

With the paint box and the brooch, and the rather bent painting-book in her hands, she marched up to the ginger man. Ruth followed, blinking with her single eye, two paces behind.

'Good morning,' said Jane.

'What yer doing here?' snapped the ginger man, glancing at the trinkets. 'Get out, yer trespassing!'

Jane stared up at him in her best regal manner, straight at his bushy red eyebrows.

'We've brought these back,' she said.

'Don't want 'em,' said the man. 'Only woollens . . . Come *on*, Sid, don't take all day!'

'We've brought them back to change for something she didn't really mean to give you,' said Jane.

'Ha! Too late, ducks! Now clear off!'

Jane took a deep breath. The more she saw of the man the less she liked him, and if it hadn't been for the golliwog she would have told him a thing or two. Only the week before, she had learnt a lovely new word when a painter at school had dropped a pot of green paint from the top of his ladder. She'd have liked to call the ginger man *that*. But she controlled herself.

'I don't mean we want *everything* back,' she said, patiently. 'We're going to give you everything back, but all we want is her Golly.'

'Her what?' said the man.

'Her golliwog.'

'Haw! That!' The man grinned in a most unpleasant manner. The painter's word rose to Jane's lips. She shut them tight. 'Sorry!' said the man. 'Can't help yer. Now clear off.'

341

'But it's only a doll thing,' said Jane. 'There's only a *bit* of wool in it. It's only sawdust inside.'

'Straw,' said Ruth. 'I saw it when I gave him his operation.'

'I told yer once,' sneered the man. 'Nothink *doin'*. I want yer Golly,' he said, sniggering at Ruth.

Jane's lip curled.

'Aren't you a bit old for that sort of thing?' she said, for the second time that morning.

'Mind what yer say, *you*?' growled the man. He turned to Ruth. 'Yes, duck. He's my Golly now, he is. He's my mascot. He's gonner bring me luck. He's brought me some already. We did well this morning, didn't we, Sid?'

'Your—mascot?' said Ruth, in a whisper.

'Yer! Look! There he is! Mascotting away there now!'

They looked in the direction the thick finger was pointing. At first they only saw the back of the lorry. All the sacks had been cleared. Sid had jumped down. Then Jane's eyes widened and Ruth gasped. For there, in the back window of the cab, dangling, with a string round his neck and a sad, sad look on his face, was Golly.

'But it was a mistake!' said Jane. 'Can't you see she's upset? Can't you give it her back? We've brought you *your* stuff back!'

'Sorry, dear,' said the man. 'I told yer. He's lucky. Can't part with him now. Impossible.'

Jane stared at him. She looked him up and down, from the top of his head to the tips of his dirty pointed shoes and back again.

'Really!' she said. 'We'll see about *that!*'

And, thrusting the toys into Ruth's hands and giving her pigtails two right royal flicks, she stalked out of the yard. She looked even haughtier than a princess this time. She looked as stern and stony as a queen—a queen who has just declared war.

342

'I'll get that Golly back if it's the last thing I do!' Jane announced, as soon as they got out into the street.

'How, Jane?' asked Ruth, timidly, for Jane still looked very stern.

'Easy!' said Jane. 'I hadn't meant to do it this way, but he's asked for it, the—the—' Again the painter's word rose up. Again Jane quelled it. 'The pig!' she made do with saying.

'Which way, Jane?'

'With a pair of scissors.'

'But—'

'Be quiet while I tell you. We'll go home now, have our dinners and, as soon as we've finished, come back here. On our bikes, so we can follow them. O.K.?'

'Yes, but—'

'I'll bring the scissors—all you need do is bring this junk of theirs. O.K.?'

'But what for, Jane? The scissors, I mean...'

'In case the knot's too tight. We'll have to do it quickly, you see. Snip! Cut him down. While they're busy collecting their rotten old woollens somewhere.'

'You mean *take* him back?'

'I mean take him back. Just like that. Snip! Snip-snip!'

'While they're not looking?'

'Of course while they're not looking! Stupid!'

'But—but ... Jane ... that's stealing!'

'Stealing *nothing*! How can it be if we leave all this stuff of theirs on the seat after we've cut him down?'

'No—but ...'

'Look—do you want Golly back or don't you?'

'Oh, yes!'

'Well shut up then!'

However, in real life things don't always go according to plan, even when the planning is done by coldly determined queens and princesses. And although Jane and Ruth were back in time to see the lorry leave the woollen men's premises, with Golly swinging helplessly in the back window, and although they had come on their bikes with the necessary scissors and trinkets in the saddlebags, they soon lost track of the men. Jane had been hoping that they'd turn into the streets and start collecting at once. But instead of that the lorry went straight along the main road out of town.

Jane did her best. Very nearly choking with fury at the way things were going, she pedalled hard. Ruth, on a smaller bike and feeling all upset again at the renewed sight of the captive golliwog, fell far behind. Not that it made much difference. As soon as the lorry left the last set of traffic lights at the edge of town it picked up speed. It was hopeless going on with the chase.

Jane waited for Ruth to catch up. Angry and disappointed as she was, her determination was as firm as ever.

'There's only one thing for it,' she said. 'And I'm a fool for not having thought of it first.'

'What's that, Jane?' asked Ruth, encouraged by the confident look in her friend's eyes.

'We'll have to go when they've finished work. When the lorry's parked for the night in that scruffy old yard of theirs.'

'But—but it'll be locked up.'

'Of course it will, but we can soon get over the wall, or through the railing at the back.'

'But, Jane—Someone might see us!'

'Not if it's dark they won't.'

'But—but it's not dark till long after nine, after bed-time . . . *My* bed-time, anyway.'

'And *mine* this week, as a matter of fact,' said Jane, remembering something her mother had said about the cigarette-chewing episode and the results of sitting up watching television. 'But that's nothing. We'll just have to sneak out, that's all.'

'*Sneak out?*'

Ruth nearly fell off the bike she was straddling.

'Yes. Why not? If I can manage it, you can. *I'd* sneak out every night if *I* lived in a bungalow. Simply climb out of the window.'

Ruth's one good eye did the work of two, it opened so wide.

'Ooh, *Jane!*' she gasped. 'Sneaking out of the house and breaking into that yard! After dark! That's burgling!'

But she said it with such relish that Jane knew she wouldn't have to argue any further—which was a good thing because this time they needed to get down to some very careful planning indeed.

'Let's see,' she said, 'we'll have to have a proper burglar's kit, of course...'

* * * *

When Jane implied that it was so much harder for her to sneak out after dark, she was exaggerating a little. Most nights it would have been harder, yes, but this wasn't one of them. For this was one of the evenings her mother and father went out to visit some friends in the country, and on these occasions they left the house in the care of Beryl, Mr McNulty's secretary.

Now Beryl was a nice girl, but a bit on the quiet side. With her, you wouldn't, for instance, dream of pretending to be a ghost, or to have a peculiar kind of complicated fit, the same as you would with some child-minders. But on the other hand you couldn't very well make a friend and confidante of Beryl and sit up half the night eating chocolate creams and sipping your father's sherry with her, as for example Jane had done with her father's *former* secretary, Deirdre. For Beryl was a great letter-writer. Her boy friend, Fred, was in the Navy, and Beryl's entire leisure time was filled with the writing of what seemed like one long everlasting letter to him. Naturally, on a job like this she took the opportunity of adding another six or seven chapters to that work, with the radiogram on low, playing the sort of elderly swoony music Jane hated.

So Beryl was all right, but a bit dull; unapproachable but not a bit interfering. And, tonight of all nights, that was exactly what Jane required. She could sneak out and return after half an hour or even an hour, completely secure in the knowledge that Beryl would never have glanced up once from her prose-poem to Fred.

She was thinking all this as she softly stepped out of bed and slipped her jumper and trews over her pyjamas, at a little after nine-thirty that evening. Sally was sleeping soundly in her bed at the other end of the room. Her breathing was deep and regular and, to Jane's ears just then, musical. No need to worry about *her*, she thought. All the same, just to make absolutely sure, as every true burglar should, Jane wriggled her bolster down between the sheets to make a sufficiently realistic hump. Then, from under the bed, she drew her burglary kit.

She was very proud of this. She had spent much of the afternoon secretly assembling it. Admittedly she'd have preferred a more burglarious-looking bag then the old vanity case, but after all it was what it held that mattered. And what it held was: one pencil torch that she'd found in the tool-chest in the garage; one pair of pliers from the same place; one pair of rubber gloves, burst in three places but serviceable nevertheless, that she'd salvaged from the kitchen waste-bucket; one piece of thick wire; one pair of scissors and one nail file (part of the case's original equipment); one apple the survivor of two; and, just to be on the safe side, a card she'd found behind the clock on the mantelpiece bearing the name, address and telephone number of her father's solicitor.

She was so proud of this collection that she couldn't resist having another look at it now, on the pretext of checking every detail.

The torch was on top. She took it out and, screening it from Sally's end of the room, switched it on. Then, lovingly, she gazed at the rest of the contents of the case.

Only the apple bothered her. All the best burglars she'd ever heard about took snacks with them on a job. Usually it was a flask of coffee and ham sandwiches, but Jane had felt that to prepare things of that sort would have been to attract too much attention. So apples it had had to be—one apiece.

Now, however, she wasn't so sure. Having been unable to resist the temptation of eating her own, shortly after tea, there was only Ruth's left, and she wondered if it was worth bothering with. Apples made a scrunching noise, anyway, and there was always the danger that this might give them away. She decided to take it out and put it under her pillow for later. After all, Ruth would have Golly himself to celebrate with, so why shouldn't she have the apple?

Feeling glad to have thought of this, she put her hand in the case and pulled out the apple. That is, she *intended* to pull out the apple. What in fact she did pull out was the apple *plus* the scissors, one of the points of which had become embedded in it, *plus* the pliers, which had somehow become entangled with the scissors.

Too late, the weight of the pliers jerked the scissors from the apple, and both implements fell to the floor with a crash.

It wasn't a *very* loud crash. The carpet muffled much of the noise and no doubt Beryl never heard a thing. But it was loud enough to wake Sally and that was what mattered.

'Oh!' gasped that girl—and sat bolt upright.

Jane never ceased to wonder at the rapidity with which Sally used to crash into gear on waking. It seemed that while normal, healthy, decent people always took several minutes to come to themselves, nuisances were ready for action the moment they opened their eyes.

As now.

'Oh!' gasped Sally and then, with hardly a pause, she followed it with: 'It's you! Our Jane! I can see you! Where are you going? You're dressed! What's in that case? I'll tell Beryl!'

Jane sighed.

She picked up the apple. She dusted it. She took it to Sally's bed. She gave it to her sister. She sat down on the edge. Then she said:

'Eat that while I tell you a story. It's about a golliwog. Called Golly...'

Ten minutes later, two fully dessed girls with a vanity case full of burglary equipment tiptoed down the stairs and out of the side door. It was a terrible price to have to pay for silence, Jane knew, but what else could she have done?

Ruth wasn't too pleased. As they approached the woollen men's yard she said, for the sixth or seventh time, 'I don't know what you brought *her* for!'

'I do,' grunted Jane. 'And it wasn't for companionship.' She gave Sally's arm a tug. 'Come *on*!'

The place was in darkness. To the left, next to the yard, was a long stretch of waste-ground. To the right was a ball-pen factory. The nearest sign of life, apart from a cat on the factory's front steps, was about a hundred yards up the road, where there was a public house. Raucous singing noises drifted down.

Intending to peer throught a crack, Jane went up to the yard's big wooden gates. She found they had been pulled to, but left unfastened.

'That's a bit of luck, anyway,' she said, pushing them open a little.

'Yes,' said Ruth, squeezing through. 'And there's the lorry!'

'I'm *frightened*!' moaned Sally, half in and half out.

Jane dragged her in.

'Shut up!' she snapped. 'Or I'll give you something to be frightened for. You *made* me bring you, didn't you?'

All the same, it was rather eerie in the deserted yard. The shadows were deep and had strange shapes, and the lorry loomed large and somehow—well—*menacing,* as if it were a bull-headed beast waiting for them to get nearer.

Jane switched on the torch and the beast became a lorry again. It was empty except for a heap of loose sacks on the back—and, of course, the object of their mission. It was just above the sacks, gazing down from the rear window.

'Aw!' said Ruth. 'Golly!'

'He looks as if he's saying Hush,' said Sally, forgetting her fears.

'Yes—well, do what he tells you then!' said Jane, going round to the cab.

She tried the door on the driver's side. It was locked. She tried the other. So was that. But she didn't feel a bit put out. She was glad, even. It gave her the chance to use her kit. She opened the vanity-case and took out the rubber gloves.

'Stand back,' she said. 'Don't touch a thing.'

What she hoped to do wasn't clear to herself. She wasn't even sure *which* instrument to apply first—wire, nail file or pliers—let alone *where* and *how* to apply it. The key-slit in the handle of the door looked ridiculously tiny and the side windows were stolidly unyielding. She was just beginning to wonder if there was a way in through the windscreen, or under the lorry and up through the floor of the cab, when Ruth clutched her arm.

'Jane!' she gasped. 'There's someone coming!'

'Nonsense!' hissed Jane, but listened nevertheless.

She heard footsteps out in the street and the mutter of men's voices. Then the footsteps slowed down, outside the gate and—oh dear!—stopped.

'Quick!' said Jane. 'Up on the lorry! Go *on*! Under those sacks!'

She tossed her case on to them. Ruth followed, a close second. Sally was slower. She might even have stood where she was, as helpless and useless as only a younger sister can be, if Jane hadn't grabbed her by the waist and heaved her up after Ruth. Then she got up herself and, huddling close to the others, pulled another sack over her head.

'Thought I told yer to keep this shut?' one of the men was saying.

It was the ginger man's voice.

'So I did . . .'

'Yer—looks like it, don' it?'

'Sorry. Mus have been the wind.'

There came a creaking and scraping as the gates were opened wider.

'Keep quite still!' whispered Jane. 'They're only checking up.'

'I—want to go—' began Sally, an ominous sob in her voice.

'Shsh! Or they'll shove us in the wool-shredder!' urged Jane, naming a diabolical instrument with a hundred and fifty long steel teeth, barbed at the tips, with which she'd coloured Sally's bed-time story.

There was a little moan, but nothing more from Sally. Whether or not she'd fainted clean away, Jane wasn't sure, but at least she was quiet. And that was important, for now the men were very close to the lorry.

'Got the clippers, Sid?'

'Tool box.'

'Right!' There came a scratching sound, a click, and then the lorry lurched. 'Get in.'

'Shall I get on the back?' came a third voice.

350

The girls stiffened. Ruth was clutching one of Jane's pigtails. Jane clamped a cautious hard over Sally's mouth. Then:

'Naw!' said the ginger man. 'It's draughty up there. Want to catch yer death of cold? We got a long ride in front of us . . . Naw—get in. Shove up next to Sid.'

And with that the engine was started.

There was nothing they could do about it.

Before they knew exactly what was happening the lorry had moved out of the yard and into the street. It might not have been so bad if it had stopped to allow one of the men to get out and shut the gates. They might then have been able to slip quietly over the side. But it didn't. Into the street it swung and straight off down past the public house.

'At least it means they're coming back,' Jean murmured. 'Leaving the gates like that.'

'Yes, but *when*?' said Ruth.

Jane didn't know. But as the lorry sped on, with Golly dancing over them—seeming now actually to be rather gleeful at having got them into such a mess—she had a nasty feeling that they wouldn't be returning to the yard for hours.

'Maybe they'll stop at a traffic light soon,' she said hopefully. 'So be ready.'

But they stopped for nothing. The girls had barely had time to sit up and look cautiously round before they were out into the dark countryside. There the lorry went faster still. The girls clung together. Golly leapt and twisted. They went past roadhouses and through villages, up hills and down them, over rivers and under railway bridges, along narrow crooked jolting lanes and back on to smoother ones. It seemed as if they were never going to stop at all.

Ruth fell silent. Sally began to whimper. Once she threatened to thump on the cab and make the men stop, but Jane pulled her down.

351

'Wool-shredder!' she warned her sister.

That silenced Sally, but it started Ruth whimpering.

'I—I'm sorry!' she said. 'It's all—it's all my fu-fault...'

'We'll be all right,' said Jane. 'They'll—oop!'

The lorry had lurched into the narrowest bumpiest lane yet. Branches scraped the sides of the cab. Sally went sprawling forward. Jane caught her. But at last the journey was at an end. With a final lurch and a grating of brakes the lorry stopped, and suddenly there was a complete silence. Ruth and Sally needed no telling to keep quiet. The three of them had just time to get back under the sacks when the doors of the cab were opened and the men jumped out.

'Get the cutters, Sid,' came the ginger man's command.

Someone fumbled at the side of the lorry. A hinge squeaked. The girls kept very still.

'Here y' are ...'

You're sure this it the right church?' said the ginger man.

'Yes,' came the third man's voice. 'Round the back. There's a jutting-out part. Dead easy to get at. There must be nearly a ton of lead up there. All in nice strips.'

'Strips! Heh-heh! *We'll* strip it! We'll strip the lot!... Sure we won't be heard?'

'See for yerself, can't yer? Since they pulled the old Vicarage down the nearest house is about a quarter of a mile away.'

'Right, well ... let's get going.'

There was a snick of a gate. Then footsteps, fading.

Jane threw off her sack. She knelt up and peered into the darkness. A square tower rose black against the stars. At its base, dull white gravestones gleamed softly.

'Hear that?' she said. 'They're going to strip some lead off a porch or something.'

'Oh dear!' said Ruth. 'They'll load it on top of us!'

'I want to go home!' moaned Sally.

'Of course they won't load it on top of us!' said Jane.

'They won't get the chance. We've got to stop them. Give the alarm.'

'But—but what about getting back? We—'

'That's all right *now*!' said Jane. 'We can't get into trouble *now*. Not if we prevent a robbery. They'll probably take us home in a police car... And give us fish-and-chips on the way,' she added, rather wistfully. 'Come on!'

Jane clambered off the lorry. The others followed.

'First of all,' murmured Jane, fumbling in her case and taking out the scissors, 'we'll make sure of *this*.'

The cab doors were unlocked this time. Ruth and Sally watched the pencil of light darting about the back of the cab. Then there was a snipping noise.

'Catch!' came the whisper, and something soft flopped against Ruth's chest.

'Never mind cuddling him now!' said Jane. 'We've got to give the alarm. I wonder which way the village lies?'

They stared about them. All at once they felt very helpless again. Up the lane, down the lane, it seemed just as dark, just as desolate.

'We—we might wander about for *hours*!' whispered Ruth.

'I want to go home!'

'Shut up!' snapped Jane.

She turned to the church. The men were setting to work very quietly. All that could be heard was the hooting of an owl, somewhere beyond the black bell tower. And it was then that Jane had her idea. In the darkness, her eyes went nearly as wide as that owl's.

'I *know* ...,' she murmured. 'I know how to give the alarm. Something I've *always* wanted to do...' A faint cough from the other side of the church reminded her to keep her voice down. 'Listen...'

Sally, Ruth and golly clustered nearer. There then arose in the night air several 'Oohs' and 'Ahs' and one stifled squeal of delight, as Jane whispered her plan.

'All we need do is slip into the church from this side,' she concluded. 'But first—wait—listen ... First we'll let down these tyres!'

* * * *

Up to then it had been a typical perfectly normal evening in the village of Little Yittersley (population 203). In the tap-room of the Blue Boar, half a mile from the lovely but secluded village church (carvings by Grinling Gibbons), some of the regular customers—including Mr Percy Donger, verger and gravedigger—were having their last drinks. Along the road at the rebuilt Vicarage, the Reverend Phillip Prinkett was spending a quiet half-hour with his stamp collection. Colonel Rabley up at the Hall was just climbing into his complexion-matching purple-striped pyjamas, after giving his wife a long talk on what *he* would do to football crowds and other vandals. In the woods behind the Hall, Mr Foxy Williams, part-time poacher, was just stretching out a hand to collar a snared rabbit; and in the same woods, one yard behind him, P. C. Taplin was stretching out a hand to collar the unwitting Mr Williams.

At the new bungalow, not far from the Hall, the people there had been entertaining old friends from the town. During the course of the evening, the lady visitor had had a great deal to say about her daughter, something of a problem-child, called Jane. There had been a rather revolting incident concerning a cigarette and some syrup, and Mrs McNulty (for it was she) was just concluding with the words: 'And to think she'll be lying in bed now, fast asleep, looking just like an angel!' when the peace of the village was broken into a million bits.

By bells.

Church bells ...

354

Three wild figures were swinging on the bells

They began somewhat hesitantly. There was one shattering clang, then a slightly fainter one; then, about three seconds later, another, lighter than the rest, with a rather plaintive, almost peevish note. Then another great clang, and the fainter one, and the great clang again—then a gap—and *two* of the peevish ones. Then the big one again ... and so on, this time in strict rotation.

In bell-ringing circles they have special names for certain peals. Some are called treble bobs—some bob minors. There are also bob triples, bob majors and bob royals, with bob maximus as the greatest. The peals that were belted out over the village of Little Yittersley that evening had no special names, though for those who are interested they might well be described as varying from a jane triple reversed to a mighty jane maxima.

They were loud anyway—and that was what mattered. They penetrated into every crack and corner of that village. They broke into the loudest conversation and pierced the thickest walls. And the villagers—who had recently had the churchyard desecrated by a gang of motor-bike vandals—responded at once, thinking the same lot had struck again.

At the Blue Boar, pints were put down and pitchforks, poles and other weapons picked up—the whole assembly being led forth by a rather unsteady but nonetheless determined Mr Percy Donger. At the Vicarage, The Reverend Phillip Prinkett dropped the Penny Black he was inspecting and made straight for the door, snatching up his stoutest umbrella on the way. Colonel Rabley, over at the Hall, chose a croquet mallet and, still in pyjamas, leapt on to his bike with a cry of 'Vandals, eh?' closely followed by the painter's word. Behind the Hall, P. C. Taplin and Mr Foxy Williams sank their differences in the face of this threat from a common enemy. Announcing to Foxy that he was pardoned conditionally, the policeman told him to get on the pillion of his scooter 'while we see what this here's all about!'

Only in the new bungalow was the reaction slow.

'Bells?' said Mrs McNulty. 'Whatever's it all about?'

Her host shook his head.

'One of these crazy rural customs, I suppose ... I say, shall we drive round? It might be rather amusing.'

'Yes—let's!' said Mrs McNulty, all for some amusement after a particularly trying day with Jane.

* * * *

The lead-snippers never had a chance.

True, after the first few peals, they realised they would have to abandon their job. True, they didn't even stop to find out who was giving them away. But with three flat tyres they couldn't get very far, and they were just thinking of making off on foot when the villagers descended upon them. Lights flashed; whistles blew; pitchforks, mallets, shotguns, poles, umbrellas and even a dead rabbit, held by its hind legs, were brandished. And ginger man, with the points of an alarmingly wavering pitchfork at his throat, surrendered.

Meanwhile, over in the bell room of the church, three wild figures continued to swing on the ropes in the dim light of a pencil torch. By this time there was something abandoned about their cries. One—the smallest—had twice nearly been sick with delight. Another—a girl with what looked in that light like a single glowing red eye—was beginning to feel dizzy. But the third, pigtails flying, went from strength to strength, urging them on.

They had even forgotten exactly *why* they were ringing those bells, and if they hadn't been interrupted by the vicar they would probably have gone on until they dropped from sheer exhaustion.

'So—ah—these are our benefactors?' said the Reverend

Mr Prinkett, switching on the light. 'We—oh!—*children!*'

The *children,* still clinging to the ropes, blinked at the crowd of faces. There was a murmur.

'Whose *gals* are they?'

'Never seen 'em afore...'

'Look a bit young...'

'JANE!'

The voice—half cry of amazement, half scream—came from the back of the crowd.

Then the villagers parted as Mr and Mrs McNulty, looking like a pair of sleepwalkers, went up to make sure they *weren't* dreaming.

* * * *

So the three girls didn't return home in a police car, after all. But they had their fish-and-chips—good country fish-and-chips, specially cooked for them by the vicar's housekeeper—and when they finally did leave Little Yittersley in Mr McNulty's car, the villagers' congratulations rang, with the echoes of the bells, in their ears. It had been a great triumph. As Jane Rebecca McNulty settled back and closed her eyes, with Sally's head on her right shoulder and Ruth's golliwog's hair brushing her left cheek, she smiled.

'What's the population of that village, Dad?' she inquired.

'Two hundred and three I think, dear,' said her father. 'Why?'

Jane didn't reply. She was dozing off. Instead of sheep she had started counting good deeds. Two hundred and three of them at one go. Two hundred and four altogether, of course, including the rescue of Golly...

The car jolted at a bend. Jane blinked. She twisted a pigtail into a loop and peered through it haughtily at the back of her mother's head.

'Impossible, eh?' she murmured.

Then she yawned and fell fast asleep, still smiling.